FELL THE ANGELS

Abby and her team mates at the Society for the Security of Reality stand between mankind and the "other." Faeries, selkies, werewolves, ghosts, ghouls... all of the creatures mankind refuses to admit exist. Abby knows firsthand that they are real. She fights her personal demons as she fights the "other" — with determination, hope, and spunk. After solving the disappearance of hundreds of children only a month ago, Abby is suddenly thrust into fighting the unknown once again.

This time, it's the faeries who have invaded Chicago. And these are not the fae of your childhood stories. These are dark magic-wielders, capable of murder and committed to obtaining power over the mortal world. All Abby needs to do is find out who is helping them, solve the gruesome murders, and rebuild a relationship with her teenage son while keeping herself and her team mates alive.

Catherine Butzen fills the streets of Chicago with fantasy and horror in this, her second book.

CATHERINE BUTZEN BIBLIOGRAPHY

Thief of Midnight (2010)
The God Collector (2015)
Fell the Angels (2015)

FELL THE ANGELS
by Catherine Butzen

Stark House Press • Eureka California

FELL THE ANGELS

Published by Stark House Press
1315 H Street
Eureka, CA 95501, USA
griffinskye3@sbcglobal.net
www.starkhousepress.com

FELL THE ANGELS copyright © 2015 by Catherine Butzen. All rights reserved, including the right of reproduction in whole or in part in any form. Published by Stark House Press, Eureka, California, by arrangement with the author.

"Fell the Angels: Myths to Live By" copyright © 2015 by Cynthia L. Shepard

ISBN: 1-933586-89-3
ISBN-13: 978-1-933586-89-2

Cover design by JT Lindroos
Cover photo by Heath Cajandig
Additional design and text layout by Mark Shepard

PUBLISHER'S NOTE:
This is a work of fiction. Names, characters, places and incidents are either the products of the author's imagination or used fictionally, and any resemblance to actual persons, living or dead, events or locales, is entirely coincidental. Without limiting the rights under copyright reserved above, no part of this publication may be reproduced, stored, or introduced into a retrieval system or transmitted in any form or by any means (electronic, mechanical, photocopying, recording or otherwise) without the prior written permission of both the copyright owner and the above publisher of the book.

First Stark House Press Edition: October 2015

FIRST EDITION

For Zellie, who dreamed enough for all of us.

Fell the Angels: Myths to Live By
By Cynthia L. Shepard

Throughout history, mankind has sought to understand the world, the stars, and our place in them. We have created mythologies and gods in an effort to explain the unknown. We are intrigued, worshipful, awestruck, and captured by that we do not understand. From the ancient Egyptian worship of the sun God, Ra, to the current popularity of paranormal reality TV, we continue our quest to understand who and what we are.

Some of our most prevalent mythologies are based upon what we were told as children. Oral histories, including mythologies, have been shared around campfires and in nurseries. Some stories and poems are used to teach children to behave,

> "An' one time a little girl 'ud allus laugh an' grin,
> An' make fun of ever' one, an' all her blood-an'-kin;
> An' wunst, when they was "company," an' ole folks wuz there,
> She mocked 'em an' shocked 'em, an' said she didn't care!
> An' thist as she kicked her heels, an' turn't to run an' hide,
> They wuz two great big Black Things a-standin' by her side,
> An' they snatched her through the ceilin' 'for she knowed what she's about!
> An' the Gobble-uns 'll git you
> Ef you
> Don't
> Watch
> Out!"
> (*Little Orphant Annie* by James Whitcomb Riley)

Other stories are used to sooth and calm children to sleep,

> "When at night I go to sleep,
> Fourteen angels watch do keep,
> Two my head are guarding,
> Two my feet are guiding;
> Two upon my right hand,
> Two upon my left hand.

Two who warmly cover
Two who o'er me hover,
Two to whom 'tis given
To guide my steps to heaven."
(*Hänsel und Gretel* by Engelbert Humperdink)

The mythologies we learn as children follow us into adulthood. Who hasn't crossed their fingers to bring good luck, or avoided black cats on Friday the 13th? Deep in our souls, at some instinctual level, we still revere our ancestral beliefs and questions.

Science has provided answers to many of our questions. We no longer believe that the sun is a fierce god, giving us light according to his whim. We know now that it is a large ball of burning gas and that it does not revolve around our planet, but that we revolve around it. We don't truly believe that crossing our fingers will bring us luck. But deep in the hearts of those of us with imagination lives a still, small question whispering, "What if?"

Catherine Butzen gives voice to this question in her novels. Her books are based upon mythologies from many cultures and, using these ancient mysteries, she pulls them into modern day America and illustrates the possibilities of "what if?"

Catherine Butzen was born and raised in Chicago, Illinois, as the fourth of five children. Her parents instilled love of books into their children, always making time to read with them. Often, two or three people would be doing the dinner dishes while another family member read aloud. They also instilled in their children a love for history with frequent trips to the museum. Catherine embraced these two passions and uses them with great skill in her writing.

In her first book, *Thief of Midnight* (Stark House Press, 2010), Butzen defines her world—contemporary mid-west America with a twist. In this Chicago, the myths are real. With this first novel, Butzen introduces Abby Marquise, a member of the Society for the Security of Reality. Marquise and her compatriots are pitched against a child's worst nightmare—the monsters under the bed. Not only are the monsters real, but they're organized. From Baba Yaga (Russia) to El Cucuy (Mexico), Butzen combines the mythologies of various countries to create a Mafia-inspired family of monsters bent on kidnapping the world's children. Of course, any sane and rational adult doesn't believe in monsters, but the children, along with Abby and her friends, know better. They're real, they're here, and they're out to get us!

Fell the Angels, (Stark House Press, 2015) Butzen's second book in the series, deals with the world of Celtic faery. Selkies are running amok in Abby's Chicago and she must find out why—and how to stop them. Her band of coworkers, including a young psychic, a golem, and a djinn, must track down the fae and stop them before they play any more murderous games with human kind. This book is somewhat darker than *Thief of Midnight*. While *Thief* is lightened with humor and whimsy, *Fell the Angels* is filled with overtones of social issues and concerns.

Butzen's books use issues of family and union—organized factions of good and evil—as well as referring to politics to incorporate ideas of current society. Humans (as well as monsters, apparently) feel more comfortable in organized groups. We join in families, clans, and communities tied together by blood and/or common interests. Our intent is to support and encourage one another. There's safety in numbers. But joining together into groups presents opportunities for those who are interested in causing harm, as well.

Butzen's Chicago, while gray and murky in the noir sense, is certainly not black and white. Her characters are conglomerates of emotions and experiences—both good and bad—and have deep, underlying histories that affect their behavior. Are Abby and her friends working to save mankind from the monsters? Or are they a vigilante group intent on taking out those they perceive as different? What makes their behavior virtuous? Where are the limits to what is acceptable in a society as regards human—or monster—rights and responsibilities?

It is easy to draw corollaries between Butzen's characters and the current economical/political/social state of the world. In reality, there are those who focus on the similarities between peoples and nations and those whose attention travels to the differences. Do we celebrate our uniqueness and follow our own path? Or do we subjugate self in an effort to provide for the whole? Which is more important? How do we recognize the good and refuse the evil? The philosophical questions of the ages cannot be answered easily. Butzen does not try to provide the answers, but she does explore the hard questions.

The stories we tell in our groups—around the campfire, in the nursery, in the media—affect who we are as individuals and as a society. Catherine Butzen addresses them all and reminds us of their importance. As Stephen Sondheim says in *Into the Woods*, "Careful the tale you tell, that is the spell. Children will listen!"

—Eureka, CA
June 2015

Fell the Angels
by Catherine Butzen

> Cromwell, I charge thee, fling away ambition:
> By that sin fell the angels; how can man, then,
> The image of his Maker, hope to win by it?
>
> William Shakespeare, *Henry VIII*

Chapter One

Chicago, Illinois. Present day.

The man grinned as he ran. He skipped lightly over a patch of ice, overbalanced, and turned his stumble into a theatrical flip that landed him squarely on the steel fire escape. He was a selkie and his name, when he bothered to answer to one, was Luka.

Abby Marquise hitched her purse higher onto her shoulder as she dodged around the ice Luka had jumped. Sweat trickled down her forehead and clung to loose strands of dark-blonde hair. Shapeshifters were never easy to handle, but this one had more energy than most. The shoulder holster under her parka was rubbing her side raw.

"Get back here!" she panted, but the selkie just thumbed his nose at Abby and galloped down the fire escape. She reached the top just as he reached bottom. As she clung to the metal railing, trying to find steady footing for the descent, he smiled up at her and tapped one foot.

Abby tried not to swear, but it was a near thing. She clambered awkwardly down the fire escape as Luka took off again.

At least he was doing her the courtesy of letting her keep up. Most fairies could easily outdistance a human, but Luka had already killed two women in his personal quest for fun, so perhaps he was enjoying this variation on his usual game. He might have a plan, or he might not. Whatever happened in the next few minutes, Abby would have to catch him.

She didn't want to. There were other agents better-equipped to handle a takedown, but unless her luck changed they wouldn't be there in time. Of course this had to happen *today* of all days.

Luka cut left and bolted across the street, ignoring the honking car horns and shouts of passersby. Another patch of ice sent him skidding, giving Abby a few precious seconds to close the gap, but her hand barely brushed his sleeve before he twisted neatly out of the way and bolted. "No touching!" he sang out.

They streaked past the adobe-colored structure of the local clinic, following the straight line of Western Avenue. Abby's lungs burned with the cold air and her heart felt ready to burst. Luka just laughed and somehow accelerated.

There was a definite course to his run now. He veered off the central course of Western Avenue and streaked across the snow of an empty lot, heading towards the park across the street. He was about a hundred feet ahead, but Abby could see him stoop low and snatch something out of a snowdrift. Then he was off, but more slowly this time, struggling to unwrap heavy PVC sheeting from a small package as he ran.

Abby slowed a little as well and fumbled her cell phone out of her pocket. "He's got something," she panted. "Think it's his skin. Off Addison, heading down to the river."

"Hang on," said the voice of Adam Starczynski. "John and Dummy are three blocks behind you. If you grab the skin you can control him, but if he hits the water—"

"I know," she said and ended the call. Sucking in as deep a breath as she could manage, she swiped sweat out of her eyes and pushed forward.

The park sloped gently for the length of a soccer field before making an abrupt plunge into the gravel-edged shallows of the Chicago River. It was one of the best places for foot access to the river: the banks for miles around were steep and lined with trees, condos, concrete barriers and private docks. A small service offered canoe and kayak rentals for an hourly fee, but it was closed for the season.

The selkie plunged into the shallows and pulled his white sealskin over his head. A moment later, a snowy seal with golden eyes was thrashing its way into deeper water. It raised its flipper in a jaunty salute as Abby stumbled to a halt on the bank.

She had to do something. She should draw her pistol, shoot him dead in the water, but her hands were trembling with exhaustion and she could hardly see through the haze blurring her vision. She could only bend over, panting for air.

But something seemed to be wrong with Luka's getaway plan. The seal flopped backwards in the water and wrinkled its nose. It sneezed. Spluttered. Its eyes instinctively squeezed shut, and its whole body convulsed as it tried to clap its flippers over its face. Its alarmed bark turned into bubbles in the greasy water and startled a seagull perched on a nearby chunk of ice.

With a wounded yelp, the seal thrashed its tail and sped towards the shore as fast as it could. When it crawled up onto the bank, some twenty yards downstream from where it had started, the water ran in oily gray rivulets from its fur.

Gasping, the selkie ripped off his enchanted skin and began to cough in a deep phlegmy rattle. "Is that supposed to be a *river?*" he demanded as Abby came stumbling through the trees. "How can you do that to me?"

Abby shucked off her parka and drew the Beretta Tomcat from its holster. "Luka," she began as steadily as she could, "you are hereby charged with the murders of Alicia Gonzalez and Rebecca Cartwright. If you have any information that would be of use to the human authorities, please disclose it now and I might be able to help you. Hand over the skin and—"

Fairies preferred magic, but they knew what guns were. Luka grabbed his skin and bolted for the water's edge.

Abby fired twice. The first bullet zinged over the selkie's head, but the second hit home between his shoulder blades. He gasped and hit the surface face-first, his sealskin still in his arms. Blood bubbled out into the icy water.

Taking a shallow breath, Abby shook her head and holstered the weapon. The body was already sinking. She pulled out her cell phone and dialed Adam again.

"He's dead," she said. "But he's in the water, and there's no way I can fish him out myself."

"Roger," Adam responded. "Any witnesses? Dummy's right behind you, and he's got the jar …"

"Nobody saw the last part, but there might be some people who were curious about the chase." The slow current of the river was spreading the blood around, creating a reddish-brown patch in the water. "We should probably listen to the police band for a while, just in case."

"I figured. You gonna write up the case report?"

"I… no, I don't think so." It would be completely dark soon, and she had an appointment to keep. "Tomorrow okay?"

Adam's voice wasn't exactly sympathetic, but it had softened. "No prob. Go home and get cleaned up."

Heavy footsteps were coming up behind her. Abby turned. A seven-foot-tall man, pale as chalk, was making his way down the riverbank with a green glass jar under one arm. When he saw her, he waved one hand and smiled. The hand hopped down from his wrist and scuttled across the now towards Abby, where it made itself comfortable on her shoe.

"Hi, Dummy," she said. "I hope you brought rope."

● ● ●

Abby Marquise hadn't expected a lot of excitement from life. Marriage, a nice house, and kids, preferably in that order. It didn't sound very go-getter of her, but she'd been determined to make a better home than the one she'd had.

For a while, it looked like she was succeeding. She'd been married at eighteen to a handsome young football player, and given birth soon afterwards to her son Jimmy. But while she'd gotten the "happily," she'd fallen down on "ever after."

The street outside was dark. An occasional gust of December wind made the small house's windows rattle in their frames, but with the curtains closed and the furnace turned up, everything was nice and cozy. The room looked better than it had in weeks: vacuumed and swept, with the subtly mismatched old furniture cleaned and sporting new slipcovers, it had a comfortable domestic feel to it. The IKEA coffee table littered with medical supplies only slightly spoiled the illusion.

Perched in an old loveseat, Abby rolled her pant legs up and carefully dabbed her knees with disinfectant. Jeans were an excellent choice for the SSR agent who wanted to blend in, but repeatedly landing knees-first on icy concrete tended to be hard on both her and them. She'd gotten good at patching denim.

The SSR, when not at home, was the Society for the Security of Reality. According to their dearly departed founder, the name had made sense at the time. When dealing with monsters and magic, who wouldn't have thought the universe was coming unraveled? *Society* just made them sound more legitimate, putting them on the same level as a society for preserving cultural heritage or the low-tide saltwater clam. Official and normal.

"So d'you want to give the lecture, or should I?"

She glanced down at the man sitting on the floor next to her. He too wore the unofficial agency uniform of jeans and a parka, but he would never be anonymous no matter how he dressed: scarred-over teeth marks decorated his right cheek, twisting a little as he frowned. Tattooed letters marched across the knuckles of his left hand: *ACAB*, All Coppers Are Bastards. John Sawyer had had an interesting youth.

"I don't think you should," Abby responded as she pulled a small piece of ground-in gravel out of her knee. "Normally I give the lectures."

"Well, normally, we're not in this position," John pointed out. Only light slurring and softened Rs remained of his London accent, but it would thicken again in a minute if he thought it would impress the listener. John was good with accents. "And I didn't ask for it neither, so honestly, it all could've been avoided if you hadn't gone haring off after that selkie."

Abby shrugged and didn't look up. "I'm not going to have this conversation with you, John."

"Too bad. It could be real funny, me trying to be the sensible one." He poked her in the bare shin. "What'm I supposed to tell Mal if you get yourself killed?"

"You'll tell him to go jump in a lake. Again." Abby concentrated on her knees and ignored the latest prod.

Ordinary post-mission cleanups were done at the office. Abby would have preferred it: there she would have had a bigger medical kit, not to mention company to mediate any arguments with John. But it was almost the New Year and Abby had a vigil to keep. That left John sitting in her living room and trying to maintain a conversation while Abby used up the hydrogen peroxide.

She could have kicked him out, of course, but he was the reason for the vigil in the first place. He'd encouraged her to do what she'd done, one month ago;

now he could wait with her and see it ended. That didn't mean she wanted to talk about it.

Silence prevailed. Outside, a car alarm went off and the wind slammed a stray branch into the side of the house. Abby finished cleaning her knees and taped large patches of gauze over the scrapes.

"Heard anything from the kid yet?" John asked.

"No," she said. "Not yet."

"He's supposed to be back tonight, isn't he?"

"It's not even midnight yet." She wadded up a blooded piece of gauze and dropped it into the garbage can. "Besides, they—he—might be on Italian time."

"Italy's ahead of us. It was midnight hours ago there."

"So maybe they're not bringing him back, then." She dropped the medical kit as well. The canvas pouch failed to provide the satisfying crash she wanted. "Maybe they ate him, like the stories say. Is that what you mean?"

"Hell, no. You gave him to the trustiest bogeymen I ever met." John completely failed to wither under her glare. "Don't get nasty with me, either, 'cos you know it's true. If you want me to hold your hand and say he'll be okay... well, I don't know he will be." He scratched his long jaw idly. "But did you do the right thing? I'd say you did. He would've hurt you, bad, if you hadn't called L'uomo Nero for him."

"Maybe." She picked up the medical kit and put it back in its usual place in the china hutch. Three of her great-aunt's prized Victorian figurines concealed it neatly.

"Maybe? He gave you a concussion and threatened to have you hauled to the loony bin. Y'know, I'd call that a definite sign of hostility." John sat back. "But sure, what do I know?"

Her hand tightened on a china milkmaid. "Stop it, John."

"Oh, relax," John said with the weary cheer of a man daring the universe to make his life more miserable. "He'll turn up safe and hearty, and then you two'll have a hot Christmas tea and there'll be no mention of bogey monsters at all. Better than *my* family Christmases, that's for certain."

"Aren't you Jewish?"

"And you're saying Jews can't celebrate Christmas? Racist." That got a small laugh from Abby in spite of herself. John nodded. "See?" he said. "That's better. Have some fun. Please. Nature didn't intend me to be the nice one in this group, and it's getting on my nerves. So chin up. L'uomo owes us."

"I don't think he sees it that way," Abby said. John shrugged and said nothing.

The momentary silence was interrupted by a knock on the door. Abby jumped while John glanced sharply at her, his hand automatically going to his own shoulder holster. She could feel the blood draining from her face as she rose.

A plain young woman stood on the porch. Her steel-rimmed spectacles reflected the light from the open door, almost blotting out her deep-set eyes. Everything about her, from her sensible shoes to her tight braids, was faded brown. She might have stepped out of an old photograph.

Her hand rested on the shoulder of a teenage boy who couldn't have been more different. He still had the same jeans, T-shirt and green hair from a month ago, but his features were relaxed, his eyes were slightly glazed, and the color of his skin was warm and healthy. The blank look in his eyes made her stomach twist.

"Giovanna—" Abby began. She stopped herself, remembering the change that had taken place since she had last met this woman "La Donna Nera," she said. Her hand shook as she reached out to stroke Jimmy's hair. "Is he okay?"

"He'll be fine," La Donna Nera said calmly. Her voice was still an old woman's voice, the one that had belonged to the human she'd once been. "We never hurt him, Abigail. Wouldn't do that, not neither of us. But you called the bogeyman for a bad child, and we took him away and showed him the truth he never believed." She laid a hand on Abby's arm. The skin felt warm but plastic, a fake part of a fake body built for a moment's convenience. "He knows now."

Abby swallowed. Behind her, John gave a low rumble that might've been skepticism.

"Don't you make noises at me," the woman said tartly and gave Jimmy a small push. He stumbled over the threshold, but as he bumped into Abby, the blank look on his face cleared and he blinked.

"Mom?"

Abby's heart broke. It had been a long, long time since she'd heard the word without a sarcastic twist in it, but that didn't change the fact that he'd been gone for a month because he was with a *bogeyman*. She wrapped her arms around her son and hugged him as hard as she could.

"Mom." The word was muffled against her shoulder. "Mom. I'm sorry. I didn't know."

"No, honey, no," Abby said softly. "It's my fault. It shouldn't have got to this point. I'm so, so sorry, sweetheart."

Jimmy didn't say anything, just sagged against her. Abby hugged him, but his weight was too much for her to support. "Sweetie?" she said. "Jimmy, you're not—"

His head lolled against her shoulder. He was asleep.

"He'll be like that for a while," La Donna Nera said. "No child, 'specially not a bad one, takes the trip between the worlds very easy. He'll sleep a long time, and probably eat a lot. Growing boys are like that."

"Thank you," Abby managed to say. For what? Helping him, or just bringing him back without hurting him? She wasn't sure.

"Was my pleasure," La Donna Nera replied. She adjusted her coke-bottle glasses and stepped back from the door. "All of you be good to each other, mind. If there's one thing I've learned since moving on, it's that somebody's always watching."

She faded back into the dimness under the porch eaves. The last thing to go was the lingering glint from her glasses.

Jimmy grunted in his sleep and shifted, burrowing into Abby's arms. John appeared beside her and silently took one of his arms, taking some of the weight off her. Together, the two of them managed to get Jimmy into the house and through the living room to his poster-papered bedroom. Abby shoved the door hard with her shoulder and stumbled when it opened easily. She'd forgotten that the heaps of discarded laundry were gone.

John helped her drop her son on the bed and tactfully left the room. Sighing a little, Abby brushed the green hair away from Jimmy's forehead and pressed a kiss to his cheek.

"Sleep well," she said. He murmured something indistinct into the pillow, but that was all.

Chapter Two

"Off with her head!" the Queen of Hearts screeched, brandishing a copy of *Paradise Lost*. Abby backed away as quickly as she could, but her long blue skirts and pinafore tangled around her legs and turned a step into a stumble. The Queen advanced, oily fluid dripping from her mouth.

Abby bumped into a tree. The forest around her groaned at the contact and began to shift, the trees lying down and vanishing into the ground. In seconds she was standing in the middle of an empty field. The Queen of Hearts was gone, leaving nothing but *Paradise Lost* behind on the ground. The sky above was checkered with clouds, and rain began to fall, turning the book into a soggy mess of paper. Abby tried to scoop it up, but it fell apart in her hands. Ants crawled out from between the damp pages and vanished into the grass.

The dream-world faded into hazy memory as Abby opened her eyes. No ants, no grass, just the plaster of her bedroom ceiling. The light slanting across the bed was watery but bright.

She sat up and immediately regretted it. Her bruised muscles seemed to have silted up during the night. When she lifted her head from the pillow, her neck made an ominous cracking noise.

"Ow," she said, for lack of anything better to say.

With an effort, Abby rolled out of bed. A basket of clean laundry was sitting on the floor, still waiting to be put away, and she rooted through it for a fresh pair of jeans and a long-sleeved shirt. After a moment's hesitation, she strapped on her shoulder holster and threw a plaid flannel button-down over it. SSR policy was to go armed for the first couple of days after a takedown, in case anyone decided to get their own back. It wasn't such a worry with things like ghouls or ghosts, but you never knew which way fairies would jump.

The sky outside was the color of concrete. A thick cloud layer obscured any signs of the sun, and flecks of white drifted serenely down with little wind to make them swirl or dance. With the background hum of the city muffled by snowfall, the world seemed wrapped in a thick blanket.

She padded into the kitchen, which had apparently been attacked by a horde of locusts overnight. Dishes were piled up in the sink, the refrigerator door was ajar, and a box of frozen waffles that had been full yesterday morning was lying empty on the table. The leftover beef stew was still in the fridge, but the chocolate chips and ice cream were cleaned out. A trail of wrappers and crumbs led her down the hall to Jimmy's door, which was firmly closed. She could hear snoring.

"Well, she did warn me," Abby said. She tossed the empty containers into the garbage and flipped on the small countertop TV. The chatter of a commercial for dish soap ran in one ear and out the other while she dug another box of waffles out of the freezer.

The commercial segued into a morning newscast. Abby poured syrup on her waffles, rolled them up, and ate them standing at the sink while listening. Most of the local morning news didn't catch her interest, but one item made her turn to watch.

"... day four of the protest encampment in Daley Plaza," a news anchors was saying. An inset screen showed clusters of tents around the base of a gigantic Picasso sculpture, with protestors waving signs at the businessmen and trendy downtown shoppers walking briskly past. "Concerned parents' groups are continuing to petition the city government on behalf of the proposed Danley-Collier regulations, which would expand school security zones and mandate higher safety standards for new housing intended for families." The camera cut to a protestor waving a sign reading NEVER AGAIN in big red letters. "Opponents of the bill argue that its language is vague and could lead to exploitation. However, a current opinion poll has shown eighty-six percent of Chicagoans are in favor of the new regulations."

A field reporter was interviewing the woman with the red sign, who seemed to be the leader of the group. "There's nothing more important than our children," the woman was saying. "A kidnapping ring operated right under the law's nose, and nobody did anything about it! What would have happened if they hadn't killed themselves? How do we even know they *did* kill themselves? There's a lot we're not being told here, and I for one am not ready to sit on the sidelines and let this happen again!"

Other protestors nodded in agreement. One was wearing a button proclaiming "Black November was an inside job!"

Abby shook her head as she rinsed syrup off her hands. She missed being able to write things off as insane.

"Black November" was a good name for it. A family of powerful creatures, literal bogeymen out of dreams, had overstepped their boundaries and gone on a kidnapping spree in hopes that it would generate fear for them to feed on. They had been goaded into it by their leader, the child spirit El Cucuy, and the SSR had only just managed to survive it. The old lady, Giovanna, had saved all of their lives and been turned into the bogeyman La Donna Nera for her trouble.

With El Cucuy gone, the plan was undone and the monsters' new leader used his magic to pull together a cover story about a kidnap-mad suicide cult. It was pretty flimsy, though, and Abby couldn't blame any of those scared parents for thinking it was baloney. After all, it was.

The Cook County district attorney was speaking to the protestors now, promising her support for their cause. Hopefully it would give them some well-deserved comfort.

The newscast segued into a fluff piece about a charity bake sale. Nothing about a killing by the river yesterday or a frantic chase down Western Avenue. Abby relaxed an inch or two and went to get the morning paper.

She brushed snow off the front porch swing and sat down with the Lifestyle section, taking a deep breath of the crisp morning air. Later in the day the cold wind would feel like knives slicing at her cheeks and the endless gray sky would wear on her; for now, the chilly stillness of the world was strangely relaxing.

It didn't last long. Abby had just finished the first page when a chorus of frantic barking cut through the air, shattering the stillness and making her jump. Seven or eight dogs were going wild in her next-door neighbor's yard, howling and growling and barking and yapping and generally doing their best impression of a crazed doggy mob. A huge gray German Shepherd snapped its teeth at a Westie terrier, who yowled like its tail had been caught in a car door and backed away so fast that it tumbled into a half-backflip. Two poodles, one teacup and one toy, were squabbling fiercely over a rawhide bone almost as big as they were. The rest were keeping up a steady chorus of howls interspersed with pitiful whimpering.

Abby clamped her hands over her ears as her neighbor, dressed in colorful nurse's scrubs, dashed into the yard and tried frantically to calm the panicking animals. The teacup poodle had forgone the rawhide bone and was rhythmically slamming himself into the fence, scrabbling his paws in the snow until he hit bottom and churned up black dirt instead. Her neighbor was a vet tech and often fostered abandoned animals, but even she seemed overwhelmed by the chaos. Abby grabbed the newspaper and backed into the house.

With the door closed, the din was muted somewhat, and she could hear the jangling of her cell phone from the kitchen. So much for a relaxing morning.

"Hello?" she said, tucking the phone between her ear and shoulder.

"Abigail." The voice was a man's, deep and even with a formal cadence to it. "John requests that you come in immediately. Something unusual has happened."

She shot a glance at Jimmy's closed door. Faint snores could still be heard, but... "How unusual?"

"I'm afraid I don't know. He texted me five minutes ago and asked me to contact you. We should meet at the office, and he informed me he requires coffee."

"Great." No coffee meant John wasn't at the office yet either, since he usually didn't keep any at home. And if he'd picked up something important while at home, it meant he was listening to the police scanner. Which meant in turn that something on the cops' radar had been bad enough, or just plain weird enough, for the agency to be concerned. Maybe yesterday hadn't gone off as cleanly as they'd hoped.

Abby sighed but shrugged into her parka. Frozen waffles and high school didn't pay for themselves. She kept the phone balanced between cheek and shoulder as she grabbed her shoulderbag from the hall and double-checked the supplies hidden in the lining. "Tell him I'm on my way."

• • •

A light snowfall pattered down on the body, dotting it with tiny flakes of white. It was actually, to be precise, half a body: the left half from feet to shoulders, with a few scraps of jugular showing that the head hadn't gone easily. The single arm was missing its hand.

The remains had been discovered in the alley by a homeless man, but by the time the police arrived a couple of feral cats had added their tooth marks to the general mess. What remained was dressed in jeans and a brand-new button-down shirt. A smear of black shoe polish on the one leg of the jeans was all that was left of its footwear.

Two policemen worked to cordon off the small alley with yellow tape while the crime-scene techs examined the body. They took blood and tissue samples, searched what was left of the clothes, and were busy printing the foot for possible identification when a wisp of gray smoke drifted down the alley towards them.

One of the policemen stopped in his tracks, ignoring the snow going down the neck of his white parka. His partner frowned and glanced towards him, but before she said anything, she stopped too. A tech froze while kneeling next to the body. Another paused while preparing to close the door of the van. Their eyes glazed over.

A Toyota Camry stopped at the end of the alley and John got out, carrying an open green glass jar. The smoke coalesced in midair and a pair of bobbing yellow lights peered out at him.

"All right, I've got 'em," the smoke cloud reported. Its voice was surprisingly clear for a bodiless being. "Make it fast, though. If the weather or the light changes while they're out, they're going to be confused as hell when they wake up."

"I don't think that's going to be a problem, Harvey," Abby said as she climbed out of the car. A tall man in a long coat followed her.

The three of them got to work. Abby took the tech's camera and began transferring copies to a thumb drive. John left the jar by Abby's feet, snapped on a pair of gloves, and went through the body's pockets for anything the police had missed.

"Nothing," he reported as he stood. "Anything on those pix? Any ID they might've hid?"

"I don't see anything." The office budget stretched to only one tablet, so Abby was handling both items carefully while she worked. "Mal?"

The third man was kneeling by the corpse. The cold wind plastered his already slicked-back hair to his skull, and for a moment, Bela Lugosi lived again.

He went by Marotte, though they called him Mal. The name was as fake as the personality he sported and the past that office rumor had constructed for him, but none of that was really a career-ender with the SSR. He specialized in Shakespearean English, medicine, old-fashioned weapons and beheadings.

"I think," he said in his slow deep voice, "that you should examine this, John."

John shuffled sideways, crablike, towards Mal. The taller man was using a pair of tweezers to hold the shredded edge of the victim's shirt away from the flesh. "Huh," John said. "That's new."

The dead man had money. The shirt had a designer label, and the artfully-torn trousers and cuff bracelet were of a brand famous for its celebrity clients and discreet Indonesian sweatshops. Whoever Mr. Doe was, he'd done well for himself. He'd also been physically torn in half.

The agents were all civilians with no forensic training, but after so long on the job they had learned to recognize the marks a blade left when it cut flesh. Here, there were none. The skin around the pelvis had torn smoothly, almost as if it happened too quickly for the skin to stretch, and the pelvis itself was cleanly split. Further up the body, the tear grew clumsier and the wound was bruised and jagged. The shattered sternum was embedded in what looked like corned beef.

"Urgh," John said. "Not human. Abby?"

"Definitely not human," she confirmed. "It looks like he was pulled in half from the ground up."

John nodded. "Messier towards the top. That means the crotch was closer to the source of the strength. And to do that to a full-grown human with, what, one hand on each ankle? I'd reckon an arm span of twelve to, oh, fourteen feet."

"And it happened quickly." Mal pointed to the victim's waist with his tweezers. "Half of his belt is still there, and the tear is clean." His broad forehead furrowed deeply. "John, I'm going to examine the van. We need more than this body can give us."

Five more minutes' brisk searching, though, turned up nothing. If the authorities had found an ID for the dead man, it was well-hidden.

"Left his wallet in his other half?" John suggested. Abby made a face.

"Perhaps." Mal handed a few scribbled pages to John, who tucked them into his coat. "But thus far their own notes state that his hand was removed when he had already been murdered, likely to prevent identification. I concur: there are tool marks around the wrist and nowhere else. Now lacking face, name, or fingerprints, they have only DNA and his footprint to name him, and those will take time to process."

"So his killer didn't just murder him, they tried to keep anyone from finding out who he was?" Abby put a hand to the silver crucifix at her throat. "Someone really hated him."

Mal knelt down again and stared hard at the mangled body. "This man was well-off. Clean and new clothes, very much in style. Unlikely, but not impossible, for a wealthy man to incur a debt. Perhaps he chose to hire an ogre, and later regretted it."

"Oh, hell, I hope not." John jammed his hands into his pockets. "Last ogre case, we ended up with wedding invitations."

"That wasn't exactly a typical case, though," Abby pointed out. She shielded her eyes and glanced up at the sky, checking the light. "And we didn't attend anyway, so you can't claim you were traumatized by formalwear or anything."

"Yes," Mal said. "Perhaps if we're very lucky, this will be a case of a simple murderous rampaging ten-foot beast."

John snorted. "You lot think you're so clever. Focus, please? Ogre's a possibility. What else?"

Mal and Abby exchanged glances. "Good question," Abby said. "Harv, what do the cops know?"

The smoke cloud shifted as it was pulled by the brisk wind. "And I'm supposed to just answer that right off the bat? Come on, you know the deal. Do the rhyme."

"Do we have to go through this every time, Harv?" Abby said, crossing her arms. "Please, just tell us what we need to know."

"Nu-uh. You know the deal. If I have to live with you people, I get to at least be commanded in rhyme like a djinn with some dignity. *Capisce?*"

"A genie with dignity wouldn't be doing a gangster impression," Abby pointed out, but Harvey gave her the closest thing he could manage to a stink-eye and she sighed. "All right. Gentleman genie with eyes aglow, Tell us what these policemen know."

"Thank you." Harvey spread out and went silent. A few moments later, his eyes brightened and he recollected himself. "Nope. They think it was some kind of body dump, but there's no drag marks or anything. And it's not easy to haul bleeding corpse chunks around town, you know?"

"Yes, I know." Abby pulled on her scarf. "Do they have any idea who he might be? Any clues at all, any conjecture, anything like that?"

"Huh," John said to himself. He crouched down and turned over a couple of flattened boxes.

"Nada. The one on the left thinks it looks like a serial killer, the one on the right is already mentally consigning it to the cold case garbage dump."

John squinted at the wall. "Do they know anything about melted brick?"

"What?" Abby turned towards him.

"Dude, are you high?" Harvey said. John shook his head and pulled away a few more boxes, clearing a large section of wall.

The bricks were melted. Not broken, warped or covered in something that might have dripped, but melted. The center of the wall was a swirling pattern of brick and mortar, with heavy drips and dribbles flowing downwards and creating pools on the ground.

Cautiously, Abby moved forward and touched it. The pools were hard and rough, exactly like a brick ought to feel. Only the mortar, long white stripes swirled into the red-brown like a streak of vanilla ice cream in chocolate, was still damp to the touch.

"Harv," she said, "is it too much to hope for that you know what this is?"

The cloud of genie drifted closer. "Not a clue," he reported. "There's no magical mojo coming off it, and it hasn't got a brain, so it's out of my wheelhouse. Kind of like you that way, Sawyer."

John ignored him and prodded the wall with his forefinger. The brick was solid, but when he pressed his gloved thumb into a swirled line of mortar, it gave ever so slightly. "Whatever happened here, it wasn't too long ago. This stuff is still a bit soft."

"But the building has to be years old," Abby said. She looked up, surveying the smoke-darkened bricks and splotches of graffiti. "What the heck could do something like that?"

"Good question. You got the sample kit?"

"Right here." Abby handed it over, and John began scraping pieces of brick and mortar into sandwich bags.

They finished collecting samples, but the light was beginning to change and nobody needed to say that they couldn't hang around for long. The group piled into the Camry, and as Abby turned the key, wisps of gray swirled out of the cops' ears and poured into the open pickle jar in John's hands.

"If you drop me," the jar warned, "I'll haunt you."

"Which would be different from the usual?" John drawled. Harvey shot him a dirty look.

• • •

The SSR maintained a small office on Western Avenue. The area had gone up and down over the years, leaving a confused mess of secondhand car dealerships, vacant industrial lots, and high-class organic supermarkets that lent the landscape a patchwork quality. The office itself had once been a failed clinic, but several years' worth of haphazard weekend repairs had turned it into a serviceable if cramped headquarters.

As usual, the place was a mess. Papers, folders, books, more papers, and photographs were piled on every available surface, and a guinea pig cage sat on top of the office printer with its guinea pig valiantly trying to gnaw its way to freedom. The pig's official name was Stinker, but an escape a few weeks ago had lent it a taste for the wild life, and an informal office petition had been started to rename it Bravehog. In deference to this, its cage now sported a cartoon of Mel Gibson shouting "They can take our lives, but they'll never take our kibble!" (Mary the psychic intern had denied responsibility.)

John absentmindedly dumped a handful of timothy hay into the guinea pig's dish as he walked past with a box of files. The box was labeled in purple Sharpie: BIG&SCARY.

"Ogres?" he said, offering Abby the box. "Or ma'am prefer something a little lighter? We've got a special on belieflings this week."

"Ogres, please." Abby neatly plucked one of the files from the box and opened it as she sat down at her own desk. "If belieflings turn out to be involved in this, I'm taking a six-month vacation. Consider yourself warned."

The file was depressingly thin. They still didn't have nearly enough information on ninety-five percent of the creatures they'd encountered. The SSR's founder, the Rev. Evan Jackson Willis, had had plenty of enthusiasm but not a lot of resources; after trying in vain to link up with various government agencies (who, for some reason, didn't want to talk to a defrocked preacher about magical monsters), he'd been forced to settle for learning from whatever he could dig up in the Midwest. Since the late '80s, the SSR had compiled a fair amount of data on some things but barely confirmed the existence of others. The ogre file consisted of six neatly-typed pages and a small sheaf of newspaper clippings.

Ogres tended to be rare and usually passed themselves off as people with glandular disorders. Some chose to intermarry with humans and father half-breeds, some lived on the edges of society and bothered nobody, and some were orphans who had no idea that they weren't technically human at all. In the SSR's files, they were classified as a neutral species.

But if they were in the files at all, it was because some of them had decided to take a different route. Ogres tended to be cleverer than their looks led people to believe, and they could achieve a lot by pretending to be stupid. One—before Abby's time—had been running a real-estate scam out of Teaneck, New Jersey and covering his tracks with a series of murders that were attributed to wild animals. John's mentor Oliver Kendrick had been the one to go after that particular specimen. It was said in the SSR office that afterwards Kendrick actually took a day off, an event about as common as a spontaneous rain of fish.

Abby perused the ogre file. The newspaper articles concerned murders, break-ins, assaults, or other happenings that might have involved ogres, all compiled by Mary the intern. Others were photographs of people with distinctive ogrish characteristics, and one was a newsprint wedding announcement. The grainy black-and-white photograph accompanying the announcement showed a massive, stoop-shouldered man with a lumpy face the texture of burned bacon, grinning broadly into the camera while a short, plump woman with curly dark hair gave him a look of mixed exasperation and affection. Abby couldn't help smiling back at the familiar faces: it was rare that a case, especially one involving an ogrekin, came to such a satisfying conclusion. She made a mental note to get the clipping laminated and reluctantly turned her attention back to the rest of the file.

She found herself hoping that the victim, whoever he was, had been a decent man. The ogre connection only a hypothesis, and the truth was that the murder of a well-liked person was usually easier to investigate than that of a criminal. Fewer people would have wanted him dead.

None of the remaining articles in the file could be explicitly linked to the current case, but two clippings featuring particularly gruesome bodies grabbed her attention. The most recent one had been filed only six weeks before, just ahead of the first bogeyman attack. According to the article, a man had been thrown from the 56th floor of a downtown skyscraper and landed in the river, cut to pieces and quite definitely dead. What had made Abby note it was the fact that the victim had made his exit *through* a thick pane of safety glass. That strength of glass was put into tall buildings specifically to keep people from falling, and if something was thrown against it, the frame would give way before the glass did.

The article said that the police were investigating the possibility of a defect in the pane, with the added hint that a lawsuit might be in the offing. But no, nothing seemed to have happened with that, likely because the victim had never been identified as an employee and no family could be turned up that might press charges. The only clue to his identity had been the broom thrown out of the window with him. Had he sneaked into the building for some reason, or was he just a janitor working under questionably legal circumstances? Janitorial work was sometimes the last resort of illegal immigrants or ex-cons.

Nothing definite. She circled the paragraph mentioning the safety glass, moved it into a separate folder and added it to the pile of material for Adam to go over. Pulling a random piece of paper towards her, she began to make some notes.

When she turned it over, though, Abby wished she hadn't. It had been on her desk for days, being ignored for a reason. The paper was a formal notice from her ex-husband's lawyer, warning her that *"any further attempts to restrict communication between my client and the minor dependent"* would result in possible arrest.

Further attempts? She hadn't even tried it once. But her ex was supposed to get their son one weekend a month, and even friendly bogeymen wouldn't take a break halfway through their work because of a court order.

Lord, she didn't need to think about this. She pushed the letter away and focused on her screen again.

The SSR office used a shared server, and the crime scene photographs had been loaded onto it. She pulled up three of them—one wound closeup and two overall shots—and hit 'print.' Ogre speculation was one thing, but they still didn't have any actual solid information; at this point, their best clues were in the murder scene itself. The clipping would go downstairs to Adam for his point of view later. Abby fanned out the printouts and grabbed an anatomy textbook from the communal bookshelf, hoping something would jump out at her.

Chapter Three

It was almost eleven PM when Abby locked her front door behind her and put down her overstuffed shoulderbag. As usual, the hall lights were out. She bit her lip and flicked them on, glancing down the hallway as she did so. Would she be waking him up?

Apparently not. The kitchen was lit up, and the first floor smelled like microwave pizza. Abby kicked off her dirty sneakers and cautiously made her way to the kitchen door.

Jimmy sat at the table, taking bites from a small pizza that he'd folded in half like a taco. Plates, silverware, and napkins were evidently not needed, and there were several drizzles of tomato sauce on the scarred wood. Jimmy probably hadn't noticed. He was engrossed in his cell phone.

"Hi," Abby said. Jimmy didn't look up.

"Hi, Mom," he said. "I've got a hundred and forty unanswered texts. My friends all want to know if I've been in rehab, and Dad is *seriously* pissed off."

"He is," Abby admitted. "I had to tell him you were really sick and reschedule his weekend. He threatened to call the judge."

"Good thing he didn't." Jimmy swiped a finger across the screen and tapped out a message. "Considering how I wasn't in this dimension or anything."

Abby paused. "I don't think he would've accepted that excuse," she said finally.

"Yeah."

The silence stretched between them, nasty and infinitely awkward. After staring at the back of her son's head for a minute more, Abby turned around and left the kitchen.

Her bedroom, like every other room in the house, was immaculately clean. She'd told herself that she was making a fresh start with her son, and their home reflected that. Ironing the curtains had probably been going a little overboard, though. It all seemed fussy and shrill.

She lay down and watched the shadows flit back and forth. More silence. Even the small sounds of Jimmy in the kitchen were muffled by the walls, and Abby might have once again been alone in the clean, neat, empty house.

It wasn't going to work. Groaning, she rolled off the bed and grabbed her shoulderbag and car keys. There might be endless work to do at the office, but at least it wasn't full of judging silence.

· · ·

The SSR office occupied a plot of land too large for it, leaving bumpy expanses of asphalt overgrown all around the building. A couple of large trash bins rested on the edge of the back lot, facing across the alley. Several businesses and apartments occupied the buildings one street over, and their own back walls formed an uneven border to the world of the backyard. At this time of night, most of the windows were dark, and only one business showed signs of life. It was the usual one.

Several small garages and car-customizing shops were dotted around the neighborhood, and Tribeca Classic Car on the next street tended to keep late hours. Their massive corrugated-steel garage door was propped open despite the cold and Pete, one of their painters, was taking in a delivery of Chinese food. He waved to Abby as she pulled up.

"Working late again?" he called out. "Demons keeping you up?"

"Worse," Abby responded as she locked the car. "Quarterly tax filing."

Pete made a face and retreated into the warmth of the garage with his bag of food.

As far as Pete and his coworkers were concerned, the SSR building was actually shared office space for a small group of academics, translators, and other self-employed types. The lot now occupied by Tribeca had been abandoned for a long time, so the agents hadn't bothered with spreading much of a local cover story until recently. The situation had become complicated when Mary, who was newly recruited and only fifteen at the time, had gone across the alley to ask the Brazilian-German Pete to translate a piece of old German writing found at the scene of a potential magical crime. Abby had only learned about this complication two days after the fact, when she'd overheard Pete talking to his buddies. "Young girl with braids, big smile, looks very like my little sister, and her paper says 'The unrighteous liars who persecute me shall perish in the fires of Moloch and Balaam—'"

That had been a slightly awkward conversation. Unable to completely explain away Moloch or Balaam, the agency had settled for being nonaffiliated academics with a folklore emphasis. Around the same time, John and Mal had put up a small car shed in front of the back door so they could switch license plates and unload bodies without anyone being the wiser.

Abby let herself in with a minor sense of relief, enjoying the warmth and liveliness of the office. A few weeks before, Mary had decided that the newly rebuilt south wall clashed with the grungy decor of the rest of the place and tacked a fleece blanket up over the plaster, adding a bit of color to the room. The furnace was turned up against the end-of-the-year chill outside, and a fresh pot of coffee was waiting in the kitchenette. Abby dropped a couple of miniature candy canes into her cup and took a grateful sip.

John and Mal were both still at their desks, clearly in deep research mode. Mal had logged into JSTOR and was scrolling through a list of articles from the *Journal of Forensic Sciences*, while John was looking through what seemed to be a late-'90s web site with red text on a black background. Several dozen sheets of paper were stacked on the office printer.

"Wow, that takes me back," she said, peering over John's shoulder. "Do you want any help?"

"Absolutely," John said. "Just pulled some info off the cop chatter. Victim's name thought to be Richard Francis Neill of Anamosa, IL. I'm checking the hits on the dating and networking sites, and Mal's following up the crime angle. This guy's name is all over some pretty bonkers stuff." The printer whirred and spat out another six pages. "Mind taking a look at those papers and sorting them out?"

"I'm on it."

Hours passed. Abby waded into the sheaves of paper with willing eagerness, which gradually morphed into generalized frustration and an exasperated hatred for all online stores, blogs, and role-playing sites with the word "mystic" in their names. Richard Francis Neill had been heavily active under his standard screen name of EctoplasmAngel, and if his various blog posts were to be taken seriously, he was phenomenally powerful as a sorcerer. Richard Neill had seen ghosts. Richard Neill had seen vampires. Richard Neill was friends with a werewolf. Richard Neill knew that the Angel of Death was stalking him. Richard Neill had been asked to do sorcery for the Mafia. Richard Neill was making magic for a dark queen. Richard Neill had a Hand of Glory.

Richard Neill was, most likely, lying. John called it Sawyer's Law: the more a magician talked about his powers, the less likely he was to have any. But no matter how much Neill had actually known about the supernatural in life, his death reeked of it.

"Corollary of Sawyer's Law," John said promptly when Abby pointed that out. "The First Rule of Active Irony. The more you tempt fate by talking loudly about your magic powers, the more likely you are to have magic bite you in the arse."

Around two AM, Mal joined Abby in the piles of paper. The two of them read through every printout and marked what was likely, what was unlikely, and what could be discounted out of hand. Abby, wielding a red pen, had to stop herself from correcting the grammar and spelling on Neill's posts.

By three-thirty, John ran out of Google hits and a picture of their mysterious murder victim was beginning to emerge. Richard Neill had, as far as they could tell, begun his online career with an alt.newsgroup posting in 2001, claiming that he had seen ghosts when he was younger. The creature he described—a shining white-and-silver angel with a sword dripping black blood—was like nothing the SSR had ever encountered or documented. That didn't mean it wasn't real, but after three pots of coffee none of the agents were feeling terribly charitable.

From there, Neill had moved on to the realms of modern Hellenistic paganism and Wicca. Or tried, anyway, since his claims about contacting gods had annoyed the genuine polytheists so much that he'd been banned from half a dozen communities. A turning point came in the fall of 2003, when he announced that he'd contacted spirits "across the burning pit" and that they'd given him the secret to true power. Neill subsequently started his own website and began offering his magic to any who could afford it. Given how he'd been dressed when he died, he seemed to have had some success.

"Unfortunately," Abby pointed out to the others as she sipped her coffee, "We can't entirely write off the possibility of him having real power. This entry, June '07, references actual books of magic. He might've started out wanting to do magic, and ended up actually doing it."

His website had page after page on what Neill could supposedly do. Some items, such as journeying to the likely-nonexistent Realm of the Faerie, could be dismissed out of hand. But a few more were believable for a sorcerer of several years' practice: creating charms to guard his home, conjuring illusions, and speaking to ghosts.

It was while paging through his site's archives that the agents found something of interest.

"'Current projects,'" John read aloud. "Find an effective familiar. Commissions: Staff of Resurrection, magic boots, magic bracelet, enchanted kevlar vest, amulet of warding.'"

Mal frowned. "Magic boots. The body was barefoot."

"But he had a bracelet," Abby said. "We should have grabbed it for testing when we had the chance."

"No way we could've known at the time." John put the paper down and made a few notes. "But add it to the list of things we might nick later on. None of that explains how he got ripped up, though, or why his hand was chopped off. Or, for that matter, where the rest of him is. Did he have any friends we could interview?"

"His blogs don't mention anybody." Abby held up one of the printouts. "It looks like he had a hard time making and keeping friends. Even the people who commented on his journals seemed not to like his attitude."

"Not the sort to take an apprentice, then."

"It may have been a helper spirit," Mal suggested. "A djinn or some other form of familiar. Perhaps we should ask Harvey?"

"I think we should," John said. He stood up and cracked his back a little, working out the kinks in his joints from several hours of sitting. "Where'd he go?"

Harvey's jar usually sat on a steel shelf next to the gun cabinet, but since that afternoon's expeditions, he hadn't been put back in his usual spot. Fifteen minutes' hunting found the jar perched on the edge of the sink, with Harvey swirling angrily inside. Mal quickly composed a few lines of doggerel while Abby and John brought the grumpy genie into the main office.

"Tell all you know of monsters, spirits currently afoot," John read from the paper Mal had scribbled on. "Perhaps a ghoul or a ghost who'd slay a master mage, Then take his hand, but not his foot, Come now, and aid us at this stage."

The bottle cap unscrewed, and Harvey drifted out. "I liked that one," he admitted grudgingly. "Not great, but at least it wasn't a limerick. You want to know about, what, servitor spirits?"

"That's it," Abby put in. "Something that would serve a magician, but have enough autonomy to either attack him or damage his body afterwards. It's probably within a few hundred miles right now."

"There isn't one."

John's brow furrowed. "What, that's it?"

"That's it," Harvey confirmed sourly. "Nothing. If there was a servitor spirit anywhere near here, any kind, any breed, whatever, I'd have sensed the ass-kisser and gone after it myself. Those little shits devalue djinni currency like nothing else. Everybody wants their three goddamn wishes."

Mal retrieved some of the murder scene photos and showed them to the genie. "Something cut this man's hand off after he died. Have you any ideas?"

"Sorry, can't think of anything." Harvey was drifting up towards the ceiling, trying to resist the pull of the heating system intake vent. Abby moved to the wall and turned down the heat, letting the genie collect himself. "They use any tools?"

"Yah. Probably a hatchet."

"Then it's... well, it might not be anything inhuman. Small monsters have claws and fangs, big ones can just tear things off people they don't like." He paused, considering. "Okay, some of them are tool users. Depends on how civilized they are. But when you're looking for pointless, petty nastiness, my advice is to look for a human. Usually Sawyer."

"A human. Maybe one of his clients?" Abby held up another paper, this one Neill's advertisement on Craigslist. "He did once claim he was being stalked."

"Taking the fantasy life a bit far, I think." John began flipping through the blog printouts, his expression skeptical. "He said he was in contact with his various supposed stalkers, his clients, the government, and his Internet girlfriend."

"The girlfriend," Harvey said instantly. "It's always the chicks. If you want ideas, break into her house and find out all her secret lifestyles and shit."

Abby shook her head. "She didn't seem to be into anything strange. Her Facebook and Twitter are all cat memes."

"We'll have to find the stalkers and the government men, then," John said. "We'll start out at the end of the rainbow and work our way through Fairyland."

"You'll be right at home," Harvey muttered.

"Bite me, muppet."

"Bitch, I will curse the *shit* out of you. Ten thousand years from now your distant descendents will still have boils and sores in all the worst places—"

"A'ight, Yahweh, back in the jar." John held it up and, with a glare that could have peeled wallpaper, Harvey whooshed back into it.

John capped up the jar and tossed it into the air. Abby's annoyed expression nearly made him miss his catch, but he snagged it with the tips of his fingers and stumbled back against the wall. "Watch it! What's that look for?"

"Don't tease the genie." She took the jar and settled it on the nearest shelf before covering a yawn with one hand. "It's been a long day, and there's no point in picking fights just because we're tired. Are we done for now?"

John and Mal exchanged a look. "I'll warrant so," Mal said. "There's little more we could do tonight with what we have. Perhaps the finding of the other half of Mr. Neill may yield some clues, but that is the business of the police. We'd do well to rest."

"Agreed." John cast a look around the messy office. "This place looks like a council estate, but Mary and Dummy can clean it up in the morning. Go on home, Abby. Back to your coffin, Mal."

Mal looked like he wanted to say something cutting, but was cut off by a yawn of his own. He seemed surprised at his own exhaustion; not given to acknowledging his own weaknesses, Mal was the ideal workaholic when it came to SSR business. Nevertheless, he gave a nod to John and Abby, and turned to go.

Dawn was beginning to break by the time the lights went out in the office of the Society of the Security of Reality.

Chapter Four

Richard Francis Neill, or what remained of him, was autopsied at the Cook County morgue. The coroner's report was compiled and duly made available. The *Chicago Tribune* gave it a colorful write-up, likely because it was a juicy story that didn't have anything to do with the usual depressing city news. The conclusion was death by misadventure unknown.

John read the article, snorted, and tore the page in half before tossing it into the trash. Abby wasn't sure why he bothered, since he'd only print it off the *Tribune* website later and rip it up again. Maybe he just needed something to do with his hands, but if that was the case, he should probably take up knitting.

It had been three days since Neill's body was found in the alley, and the agents hadn't turned up anything helpful. The mysterious brick samples turned out to be composed of nothing but brick, the police weren't releasing any more details about the murder, and none of their own inquiries were producing anything useful.

The ogre route had hit a dead end. Most of the ogres they'd ever met had gotten onto their radar for murder, and given that there wasn't any way to imprison or discipline an eight-foot supernatural cannibal those ogres were no longer available for questioning.

Only Paul LaCroix, the ogrekin from the wedding photo, could talk to them. Abby had called him that morning, but while he was willing to share information, he had nothing for them.

"I don't go with those people any more," he'd rumbled, slurring his words a little through scarred lips. "The ones who find out they're not human want to be special, and the ones that grow up knowing it are slaves to the ugly clan system. If an ogre killed a sorcerer, that sorcerer had some bad stuff going on."

That wasn't reassuring. Abby was looking at the crime scene photos again, trying to come up with an alternate explanation for the ragged wounds on the corpse, but nothing suggested itself. For the moment, they were stuck.

Their best hope lay with Mal. He'd found one of Neill's e-mail addresses from the website and was trying to get into it by any means necessary. Normally he had an uncanny knack for guessing peoples' passwords, but Neill's seemed to be defeating him, and it was clearly getting on his nerves: Abby heard a soft sigh as his latest attempt failed. She left him to it.

She looked around the office. John had gone into their small library to look for a book on the folklore of the Americas. Mal was still glaring at the computer. From the hair metal blaring through the floor, Adam was hard at work in the basement. Mary and Dummy were sorting through files. Judging by

Dummy's expressive hand movements, he was giving his own theories on what happened to Mr. Richard Neill.

Mary was seventeen and small-boned with bright red-blonde hair tied into complex braids and fringed with dyed feathers. Most days, she haunted the office and left the imprint of her personality in the form of décor, tidied-up desks and passing sarcasm. Sometimes she went into the field and used her psychic talents to read the minds of victims and monsters alike.

Recruiting her had been the smart thing to do. Psychics were hard to find and endlessly useful once they were in hand. Mary might be young, but she hadn't been damaged by the work as far as Abby knew. There was no point in borrowing trouble by worrying about a teenager looking at corpse photos.

And if Abby told herself that often enough, she might just start to believe it.

The case had stagnated, and it might stay that way for a while. It was a good time to make some changes. Thank God their only other teenage employee was on vacation; she didn't know if she could wrangle two of them at once.

"Mary, Dummy," she called out. The two looked up, guilty expressions quickly flashing across their faces like kids who'd been caught talking in class. "Come here for a minute."

By the time John had returned from the library, carrying two books and an unexplained box of peanut brittle, Abby was helping them pack their things. Mary kept letting out little squawks of complaint.

"Huh," John said, stopping in the doorway of the main office. "That's new. What, is there a flood warning? Bit early for spring cleaning."

"They're going home," Abby replied. There was a certain amount of flatness in her tone, more than she intended. "This isn't a good case for a seventeen-year-old to be on."

John leaned casually against the lintel, putting on a show of calm. "So something out of hand, and you think the best possible thing is to get rid of our psychic and golem? Not quite followin' your logic."

"We don't need a psychic right this second, and Dummy goes where Mary goes." The pale figure just nodded and handed Mary her backpack. She muttered something that sounded very much like "traitor." "*Seventeen*, John. You can't seriously argue with me on this."

"I can and I will, thanks." John detached himself from the door and stalked towards them. "We need every resource available right now. Melty brick, dead man, maybe ogres? Not a good time to let your guard down. And she's been doing this for a while already. She can't be scared of a bit of blood."

"If she isn't, maybe she should be," Abby said briskly. He had a point, but this wasn't one she was willing to concede. "I know what's going on. But when we hired Mary, we promised that we wouldn't be putting her in any danger. And last month she was right here when the bogeyman smashed right through that wall." She jerked one shoulder towards the fresh plaster. "If this case goes wrong too, the last thing we need is for these two to be in the middle of a fight."

That got a snort from John. "They've got to learn sometime, don't they? And before we get into any other arguments, try remembering that I'm the boss here, and I didn't authorize this shite."

Abby crossed her arms. "Are you really going to fight this? Fight sending *underaged agents* to safety?"

"They're not your fucking kids, Abby!" John exploded. "They've been there and done that, they know what's going on! You think they'll be any safer at home? If something magical wants you dead, it doesn't matter where you are! You ought to know that!"

There was a long, frozen moment of silence. Abby wanted to scream at him, but even if John wasn't going to be the mature one and hold his temper for five goddamned seconds (Lord, she wanted to kick him sometimes) she wasn't going to follow his example. Maybe he was technically the leader of the group, but she'd been with them for years and knew her own mind well enough. She didn't break the staredown.

Her resolve was rewarded when John grunted and looked away. "Fine," he said, waving a hand as if dismissing something so trivial he couldn't even be bothered with it. "On your own head be it, etcetera, etcetera. And Mal—" This was directed with sudden violence at the thespian, who hadn't even said a word or moved from his chair since the argument began "—if you're about to say one fucking word about the winter of our discontent—*don't.*"

And with that he stalked off again. He didn't bother with slamming doors, but he was probably close to it. He vanished into the basement.

"He's getting worse," Mary said softly.

Dummy frowned. *Winter of what?* he spelled out. Abby distractedly muttered something about Richard III, but her attention was focused on Mary.

"Are you sure?" she asked.

Mary nodded. "He hates everything. It's like, you know, that crappy dry-ice fog you get in clubs and stuff. When he walks into a room, anger just clings to everything. Has he been taking his pills?"

"I think so. I haven't been watching." Because she was wrapped up with Jimmy coming home. But really, was she supposed to watch what all of her coworkers were doing every minute of the day? "Do you think it's his condition?"

The issue of John's mind was a strange one. She wondered sometimes if he wasn't bipolar; he did seem to flip from high to low, but there was no visible depressive part of the cycle and as far as she knew he had never been diagnosed with anything. Mary could confirm that there was something unusual in his brain, but it never seemed to be the right time for a discussion about it. Not when he was a good agent and things usually got done.

Mary just nodded. "He needs a shrink, Abby. Pronto." She tossed one of her braids. "And I'm not joking. It used to be all inside his brain, you know? Less fog, more like a fungus or something, all in one place. Now he walks in and it broadcasts everywhere. When I say shrink, I mean, like, one of those industrial-strength shrinks. Get Dr. Sweets in here."

"I don't think we have the budget for him," Abby said. "But now do you understand why I think it's best if you leave the office for a while? I'm not trying to be a control freak. This is serious business." The phrase made Mary smile for some reason. "And that means getting those of us in high school out of the line of fire."

"You're not gonna need Dummy?" Mary pointed out. "He's eighty-five. Uh, eighty-three. I think. Dummy, how old are you?" The pale golem responded with a flurry of gestures that Abby couldn't translate and evidently followed it up with a thought, because Mary laughed. "Okay, close enough, right?"

"You know Dummy wouldn't leave you," Abby replied firmly. Dummy and Mary were a unit, and had been since day one. But even if they hadn't been, Abby would have sent him with Mary anyway. There was no way she would separate the psychic from a good bodyguard. Heck, she wished she had one for the rest of them, too.

She must have thought that a little too loudly, because Mary raised an eyebrow and whispered something to her companion. After a second or two of contemplation, Dummy removed one of his hands and solemnly presented it to Abby. She nodded and set it down on the desk, where it began to twiddle its singular thumb. No matter where he went, his scattered pieces would stay alive and in contact with each other.

Line of emergency communication thus established, Abby bundled the two of them into her Camry. She didn't say anything, but Mary of course knew what she was thinking: she didn't want to risk John coming back. Some types of confrontation Abby still wasn't much good at.

• • •

Mary's aunt, Georgia Morales, lived on the north side in a small one-story bungalow. Like most members of her extended family, she was familiar with Dummy; the huge albino had been part of the family since Mary's great-grandmother had discovered him in the late 1920s. Georgia's husband was somewhat less comfortable with him, but as long as Mary and Dummy were going to be living in Chicago, he tolerated him for family's sake. It had been part of the deal struck with the Scales/Morales family when the pair had first been headhunted by the SSR: Mary would live with relatives, and the organization had to promise not to involve her in illegal or dangerous activities. The "illegal" part had fallen by the wayside a while ago, but with luck, the "dangerous" part would still hold.

Georgia met them at the door. She and Abby knew each other peripherally, and as Mary's twin ten-year-old cousins tugged the young psychic into the house, Abby took the other woman aside. Dummy followed at a steady pace, carrying the baby of the family on his hip.

"Is everything all right?" Georgia said. "Or perhaps I should ask what isn't all right, and why not?"

"It's a long story," Abby replied. "But I know everyone will be a lot happier if Mary stays home for a while."

"Things are that bad?"

"Not exactly. But something may be happening."

"You know I'm going to have to tell my sister about this," Georgia said. "If you're getting Mary and Dummy in trouble, she needs to know."

"I'm sorry, I'm sorry. Believe me, if we could avoid this, we would. But it looks like things might be getting difficult soon, so—" Abby nodded towards the house. "Better this way."

Georgia gave her a long, hard look. "I'm trusting that nothing is going to come looking for her."

"You know I can't promise that," Abby said softly.

Without a word, Georgia turned her back and went into the house. Abby sagged as the front door closed.

• • •

When Abby walked back into the office, she was greeted by John. He was carrying a cup of coffee in one hand and an uneaten roast beef sandwich in the other, and he silently held out the sandwich to her. She considered ignoring it, but she was hungry, and recognized a peace offering when she saw it.

Mal, though, had something even better. He'd finally wormed his way into one of Neill's e-mail accounts, and the results were telling. Either Neill only had two clients, or he deleted a lot of his messages, because the only e-mails were from contacts labeled OP and C.

"OP is probably this man, Owen Petrovich," Mal said, pulling up Neill's links page from his website. "He has a small site advertising charms and sigils, and claims to be an academic."

"Everyone's an academic on the Internet." John peered over his shoulder. "What were they talking about?"

"Difficult to say. The messages were short, and contained a minimum of information." Mal clicked on one from two months ago.

From: OP
To: RN
Re: C

What makes you think the crystal lady will say yes to the project? She has more sense than that.

From: RN
To: OP
Re: C

Don't get jealous. It's a valuable proposition & the aura is good.

"Suitably mysterious, while still managing to tell us nothing." John raked a hand through his hair. "What about this C character? And who's the crystal lady? Sounds like the name of a drink."

"Anything else?" Abby said.

"Just strings of letters and numbers." Mal opened one e-mail and pointed. "With no pattern or code that I can discern."

"So Petrovich and Neill were talking about a project, someone called the crystal lady was involved, and someone else was playing Bingo long-distance. Not much of anything to go on." John's shoulders sagged a little. "All right, I suppose we'll have to do this the hard way. Mal, do we know where this Petrovich character lives? Public mailing address? Good. Head on over there and see what you can dig up."

Mal inclined his head slightly. "Immediately."

"Wait, wait. Stop." John held up one hand. "Look, just be *subtle*, would you? Maybe slouch. Change your clothes. Use abbreviations. Understood?"

Mal frowned at him, and Abby sighed and shook her head. John had a point, in a manner of speaking; you could try hiding Mal's light under a bushel basket, but the man himself was six-foot-five and looked like a Hamlet who had grown up and traded his puffy pants for a business degree.

"Why don't I go?" she said. John shot her a slightly pained look. "Look, Mal sticks out. We all know how this is going to end, so why don't you let me have the address and we can save a lot of arguing?"

"I was going to say you're taking too much field work," John said carefully. "Especially now that Junior's back."

"It's barely two o'clock. I'm sure I can go knock on a door and be back here by six." Abby crossed her arms, keeping her gaze level. "Next objection?"

"He's an actor," John pointed out. "You're not. He can pretend to be, I don't know, a mailman or something."

"Mailmen can still be suspicious. I have my secret weapon."

"Not the—" John began, but Abby had already opened her desk drawer and whipped out The Sweater. It was patchwork red-and-green, with a hand-stitched felt Santa's workshop featuring smiling elves. A little felt door opened to reveal an apple-cheeked, impossibly jolly Santa.

John loathed her holiday sweaters. No one could look at them and imagine that she was carrying a handgun, and he admitted that, but he claimed that felt candy cane trim would rot her brain. She'd retaliated by buying him one every year.

"Can Mal wear something like this and still be invisible?" Abby said. "Don't even argue with me, John. I'll go scope out this Petrovich person and be back before you can get lonely. All right?"

"All right," John said reluctantly. "But for fuck's sake, don't wear that. Get yourself up in spikes like an aging Goth or something. Just not that. All the other secret organizations will be laughing at us."

After some wrangling, Abby agreed to a pentagram necklace and dark colors, but no spikes and no Christmas sweater. It would be easy to do: the SSR kept a few boxes of disguise supplies in the basement.

The basement stairs were tucked away in a closet-like space between the two largest rooms of the office, and a faint smell of salt rose when Abby opened the door. She picked her way carefully down the concrete steps, moving slowly and making more noise than usual. A pair of hundred-watt bulbs shone through thick old-fashioned glass dish fixtures, illuminating the dusty corners and slightly stained drywall. It was, to quote one of their former members, "very mad-scientist chic."

On one side of the divided basement was a small workshop where Adam Starczynski lived and worked. The other side consisted of a single broad white room with a hatch in the floor and several long tubs heaped with gleaming mounds of salt. Sooner or later, every creature the SSR caught wound up down there.

The stairs took her straight into Adam's half, and she knocked on the wall before reaching bottom. "Hello?" she called out. "Are you awake?"

"Yeah," a gravelly voice said from beside her. Abby only jumped a little this time.

Adam was sitting on the end of his cot next to the stairs, half in shadow. He was just shy of six feet and, with his wavy blond hair and china-blue eyes, should have been good-looking in an all-American way. But there were deep, dark circles under his eyes, and his BDU jacket and paint-stained T-shirt hung loosely from a frame that had lost some muscle since he had been discharged from the Rangers. These days he looked less like a Ranger and more like a strange man living in a basement with lots of guns. Which, to be fair, he was.

"Jesus, you scared me," Abby said. "How are you feeling?"

Adam shrugged one shoulder. "Better today. Did you guys really bring me a sample from some brick that melted?"

"Yes, we actually did." Abby glanced around. The walled-off basement half had three separate workbenches, two closed wardrobes she knew contained weaponry, and piles of miscellaneous boxes and plastic bins everywhere. "Do you know where the clothes are? I need to be an unsatisfied suburbanite looking for a spiritual consultation."

"Not sure. You gonna need gear? What are you carrying?"

"Just the Tomcat." Abby made a face. "I'm not sure how much I'll be able to hide, since John vetoed the Christmas sweater." She knelt down and began sorting through some of the boxes stacked under one of the benches. There was a thick layer of dust scattered around, and she sneezed hard enough to almost bang her skull on the underside of the bench.

Eventually she spotted the box she needed. Adam tactfully turned his back as she shucked out of her outermost shirt, leaving her in her tank top and sports bra. She packed a money belt with extra clips and a few other supplies, then layered several tops and some heavy jewelry over it. When she looked for the pentagram, though, she couldn't find it.

"That's weird," she muttered, pawing through the bottom layer of detritus in the box. "Adam, have you seen that pentagram? The one Mary used for her Madame Leota costume?"

"Huh? Oh." Adam blinked vaguely and scratched his shoulder. "Yeah. I took a bunch of the jewelry to fix up. It should be... over there." He waved a hand towards one of the equipment cabinets.

The items Abby found scattered in one of the cabinet's drawers weren't quite what they used to be. When she picked up a pocketwatch (Dummy's, which had gone missing a few months previously) the back of the case flipped open, revealing soldering scars. Adam had gutted the watch, removing the old windup system and installing a tiny battery-powered motor. He'd filled the new empty space by inserting a GPS chip and a coil of something shiny.

"Adam? Is this concertina wire?"

Adam shrugged again. "Yeah, but I haven't figured out how to fit the handles in yet. If you tried to use it now, you'd cut your fingers off."

"Well, give it back to Dummy. He's been looking everywhere." She took the pentagram necklace, which had another tracking chip on its back and dangled from a rubbery loop of thin black detcord. "Do these actually work?" she added, pointing to the chip. Adam shook his head and made a gesture along the lines of "shit happens."

"It was one of the kids' ideas," he continued as Abby slipped the pentagram on. "Not sure which. But me, I'm not so good with computers. Might be able to make it work eventually, but it'll take more of a budget than we've got right now. 'Specially if you don't want anyone else with a GPS to be able to find you."

"Maybe you can ask the Director to increase the equipment budget?" Abby suggested. "I wouldn't mind some low-profile body armor. Sweaters can only do so much."

Adam grinned. The sudden expression brought life to his face and made him look almost normal. "It's not gonna happen," he said. "I think he has more fun watching us MacGyver our shit together."

With that cheerful thought, Abby left him. As she climbed up the stairs, she could hear him humming tunelessly as he moved further back into the basement, doubtless to MacGyver something else. She shook her head at the thought. It might not be right to keep Mary involved with their group, but at least Adam had work and a place to go. He hadn't had either before he joined.

• • •

Abby's off-white Toyota Camry was normally the SSR's choice of transportation; with a periodic switch of license plates, it was the most perfectly anonymous vehicle possible in a city of three million. This time, though, she chose to borrow John's black Saturn instead. It fit the character she was trying to portray. Abby Marquise liked a sensible Camry because she could fit her groceries in it, but the Saturn had low ground clearance and not much in the way of seating. It was a car that said "I buy cheap, but have no responsibilities."

Hm. Maybe she was projecting.

According to the mailing information Mal had dug up, Owen Petrovich lived in Wrigleyville. Apartments in the area tended to be expensive, especially since top-floor residences across the street from the baseball field could make tidy sums renting rooftop space to people who didn't want to be crammed into uncomfortable stadium seats. Further away from Wrigley Field, the apartment buildings and storefront delis were replaced by plain residential streets.

Several of the houses appeared to be clones of each other. Most didn't have much of a yard to landscape as the houses themselves filled up almost all of their plots, leaving thin strips of greenery edged with weeds or a single row of flowers. Some people had ripped out the lawns entirely and replaced them with flagstones or rock gardens, which Abby liked better. The half-sized patches of grass just looked sad.

Petrovich's house was smaller than the rest. It was white with brown trim and a large angled bay window looking out onto the street. The exterior was clean, low-maintenance and completely lacking in personality: no flowers or plants, no flagstones, no decorations of any kind. Every window had its shades drawn.

Abby double-checked the address, parked, and marched up the front steps as if she belonged there. People in the city rarely kept an eye on what their neighbors were doing, but it was still a good idea to act confident. Body language made a much bigger impression at a distance than clothing.

She knocked and rang the doorbell, but nobody answered. The glass panel in the door was just wide enough for her to peer through at the hallway beyond, showing her several closed doors and no sign of life. Something was lying on the floor by the front door, and by craning her neck, Abby could just see the edge of several pieces of paper. Letters? Was it a pile of unopened mail?

It was. And it meant he probably wasn't home, which was good news for Abby. She stepped off the porch and circled around the side of the house, checking for any signs of an electronic security system.

There was none. Petrovich, it seemed, had gone for the subtler forms of security: small rune-like symbols were scratched into the lintel at every door, setting up charms that would doubtless notify him when someone tried to break in. Abby moved around to the back door and examined the wood, finding more of the symbols there. She couldn't help but be impressed at the obscurity and antiquity of some of them, but the execution was awkward and the symbols were only lightly scratched into the paint. Would they even work? Possibly not. Still, best to be safe.

She reached into her hidden money belt and retrieved a packet of salt. Pouring a bit into her palm, she said a prayer and blew the salt over the symbols. For a second, sparks flared, and there was a smell of burned wood.

The theory was that some magical symbols were like computer chips, storing patterns of energy coded for a specific purpose. Disrupt their energy flow—for example, with a large number of tiny crystalline particles—and you short-circuited the chip. Abby had learned not to assume that any piece of magic would work the same way twice, but triggered symbols tended to be reliable. Petrovich seemed to be more creative in design than execution, which was lucky for her.

With the protective magic out of commission, it took only a moment for Abby to pick the lock. She carefully eased the back door open and stepped into the kitchen.

The kitchen was clean and top-of-the-line, with sleek brushed-steel appliances and granite countertops polished to a mirror sheen. She didn't have to be psychic to know that the fixtures were both expensive and mostly unused. Dust was gathering in the corners of those nice counters. A quick check of the refrigerator revealed nothing except a bottle of Rolling Rock and two half-empty cans of cream cheese frosting. One had a spoon in it.

She slipped her Tomcat out from under her jacket and softly stepped into the hallway. There was indeed a pile of mail in front of the door: catalogs, letters, and bills, all lying where they'd fallen after being pushed through the mail slot. Several magazines had slid down the small heap and ended up in the path of two other doors. They lay where they had fallen, undisturbed, which meant nobody had been home to move them. She still kept the Tomcat out.

The first door revealed a guest bedroom, sparse and untouched. Next came a linen closet, a small pantry, and a pair of doors with better locks and more runes scratched into the paint. Abby gave them a quick look before moving on: she'd come back when she was sure the rest of the house was empty.

She paused as she reached the mail pile. Something tugged at the edge of her awareness, like someone was whispering and trying to catch her attention. She took a deep breath, wondering what was wrong.

Something smelled familiar. Rust, copper, salt ...

Flattening her back against the wall, Abby thumbed the safety off her Tomcat and took another breath. Then she carefully peered around the lintel.

It was worse here. After years on the job, Abby had learned to recognize any number of worrisome smells. This one was much too familiar: that tinge of copper and salt in the air, almost like sweat, with the twist of strange sweetness that rot always carried. Even before she looked, she knew what she'd see.

The living room was filled with expensive imported furniture, all elaborate items from designer catalogs. Like Neill, their owner had money, but he'd used his to buy things that would last. An old Victorian fireplace had been closed up, leaving a mantel flanked with floor-to-ceiling mirrors in mahogany frames. The coffee table was rustic reclaimed barnwood, set against a deep wine-colored couch with curlicued armrests.

The corpse lay on a diamond-patterned Persian rug. A hand-painted copy of a Degas dancer hung on the opposite wall, and the calm eyes of the little poised ballerina looked down on the scene with complete impassivity. She seemed to be pondering it.

It wasn't a clean body, but it was a scientific one. Every inch of skin below the jawline had been carefully peeled away, leaving glistening muscle and yellow fat laid out as neatly as an anatomical diagram. No sign of clothes, or of skin either. That dancer probably would have wondered if any of his blood—and there was plenty of it—had gotten onto her canvas.

Abby's mouth tasted like bile, but she swallowed her fear and pulled out her cell phone.

There was a click, and to her surprise, Adam picked up. "Thank you for calling Moe's Crematorium. You kill 'em, we grill 'em."

"Go get John, please," Abby said as she carefully circled the body. The blood hadn't traveled further than the edge of the rug, she noted. There were no footprints or signs that the body had been moved. No splash marks, no drips, not even arterial spray. Abby rubbed her face. "I might have another dead sorcerer here, and he definitely didn't die naturally."

The line was silent for a moment. Then, faintly distorted, came the sounds of footsteps and a door slamming as Adam toted the cordless phone upstairs. Abby knelt down near the edge of the blood zone.

She tucked the phone between her cheek and shoulder, then unfolded a fresh pair of cheap rubber gloves from her money belt. They had come in a hair dye kit, and later on she would take them home and actually use them for their intended purpose. If it ever came to a search of her house, the only gloves the authorities might find would be soaked in L'Oreal and completely useless as evidence. Maybe that was paranoid of her, but only a month before she had met the actual things that went bump in the night. Safety first.

The phone buzzed and thumped as Adam sprinted through the office. "Sawyer! Hey, Sawyer!" he was yelling. Abby took a pencil from Petrovich's desk and carefully lifted up the edge of the rug to check the depth of the stains.

John said something she couldn't understand, there was an indistinct conversation, and he took the phone. "Petrovich is dead?" he said.

"I don't have a positive ID," Abby told him. The blood had soaked all the way through the center of the rug, but closer to the edges, it hadn't penetrated the twill backing. "Though there doesn't seem to have been anyone else here for days. The mail hasn't been picked up, and somebody's been skinned in the living room. I had to salt the door charms."

There was silence on the other end of the line.

"Huh," John said finally.

"Precisely." Abby stepped back and pinched her nose before taking a deep breath. The dead man had fallen facedown and his legs were flexed and spread, but his arms were tightly drawn in, with the right arm tucked under the torso. She glanced up. The ceiling was rough-textured plaster, mostly clean but old enough for intractable dirt to have collected in the deeper crevices. There was no sign of a hook or a hoist of any kind.

"Any foul play? Besides the body?"

"More like a suspicious absence of it." Abby retreated a few more feet, surveying the whole room. "He's lying right in the middle of a rug. It's soaked through in the middle, but not in the edges. It all must have ..." She closed her eyes. "Sorry. It all must have happened right here. The drip and spatter patterns all look right."

Keys rattled, and more footsteps echoed down the line. "MAL! Mal, pay attention, you naff bastard! We've got a—ahh! Fuck! Make some noise next time!" There was a clatter and the slam of a door, and John turned his attention back to Abby. "I swear he ain't human. How d'you think it was done?"

"I don't know." Abby shook her head. "No signs of a struggle, and I don't see any wounds apart from the missing skin. It's like his blood just... fell out."

"Novel." Her coworker didn't skip a beat. "We're coming your way now."

Considering the way John drove, she knew it wouldn't be long before her backup arrived. That didn't make waiting in a house with a dead body any more fun, though, and after walking a full circuit of the living room Abby quickly decided to check out the rest of the house.

She noted each locked room on the first floor and made for the stairs, determined to sweep the second floor for more traps or corpses. As she climbed, puffs of dust drifted up from the carpet runners and made her sneeze. Either Petrovich didn't vacuum, or he hadn't gone upstairs in a long time.

The staircase ended in a plain white door. She opened it and promptly found herself faced with a brick wall.

"That's new," she said to herself. The sound of her own voice startled her, but it was preferable to the dead silence of the empty house. She ran her gloved fingers lightly over the brick, testing its surface.

It *was* new: most of the bricks were a warm, fresh red, and when she rubbed a finger against one, it came away with a light coating of brick dust. The mortar was clean white, with no crumbled edges. She'd never had to judge the age of indoor plastering before, but if she had to guess, it couldn't be more than six months old. Why would Owen Petrovich brick up his own second floor?

She was still examining the doorway, hunting around for other possible entrances or clues, when the back door slammed. In the hall, John made a noise like "whough!" and coughed loudly. "D'you smell that?" he said. "Like old soup. Abby? That's not you, is it?"

"Very funny," she said. "Keep your voice down, will you? I'm up here."

John came tramping into the front hall, followed by Mal and Adam. The equipment guru was seemed more alert than he had before and was carrying a laptop bag bulging with tools.

"Oh," he said. "More bricks?"

John took the opportunity to start humming "Another Brick in the Wall." Abby rolled her eyes and moved back down the stairs.

"This is a first for me," she admitted. "I can't find any other way into the second story. And we can't ask him about... well ..."

"*Requiescat in pace*," Mal said. "Where is he?"

"Living room. Second door on the right. There's a few more rooms I haven't gotten into yet, too. He has pretty good locks. And watch out for charm symbols."

"If I may?" Mal said to Adam, who nodded and unzipped his bag. He handed Mal a little velvet roll, and the thespian disappeared back down the hall. John opened the door to the living room, peered through, then stepped back quickly, eyebrows raised.

"I told you," Abby said. John just shook his head as if he was trying to clear water out of his ears.

"That," he replied, "is evil. I'm impressed."

Abby, John, and Adam gathered in the living room around the corpse of Owen Petrovich. As Adam unpacked a digital camera and began to photograph the scene in better detail, John examined the carpet just as Abby had done. Abby herself, unwilling to look at the body any more than she had to, began poking through the sideboard and the bookcases.

The first thing she found was a well-worn book of Goya prints. An eyeless corpse looked back at her from the cover, sprawled sideways under what looked like a dead tree. The single word "nada" was written on a paper in the corpse's lap.

Abby liked coincidences even less than she liked bogeymen. She dropped the book, pushing it aside with one foot, and continued pawing through the collection. A book of Irish fairy stories, a copy of *I, Claudius* by Robert Graves, a reproduction of the famously cryptic Voynich manuscript, and a history of the Crusades were next.

"There's no theme here," she said aloud. "War, maybe, but I think he was just widely-read. His favorite was probably this copy of the Voynich book. The spine's broken."

John grunted as he crouched down next to the corpse. "Creepy."

"Hey, you gotta have hobbies." Adam tilted the camera, getting what must have been a rather artistic shot of John grimacing at the dead man. Abby quickly looked back at the cabinet.

The rest of the findings were sparse. A few old water and power bills had been tucked into the back of a drawer, as well as an invoice from a pest-control company. Apparently Petrovich had paid them, in cash, for dealing with a termite problem. All of his business seemed to have been conducted by cash or check: Abby found check numbers listed in the margins of a few of the bills. No sign of a cell phone and no cable service. Owen Petrovich was living as far off the grid as one could in the middle of a city.

All too soon, the drawers had been inventoried. For a living room, it didn't look like a place where anyone had done much living. Aside from the corpse laid out on the rug and the handful of books, the place was in almost showroom condition.

Abby turned back to the body and forced herself to look at it as detachedly as possible. "What do you think?" she said to John. "He doesn't look like he was fighting anything."

"Maybe not. Fingers dug into the carpet, look." John prodded the bloodied carpet an inch or so from the dead man's left hand. "But all this blood doesn't just come out of nowhere. No footprints, no signs of things bein' done to him, nothing. Remind you of anything?"

"Yeah. Blankets."

During the Black November crisis, the agents had gone to the scene of an abduction. The victim's blankets were still lying on the bed, forming a pocket around the body that should have been there. The only way to remove someone from their bed that neatly and quickly, while an alert guardian was in the next room, was to use magic.

And real magic was rare. Most of the time, the agents found themselves looking for angry ogres, hungry doppelgangers, or kill-happy fairies: the creatures living in the corners of the world who liked to have their fun or simply viewed the human population as food. Sorcerers popped up occasionally, but the agents didn't have much data on them and they didn't stick around for interviews.

But a few types of creatures could vanish someone out of a bed or teleport a bleeding body into the middle of a room. Bogeymen, for example. The same bogeymen who'd just handed her son back.

John was clearly thinking along similar lines. "Not likely this all happened here. There'd be arterial spray, for one. And not likely it happened elsewhere and got brought here, 'cause you don't ship a corpse around without leaving a mess. So if he was brought here, it had to be by someone who didn't need to use the door." He glanced at her, his voice oddly plaintive. "Tell me I'm being paranoid, Abby. Not the fucking bogeymen again."

"You're being paranoid." She hoped. "They take kids, not fiftysomething sorcerers."

"They made exceptions." John rubbed his face, touching the scars a bogeyman's teeth had left behind. "But please, when we get back, do some looking-up on that. Teleportation. Magic that zaps people into new spots. Anything that isn't bogey-related."

"Got it." Abby turned away from the corpse. "I'm going to go find Mal, okay? There has to be more going on here than just some bills and books. You do your thing."

"Have fun." John crouched down again and eyed the body, as if he was expecting it to talk to him. Maybe he did. She backed out of the room and went looking for Mal.

He was easy to spot. All but one of the locked doors had been jimmied open, and Mal was kneeling in front of the last holdout with picks in hand. He slipped a hook into the lock, worked it back and forth, and nodded to himself as something caught.

"How's it going?" Abby said quietly, crouching down next to him. "Find anything interesting?"

"Not yet." Mal slipped the hook out and selected another one, identical to Abby's eyes. "The other rooms were benign. But the lock here is much better, and I had to salt it first. I think this may be his workroom."

"That would be a big help." Abby sat back on her haunches. "John thinks bogeymen killed Petrovich."

She'd been hoping for a flat denial, but Mal just frowned in thought for a moment."Unlikely, but not impossible, I would say. What do you think?"

"I don't know. What else teleports?"

"Nothing that I can think of." The lock clicked slowly to the side, and the door swung ajar. "Aha! 'Wonderful things,' said Carter as he opened the tomb of the pharaoh."

"Gold and jewels would be nice, but I'll settle for answers." Abby stood up and stretched, cracking her back. As Mal put away the picks, Abby put a hand on her holster and peered around the edge of the door.

Here, at least, was a room that seemed used. The fireplace flue had been closed and the fireplace itself filled with steel filing cabinets, all padlocked. The room was lined with shelves, and every spare inch of them was crammed with books, CDs, boxes of miscellaneous receipts, and handmade clay statuettes that none of the agents could identify. The wallpaper was marked with a grab bag of mystic and religious signs, some real, some phony.

The dead man seemed to have focused on theory. Two hours' hard searching found exactly one cabinet filled with the tools of the trade, and very little of it had been used. His energy conduit was a plain magic wand, the plant and animal ingredients were dried up or completely useless, and the only sigil drawn on the cabinet itself was wobbly and indistinct.

"I guess he was more interested in the why than the how," Abby said, picking up a jar of garlic and squinting at it. She unscrewed the cap, gave a quick sniff, and recoiled. "I didn't even know garlic could go bad."

"Learn something new every day, us." Abby jumped. John had come quietly into the room while she was busy with the file cabinets.

"Do you mind?" she said. John gave her a lopsided, slightly apologetic grin and slid past her to the file cabinets.

Mal closed Petrovich's laptop. "Nothing to be found on the hard drive, not even a browsing history. He may have stored things on an external drive, but if so, we have no sign of it here."

"Of course not." Abby ran a sleeve over her forehead, quickly wiping away the moisture there. "We'll have to see what we can find on paper. John, do you have anything we can use?"

"Plenty. Address book, more check stubs, and, hey, adverts!" John pulled a bundle of photocopies out of one of the paper stacks. "From the Pine Forest Renaissance Fair, up in Wisconsin. Looks like he did a show about medieval witchcraft and things. Says here he was a professor of history." He handed one of the papers to Abby, and picked up the sheaf of stubs and the address book while she examined it. "And more. Shame he's dead, we could've used him," he added with bald honesty. "Look at all these degrees."

"We seem to do all right without any Ph.Ds," Abby said. "But that address book could be useful. Pass it to me, would you?"

"Here you go. Looks like it's in code, though, so don't get your hopes up. And look at these while you're at it." The thin man removed another stack of photocopies. "More papers. He did a lot of work on the fair circuit, looks like. San Diego Comic-Con, too. Heard it takes ages to get a booking there. Hold a mo, got something …"

John stood back, the new object in hand. It was a purple drawstring bag, made of satin, with gold stars stitched into the fabric. "Very Merlin," he commented, swinging the bag lightly by its string. "Very D&D. What's a professional sorcerer doing with this?"

"What's in it?" Abby asked.

"Dunno. Let's find out." John carefully unpicked the tangled string and pulled open the bag. A dry crust of bread fell into his palm. Carefully, John raised it to his nose and sniffed it.

"Smells like iron," he said. "Stale bread with iron filings in it."

Abby shivered. She'd always liked myths and superstitions, back when they were all safely in the realm of fiction, and she recognized that one. "He was afraid of fairies."

"But that doesn't wash, does it?" John said. "He was able to work enough real magic to put up charms, and maybe get himself killed. Wouldn't he know iron only works if you believe in it?"

"Not necessarily," Mal said. The tall man was flicking through the assembled copies of Petrovich's fair flyers. "Our archive of belief data only comes to us through extensive experimentation and mistakes. If he operated on the basis of tradition, he may not have even considered the possibility of belief."

"He sure looks traditional," Abby said, holding up a fresh sheaf of files. "Or he wanted the public to think he was, anyway. Look at this."

She fanned out the folders' contents on the desk. John and Mal craned their necks to look, and John cocked his head. "Fancy."

Each file folder contained a dozen high-contrast eight-by-thirteen glossies of a fiftysomething man with curly salt-and-pepper hair and a cool, confident expression. Instead of the usual magic wands utilized by single practitioners, he carried a carved staff about six feet long. Most of the other photographs showed chalked circles, knives and swords with ritual incantations etched in them, and other ephemera of the practitioner's trade. It was the same man as the one pictured on the website: Owen Petrovich.

The folders were unlabeled, but it was easy to guess that these were promotional pictures. The effect was blunted somewhat by the fact that all of the photographs had their colors reversed.

"Artistic statement?" John guessed, picking up one of the full-length pictures. It looked like a huge, professionally-printed negative.

"I don't think so." Abby fanned out some of the handwritten notes from the folder. They appeared to be in code, but they had also been scribbled hastily on orange-lined black notebook paper in white pencil. When she brushed her fingertip over one of the letters, the pencil smeared, creating grayish marks on the cheap paper.

"That *is* odd," John agreed. "Do they even make black notepaper? See, this is the kind of thing we could've asked Mary."

"I don't think they do," she said, ignoring the light jab. "Maybe the photos were printed as negatives, but this? I really don't know."

"Well, pack 'em up," John said. "We'll look at 'em later."

"Best be quick," Mal put in. He was standing beside the window, and his expression was tight. "Someone is out there."

Both Abby and John immediately dropped to the floor. Mal had flattened himself against the wall and faded back into the shadows, head still turned towards the window, his face a mask. Abby looked up at the opposite wall and squinted at the reflection in a picture's glass, trying to make out what Mal was seeing.

A black limousine was idling by the curb outside. Abby had parked a few blocks away, just in case someone did come looking for Petrovich, but that didn't really comfort her when she and her teammates had been right in front of the window only seconds ago. The car waited, its engine rumbling, but nobody got in or out.

It seemed ridiculous to hide from such a minor thing... or would be if they weren't busy ransacking a house while its owner's body cooled on the living room rug. The seconds stretched out, slow and tense, as they waited.

Finally, the limo pulled away again. John popped up from his crouch just far enough to peer over the sill, but there was nothing to see; the vehicle was too far away for him to get a good look at the license plates. He swore and slammed his fist into the carpet, raising a small cloud of dust.

"That was suitably mysterious," Mal said in a low voice, "and yet, accomplished nothing. We should leave before more visitors intrude. There is, as you may recall, a dead man in the next room."

"To hell with him, he's not going anywhere." John clambered to his feet. "But these files are. C'mon, help me."

They gathered up the folders and packed them into John's duffel bag. Adam, lingering in the doorway, watched with unfocused eyes as they did so but didn't offer to help. Instead, he blinked and wandered out of the room.

John gave a dismissive grunt and dropped into a thick Scottish accent. "He's awa' wi' the fairies agin."

"Hopefully not," Abby said as she hefted her own bag. "They've caused enough trouble already."

. . .

Jimmy was in the living room when she got home, sprawled on the couch and deeply asleep. His jacket was wadded up under his head, and one leg had drifted half off the couch and was resting on the coffee table. He'd been tired enough to not bother getting up and fetching a pillow first, then. It took her a moment to realize that she was inventorying his posture the way she had Petrovich's, and she resisted the urge to slap herself.

Nothing to worry about. La Donna Nera had said that he would be sleepy for a while, and he was still a teenage boy; most days she could barely get him out of bed with a crowbar. Especially school days. Which reminded her, she would have to call his school and let them know that his "pneumonia" was better. He'd mysteriously come down with it the day after the bogeyman case was closed, and even though the school was currently on break they'd want a confirmation that he was better before he could come back.

She took a blanket from the linen closet and draped it over him. He made a snuffling noise and shifted, burrowing into the couch.

Abby left him to it and picked up her bags again. The lights were still on in the kitchen, and her son had left the tail end of a microwave burrito on the table. She wrapped it up in, stuck it in the fridge, and cleared a space on the table for the folders and papers.

There were more black papers and negative photos than she'd first thought. Several were printouts, black-on-white, with reversed photos on them as well. The articles were all about local politics: elections, laws passed, motions proposed, lawsuits by or against the city. None of them were annotated in any way, but one— a recent revision in the city codes related to street festivals and other peaceful public gatherings—had been circled.

The notebook paper seemed to contain nothing but random jumbles of letters and numbers. Some appeared to be chemical formulas, with mathematical symbols and Greek letters scattered through strings of otherwise meaningless gibberish, but Abby wasn't much of a chemist and she knew she'd have to forward these to Adam or Mal. She tried a few simple letter-substitution codes with no luck.

On impulse, she tore a piece off the edge of the closest paper and turned on the stove burner. With a pair of barbecue tongs, she carefully pushed the paper triangle into the fire. A heartbeat later, it caught, and flames licked around edge of the paper before subsiding into glowing ash. Blue ash.

She tore another corner from a different piece of black paper and tested it. Again the flames flared up bright blue, and the pieces of burning ash left on the edges of the sample were tinged with cobalt. After a moment's consideration, she grabbed a piece of paper out of her own printer and tore a blank page from the notebook she used for recipes, hoping she was just seeing something normal. Both burned a familiar deep orange.

With a sigh, Abby checked the clock. Mal would be asleep by now. Adam, on the other hand, was even more of a night owl than the rest of them. She hesitated, but finally picked up the phone. Maybe she could just leave him a voicemail message.

He picked up on the first ring. "Welcome to the Church of Satan suicide helpline. Stay calm and take one step forward, it'll all be over soon."

"Adam."

"What?"

"That's not funny."

"Yes it is."

"Adam, what chemicals burn blue?"

"That depends." There was a noise of shuffling papers. "Do I have to answer? You sound angry, and I have a migraine."

Abby massaged her forehead and counted to five. "I'm sorry, Adam. I could Google this, but I thought you should know about it right away. There's something in Petrovich's black papers that's making them burn blue. Do you know of any chemicals that do that? It could be a hint towards what he was working on."

"Well, yeah, there's lots of options." Something rattled in the background before Adam's voice came back, slightly breathless. "Alcohol. Copper chloride, if you've got it right. Lots of artificial coloring agents. I once saw some guys make a fire with Pepsi boxes, and that stuff was like fuckin' cotton candy. It was amazing. What kind of blue?"

"Sort of tropical." Abby sniffed the black paper. "I don't think there were any coloring agents. I mean, it's pretty thin paper, and it would probably wrinkle if it was dyed. Unless it was that special scrapbooking paper." She shook her head. "Never mind, Adam. I think I'm chasing a bad lead here. Sorry to bother you."

"No prob." He hung up.

"Something wrong?"

The voice was so like Adam's that she started. Jimmy took a step back, holding his hands up defensively. "Hey! It's just me!"

"Christ, Jimmy." Abby settled back into her chair, heart pounding. "I thought you were asleep."

He yawned. "Phone call woke me up." He pulled out another chair and slumped into it, heavy-lidded and listless. Folding his arms on the table, he rested his chin on them and blinked sleepily at Abby. "Whatcha working on?"

That surprised Abby almost as much as his sudden appearance, but she tried not to show it. "Just some things from a new case," she said, fanning out the black papers for him to see. Jimmy peered at them but seemed to lose interest within moments. "These could be evidence in a murder investigation."

"The legal kind of investigation?" Jimmy said, yawning again. "Or the kind where you guys go shoot stuff that isn't supposed to exist?"

"The kind where someone was skinned." Her words came out a little sharper than she intended. Jimmy cocked his head and gave her a half-asleep "yeah, right" look, which didn't do anything for her temper. She pulled the papers back towards her, struggling to keep her sudden flare of anger under control. "I don't know if anyone's going to get shot. I hope not. Two people have died already."

"Of course they have." Jimmy rested his chin on his folded arms again. "Because people are always dying. And they're always getting killed by creepy things nobody knows exists. Right?"

"Right," Abby said. "Do you have something you want to say, honey?"

"Nah. It's not like you'd listen."

"Jimmy—"

"No, seriously, Mom, it's cool. It's not like I enjoyed not being kidnapped by ghosts or anything." His tone was bitter, and his shoulders hunched protectively. "I mean, you're always going to be freaking out about whether some guy got *skinned*. And I get to know that that's a thing my mom is into. Cool. I'll remember that next time we have Parent Day."

"It's not something I'm into, Jimmy, it's something I have to do." She flicked through the papers without seeing them, trying to keep her hands busy. "It's important."

"Sure it is. It's so importantly important that you couldn't live with someone who didn't know how important it was, right?"

"It's not like that!" Abby said defensively. "These things are real, and they could kill you! I wanted you to understand so you'd be safe!"

"Did you ever think I'd be happier not knowing?" he demanded. "Aside from you, who do we know that ever gets attacked by big scary monsters? Not Dad. Grandma and Grandpa, no. All my friends, nothing! What you did was like... like... like deciding I should be scared of cancer, so you gave it to me!"

"It's not a disease, Jimmy, it's crime. People are getting killed, and I don't want you to be one of them."

"What, you think I'm going to get *skinned?*"

"I don't know!" she exploded. "I don't know, *nobody* knows! We all have to just do what we can. And if that means scaring you to make you realize how dangerous it is, then that's what I have to do!"

"Is that what that was? Just scaring me? Like a fucking ride-along or something?" Jimmy sat up, face reddening. "Who the hell are you to try that shit with me?"

"I'm your mother!"

"*Biological* mother." The words were a growl. "Dad proposed to Diana. And you know what? She doesn't try to *scare* me."

That brought Abby up short. She'd known her ex-husband was dating someone: a woman with twin daughters, both of them a couple of years younger than Jimmy. She hadn't known Terry was going to marry her.

Her son's words carried a threat with them. Soon, Jimmy was going to have another mother. Legally, anyway. The thought stung.

"Fine," she said flatly. "But who your dad marries doesn't change the fact that those things are out there, and I did everything I did because I wanted to protect you. Is that so impossible to believe?"

Jimmy pushed the chair back and stood up, turning around. "Yes," he said. "I dunno. Maybe. Look, I don't want to talk about it." And before Abby could say anything else, he hurried out of the kitchen. His door slammed behind him.

Abby leaned back in her chair, closed her eyes, and tried to think good thoughts. It didn't work.

・・・

The knock on the door was light and hesitant, but it did the trick. Bright green eyes shot open.

"Conscript mother?" the soft voice of Phillips called out. The woman planted her hands against the mattress and pushed, forcing her stiff body to roll over. The knock came again. "Conscript mother, are you awake?"

She pulled herself up into a sitting position against the headboard and brushed her curls back over her shoulders. "I am. Come in, George."

The door creaked open and Phillips' face appeared. Normally his beauty routine was almost as extensive as hers (covering up gills took time, after all, and even on his best days the poor man never looked quite all there) but now his prosthetics were peeling and his real nature showed through. That didn't explain why he was coming to see her in the middle of the night, but she could guess.

"What's wrong?" she said, settling her hands on the bed's guardrail.

Phillips stepped into the room, raking one hand through his wig as he did so. "The team just came back."

His hesitation was obvious, and that meant only one thing. She shifted her grip on the guardrail and pushed herself further up the headboard, making herself comfortable in her nest of pillows. Her mouth tasted sour, but she knew her expression would be calm. These days, it always was. "And there was a problem with Petrovich's operation?"

"No, ma'am. He's dead." Phillips swallowed. "There was a problem with the retrieval."

"What sort of problem?" She brushed a curl behind her ear.

"There was someone at the house when the team went in for retrieval. At least two people. A man and a woman, judging by their silhouettes." He looked past her, his gaze fixing on the print of Romeo and Mercutio on the far wall. She gestured for him to continue. "Given the residential area, it seemed unwise to perpetrate a conflict at that time. The team made the tactical decision to withdraw until the items could be retrieved with the required care."

She raised her eyebrows curiously, as Phillips would expect. But her next question surprised him. "The team made the decision?"

"Yes, conscript mother."

At that, she couldn't keep a small smile from appearing. "You mean Mr. Ashwood made the decision. And there wasn't any argument from the rest of them?"

"I... yes, conscript mother. I mean no, conscript mother. The team agreed with him."

"I'm so glad to hear it. Please tell Mr. Ashwood I'm proud of him and his people."

"Ma'am?"

"They were able to eventually get the things we needed, correct? And without drawing attention to themselves or starting any unnecessary fights?" Phillips nodded cautiously. "Then Mr. Ashwood's team did a good job, and their decision-making skills are improving." She wound one curl around her finger.

Phillips relaxed a little. "Oh. Good. I'll tell them that."

"About these intruders. Were they burglars? Any indication that they were there for Petrovich?"

"The men weren't certain, ma'am. But when they went into the house for the retrieval, they found that it had been extensively searched." Her lips tightened and Phillips, sensitive to her moods, started talking to Mercutio again. "A lot of Petrovich's papers and belongings were missing, and the charms had been disabled."

"Which means they knew the charms were there in the first place." She tapped one fingernail against the guardrail. "Not a burglary. Knowing Petrovich, they would have been fried the minute they opened the first door." She gnawed on her lower lip, thinking. "Get me a complete list of everything found in his possession, and I do mean everything. Furniture, clothes, silverware, all of it. Monitor police communications, too. He wasn't much of a people person, but they'll find him sooner or later. And for the love of the old ways, George, can you tell me *anything* about these intruders?"

"Yes, conscript mother." Phillips moved to her bedside and extracted an envelope from his jacket. "There was a suspicious vehicle parked behind Petrovich's house. Ashwood managed to get a photograph of its vehicle identification number."

"Mr. Ashwood deserves a bonus, I think. Twenty percent. Make sure it's done." She extended one hand. "And I'll take that, thank you very much."

Chapter Five

Abby got up at six AM, and her son was already awake. He brushed determinedly past her in the hallway, didn't answer any of her questions, vanished into his room and locked the door behind him. A few moments later, Abby heard the tell-tale chime of the console starting up.

"Kids these days," she muttered, for lack of anything better to say. She tried knocking on his door a few times, but he didn't answer, and she wasn't sure she could entirely blame him.

What the hell had happened last night? She almost never lost her temper, especially not with Jimmy. It had always been something she was conflicted about: she knew she should discipline him, but she worked long hours and had put him into a broken home in the first place by agreeing on the divorce. (But on the third hand, who was she to blame herself for that? It wasn't her fault Terry would rather think she was insane than contemplate the existence of monsters. There were too many factors, too much confusion.) But the night she gave Jimmy to the bogeymen was also the night she had faced the demented leader of those bogeymen and slapped him in the face. It had wrenched something free, and when Jimmy had knocked her to the ground she'd stopped taking it and dealt out punishment to him as well. La Donna Nera had taken him away to show him the truth about the world. Now Abby was wondering if she'd broken what she was supposed to fix.

For a few minutes she lingered outside the door, staring at the wood. In the month her son was gone, the whole house had been cleaned top to bottom, and even the cheap old door had a fresh coat of paint on it. She'd gone to special effort to fill in the words Jimmy scratched in the wood, and now the whole veneer was fresh.

None of her options were palatable. Give him space? He might withdraw more, or worse, run away. Barge on in? She could persuade him, or just alienate him further. Try to relate to him? She'd been doing that for years, and it hadn't worked yet.

Finally, she went into the kitchen. More than a dozen take-out menus were stuck haphazardly to the fridge with magnets, forming layers like bristling scales. Her own favorites were near the bottom of the stack, but Jimmy's got a lot of use and were right at the top.

She selected one she knew he liked, did some quick mental math, and slipped a couple of bills into it. Then she slid it under his door and left the house.

· · ·

She was pulling up to the office before realizing she hadn't actually been thinking since she closed the front door. Unsure of what to do, she'd walked out of the house... and promptly driven back to work. These days, her world consisted of home and the office. She had no friends to go to, only coworkers.

Pete and a couple of his friends taking five outside the steel door across the alley. They were all wrapped up against the winter cold but chattered away cheerfully as they puffed on the cigarettes they were forbidden to smoke inside. One of them was reading aloud horoscopes from the paper. She wanted that. Relaxation and camaraderie, away from her job and the things that lived on the edges of the world.

If she quit now, she could have that kind of life. She could find a job that didn't involve illegal activity or magic, and she could find time to repair her botched relationship with her son and ex-husband. No more hiding weapons, no more chasing monsters, no more skinned knees on concrete or powder burns on fingers. It was an attractive notion.

But as she got out of the car, she felt the skin on her back itch. Whenever she moved, the thick bands of scarring there would tug at the more pliable flesh of her shoulders and sides, pulling at her like there was an animal clinging to her back. She'd been twenty-nine, married and mostly happy when a ghoul jumped her in an alley and tried to turn her into a meal.

Abby shook her head as she pushed the back door open. She'd seen the claws coming right before she blacked out, but the doctors (and her husband) had thought she was attacked by some kind of mad slasher with a railroad spike. Things hadn't gotten awkward until she insisted on what she'd seen. In divorce court, "attacked by monster my husband won't acknowledge" translated very easily into "irreconcilable differences."

She picked a book on photography off the shelf and pushed on through to the main office. To her surprise, there was no sign of John. Only Mal, unusually casual in a pullover and jeans, was at his desk. He was watching a live feed on the CNN website: more speeches at the plaza rally.

"What's the word?" Abby said, settling down at her own desk. Stinker the guinea pig plastered himself against the side of his cage and squeaked until she gave him more hay.

Mal offered her the coffee pot, but she declined. Mid-investigation caffeine headaches were not conducive to work. "The usual talk," he said as he put down the pot. "Various officials are promising to be tough on crime and clean up the city."

"Good luck with that," Abby sighed. "Anything about our case? Have the police found Petrovich's body yet?"

Mal closed the CNN window and pulled up several others. "If they have, there's no word of it on the news sites or police blogs. They might keep it quiet. Or perhaps it won't be found until some well-meaning neighbor smells it, or the postal service reports unanswered mail."

"Which could take weeks." Abby shook her head. "Back home, someone would've reported him missing days ago. Bad for him, but I guess it's good for us if we need to check out his house again."

"Fortunately, that may not be required right away." Mal smiled as he turned and put an open book on her desk. "I found something."

A jolt of energy shot through Abby, and she pounced on the book. It was a familiar plastic-backed day planner with a Degas dancer on the cover. "Petrovich's address book?" she said. "But it was all in code. You broke it?"

"Only part of it." Mal handed her a sheet of paper. Several short lines of prose had been transcribed, with tiny numbers appended to certain letters and a lot of scribblings and crossings-out underneath. "His copy of Graves reminded me of a conceit within that work—a cipher employing letters and numbers linked to a key book. I could find no particular key for most of the addresses and notes, but the broken spine on the Voynich suggested that it might be utilized in such a manner. It was somewhat difficult, given that the Voynich isn't written in English, but there are letters that resemble the English equivalents. Once I had the idea, it followed rather easily."

At the bottom of the page was a single neatly-written line. *Sarah L. Mulsey, 1C, Greenview Terrace Apartments.* Then came an address in the Bridgeport area of the south side and the words *knock loudly and never apologize*.

"Mal, you're a genius!" Abby said eagerly. "This woman could tell us about Petrovich. And if she knew him, she might know Neill too! We have to go talk to her right away."

"Agreed. But Abigail, I would counsel caution." Mal's brow furrowed as he took the paper back. "We know nothing about this person. Indeed, she could be Petrovich's killer. The fact that he used the Voynich manuscript to encode her address suggests unsettling possibilities."

"Maybe he just wanted that extra layer of security. Anyone picking up a copy of Voynich usually puts it down five seconds later unless they're a hardcore cryptogram fan." Abby knew that for a fact. The Voynich manuscript had been written sometime in the early fifteenth century and was over two hundred pages of undecipherable writing and diagrams of things that didn't exist, so of course the SSR owned at least two copies. Finding them under the hundreds of other books would be a challenge, but they were there.

"That may be," Mal conceded with obvious reluctance. "Nevertheless, I'm unable to entirely discard my feelings of apprehension."

"Me neither," Abby said. "I think that's called 'being sensible.'"

When John came in thirty minutes later, looking rumpled and sleepy-eyed,

Abby had pulled up a satellite photo of Mulsey's neighborhood and was checking their archives for any records of trouble in that area. The results were reassuring: Bridgeport clocked in the medium-low range for street crime, and they had no records of ever investigating supernatural threats in the area.

"Undercover cops, then," John said when Abby had finished bringing him up to date. "We'll just be civilians until anyone asks questions. Where's the new badges?"

"I think Dummy left them in the gun safe. Top shelf." Abby dug through her drawer and tossed him a box of Band-Aids. "Don't forget to cover up your tattoos."

He gave her a look. "Yes, mum."

"And tuck in your shirt!" she called after him as he headed for the door. "You weren't born in a barn!"

"As far as you know!"

"Good point. Should I be putting down some tarps?"

John rolled his eyes and extended two fingers in her direction. She just laughed and tossed an eraser at him, which he dodged as if it was a bomb. "Death to the oppressors!" he shouted and ducked into the basement staircase before she could retaliate.

"Vive le roi!" Abby yelled after him. It was only as the door closed that she remembered Mal was still in the room. A momentary blush of embarrassment crept over her cheeks, but she shrugged a little at Mal's expression and settled back into her chair.

"So," Mal said. "You're a monarchist?"

"Well, if he was a revolutionary, I couldn't be one too," Abby said. "Unless I wanted to be someone like Robespierre, and I like having my head not cut off."

"Sensible indeed."

• • •

Sarah Mulsey's apartment complex was one of three identical buildings on a single city block. Patches of siding had fallen away, and more had been covered with several layers of eggshell-colored paint. From the way it was peeling, it was probably not meant for outdoor use.

Inside, the hallway was painted a color Abby could only describe as off-beige. Every door was closed, and the muted thud of bass reverberated through the walls. One door had several lines graffitied on its lintels in Sharpie, including a couple of Twitter hashtags apparently put there out of boredom.

Mulsey's door was easy to find. It was the one with yellow crime scene tape on it.

"Hell," John murmured as the two of them stopped in front of it. The door was closed and locked, with no signs of being forced or having a lock recently replaced. The tape, on the other hand, had clearly been moved several times. "Someone been in and out, but if this stuff is still here, it probably ain't our girl."

A hollow feeling settled in Abby's stomach. "Maybe she got burgled and went to stay with relatives," she suggested, but didn't believe it any more than John did. The two of them stood silently for a moment, looking at the door.

Finally, John let out a soft breath and fumbled in the pocket of his parka. "Well, wherever she is, we should have a look," he said, withdrawing the little velvet roll of lockpicks. "Let's hope no one decides to get inquisitive."

"Amen." The hallway was empty except for them, but Abby still moved to the side of the door and casually blocked John from the view of any nearby apartments while he picked the lock.

The door swung open. Despite the early hour, the place was completely dark, and Abby's gloved hand fumbled awkwardly along the wall for a light switch. She could hear John sniffing at the oddly fragrant air while she searched.

Finally, her fingers touched the switch. The overhead lights blinked on. John whistled. "Looks like playtime's over."

"John," Abby said automatically. "Close the door behind you."

"I don't want to. They might eat me."

"*John.*"

"All right, all right." John pulled the door closed and locked it again. "Just keep your eyes on them, and don't blink."

Abby had never been afraid of clowns or dolls. She had some minor issues with large bugs, especially centipedes and anything else that had been first in line when the legs were handed out, but the unwavering fixed smiles that populated other kids' nightmares didn't really do anything to her. Movies about evil puppets had become a lot less scary after she learned to shoot straight.

That being said, she could sympathize with John right then.

Sarah Mulsey's apartment was filled with dolls. Not just the eerie, staring Victorian dolls one might expect in the home of someone possibly linked to a mysterious death; that would actually have made Abby feel better, since it was hard to be scared by something that reminded you of the rummage sales Grandma frequented. But Mulsey had owned big dolls, small dolls, human dolls, animal dolls, expensive dolls, cheap dolls, cloth dolls, plastic dolls, exquisite little confections of antique lace and Dollar Store made-in-China, close-enough-to-confuse-well-meaning-toy-buyers polyester knockoff stuffed toys. Dozens of them. *Hundreds* of them. They were lined up against the walls, stacked seven or eight deep in all directions.

Underneath the empty smiles and staring black eyes, Abby could detect order. The gray-brown carpet, exactly the same as the stuff in the hallway, had been covered with several large rugs in bold modernist patterns. Rust-red, yellow ochre and saffron predominated, and the worn, sprung couch was chocolate-brown leather with a colorblock throw on the back. Small tables were set at each end of the couch, and on each one (nearly hidden by the heaps of dolls) was a yellow-orange crystal the size of a large cat. The base of each crystal was lodged in rough dark rock, and the irregular spikes and blocks of flame-colored stone reflected and refracted the lamplight.

An odd little tableau dominated the center of the room. A small coffee table and two chairs sat there, but one of the chairs had fallen backwards onto the rug. Just above the fallen chair's headrest, a plate-sized patch of carpet had been cut away. A few dappled stains on the wood underneath showed brownish-red.

"Well, this doesn't look good," John noted, crouching down next to the chair and taking a quick photo with his phone. "What d'you think? Blood?"

"It certainly looks like it." Abby took her silver crucifix between two fingers and rubbed her thumb over the worn metal, silently hoping they were wrong. "Something happened to someone sitting in the chair. They fell backwards and lay there, but only bled a little. The blood would have gone everywhere if they'd been struggling, so it must have been quick."

John frowned. "That's assuming this is all as it was, mind. The cops've been all over the place."

"Right. Maybe we should've brought Harvey." Abby sniffed as well. "What's that smell?"

"No idea, but it stinks." John wrinkled his nose and glanced around. "Sort of warm and spicy. Think she's a cook?"

Abby stepped carefully around the overturned chair and looked into the kitchen. The dolls were here too, crowding the minimal counter space and lounging on top of the refrigerator. "No way," she said. "You could probably heat up soup in here, but that's about it. I think it's an air freshener."

"Aw, shite, can we get rid of it? Those things make me sneeze." John wrinkled his nose again and sniffed wetly.

"Check the wall sockets. If it's still lingering with Mulsey gone, it's probably one of those plug-in vapor things." Abby knelt and brushed aside a family of ragdolls propped against the baseboard. The largest doll, outfitted as a 1950s sitcom father with a newspaper, pipe and slippers, thudded heavily as it landed on the carpet. She nudged it with the toe of her shoe. It was filled with sand.

"Not here." John was scuffling around on the other side of the living room, pushing through a small mountain of dolls with his gloved hands. A muffled sneeze exploded from the pile, sending two toy cats and a Pierrot clown tumbling to the floor. "Fuck!"

"Keep it down," Abby cautioned. The baseboard wall sockets were clear. She poked her head into the bedroom, but there was no sign of anything there either, and the spicy scent was weak at best. John sneezed again and muttered dire imprecations, making Abby sigh.

Finally, she opened the tiny coat closet by the door. "Got it!" she called out, kneeling down to yank the little scent vaporizer out of the electrical socket. Another sneeze was her only response. Abby looked around for something to wrap the vaporizer in and spotted a box of plastic bags in the back of the closet, perched on what looked like an older-model Roomba.

"Ow!" The back wall was closer than she realized. Abby massaged her bruised forehead. The wall was rough, and had left tiny pieces of grit stuck in her skin. "More darn brick," she muttered.

Which was odd, because the apartment walls were plaster.

Abby shuffled backwards out of the closet and pulled the door open wide to let some light in. Yep, brick: fresh and new, almost unrealistically bright red with clean white mortar. The lines were so perfect that it was easy to notice where the bricks seemed to twist and the mortar dripped.

Perfectly solid, but almost... melted-looking.

Hell.

"John," she said, "I think whatever got Neill's been here."

Her partner's only response was another choked sneeze. John came loping towards the closet, wiping his nose on a bit of toilet tissue. "Well, fuck," he said damply before stifling another sneeze. "That's just what we needed. Let's have a look." He briefly inspected the brick, swore for no apparent reason, and took out his cell phone.

"Adam? C'mon, you daft bastard, pick up... Adam! Thank you. Did you ever get a chance to look at those bits of brick we gave you? Yah, the melted stuff..." He nudged the brick wall with the toe of his shoe while he listened. "Really? Goddamn it." He hung up without further ado. "The brick was just brick. So either this is just brick too, and we're seeing an amazing coincidence as evidence, or it's not and we're not." He snuffled into the tissue. "Fuck."

"Has anything ever been recorded as melting brick this way?" Abby pressed. "I've been through the whole Anthology, and I never saw it."

"Reality disruption?" John offered through his tissue.

"I don't know. Reality disruptions usually move things, not reshape them." She frowned at the wall again. "But I just don't know. It's not like we have a whole lot of information. But it's a link. Melted brick by Neill's body, and an unexplained brick wall in Petrovich's house—"

Her words were cut off by another thunderous sneeze from John. "Fuck," he said damply. "Sorry. Look, is there another one in here? I can't breathe."

Abby and John plowed through the silt of plush toys around the edges of the room. In quick succession they uncovered three more plug-in air fresheners, a jar of perfumed oil with diffusing reeds in it, and a magnificently chintzy wine-bottle lamp that appeared to have been coated with some kind of scented wax. John was sneezing too much to get a sentence out, so Abby bagged the various items and dropped them in the empty kitchen garbage can. Her partner ran to the kitchen window, opened it, and panted in the cold wind like an exhausted dog.

Gradually the sniffling and wheezing began to decrease. A watery-eyed John scrubbed his face with a handful of snow from the kitchen window as the fresh air swept the offending scents away.

Abby was kneeling by the wall, examining the spot where she'd found one of the air fresheners, when John came loping back into the living room. "The fuck was that?" he demanded of nothing. "Who needs that crap?" He stifled another sneeze, mopped his eyes on his sleeve, and finally managed to take a deep breath. "Abby? What're you doin'?"

"Finding a mystery, I think," Abby said. Instead of brushing aside the piled-up dolls this time, she carefully began to stack them. Sections of carpet came into view. "I thought so. John, look at this. I spotted it when I was checking the wall sockets."

"Huh." He knelt down next to her and prodded at the carpet. "Shoe prints. So?"

"Shoe prints *under* the dolls." Abby moved more of them out of the way. Her heart was beginning to pound, but not in fear. "When we came in, these dolls were all lined up perfectly. And look." She shifted another pair of toys. "Vacuum lines. I spotted more of these on the other side of the room, too, and they go over the shoe prints. Someone was vacuuming in here recently."

John made a face. "Less of the twenty questions. What're you getting at?"

"There was a Roomba in the closet, but I can't see someone shifting over a hundred dolls just for the sake of vacuuming the edges of the room. Some of these things are filled with sand, too." She nudged the fifties father doll with the toe of her shoe. "And they're clean, too. No dust or carpet fluff or anything. I don't think hoarders are normally so careful about their possessions."

"So they shouldn't be here?" John scratched his chin. "Not that I'm not open-minded, but that's a little far-fetched. What, did they just pop into existence?"

"I'm not saying that. But I am saying they probably weren't here until recently, and a big change just before something weird happens is suspicious." Abby glanced around, taking in the rows and rows of staring eyes. "In one of the stories my grandpa used to tell me, there was a magic doll. It could do anything its owner wanted, even things that were supposed to be impossible. Even Baba Yaga couldn't beat it. Maybe …"

John winced. "Wish you hadn't said that. Now I'm gonna be imagining that hairy old bat hanging over our shoulders."

"Maybe she is." Abby turned over another of the toys, a dough-faced Cabbage Patch knockoff. "But Russia isn't the only place with stories of magical dolls. Plenty of people have looked at fake humans and said 'that's creepy.' And then there's their use in rituals, like with poppets."

"You mean a voodoo doll? But we were never able to get any of that stuff to work."

"We weren't exactly testing it scientifically," Abby pointed out.

John glanced around, making a face at the rows of dolls. "I don't see anything here that looks like it could do that. But if I say it's impossible, the gods of irony'll drop an anvil on my head. I fucking hate dolls."

"I'm starting to see why." Abby dusted off her hands. "Maybe we should ask the neighbors if any of them know anything about Mulsey or the dolls? I don't think any of these things are going to talk."

"If we're lucky." John eyed the nearest heap of toys as if expecting them to object. "I think we can safely say something bad's happened to Mulsey, though. Let's start with next door. If there was a murder or something here, they have to have heard something. Are we still cops, d'you think?"

"Depends on who's in there. Maybe private investigators? District attorney's office?"

"DA's office, yah. She's making all kinds of promises about cleaning up police misconduct, after all." John rifled through his pockets again and located the appropriate ID, tossing another one to Abby. "Let's go be concerned about stuff."

Abby nodded. "Let's."

Chapter Six

1B's door was heavily scuffed around the edges and the marker vandal had struck again, this time with a selection of Jay-Z lyrics. John corrected a couple of spelling mistakes while Abby rapped on the door. Heavy footsteps sounded, and the door creaked open.

The occupant of 1B looked like a fighter: medium-height and leanly muscled, with a sparse quarter-inch of dark brown stubble on his scalp and what looked like a fresh cut on his lip. He glanced between John and Abby with mild suspicion.

"Hi," Abby said. "I'm Brittany Douglas and this is Joe Acton." She flashed the fresh ID. "We're from the district attorney's office, investigating allegations of police mistreatment of civilians in this ward. We'd like to ask you a few questions."

The man's eyebrows shot up. "Seriously?" he said. "I mean, wow. I didn't know. I mean, I haven't seen anything."

"What's your name, sir?"

"Uh, Leonard Scott."

"According to our records, there was an altercation in apartment 1C not long ago," John said. Despite the seriousness of the situation, Abby had to work not to smile. The bureaucratic double-talk sounded so bizarre coming from him. "It would greatly assist our investigation and report if you would spare us a few minutes of your time."

Scott hesitated for a moment, then nodded and stepped back. "I... sure. Okay. Do they know who hurt the old lady?"

Confirmed. Abby's temporary burst of good humor died even as she spoke. "We can talk about it inside," she promised. Scott made room, and the two agents stepped into the apartment.

Unlike Sarah Mulsey, Leonard Scott had a very utilitarian view of apartment decoration. The carpet had been ripped up and replaced with stick-down linoleum tiles in a flat beige, and the walls had been painted the same color as the exterior siding. Probably from the same can, too. A treadmill sat opposite the TV, and most of the remaining living room space was taken up by a weight bench, a large stereo system and several stacks of DVDs and paperbacks. There was a bookshelf, but it was full of more DVDs and classic vinyl. Several half-full cardboard boxes indicated that Scott had either recently moved in, was planning to move out soon, or just never bothered to fully unpack.

"Thank you," Abby said. "Can you please tell us what exactly you know about the incident with Ms. Mulsey?"

"Uh, sure." Scott perched awkwardly on the back of a battered futon. "I always see her around. She's pretty old, you know, and she lost her legs a while back. Car accident, she told me. And there's all that snow and shit, so she only goes out when it's nice. I can always hear her rattling around next door." A thought struck him, and he swallowed. "I mean, uh, I used to."

"And you stopped hearing her?" Abby prompted as gently as she could.

"Not really. I was asleep, but my bedroom's right over there—" he pointed "—and they share a wall. So I heard this scream, sort of like a cat, and it woke me up. It went on for a couple of minutes, I think." He scratched his neck and shifted. "I wasn't sure if I was imagining it or not. I mean, there was a big party at my sister's, and I was kind of wasted. My head was killing me. I went back to sleep. But when she didn't make any noise for the next couple of days, I figured I should call someone, y'know?"

"And what happened when the authorities arrived?" John said. He was standing by the wall with an expression of terminal alertness. "Did you observe their activities?"

Scott eyeballed John. *You're weird*, the message of the eyeballing was. "Sort of. I mean, the cops came to ask me questions. And I saw the... body get taken away." He swallowed again but tucked his hands into his pockets, trying to look casual.

"Are you aware of what happened to the victim?" Another confirmation: Sarah Mulsey was dead. Phrasing the question as a test would make it look slightly less suspicious, but if Leonard Scott was quick on the uptake he might ask for more than an ID. Abby wished again that they'd brought Harvey.

Scott didn't seem too surprised by the question, but he did look somewhat disturbed. "I... yeah. I mean, something weird happened to her eyes, right?" he said. "Her eyes and brain. One of the forensic guys said they were just, like, *gone*. They thought she might've been messing with dangerous chemicals or something. They asked me if she was cooking meth."

His head ducked a little at the thought, so Scott didn't see John shoot Abby a look. *Eyes and brain?* he mouthed. Abby replied with a quick grimace and a shrug: she'd never heard of anything like it, in fairy tales or anywhere else.

"Thank you for confirming that," Abby said gently. "I know it has to be tough to talk about these things, but we need to double-check everything. Do you know if there anyone who might have wanted to hurt Ms. Mulsey?"

Scott's head came back up, and the eyeballing was transferred to her. "I told the cops all that stuff already."

"Just answer the question, please," John told him. Abby frowned at him, doing her best to convey that he was behaving inappropriately. She always worked best as the Good Cop.

"No. No one I know about, I mean. My rule is, no matter what there's someone out there that wants to screw you over. That's life." He shrugged. "But I didn't see her piss anyone off. She was nice."

"Did you know her?" Abby asked. "Did she mention anyone to you that she might have been concerned about? Friends, relatives, business partners, members of a church?"

Lenny shrugged again. "Don't think so. We didn't really talk."

"Did she have any visitors?"

"Nope."

"Sir," John interrupted, "we found men's shoe prints in her apartment. Unusual in the home of a woman with no legs."

"So what?" Lenny shot back. "What's with you guys? The cops probably left 'em."

"Shoe prints under the dolls," John clarified.

"What dolls?"

John and Abby exchanged looks again. John quirked an eyebrow at Abby, his only visible reaction to Lenny's statement. The witness glanced back and forth between the two of them, surprised and a bit defensive. "What? What'd I say?"

Abby took the lead this time. "My partner was referring to the toys in Ms. Mulsey's apartment," she said. "Were you familiar with them?"

"Oh! Uh, yeah. The dolls. They're new, but she had them the last time I saw."

"So you visited her apartment?" Abby said. Gotcha.

"But you said you didn't talk to her. Mr. Scott, let me remind you that it *is* a crime to conceal evidence from a federal officer in the execution of his duty," John added his tone beautifully bland.

Scott threw up his hands. "Fine! Fine! Fuck. Look, I helped her occasionally, okay? *That's* not a crime. She wasn't exactly fast, you know? She was on one of those little scooter things. You're not gonna arrest me for that, are you?"

"No, we're not," Abby reassured him. "I'm sorry for the trouble, Mr. Scott, but we have to get this as clear as possible."

"Look, there's not much I can tell you. She lived alone. She went shopping sometimes—I took her mall-crawling up at the HIP once. She loved it."

"There was a computer in her bedroom," Abby said, making a show of checking her notes. "Did you know of her e-mailing anyone? Did she know anyone online?"

"I dunno about e-mail. She bought stuff off eBay a lot."

"Like what?"

"Mostly crystals. She was really into that New Age stuff. She kept getting these big boxes of geodes from New Mexico or something."

Abby made a few more meaningless notes, but her brain had begun to spark and she resisted the urge to glance at John again. No sense in acting suspicious. But crystals? Owen Petrovich had been in contact with someone he called the Crystal Lady, and Abby couldn't think of a better person to carry that name than a woman who put hundred-pound blocks of quartz on a side table like it wasn't anything.

"Everyone has their hobbies," was all she said. "My aunt used to collect Coca-Cola merchandise. We had to step in after she retiled her kitchen red and white." That got a small grin from Scott, and the tension eased slightly. "Did she buy her crystals or toys from any local suppliers, or was it just the Internet?"

Scott hesitated before answering this time. "There was one place she'd go sometimes. It's like a costume store, kind of, but they had some of that pagan shit in the basement. She wanted a ride once 'cause she had an order for something huge and couldn't bring it back on her Rascal."

"When was this?" John said.

"Uh... about two, three weeks ago. She said it was important."

"Do you remember what this store was? Where it was?"

He hemmed and hawed before finally coming up with an approximate address on Montrose Avenue. "You can probably Google it," he offered. "It was called, uh, Le Masque. And it had these big faces, like Mardi Gras stuff, on the front."

"Thank you for your cooperation, Mr. Scott," Abby said. That information could be helpful in the future, but they couldn't risk pursuing something that didn't have to do with their supposed reason for being there. "Now, about the night of the incident. When the police spoke to you, how were your concerns addressed? Did you feel marginalized or mistrusted?"

The two of them followed the police-misconduct line of questioning for a few more minutes. John made a point of prodding Scott for any information on the officers who found the body, but Scott had nothing but good things to say about them. That was a relief. The agents might impersonate the authorities, but in most ways they couldn't be further from legitimate law enforcement. If there was actual police misconduct one of them could call in an anonymous tip, but beyond that they had no real legal recourse. Pretending to be able to solve someone's problems had always made Abby feel a little sick.

They finished up with John encouraging Scott to call the police station if he thought of anything else pertinent. Scott closed his door and the agents moved down to the end of the hall for a whispered consultation.

"He's lying," John said instantly.

"About what?"

"I don't know. Something. He just feels off." John's forehead wrinkled. "Didn't you notice it?"

Abby shrugged. "Sort of. I don't think he ever saw the dolls, for one thing. But even if he's hiding something or lying to us, I don't know how many other sources we have on this one."

"Maybe Mal and Adam will get something else from the address book?" John said hopefully.

"Maybe. But for now, I don't think we can afford to not follow this up."

Unfortunately, the other neighbors either weren't at home or didn't have much to say. The woman occupying the apartment on the other side had been in Oahu with her girlfriend when the crime happened, and she had the receipts to prove it. The Sikh couple across the hall worked long hours and, while they'd given statements to the police during the body discovery, weren't at home when Sarah Mulsey likely died. The apartment above her on the second floor was currently unoccupied.

That left them with only one lead.

Chapter Seven

When Mal heard about what they'd found, he immediately turned to their backdoor into the state coroners' database. According to the sparse reports, Sarah Mulsey had been autopsied already and had no known next of kin. No one had arranged to retrieve the body, and there was no contact information for anyone with power of attorney.

"So if their time of death is right," John said as he looked over Mal's shoulder, "she died before Neill but after Petrovich. Melted brick at her place and in the alley by Neill, but no sign of it at Petrovich's. Yet Petrovich was the one in contact with her. What the hell was this lot up to?"

"Magic, maybe." Abby was making notes in the file. "Magic that got them killed."

"And no one to come pick 'em up afterwards. That's just fucking depressing. If I wind up on the floor with my brain out, would you mind taking care of that?"

"As long as I'm not in custody for doing it."

"You think you're clever, but you're not," John said with a look of wounded dignity. "But that just leaves us the shop, doesn't it. Mal, go warm up your car, would you? I don't trust Dame Edna Everage here to drive."

• • •

Some days, Chicago looked like it did on the postcards. Souvenir kiosks would be set up all over the Loop, each displaying the same pictures on keychains and T-shirts: gleaming buildings against a clear sky, the lake a placid wash of blue-gray in the foreground. Huge pieces of public art—beautiful, twisted and incomprehensible—made striking outlines against the glass Mies van der Rohe buildings and post-Fire classical colonnaded banks and law offices. Some days, the city was beautiful.

The Le Masque costume shop was not part of that world. It lived in the other Chicago, where two-and-three-story brick buildings sported decaying ads for long-gone businesses and glossy chain stores were crowded in next to fortified jewelers and payday loan merchants. The shop itself had boarded-up windows, and the inside of the glass door was dirty and opaque.

Mal eased the door open, and promptly inhaled a lungful of dust. He stumbled forward into the store, muffling his coughs in his coat sleeve, while John and Abby followed close behind and made sure the door was locked behind them.

Halloween was the prevailing theme. Several long racks of mass-manufactured costumes in clear plastic lined the walls, mostly superheroes and impractical bikini versions of classic monsters. John picked a tub of black greasepaint off one of the shelves and pried open its pack.

"I don't think anybody's been here for ages," he said. The greasepaint had solidified into claylike chunks.

Mal wiped his mouth on a handkerchief. "And the dust is undisturbed," he said hoarsely. "I am afraid you were lied to."

"We'd still better check it out." Abby pulled a flashlight out of her bag and shone it around the store, trying to squash a sudden fluttering of nerves. "He said Sarah Mulsey came here, and if she did, she was here for something."

The three of them moved behind the counter. The back rooms of the store were sparsely furnished and looked as if they had never been inhabited; there was no running water, and the furniture had been covered in dust sheets. Mold had collected under a faucet but long since died, leaving nothing but a black stain on the porcelain. Abby opened a cupboard and found a pair of men's shirts wrapped in yellowing plastic, a laundromat receipt still pinned to them.

"Hey guys," she said, "I think I found Edward I's dry cleaning."

"What?" John peered over her shoulder. She pointed to the date on the receipt: 23/42/1299. "Would you look at that," he said appreciatively. "It takes some kind of artistry to get every single number wrong. That's quality work, right there."

She rolled her eyes at him and stepped away, dropping the package back onto the counter. John muttered something and moved to investigate a small janitor's closet.

"Burnt-out telly in here," he reported, backing out again. "Got an M-80 in it."

"Teenagers playing." Mal pulled open a cupboard and ran a hand along the top of the door, inspecting the thick layer of dust. "More likely that than any owner. This place has been abandoned for at least two years."

Abby waved a hand in front of her face, trying to clear the clouds of dust that their steps were kicking up. "We'd better keep looking," she said. She reached up and tapped a nail against a vent high in the wall. Flakes of rust floated down. "An abandoned store is a great place for making illicit deals. Maybe Sarah Mulsey was buying something besides crystals."

"Dump like this'd be perfect for it." John wandered down the hall and into the tiny kitchenette at the end. He opened the refrigerator door with a horrible squeal of hinges and peered into the crisper drawer. "Oh, yah. We got a sorcerer around here somewhere. Throw us a bone, eh?" John reached into the drawer and pulled out a long yellow-white object.

"A femur?" Mal said.

"Looks like a bone to me, but I'll take your word for it." John flipped the object over in his hand, examining it. "'S broken. Looks like it was polished."

"That isn't polish." Mal shook his head and took the bone, peering at the end. "Bone regrowth, I think. Look at this. It's weathered and yellowed on the interior of the broken cavity, and regrown over the yellowing."

"Mal?" Abby began. A nasty idea was taking shape in her mind.

"It seems there was no skin over it when it grew."

He said it calmly, but he might have shouted for the weight it had. The three agents drew closer together as John's hand flew to his jacket pocket. Eyes flicked to the shadows. Abby thumbed the safety off her Tomcat and tried to control her breathing.

"Ah, fuck," John said quietly. "Was half convinced the Rev got sold a dummy when he picked up that book. Don't suppose someone knows anything else that grows bone without skin on it? Abby?"

"Nothing's coming to mind," she whispered back.

The two men drew together shoulder-to-shoulder and blocked the doorway. Abby drew her Tomcat. "Should we run?" she asked, doing her best to keep her voice steady. Sweat began to collect around the collar of her coat.

Mal shook his head. "If there is such a creature, that would be cowardly. Who knows what it may do to others?"

"All right, then, let's blow the fucking place up," John said. He had already loaded his Desert Eagle and was glancing left and right where the dusty shadows were deepest. "Say it was a gas leak."

Abby rearranged her grip on the Tomcat. It felt silly to be standing huddled in a dusty room, broad daylight leaking through cracks in the boarded-up windows, while they spoke in hushed whispers. But their founder had spent an exorbitant amount on the agency's collection of magical books, and the most expensive volume of them all had been one slim quarto bound in old leather. Only that battered little book had ever spelled out exactly what would make naked bone grow by itself.

A clatter made Abby and John jump, but it was only Mal dropping the bone onto the countertop. John let out a gusty sigh. "Jesus fuck! Mal, d'you mind?"

"*Mea culpa.* What now?"

John let out a breath. "Good question. Where would one of them hide? Basement?"

"It's as good a place as any to start." Abby double-checked the magazine in her gun and brushed a stray strand of hair behind her ear. Her heart thudded painfully as they moved forward.

The stairs to the basement were narrow and dark, and the door was hidden behind a stack of cardboard boxes. The uneven steps wobbled slightly when the agents stepped on them. At the bottom a bare corridor branched left and right. Damp stains covered the concrete from floor to ceiling. A little light came in through a vent set high in the wall, but the light bulbs hanging from the beams had burned out long ago.

John switched on his Maglite and played it over the scene. Something tiny went scrambling out of sight with a high-pitched chittering noise.

"Rat?" he whispered.

"Mouse, I think," Abby said. "Don't tell me you're afraid of rats, John."

"I'm not! But if something's going to bite me, I'd like to know about it. Professional courtesy and all."

The right-hand corridor led only to a wall and another pile of cardboard boxes. The agents, moving cautiously in the murky damp, turned back left. A low doorway there led out into a wide basement. Only Abby could walk comfortably; John found himself ducking under the thick ceiling beams, and Mal bent unhappily.

The room was filled with junk. The beams of their flashlights revealed piles of black garbage bags, an abandoned mannequin, stacks of drywall, and boxes of old books and clothes. Several lengths of pipe were propped up by the wall. A workbench stood against the far wall, but the bottles and jars on it contained only grimy residue of whatever had been there. There was a large circular burn on the worktop.

A chill ran down Abby's back as she touched the scorched area. The men were glancing left and right, eyeing the stacks of debris uneasily and trying to look everywhere at once. Her hair was falling down out of its practical knot and loose strands stuck to her cheeks.

"Bunsen burner," she said. "Someone let it go too long."

"If I had to work in this dump, I'd try to burn it down too." John prodded one of the garbage bags with his foot. It made a hollow scraping noise. Taking out his clasp knife, he slit the bag open.

A second later, he leaped back. Bones poured out of the broken bag, clattering onto the cement. The sound echoed in the dim basement like the chatter of teeth.

Something moved in the heap of bones. A tendril of limp gray string came wriggling out of the morass and twined itself through the pile, slipping through holes bored in the end of each bone. John backed further away hurriedly, groping hurriedly in his pockets.

"Matches!" he shouted, rounding on the other two as he pulled a flask out of his coat. "For fuck's sake, give me some matches!"

Abby dropped her bag and fumbled through it, searching. It was a futile gesture: she knew they hadn't packed any accelerants. Mal took a different route and scrambled over the pile of drywall towards the charred bench. As John untwisted the cap on his flask and poured Scotch over the slithering pile of bones and string, Mal grabbed a slightly melted lighter and tossed it to John.

Light flared as the alcohol caught. Something in the blazing pile shrieked. A claw lurched out of it and swiped at John's trailing trouser leg, striking sparks as the scorching bone scraped across the floor. The three agents drew further back. Abby took aim and the two men followed suit, watching the shape in the leaping flames.

It dragged itself together and rose. Unable to stand upright, it crouched like an ape, too-long arms and legs skewing sideways. Abby kept both hands on her gun, fresh sweat beading on her forehead and cheeks as the fire began to die and patches of ash fell from the undamaged bone.

Her throat was dry as she looked at it. A thing that none of them had ever thought they'd meet, right there in front of them. The one whose file was just pages copied from a book called *Les morts-vivants en guerre*. Or as Mal had translated it, *The Undead at War*.

"Fucking bonepicker," John said.

The bonepicker tilted its head to one side, watching the agents inquisitively. It was old: the bones had thickened as it grew, leaving ropes of ivory spreading across the once-smooth surfaces. Its skull was deeply pitted, and the eye sockets were laced with delicate tendrils of growing bone. In the depths of its buckled ribcage a small lump of gray flesh pulsed fitfully. Long spines protruded from its shoulders and back, vibrating with every sound in the enclosed basement.

For a moment, they had a standoff. Then John took a step back and the bonepicker reared upwards, slamming its head into the ceiling and losing a few trailing pieces of bone. Its jaw sagged open as it raised one hand, pointing to the SSR agents.

Without another word, the agents scattered. John fired three times as Mal and Abby split to the left and right. Two of the shots missed. The third struck the bonepicker on the right shoulder, shattering one of the spines of bone. Its arm unhinged, trailing more of the grayish tendon as it fell. It ground its teeth and charged.

It moved fast, knuckling along like an orangutan on its overlong arms. With one swat, it sent John staggering backwards. The Englishman sprawled backwards over a box of books, head landing on an encyclopedia with a dull thud. His gun flew out of his hand and skittered across the pavement.

The bonepicker rounded on Abby, who trained her Tomcat on its chest. It ripped off its hanging arm and threw it overhand towards her. Surprised, Abby caught the arm in the stomach. It flexed and reached for her throat, giving her the sensation of being throttled by Dummy as she grappled with it. With a heave, she flung it away and scrambled back.

That gave Mal the time he needed. He had grabbed the mannequin and, crouched as he was under the short ceiling, hurled it overarm. The bonepicker let out a wordless groan as the mannequin slammed into it. With a brittle series of cracks, the skeleton's fan of bone snapped like dry straws. It flailed, slapping at the walls and seeking blindly for the agents. Eyeless and without its spurs to sense vibration, it was blind.

John rebounded. Scrambling to his feet, he seized one of the volumes of the encyclopedia and shoved it at the creature. The book struck it in the torso, snapping several ribs and sending the blind thing stumbling.

"Grab it!" Mal shouted. "Abby!"

She threw a length of pipe, hitting the skeleton in the back of the knee. John grabbed the thing by the shoulders as it stumbled, and Mal seized the pipe from the floor and swung it like a baseball bat.

It thrashed like a cockroach as its skull cracked. Its legs kicked and jaws snapped, lashing out for anything they could reach. John lurched as he struggled to hold it, but it lunged just far enough forward. With a crunch, the teeth fastened themselves onto Abby's right arm.

"Fuck!" she gasped. Bolts of white-hot pain shot up and down her arm, and she shuddered as she tried to wrench herself free. Something twisted. With a sick crack, she pulled the skull off the spine. Droplets of blood went flying.

John grabbed the pipe from Mal and snapped the bonepicker's flailing arm in half. Mal was more sensible: he knocked the enraged John backwards and fired two more shots into the ribcage, where the dull lump of flesh pulsed. As the ribcage exploded into shards, the thrashing limbs slackened. The skull's jaws opened, and Abby stumbled backwards, clutching her bleeding arm to her chest.

"Fuck," she repeated in a hoarse voice. Some part of her couldn't believe that she was actually saying it, but "oh no" didn't seem to fit when war zombies were involved. Her face felt oddly stiff, and she wondered vaguely if she was going to cry.

"Abby, you all right?" John said, loping towards her. Abby could see sweat standing out on his forehead and his hand trembled on the pipe, but his outburst against the bonepicker seemed to have calmed him somewhat. He bent behind one of the drywall piles, and rose a moment later with the twitching disembodied arm in one hand.

Mal was fumbling in his bag. He found the medical kit and gently but firmly took Abby aside. "You'd best have this looked at," he said as he wiped the blood off her arm. Abby nodded mutely. "The bite is deep. We should take you to the hospital."

Something scraped, and the three agents jerked. But as they looked around they saw the broken skull of the bonepicker rocking back and forth, clacking its jaws as it scrabbled on the concrete.

John moved towards it with murder in his eyes. To Abby's surprise, though, he stopped halfway and looked down at the arm he was carrying. It was making frantic gestures—the OK sign, and then SOS in Morse code.

"Can it understand us?" Mal said. The skull's rocking redoubled, and the arm flapped. John raised the pipe, but Mal cut him off. "We should question it," he said.

"How about no," John said flatly.

"It may have information," the thespian argued as he wrapped up Abby's arm and bruised hand. "It was here for a reason. Perhaps it was created by a sorcerer who lived here." The skull shook itself frantically.

"We need to question it," Abby agreed. She spoke carefully, picking each word like a tool and enunciating through the numbness in her tongue and lips. Cold aches were spreading up her arm, and she had the strange sensation of being just a bit off-balance. "I think we need Mary."

John shot her a swift, challenging look. She stared back, trying to ignore the bad taste in her mouth. "Really," he said to her. "You know, I was gonna say the same thing, but it seems rude to start a fight so soon after finishing one. You're okay with that?"

"No. But this thing can't talk, and we need her to talk to it for us. We'll keep her safe." Abby's tone was flat. She cradled her arm and looked past the other two, not wanting to see Mal's disappointment or John's knowing expression.

• • •

They cleared the garbage out of the upper office, and John set the skeletal remains on the counter. The three of them gathered around. Abby's arm had been bandaged and the bleeding had slowed to a trickle, but everything still felt vague, and she swayed as she tried to focus. Mal stood ready with the pipe, a warning all by himself. John, though, didn't believe in half measures. He pulled out most of the gray tissue from the disassembled bonepicker and spread the wriggling stuff across the counter.

"All right, this is how it goes," he said to the bonepicker. "You already tried to hurt us, so we're not going to be feeling very friendly right about now. It's in your best interests to cooperate with us. Got it?"

The broken skull chattered, and the disembodied arm began to tap frantically at the table. A tendril of gray slithered across the table towards the skull. John promptly crushed it with the butt of the Desert Eagle. The skull creaked angrily.

At that moment, the door slammed open and a harried-looking Mary came hurrying in. Her clothes were streaked with lint and fuzz, and her elaborately braided and striped hair had been pulled up under a bandanna. She looked tired and annoyed.

"Now what?" she said. "You know I'm supposed to be at work, right? My aunt gave me a job, and she'll freak out if she finds out I left—" She stopped dead at the sight of the skull. "What the heck? I'm gone for like a day, and you guys turn into the Texas Chainsaw Massacre?"

"Please, Mary. We need your help." Abby tugged on the edge of the bandaging and tried not to wince at the growing stiffness and ache in her wrist. "Can you talk to it?"

Mary approached the counter hesitantly. "Look, guys. I want to be part of this, you know I do, but you sent me home and if Aunt Georgia finds out I was working with you while this is still going on, I'm going to be in so much trouble it's not even funny. She thinks she's keeping me out of trouble by letting me work at her baby boutique and *holy shit,* Abby, what happened to you?"

"The zombie did," said John. Mary looked uncomfortable and shot another look at the bandages, but she moved towards the counter.

So much for keeping Mary out of trouble. Barely twenty-four hours before they'd had to call on her again. But while Abby, John, and Mal could subdue undead if they absolutely had to, Mary could talk to anything. Creatures without brains talked to Mary. Creatures without brains *liked* Mary, which baffled every agent who had ever opened a biology textbook. Most of them just tried not to think about it. Mary didn't always like those creatures back, but she could talk to them.

The girl gingerly splayed her fingers on the broken temples of the skull, which redoubled its rocking. The tapping hand made the OK sign again, and Mary's eyes drifted closed. Abby felt her hackles rise as the skeletal hand began to make stroking motions on the tabletop, as if petting something.

Then her eyes opened again, and they were blank and glassy.

"Do not crush me," she said in a high, thin voice. "Do not snap me. Do not shatter me. Do not break me."

Abby moved closer to the teenager and reached for her hand with her own uninjured one. Mary felt the touch and responded, squeezing back to let Abby know that she was still in control. Abby relaxed an inch or two, but she didn't let go of Mary.

"That depends on what you tell us," John said to the skull, which was still rocking under Mary's hands. "What are you doing here?"

"It is the world I live in," said the voice of the bonepicker. "It is my life to live here. Why do you come here?"

John ignored that. "Who made you?" he demanded.

"Why do you come here?" insisted the bonepicker. The hand stopped stroking and curled into claws, and the shreds of fleshy cord began to move on the counter, reaching out for the remains of its body. So John dropped his Maglite on them.

The skull jerked, but the shriek came from Mary. Abby grabbed her arm as the psychic's eyes cleared. "Don't DO that!" she said in her own voice.

"Are you hurt?" John said.

"No, I can't feel it, but—"

"Then I'll do it if I need to."

Mary looked at Abby, but the older woman shook her head slightly, and Mary nodded. Her eyes closed again, and a moment later, opened in the glassy stare of the bonepicker.

"Do not crush me," the creature whined through Mary's mouth. "Do not crush me. Do not pull me. Do not tear me. Do not stab me."

"Then answer our questions," John said levelly. "Who made you?"

The remains of the zombie jittered on the tabletop. "I do not know."

"Are you sure?" the thin man demanded. His hand hovered over the table.

"I say what I know!" it yowled. "All! All!"

Abby could hear shifting feet, and Mal moved to stand by her. Glancing up, she saw that his eyes were fixed on the interrogation, and that his expression was grim.

"Mal?" she whispered. "What's wrong?"

"'But brush this dust off me, lest horror it brings,'" he said in a low voice. It seemed to be a quote, but Abby had never heard it before.

"All right, then talk." John fumbled in his pockets. "Shit. Abby, tape?"

She straightened up. "Got it," she said, and produced her handheld tape recorder. She moved towards Mary, but John shook his head and motioned her back. "Chuck it here," he said. Feeling a sudden surge of unease, Abby tossed him the tape recorder and stepped back.

"Now. Once more, with feeling," John said as he clicked the red button. "What are you doing here?"

"I was told to wait, just to wait," bonepicker-Mary babbled. "Before there was me, there was dark. I was told to wait, and sleep, and there would be things to do. I have no names for you. Only faces."

"Mary?" Abby said.

The psychic shrugged. "Got 'em," she said. Her face was beginning to look strained, and her eyes were widening under the effort of maintaining contact with the alien consciousness of the creature. "Guys? I think they were fairies."

John swore, and Abby felt her heart plummet, but Mal remained placid. "Tell us about them," was all he said.

And the skull chattered on. There were people: not his makers, but the ones who had told him to wait. They had laughed a lot, which made his poor bones ring. They were fae. They had told him to wait, and they would send people to him. He would kill those who came to him.

"Setup. A fucking setup." John kicked the counter, making the bones leap and rattle. "I am going to *kill* Scott."

"Get in line," Abby sighed. She tried to rotate her wrist and immediately regretted it: the swelling was getting worse, and the muscles of her arm felt tight enough to peel off the bone. She was definitely not a doctor, but something had to have broken. "What now, do you think?"

"We need to clean up and get out of here." His lips twisted. "And then we pay a visit to Mister Scott and explain a few things to him."

A worm of gray flesh rose off the table. Mary bent her head over the skull, which was chattering again. "He wants to know if he can go back to sleep," she reported.

"No. No, it can't." John unslung his duffel bag. "We can't leave this thing lying around for some poor bugger to stumble on when he's just looking for a quiet place to smoke. Have to get rid of it."

Mary yelped, and the reedy voice of the bonepicker came back. "Do not crush me!" it wailed, its bones rattling frantically as it tried to reconnect its pieces. "Do not break me! I want to sleep!"

"Sorry," John said. He didn't sound sorry. "We'll make it quick."

"Wait a second!" Mary snapped in her own voice. "Hold up just a second, Sawyer. You wanted me to come down here and get into his head, and I did, but you didn't say anything about killing him! That's not fair. It's not his fault someone put him down here!"

"One side, kid."

"I said *no*." The psychic put her hands on her hips and glared through her fringe of stripy hair. "It's not. His. Fault. He's not too bright—sorry, buddy, but it's true—and he got screwed over! He's *old*. I saw it in his head! He's like two hundred years old, and someone made him and then he got traded and sold to the fairies, and they put him down here and just said to attack anyone they send him! He doesn't get how it's wrong!"

John looked at her, his eyes hard. Somewhere in the last minute he had unsheathed a small, slim knife. "Someone who doesn't think killing is wrong is *wrong*, kid. This isn't hard to sort out."

"He doesn't know because no one ever tried to teach him!" Mary shouted.

"Now you're bonding with it? It's not a pet, it's a fucking zombie!" John's grip tightened on the hilt of the knife. "The only source we have on these things calls them a *war crime!*"

Abby couldn't take it any more. The pain in her arm was only getting worse, and the argument was reminding her entirely too much of her own confused thoughts over the past few days. She took a deep breath.

"LANGUAGE!" she shouted, startling both Mary and John. "Both of you! If it's capable of learning, then this is a bad place for it to start! John, for the love of God, put the knife away."

John lowered the knife, but didn't sheathe it. His gaze was incredulous. "You can't be agreeing with her, Marquise," he said. "The damn thing tried to kill us! What about your arm?"

"Hurts like heck, thanks for asking." That got a snort from John, but the tension thinned slightly. "Listen," Abby went on in a softer tone of voice, "we've only ever seen the one source on bonepickers. *The Undead at War* said making them was a crime because they were unstoppable, but we've stopped this one, didn't we? And it can think—that's not supposed to be possible. What if we, I don't know, find it someplace safe?" John's eyebrows shot up, but she hurried on before he could interrupt. "We could bring it back to the office in pieces, so it can't attack anyone. Keep the nervous system separate, put it in a jar in the safe or something, and just let it sleep like it wants. And we can study the bones. All right?"

John rubbed his face with his free hand, apparently working out some muscle aches in his temples. "This is the stupidest damn thing I've ever heard. It's a weapon, Marquise."

"Weapons don't kill people, remember? People kill people." Abby cradled her damaged arm. "So how about we go after the guy who put it down here in the first place?" A fresh bolt of cold pain shot up her hand, and she amended that. "You and Mal go after the guy who put it down here. I think I should probably go to the doctor."

"I...Yeah. Right." John glanced down at her damaged arm, and his face reddened slightly. "Maybe that should be first. Mal, can you pack up that thing and get it back to the office?"

The other man nodded. "Not difficult. Perhaps we can find a spare terrarium."

"Fuck, no. This thing is not going to be a pet." John jabbed a finger at Mary. "But you—you get to feed it and clean its cage. Got it?"

"Sir, yes sir!" Mary picked up the skull and cradled it, gently cupping the trailing gray tendons. "C'mon, you, let's get moving. I have to be back at the store soon, and hanging out with David Bonie is so not an excuse."

John groaned. "No nicknaming the war zombie."

"Too late."

Chapter Eight

The drive to the hospital seemed dim and unreal, as if something was filling Abby's head with cotton wool. But to her relief the emergency room wasn't very busy, and she was admitted almost immediately.

She had to lie, of course. Between the humanoid bite marks and the twitchy man accompanying her, the nurse's first thought was domestic abuse. Abby quickly threw together a story about a beloved but mentally-impaired cousin who'd had a fit, and though one or two of the nurses still looked sideways at John, he was eventually allowed to come in with her.

The prognosis wasn't encouraging. After poking, prodding and several X-rays, the attending doctor confirmed that she had two cracked metacarpals and a spiral fracture of the right ulna. The swelling was worse than it ought to be, and further X-rays would be needed to see if she required surgery. That meant an overnight stay. She was quickly moved into a small room on the ground floor.

As the first dose of painkillers kicked in and the hot, tight throbbing in her arm began to subside, a sense of deep weariness flooded through Abby. She sighed and slumped back against the raised head of the bed, fighting the urge to close her eyes.

With the danger past, her body had apparently decided to sign out for the night. She wanted to get up and patrol (how was she supposed to know there weren't any enemies in the building? What about the bonepicker's fairy masters? Remember the way the ghoul lured you, Abby?) but she just couldn't seem to work up the energy. Everything was limp and lifeless.

The door opened and footsteps approached. Abby slid a little further down and let her eyes drift closed. The nurses' walks were quick and brisk, their feet clicking against the tile despite their sensible soft shoes. John was no nurse, though, and after years of hearing him banging around the office she knew the sound of him immediately.

The strange thing was that she didn't have to be nervous if John was there. Her normal concerns about his health and mind were pushed aside by exhaustion and the stark arithmetic of near-death. They were in crisis mode: John's temper would need to be addressed eventually, but something had tried to kill them and John, like any other agent, wouldn't let that happen to his teammates.

The footsteps crossed the floor. A chair scraped. Cloth rustled, and cheap leatherette seat lining squeaked as he sat down.

"You look awful," he said without preamble.

"But I feel better," she replied. Her voice was still slurred, and she licked her lips and tried to make her own mouth cooperate.

"Are they going to, you know, have a dig around?"

Abby opened her eyes again with reluctance. Her coworker was sitting slumped in the chair, his shoulders indrawn. The idea of surgery seemed to make him nervous. "No. I'll be in here overnight because it's so swollen, but they cleaned up the bite mark and started me on some antibiotics. I'll be getting a fiberglass cast in the morning." With some effort, she hefted her right arm. The temporary plaster cast was heavy and clumsy.

"Had to be the right arm, though," John observed. "In movies, it's always the arm they don't use that gets it."

"I bet it still hurts, though." She slid a little further down on the bed. "What's going on with everybody? Did the others get back to the office all right?"

"Yeah, they did. Got a phone call from Mal about ten minutes ago. He's put that... thing in the spare safe. Said Adam practically creamed 'imself over the bones." John shot a suspicious glance at the curtain. "Is it safe to talk about this?" he added, coming out of his slouch and leaning towards the bed. "Those nurses all have a look on them like they've got Tasers under those scrubs."

She laughed a little. "Nobody's behind the curtain, I promise. And even if they're still suspicious about how I got hurt, they aren't allowed to kick me out. I've got insurance."

"Mary's back at her family's store. If I know her, she's worried, but you wouldn't see it if you asked. She's being a real trooper. Mal?" John paused. "Well, he's being Mal."

"Stoic?"

"Statuelike."

"Is he going to explain about why we needed her?"

John grinned. "Already taken care of. Me, I'm not so strong with the weepy family people, but Mal handled it all right. She's gonna be safe, too. I think her uncle has more guns than Starczynski."

"Safe. Good." Abby smiled at the thought and wanted to ask more, but her vision was beginning to blur. The pain and the painkillers were teaming up on her. "Kids need to be safe."

"Something on your mind?" her coworker asked in a voice of forced congeniality.

"No, not really."

"You're lying."

She held up her good hand, thumb and forefinger an inch apart. "A little."

"Well, spit it out, would you?"

"It's about Jimmy." Her partner tensed, and Abby lowered her hand. "Look, I know this is probably a bad idea, but I want Jimmy to stay at the office for tonight." She shifted, fiddling with the bedspread.

John's face had frozen while she spoke, but now he leaned forward again. "Abby," he said fervently, "I can't stand that little shit."

"I know, I know, I *know*," she said tiredly. "You'd rather have a root canal than spend time with him. But what do you want me to do? He needs to be looked after."

"Send him to Mary's. They can do each others' nails, for fuck's sake."

"Mary won't shoot first," she said. "I'm sorry, John. I know it's not agency protocol."

That made John laugh, just a bit. "You've got the wrong guy. We don't have agency protocol, we've got crap we do all the time."

"I know he's not safe with you."

"Who is?" John joked. Abby glared through her half-closed eyes, and he subsided again.

"I'll tell him to stay out of your way. But if somebody's gonna do something dangerous, I want Jimmy hiding somewhere with crazy people who'll kill whatever comes through the wall."

"That's us." John shook his head, but his expression softened. "All right. But if he kills me in my sleep, I'm going to haunt you."

She smothered a laugh with her good hand. "I wouldn't expect anything else."

• • •

The office was clean and sparse, but a few personal touches had sneaked through. Pictures of her friends, of her pets, and of her departed husband crowded the desk, all marked with dozens of fingerprints and scuffed at the edges. A coffee mug with a picture of a tongue-out Albert Einstein on it was parked next to the computer.

She rolled her chair up to the desk and booted up the computer. The background was another photograph, this time a picture of Highland dancers caught in mid-leap with their kilts flying and hints of smiles breaking through the stoicism required by a formal dance exhibition. She'd taken the photo herself almost ten years before, when she and her husband had been on their honeymoon. He laughed wonderfully at the dance, she remembered, but the highlight of the trip had been the journey up Sgùrr nan Gillean: her clinging to his back, him carrying her as easily as if she'd been a feather pillow. He had opened her world up in so many ways. Helped her get in touch with her true heritage.

Her e-mail icon was blinking: sixteen new messages, none of them spam. That was the problem with her chosen career. People all needed things, and even she couldn't do everything for everyone.

No matter how much you bled, you couldn't give enough for all of them. There wasn't enough in her body.

The phone rang. She pushed the thought aside and checked the caller ID. Her brother? What did he want?

"Is everything all right?" she said. Maybe his condition was acting up again.

"I'm fine," he said shortly. "Two for Wormwood. Blonde woman, skinny guy." And before she could say anything, he hung up.

She leaned back in her chair and laced her fingers together, thinking. Considering all the various wiretapping scandals lately, it was smart to keep things quick and opaque when talking on the phone, but she still wished he would have said something more. Men, especially men with his particular problem, had trouble using their words. She wondered if she ought to have put a tighter leash on him.

Still... two for Wormwood? That would be interesting. She'd have to send someone to pick up the bones later.

• • •

The nurse had tried to turn the room's lights off, but Abby asked her not to. "It makes me feel safe," she said, and the nurse nodded sympathetically and left them on.

Of course, the hospital was supposed to be safe. It had to be, with its guards, visiting schedules and thick walls. Nothing undead could just wander into her room. She shifted on the mattress, feeling the pull of the scars, and tried to relax. Everything had to be safe.

Except that this was St. Luke's, where Giovanna DiFrancesca had spent some of her last days as a human. Where a bogeyman had come crashing through the wall, not giving a damn if there were guards or metal detectors or not. She pulled the blanket up and wrapped it around her shoulders, trying not to think about it.

She dozed for a while. With her eyes half-closed, the world was a grayish blur through the fan of her lashes. Every so often she would remember herself and straighten up, checking the corners and noting the time on the clock.

When she was young, Abby spent a lot of time in hospitals. Her mother's epileptic spells came and went for years, sometimes better, sometimes worse. There'd been a routine to it: Aunt Gail would take her down to visit, and they'd stay exactly thirty minutes while making small talk about school or housework. Then her aunt would shepherd her home for dinner, where nobody would talk about anything. Hospitals were just places where Mom went to get better, and the routine of the visits leached away some of the fear.

Later, the hospital had become the place where her marriage hit the rocks. The beginning of the end for the Marquise family, as a unit anyway.

Abby turned over onto her left side, carefully propping her injured arm against her hip and blinking rapidly to forestall the dampness in her eyes. No point in thinking about that.

No, lying on her side wasn't working. With a sigh, she turned back over and resettled her arm on top of the blankets. There was a call box tucked into the blankets, its cord wrapped around an IV stand propped by the wall. Probably due to some hurried equipment rearranging with the room's previous occupant. She patted the call box with her good hand, somewhat relieved by its presence.

Time passed. She heard a shift change somewhere down the hall, cutting into the usual background chatter of announcements, equipment beeps and phone calls. Someone a few rooms away seemed to have their TV on, because she could catch a few scraps of monologue from a sports announcer. When she tugged on the call box, the tangle of cords made the IV stand against the wall rattle and sway.

The night nurse, Sunita, came to check on her and tsked a little at the sight of her swollen hand. "Not good," she said, bending back one of Abby's fingers and making a note when she winced. "If that hasn't started to go down by morning, you might have to stay another day for observation. Are you in pain?"

"Yes," Abby said, leaning back against the pillow.

"As bad as it was before?"

"No, not as bad. The doctor gave me some pills... Uh, yellow ones, I think?"

Sunita checked her chart. "Right. If it starts getting worse, or if you're having trouble breathing, use the call button right away."

Abby nodded and the nurse swept out, leaving her alone to brood. She contemplated taking another pill, but just one had left her without a sense of balance for half an hour. Sighing, she made herself as comfortable as she could and drifted off.

• • •

Someone had turned off the light after all, and the room was shadowy and gray when she awoke. It was a little too dark to see the hands of the clock, but from the color of the sky outside the window and the quiet all around her she could guess it had to be after midnight. A sliver of light slanted across the floor from the open door of the bathroom. She frowned, struggling to sit up. She hadn't left it open.

Footsteps. Two pairs of them, and not out in the corridor. Footsteps in the bathroom, slow and light, trying not to be heard.

She barely had her hand out for the call box when the fairies emerged. They moved smoothly, with the slow mechanical glide of computer animations. Two of them: at least one too many for Abby.

The woman was the taller of the two. The dim light turned her pale skin sickly and made her green eyes glint, reflecting in an oily mirrorlike sheen. Every inch of visible flesh was sketched with dark, angular tattoos in slanting triangle patterns, and her long copper hair was braided with ornaments in the same designs.

The man's eyes reflected the light just the same, but he was dark-haired and tattooless. Like the woman, he wore plain, cheap dark clothes with signs of hard wear on the elbows and knees. What worried Abby more was the white sealskin slung casually across his shoulders.

"We thought you'd be awake," said the man with a smile. "Are you scared?"

"Yes," Abby said. There was no point in lying; fairies' senses were too good, and they all knew what fear smelled like. "Not of you, though."

"That's not very smart." The selkie rearranged his sealskin. Its empty paws dangled down onto his chest like the sleeves of a trendy cardigan. "After what you did to my brother Luka—"

"Close your mouth." The woman's voice was cold and flat. "She wants to keep you talking, idiot."

"Maybe," Abby said. The selkie's brow furrowed at that.

"Shut up." The woman brushed a finger over a design on her forearm. A web of shadows spread from it, filling the room with stripes of angled darkness. Sparks flew from the TV, wisps of smoke curled up from the electrical sockets. The call box under Abby's fingers grew hot, and its light went out.

Abby's stomach dropped. The idea of a lot of hospital equipment suddenly breaking wasn't a pretty one, and her one discreet way to signal for help was suddenly out of the game. Now the only thing she could do was scream, and she was willing to bet that the fairies wouldn't be happy with that.

"More fear," said the selkie. "Very nice."

The thin plastic of the box warped and split in her grip. "You're not very good at this," she told the selkie. "Luka was a lot more trouble."

To her surprise, the selkie smiled. "I bet he was, too. He always was a dumb fucker."

That wasn't the way he should have responded. Abby tensed, trying to keep the calm expression as she thought rapidly. Stripes of the woman's shadow magic lay across the bed, and purplish bruises were beginning to rise wherever they touched her skin.

Two fairies was too much. Abby wasn't a fighter, but she had spent years with the agency and learned more than a few things about hurting someone who wanted to hurt her first. Fairies, though? Fairies were stronger than humans, with no certainties about what they might do for the sake of amusement. Worse, the woman's magic was a completely unknown quantity. Attempts at the usual distraction (fairies *loved* to talk) had fallen flat.

Which left her with exactly one option.

She yanked on the call box. The cord snapped like a whip and sent the IV stand crashing to the floor. It clattered against the visitor's chair and knocked it over too, making the room echo with the sound of metal hitting wood and tile.

The woman jerked and instinctively whipped a rope of shadow at the clattering stand. The selkie flinched, and Abby flung her blanket over his head.

She tried to leap off the bed, but the medicine was still in her system and she sprawled sideways onto the floor. The temporary cast thudded heavily and split.

The selkie started forward and bumped into the sorceress. She hissed impatiently and slammed a palm against his face, leaving a bruise in the shape of her palm tattoo. "Jackass!" she snarled. The word was almost lost in the yelp of pain from the selkie.

Abby struggled to her feet. The bruises on her skin were growing darker, and every muscle seemed to be screaming. The cheap plastic of the call box was just shards in her fingers.

She half-hoped the selkie would turn against his partner, but no such luck. The sealskin began to melt into his shoulders as he dove for her, his hands turning into paws, eyes going gold. She lurched sideways, pulling herself under the bed. The selkie let out a hoarse bark as he scrambled after her with bared teeth. The plastic shards stuck between her clenched fingers.

Her arm was throbbing, white-hot. Her head reeled. All she could see was those gleaming gold eyes coming straight at her—paws out, a predator hiding behind a white coat—

Her hand came up. Her fist shot out. The broken plastic stabbed into the selkie's eyes.

The creature howled like a man being torn in two. He reared back, trying to clutch his face with his paws, and banged his head into the underside of the heavy bed. Half-stunned by the blow, he collapsed forward again. As he wavered, his sealskin loosened, and Abby snatched it off his shoulders.

A cold, biting energy flooded her, chasing the fuzziness out of her head. As she lay there, she could feel the ache of the selkie's bruised head. She *knew* him now: the agony in his eyes, the reeling confusion of the loss of his skin, the memories that rattled through his head. Orders, his brother, his name.

"Kotik!" she choked out. "Protect me!"

The sorceress's eyes blazed, but whoever held the skin controlled the selkie and Kotik moved like greased lightning. Without thinking twice he rolled out from under the bed and dove at his partner. Sparks flew from the woman's hands and caught in Kotik's hair, but he didn't seem to notice.

"Jackass!" This time a scream. White smoke streamed from her nose and mouth, wrapping around the selkie's head and solidifying instantly into a crystalline block. Kotik collapsed like a marionette with its strings cut.

Abby clambered to her feet, still clutching the sealskin. The shot of energy was fading fast, but it had given her a few more moments and she had to use them. The sorceress was now focusing on her again, more mist gathering, and Abby was almost out of tricks.

"You're the smart one," she said hoarsely. The sorceress's eyebrows knitted. "It's pretty obvious. So you have to know that after all this, there's gonna be security here any minute." She braced herself against the wall and raised her chin, meeting the other woman's stare. "Do you want to get into a fight with a whole bunch of humans? You can't kill everyone in the city just to get to me."

The sorceress looked like she would have gladly committed mayhem. Abby faced her across the body of the selkie, green mirrors burning into brown, and wondered if she was about to die. All she could do was hold the skin and keep looking back.

But the sorceress *was* smart. With a wordless hiss, she flung Kotik over her shoulder and darted back into the bathroom. There was a small thunderclap, then—nothing.

Heart in her mouth, Abby counted to five before following. They were gone. The wall, painted plaster over cinderblock, was warped and melted.

She gently touched it. The plaster yielded under her fingertips as easily as dough.

Something rippled down her arm. Her fingers trembled and turned numb as the nails started to grow. In seconds they were an inch long.

Abby jerked her hand back. Her index and middle fingers looked almost like claws, and the very tips of the overgrown nails were warped and speckled with white plaster. The nails were thin and razor-sharp like a baby's.

"Well," she murmured. "That's interesting."

The door of the room slammed open, and Abby jumped. Three people came hurrying in. She quickly wadded up the sealskin and shoved it behind the toilet before emerging from the bathroom, her mysteriously overgrown fingernails concealed in the folds of her hospital gown.

Two security guards flanked Sunita the nurse, who was looking at the knocked-over furniture and smoking TV with a mix of surprise and exhaustion. It was pretty obvious to Abby that Sunita had had a long enough night without fairy bullshit, and she empathized.

"What the hell happened?" one of the guards demanded. "Was there a fight in here?"

Abby shuffled out of the bathroom, doing her best to look ashamed. "I'm so sorry," she said. "I... there was some kind of fuse thing, it all started sparking, and all the lights and stuff blew. I get night terrors sometimes, and …"

It was a pretty weak explanation, but with no cameras in the room and no witnesses to anything, all they had was her word. Sunita seemed more concerned with the busted cast and rapid bruising than anything, for which Abby was grateful. The nurse snapped a few words to the guards, and they vanished into the hallway.

"If this happens again," she said as she ran expert fingers over Abby's broken arm, "we might have to give you a sedative. I understand night terrors, but we can't have patients breaking furniture and hurting themselves. Are you on any medication for it?"

"I—no, not really." Abby shook her head. Explaining about the fairies, or even just calling it an attack by people that somehow got into the room without actually entering the hospital, might result in one of those involuntary psychiatric holds.

The nurse was a whirlwind of efficiency. In no time at all she had the plaster cast re-made and the room set to rights. An electrician was called to deal with the mysterious failure of the electronics.

When the room was dark and she was finally alone again, Abby crawled out of bed once more and checked the bathroom. The wall had dried, and there was only a melted place where her fingers had sunk into it. When she touched the sealskin, there was no bolt of energy or cold flowing thoughts. Just soft fur.

She grabbed her cell phone, but it too had been fried by the sorceress. Her head was swimming as the last of the adrenaline ran out and the pills ganged up on her. Holding the skin, she collapsed back into bed.

Chapter Nine

"You look like hell."

"So do you."

There was a moment of silence as Abby and John eyed each other. Both were sporting fresh bruises, and half of John's cheek was covered with a gauze patch. The geometric marks left on Abby's skin by the fairy's magic had settled into purplish-blue. The two of them didn't look as bad as many of the other people in the hospital's lobby, but that wasn't saying much.

"Rough night?" John said finally. He crossed his arms and tried to sound casual, but the words were slurred by his efforts not to speak out of one side of his mouth. Definitely much more than just bruises under that gauze.

She wanted to burst out with everything she'd seen and learned, but not in public. With an effort, she swallowed the words and instead opened her bag. Kotik's sealskin, with its empty paws wrapped neatly around itself, sat in the bottom.

"Well, fuck," John observed. "Are you all right?"

"I'll be fine." She closed her back again and slung it over her shoulder. "What about you?"

"You know, the usual shite."

"How's Jimmy?"

"Fine. Sleeping in the basement last I saw. He nicked Adam's cot. Ate everything in the fridge, too."

"Yeah, that sounds like Jimmy." Abby smiled. "So what exactly did happen to you? You're being more evasive than usual."

"In the car."

Once they were settled and John had pulled out of the parking lot, Abby shot him a meaningful look. "Well?"

"After what happened in the basement, we went to go have a talk with Scott. He went a little off the rails." John shrugged with one shoulder, rather stiffly. "He fed us the basement thing on purpose, hoping we'd die. We brought him back to the office. Oh, and he's a therianthrope. "

Abby leaned back. "What?"

"Therianthrope. He turned into a coyote."

There was silence in the car. Then Abby said "Well. That sounds interesting."

A shapeshifter. "Therianthrope" was the technical term, at least according to the Rev, but it was hard not to make the jump to "werewolf" when somebody got ripped in half. The SSR had been formed during an outbreak of werewolf attacks in the late '80s, and to the end of his days the Rev had been particularly worried about therian activity. He'd insisted that the Southwest was lousy with werecoyotes, and the famous chupacabra stories were just therians using a fake monster to cover for eating other people's livestock.

A human-born therianthrope was different from a shapeshifting fairy. Something like a selkie might have been human at some point long past, but the selkie required its sealskin to change its form. And if you took that skin, as Abby well knew, you could control it. Therianthropes needed no outside artifacts to change into their creature of choice, and they could interbreed with normal people easily enough. Fairy-human breeding tended to have unpleasant genetic consequences.

None of the current members of the agency had been there during the '80s killings, and Abby herself had only met one therian: Iris Liu, a werecobra who'd accidentally left scales at the scene of a mugging she interrupted. Iris was living in San Francisco these days, though they still got e-cards from her sometimes. Mary had added her as a Facebook friend. But most therianthropes typically kept their heads down, and the SSR's files on them were thin because they rarely had a reason to meet them. Even Iris hadn't told them much.

Now they had a werecoyote in custody. Maybe some of those questions could be answered, but the more important thing was pumping him for information about the mysterious deaths. And the war zombie in the basement. And the two fairies that had come through the wall.

She didn't say anything else until the car pulled up behind the office. She had to gather her thoughts, and as strange as the werecoyote was, she had something else just as important to share.

"Mal's put him in the basement," John was saying. "Got him good and tied up. Covered his eyes and nose, too, 'cause we don't know how good he can smell in human form. Mal thinks we should take the bandaging off, let him see us an' know he's not getting out. What d'you think?"

"I think I need to ask him about brick walls," she said. "I know what caused those melted patches at the crime scenes."

"Wait, what?" John frowned, stopping in the middle of opening the car door. "You sure about that?"

"I'll explain inside." Abby's shoulders hunched as she clambered out of the car. The office and its parking lot were familiar, but now the scars under her shoulders itched whenever she turned her back on an open space. They couldn't be feeling anything, but with too many fresh bruises and aches to count, it seemed like even the dead tissue was getting in on the action. Turning her back on anything these days felt like an invitation.

It was a relief to get back inside the office. She stripped off her coat and tossed a few pieces of hay to Stinker, who quickly gobbled most of it before standing on his hind legs and taking another experimental bite at the cage bars. The room was warm, almost stuffy, but everything was familiar and there were walls she could put her back against.

There was no sign of Mal, but Adam was there, looking tired and drinking coffee from a travel mug labeled "Rangers Do It in the Woods." He nodded to Abby when she sat down and offered her the half-full coffeepot.

"Thanks, but I'll need to get a straw first," Abby said. Adam grinned and put the pot down.

"All right," John cut in, "let's recap. Lenny Scott is a werecoyote and he tried to have us killed. So what came after you last night? Dracula?"

"Another selkie and a fairy... something. I think we need to recheck our fairy file, because they don't just have sorcerers, they *are* sorcerers."

She told the story as quickly and plainly as possible. The sealskin was passed around, but no one liked to look at it and it quickly went back into her bag.

By the time she finished, Adam already had his notebook out and was scribbling frantically. "It shouldn't be possible," he was saying, "but there *are* limited references to travel magic in the old stories. Fairies came out of trees a lot. Vivien and Merlin, that kind of thing. Maybe?" He turned the pad around and showed Abby a mess of mathematical symbols and Greek letters. "What do you think?"

"I didn't pass algebra," Abby said. "John?"

"I didn't pass anything. Adam?"

"You guys should take some night classes. Point is, yes, it's possible. Unlikely, but possible." Adam tapped his chin. "The samples were plain brick, but maybe the atoms had been rearranged. If fairies passed through it, that means they used some kind of spell that turned a solid wall into a portal. Then once they were gone, the wall solidified in its new shape."

"And the magic affected more than just the bricks." Abby held out her hand, showing them the overgrown nails. "That happened when I tried to touch the place where they'd gone into the wall."

"Reality ripple?" Adam took her hand and examined the nails curiously, poking one with the tip of his pencil. "Cool."

"Not really. Fairies playing with magic is never gonna be good news." John leaned back against the wall, tapping his own fingernails against the plaster. "But it means we have some information. Those melty patches, we found those by the dead bodies."

"So the fairies use the wall portals to attack and kill the human sorcerers," Abby hazarded. "Like trapdoor spiders pouncing and disappearing again. Or just to dump the bodies."

Adam nodded. "I'd buy it."

"Question is, why?" John added. "What's the angle?"

"It's probably too much to hope that it's just random killings." That got murmurs of assent from Adam and John.

Fairy crimes were usually unplanned. The selkie Luka had committed a pair of murders, but he'd done them out of a very straightforward motive: fun. Human psychopaths obsessed over their work or even thought of it as an art form, but when fairies killed, they usually saw it as something to do on a Saturday night. Using magic to enter a sorcerer's home and *skin* them, or dump someone's body in an alley afterwards and cut off a hand postmortem? Never.

Plus, if a fairy had dropped a body they probably would've posed it first. Or pantsed it.

"Someone else must be involved," Adam was saying to John. "Someone hired them to off the sorcerers, maybe. Fairies can work for cash. Remember the Fond du Lac incident?"

"That's a good point. We should check the files on our extant fairy cases, see if there's anyone still at large we could be looking for. Is Creepy Ivan still working at the toy store in Lincoln Square?"

Adam shook his head. "Vanished two months ago. It came over the police band and I put a note in the file."

"I don't think we have time for research right now," Abby interjected. "Not all of us, anyway. Don't we have a prisoner in the basement?"

"Oh, right. That." John scratched one stubbled cheek. "I vote we let Harvey go mad and see what happens. He said he can't really do nonhuman, but I bet you if we let him get to work things'll turn up."

"Good idea," Adam said. "Especially if we ask him in rhyme. Where'd the kid leave the jar?"

Abby sat up. "You didn't let Jimmy talk to Harvey, did you? I really don't think they should meet yet. Harvey really isn't a good influence."

At that, Adam and John exchanged glances. "Hang on," Adam said. "You didn't tell her?"

"Tell me what?" Abby's heart stuttered a little. "John, I asked you to keep him safe. You let those two spend time together?"

"Not exactly." John shrugged, crossing his arms. He looked her right in the eye, which was usually a sign that he was getting ready to lie. "It wasn't much of a problem, really. All sorted out."

"Jimmy rode along when they went to grab Scott," Adam supplied. A cold hand seemed to close around Abby's guts. "He told me John tried to shoot the guy in the crotch, too. That was weird."

Abby sat down hard. For a moment, the aches in her head and and the tightness in her arm seemed to gang up on her, and the world swayed. The silence between them pressed in on her ears like water. Her stomach lurched and she fought to keep her breathing steady.

She was used to thinking about consequences. Not thinking had had consequences of its own in the past, after all, and ever since then she tended to weigh and worry over every decision. It had scared her, even through the pain and confusion of her injuries, to hand over her son to John—but she'd thought it was the smartest thing to do. She needed someone she could trust to annihilate a threat.

Something shifted in the corner of her eye. John crouched down next to her, putting himself just below her own eye level and forcing her to look down at him. There was a strange expression on his face that she couldn't identify.

"Abby," he said. "Abby, listen. He's fine. Abby, can you hear me?"

"... yes," she said finally. The words felt as if they were dragged out of her. Distantly she registered that her grip on the edges of the desk was white-knuckled. "I'm sorry, what were you saying?"

"Jimmy's fine. Little bastard, but he's always been like that, ain't he? Wasn't hurt, I swear."

"That's ..." What was it? The words weren't lining themselves up to be used like they usually were. "That's good. I just don't think we should do this again in the future. Okay?"

"Okay." John stood up, a look of relief on his face. "Right. Now, where *did* he leave that jar? Interrogation just isn't interrogation without a great big cloud of attitude over our heads."

"John," Adam said quietly, "now'd be a good time to shut up."

With an effort, Abby pulled herself together and stood again. Wood from the cheap desk was digging into her fingertips, and the feeling of a dozen splinters in her skin was breaking through the fog that filled her head. She took a deep breath, blinked several times, and let go of the desk. "Sorry about that," she said, carefully extracting the first of the splinters. (Extra-long nails were good for something, it seemed.) "Just so long as everyone's safe. You said Scott is in the salt flats, right?"

"Abby, wait." John stepped into her path. "Maybe we should let Harvey and Mal do the interrogating. They're spooky bastards, after all. They know how to do that sort of thing."

She met his gaze head-on. "John. That son of a bitch ran us into a zombie nest, got my arm broken, and put me in a situation where I had to leave my son with you. Trust me when I say that I'm feeling God-damned spooky right now."

Neither of the men seemed to have anything to say to that, which was fine with her. Some part of her still couldn't believe she'd said *God-damned,* and if she kept moving she would have something think about besides what was happening.

Well, as far as commandments went, "thou shalt not kill" had already been blown. Taking God's name in vain was pretty minor in comparison. She grabbed her bag and went to the basement stairs.

By the time she reached the bottom of the stairs, Abby could smell the salt flats: a thick, almost musty scent, the same that rose when she tore open a bag of rock salt for the driveway. With it came a sharper tang, an edge of caustic chemicals that reminded her of a freshly-cleaned bathroom.

Edged into a corner by the door to the salt room was a folding cot, and sprawled on that cot was Jimmy. He'd somehow managed to prop both his legs against the wall, leaving his boots resting against a worn safety poster, and slept with his left arm flung over his face like he was trying to block out the world. His blanket had somehow wound up wadded under his left shoulder. His right arm was curled protectively around a familiar green glass jar.

Abby coughed, but Jimmy didn't even stir. She hoped it was just more of the aftereffects La Donna Nera had mentioned and not a sign of being worn down by something John had involved him in. Even with his face covered, he looked too young to be in the office, let alone cradling a jar full of genie.

This shouldn't have happened. He should have been safe, not getting involved with the work. Fear and fury bubbled in her stomach, and she lowered her head and closed her eyes. If she took her rage out on John and the others—God, she wanted to, but what would that accomplish? She had to crush those feelings, bury them deep and never let them out. It was the safest thing to do.

They had a prisoner, and that prisoner could have crucial information about the fairies and the strange killings. She couldn't trust John to do the questioning, not now, but the sooner it was done the sooner she could have some peace. Settling her bag against her hip, she slipped through the dividing door and into the salt flats.

Back in the early '70s, the SSR's building had been owned by a charitable group aiming to build a free clinic. The construction had been somewhat shoddy (resulting in, among other things, the hexagonal kitchen) and the clinic itself lasted only a few years, leaving the building essentially derelict by the time the SSR bought it in the '90s. When the agency first started cleaning the place out, they'd found a wide, one-room basement filled with filing cabinets of moldering patient records and piles of vintage junk. Later on, when body disposal became a problem, they'd walled off a little over half of the basement and moved all the miscellany to the smaller side. The larger side became the white-painted room known as the salt flats.

To Abby, it looked like a mad scientist's laboratory. There was a broad stainless-steel autopsy table backed by several racks and cabinets of tools. A heavy hatch in the floor covered a drain that led directly to the nearest sewer main, and an oversized tub with attached pumps and filters served as an improvised chemical bath. All of it was scrupulously clean, thanks to Dummy's industrious scrubbing.

Set against the dividing wall were the things that gave the room its name:

six coffin-sized metal tubs filled with glittering whiteness. Adam had devised the special mixture of salt, soda ash and a few other things Abby couldn't name, and in controlled circumstances it would fully dehydrate a corpse over the course of a few weeks. Once a dead ghoul or doppelganger was brought back to the office, they would be autopsied, dissected and then left to dry in the salt for a while. The process not only removed fluids and cut down on bad smells, but made the bodies look less recognizably nonhuman in case of a raid on the office. Then the dried body would be cut up and placed in the chemical bath to be broken down into liquid form, where it could be poured into the sewer. Methodical. Careful.

She sometimes wondered if there were ghosts in the basement. None had been seen, but that didn't mean a lot with ghosts.

Lenny Scott was tied to a chair in the center of the room. The legs of the chair were anchored to the heavy drain hatch, and his wrists and ankles had been tied with coarse nylon rope. His eyes, ears and nose had all been covered with gauze bandaging and secured with duct tape. Dried blood streaked his clothes, and there were bullet holes in his shirt but no visible wounds. The Invisible Man à la Tarantino.

Leaning against the wall was Mal, looking unusually pale and tired. He wore a T-shirt and khakis, which surprised Abby: even on the worst days, Mal was a waistcoat kind of man. A battered paperback was tucked under his arm, but his eyes were fixed on Scott.

The prisoner cocked his head when she closed the door behind her. "Let me guess," he said, hoarse voice heavy with sarcasm. "Waterboarding time?"

"Sorry, no," Abby said. "How's he doing, Mal?"

"Belligerent and intransigent." That got a snort from Scott, which Mal ignored. "He also called me a faggot and likely did not mean a piece of wood. When I corrected him, he reiterated the sentiment."

"So I see," she commented. What little she could glimpse of the therian's expression was sour. "Has he shared any information yet?"

"Just graphic, though unimaginative, descriptions of what he'll be doing to us once he gets free," Mal said. His tone was casual, or as casual as he ever was anyway, but his expression was concerned. "He favors crude sexual taunts."

Oh, great. There was a hint of a smirk on Scott's face at that, and for a moment, she reconsidered her plan. She didn't like the thought of being threatened with a second attack so soon.

On the other hand, she didn't plan on letting Scott intimidate her. He was definitely smirking now, either pleased with himself and his behavior or trying to make it look like he was, and it did wonders for putting her ethical doubts to rest for now. Clearly this was someone who needed to be dealt with firmly. And she was just petty enough to care that he had tried to have them killed.

"Well, that's not very original of him," she said, moving over to the autopsy table. The metal buckle on her shoulderbag clicked loudly against the table's surface, and Scott straightened, his head turning as he searched for the cause of the noise. Abby raised an eyebrow at Mal and repeated the click, louder this time.

Hmm.

"Okay," Abby added, "I can take over now. Would you mind giving Leonard and me some privacy?"

"Not at all," Mal said, but his glance between them said differently and his expression was questioning. She gave him a reassuring smile and mouthed *Don't worry,* drawing a cursory nod from him. Still, he mimed waiting outside the door. She shook her head at that. If it turned into an emergency, the whole building would be able to hear anyway, but she wanted the illusion of privacy for what she was about to try.

Scott's expression shifted as the door closed. She couldn't quite figure out what had changed for a moment; with his eyes and eyebrows covered, figuring out his moods was going to be a challenge.

"Hi," she said. "Comfortable?"

"Seriously? I'm tied to a chair. In a basement. You're really funny, bitch."

"Sorry about that. Here, let me help." Leaning forward just far enough to touch his head, she peeled off the bottom two strips of gauze. The bloody marks on the bandaging matched up to spots on his nose that were only lightly bruised. Apparently, therianthropes were pretty good healers.

He sniffed at the air and promptly choked. "What the fuck're you people doing down here, cooking meth?" he demanded, the words half-strangled by a coughing fit. "Smells like crap in here!"

"I'm surprised," Abby said as she stepped back with the soiled gauze in hand. She quickly fished a clean sandwich bag out of her satchel and folded the bandage into it. A good sample of therian DNA shouldn't be wasted. "That selkie had the same problem the other day, when he jumped into the river. Do you know if all shapeshifters with enhanced senses have the same problems? It's strange, isn't it? If I had such a good sense of smell, I don't think I'd be living in a city."

From the set of Scott's jaw, he was trying to glower at her. Difficult without being able to see. "Fuck you," he rasped, stifling another cough against his shoulder. "What's that *smell?*"

"I mean, Chicago kind of has a reputation, too," Abby continued. "Fifty years ago, rats could run right across the river when it was cold. The scum on top of the water would freeze solid. Even today, it's pretty... well, you know. Not as bad as a manufacturing town, though. Do you know any therianthropes who live in more highly-polluted areas? I'd love to get their statements."

His expression was incredulous. "Are you retarded?"

"No, just curious." She perched on the edge of the autopsy table, wadding her jacket underneath her to protect her behind from the cold metal. A strange numbness was creeping through her limbs, and she looked over Scott's head as she talked. "And you know, you really should think about watching your language. I know it sounds cheesy, but swearing all the time really doesn't do anything to make you sound scarier or smarter. It just makes the words lose their power."

"Fuck you, bitch."

"Thank you for demonstrating." She tapped her fingers against the metal surface of the table. "You know, I'm really not sure what your end game is here. I guess you could be stonewalling by just cussing at me until whoever you work for shows up to rescue you, but I don't think that'll work." He laughed at that, loud and hoarse with a strained edge, trying to cut through her words. Perhaps an attempt to assert some kind of control and run the conversation. Instead of shouting or arguing, Abby let him keep going until his breath ran out and the laughter died in an undignified, patently insincere chuckle.

"As I was saying," she continued, "it's not going to work. I'm sure you have a perfectly good reason for—" Again he interrupted, this time with a string of nonsense sounds and mixed profanity, and again Abby waited for him to finish. He'd need to breathe, after all.

Soon, though, it became clear that her approach wasn't working. Scott didn't seem like the type to get frustrated by someone else's cooler head. That had been a miscalculation on Abby's part: she'd taken one look at the cocky grin and decided that he should be treated like a teenager.

Plan B it was, then. She slid off the table and moved over to the nearest salt tub. It had been occupied for almost six weeks now, and patches of the glittering white were stained yellow by the fluids that had seeped from the corpse. She ran her good hand through the top layer of salt, breaking up hemolymph-stained chunks and releasing a fine white dust into the air. Her fingers scraped lightly over the desiccated remains. A chitinous feeding spike emerged, jutting upwards as if still hungry in death. The smell of salt and death grew stronger.

Scott shifted in his chair, straining as he tried to turn his head and follow the source of the scent without actually showing that he was doing it. Abby wondered what the smell was telling him: did he know what kind of creature lay in the salt? Could he tell how it had died, or who it had killed?

She moved to the next bin and raked her fingers through the salt, noting the gray and reddish-purple clumps there. It was the tub where they'd planted the Luka the selkie. She took another breath of her own, steeling herself, and brushed back the first layer of salt. The face that appeared was already drying and sunken: eyes closed and eyelids wrinkled, lashes crusted with tiny crystals stained a very faint yellow. The vitreous liquid in the eyeballs was supposed to be clear, but it didn't always stay that way after the body died.

All things considered, Kotik's brother looked rather peaceful. More peaceful than his victims had, anyway. Abby picked a clump of crusted salt out of one eye socket and flicked it onto the ground between Scott's feet.

He didn't say anything, but his jaw worked reflexively as he caught a whiff of the salt. Abby leaned against the tub and watched him, studying the deepening lines at the corners of his mouth and the faintest beginnings of sweat dampening the gauze over his eyes.

"I have some questions for you," Abby said, pressing her fingertips against the sheet metal. "If you answer them, you'll be treated fairly. We'll have to hold you until this mess is cleaned up, but afterwards, we can make you a deal." Her stomach twisted a little at the lie. It was true, they could make him a deal, but it might not be one he'd like. They really didn't have any procedures for dealing with prisoners. Fortunately, the smell of the salt flats should cover any hint of nervousness in her scent. "But right now, people have died, and you tried to double down on that by running us into a bonepicker nest. If you don't help us out now, things aren't going to go well for you."

"Bullshit." Scott's voice was slightly muffled as he dug his face into his own shoulder in an effort to squash his nose closed. Just looking at it gave Abby a shooting pain in her neck. "You don't have anything on me."

"Don't we? You admitted to knowing one of the victims. Fairies are going through brick walls to kill people, and we found evidence that they'd been in Sarah Mulsey's apartment recently. And when we asked, you sent us to a war zombie. That's a heck of a coincidence."

He tried to reply, but his words were strangled by a cough. "Get rid of it," he managed to wheeze. "Get rid of it!"

"In a minute." Abby moved to the next bin. Tears were dampening the gauze around Scott's eyes, and something wrenched deep in her chest at the sight. "We need to know this, Leonard. People are being murdered. Someone was *skinned alive*, Leonard. We need to know why."

"Why do you care?" Scott rasped. Tendons bulged in his neck and shoulders as he twisted in his chair. "Or are you just pissed off you couldn't get to 'em first?"

The jab hurt, but Abby wasn't going to let him see know. "That depends," she said. "What did they do wrong?"

"Nice try, bitch. I'm not saying anything."

Abby's heart sank. "Oh, well," she said. "Let's see what's in tub number three, then." Scott made a gulping noise, manfully stifled, and she moved on.

Tub number three contained a collection of animal zombies in various stages of decomposition. Two sparrows, a crow, and a stray cat were in the first layer, but Abby wasn't about to dig deeper. Even after days in the salt, the smell wafting off them was enough to make her eyes water. Zombies were her least favorite form of natural disaster.

The crow was the newest. It had been picked up a week ago in Elgin, squawking and hammering itself against the glass of a deserted house despite a broken wing and a golf-ball-sized cavity in its chest. A small colony of maggots extracted from the wound were currently being incubated on Adam's side of the basement in hopes that they'd provide some clues about the nature of the bird's life after death. They probably wouldn't, but it had to be tried. In the meantime the bird itself might be able to help.

Its head had been separated from its body to stop it moving. She picked the head up, blinking fresh tears out of her eyes at the smell, and tossed it onto the ground next to Scott.

He lurched. Sneezed. Swallowed. A red flush spread across his face, and as he swallowed again, he bit his lips until they turned white. It didn't work. Abby barely had a chance to jump back before the vomit hit the floor.

"Well, that's not helpful," she said, mostly to keep down her own bile. Scott retched again, spitting onto the concrete.

"I'm gonna fuck you up," he gagged. "Bitch! Fucking bitch! Fucking—!" Then came more words, the kind that Mal had warned her to expect. Graphic and detailed threats of what he would do to her if he ever got his hands on her. She did her best to tune them out, focusing on Scott's face and the desperate way he wrenched at his bonds.

Muscles bulged as fur rippled across skin and red froth welled up in his mouth. Skin shifting. He was trying to transform, and if he did, she would be dead meat.

So she tossed the rest of the crow into his lap. He choked on his own saliva and spasmed, spitting blood into his lap. His next words were more in the same vein, but they were cut off by his closing throat.

After a slow count of thirty seconds, Abby retrieved the crow and dropped it back into the salt tub. Scott's ragged breathing evened and he sagged forward against his bonds, pallid and sweaty.

"Zombie," Abby said, smoothing salt over the pieces. "This seems to be the best time of year for them, you know. Things don't rot as quickly in the cold. Your friends probably could've put a plain category-two twitcher down in that basement, and it would've had the same effect."

Scott spat again, onto the concrete this time. "They're not my friends."

"Accomplices, then. But you're involved in something, aren't you? Something strange is going on here, and it's a lot bigger than one therianthrope." Abby wadded up several paper towels and swiped at Scott's face, wiping away some of the vomit and blood. He snarled at her, and she quickly jumped back again. "Hold still! If you don't get your face clean soon, it's going to get crusty."

He muttered something but, to Abby's faint surprise, actually held still. She mopped off his face, carefully avoiding his teeth while she did so, and wrapped up the paper towels to use as further samples.

"I don't fuckin' believe you," he said finally. "I don't. What's wrong with your head?"

One side of her mouth quirked, though it couldn't have been called a smile. "If you don't believe me already, what makes you think you'd believe me if I told you?"

"You think this is gonna make me tell you anything?" he demanded raggedly. "It's not. You're crazy, and you're all gonna regret this the minute I'm out of here. Get me?"

"Yes, I get you. In fact, we've had you for some time." Scott opened his mouth, but she picked up the crow body again, and the smell wafting off it made him pause. "Now let me help you get something. You're tied up in a location you don't know. My friends have already searched you for tracking devices. There's enough of us to keep questioning you around the clock, and not all of us are as nice as me." Dimly she registered a sense of the disturbingly ridiculous at the words. The problem was that there wasn't much else she could say. Except— "We're not doing this because we're crazy or sadistic, Leonard. We just don't want any more people to die. There's been enough of that already."

There was a long moment of silence from Scott. His breathing was shallow, and despite the blindfold, his head turned to follow the crow in Abby's hand. The reek of coppery blood and vomit was thick in the basement.

"It's not gonna work," he said finally. "Even if I wanted to talk, I couldn't. You have no idea of the level of shit you're dealing with here."

"Let me ask you something," Abby said. "Does the name Baba Yaga mean anything to you?"

"No?"

"How about L'uomo Nero?"

Scott pulled a face. "Was that the historical guy with the fiddle?"

"No."

"Then I don't know what the fuck you're talking about."

Abby shook her head, remembering a creeping cold and a bright-eyed, hunchbacked figure attended by floating hands. "Trust me, Mr. Scott. If your boss isn't Baba Yaga, we'll manage."

Scott seemed unsure of how to react to that. Fine by her: she wasn't sure what she was doing any more. All of her thoughts—plans, resentments, confusion—seemed to be clashing together, knocking pieces off each other.

"All right," she said after a long pause. "It's too bad you can't help us. Kotik was actually pretty helpful, but I suppose that was just fairy chattiness."

The prisoner couldn't hide a twitch. "You met *Kotik?*"

"'Met' is sort of generous. He tried to kill me in the hospital last night." Abby leaned against the workbench. "But you wouldn't know anything about that, right?"

"Uh... no, not really. That's not my department." What she could see of his expression was incredulous. "But why should I believe you? Kotik never leaves any survivors."

"I'm surprised. He seemed pretty flaky to me." Abby rubbed her right shoulder, massaging the remaining aches in the muscle there. "But if you don't believe me, smell for yourself."

She opened her shoulderbag and held it under Scott's nose. He inhaled and immediately recoiled.

"I think," Abby said slowly, "that this is the part where I'm supposed to say he seemed like a nice guy, and it would be a shame if anything happened to him. I'd be lying."

"Jesus Christ," Scott said faintly. His exhalation ruffled the white fur. "How?"

"Sorry, I can't say." Abby pulled her hand away and made a mental note to bag some fur samples as well. Adam would have a lot of work to catch up on when this was all over. "Now if you were willing to share ..."

"No way. I can't. I *can't.*" Scott's face was turning sickly pale. "There's a gayass on me. If I talk, I die."

That gave Abby a moment of pause. "A what?"

"A gayass. You know, g-e-a-s-s. I'm pretty sure she named it that just so I couldn't talk about it without sounding like a dumb shit." Scott took a deep breath. "I'm serious, she warned me about this, it's bad mojo. Karma. Whatever it is."

Abby knew a bit about *geasa,* but only in the context of fairy tales. It was a sort of magical vow laid on someone that would kill them if they broke it. It was also big magic, an idea much larger than simply channeling energy through a small charm or even the disturbing-but-comprehensible shapeshifting process used by therians and fae. Being under a geas was just like being under a curse, and they had no evidence of curses.

This you balk at? she thought. Her inner voice sounded remarkably like her grandfather George, raising one graying eyebrow at her from behind his beer mug. *Bogeymen, werewolves and fairies are all to the good, but you dig your heels in at one small curse? Pour me another one,* Galya, *you make my head hurt.*

Think logically, she told herself. If geasa existed, and if he was under one, it couldn't be a perfect one. After all, he'd already given her something.

"So you have a boss, and she can use magic," she said. "And she's a she. Thank you, Leonard."

He froze and turned, if possible, even paler.

"That's actually a big help," Abby continued, mentally apologizing to the universe for yet another lie. "Magic-users aren't very common in this part of the country, and with the body count so far, there won't be many left to sift through."

He sputtered, the words slightly mangled by his overwhelming need to swear. Abby sympathized.

"I didn't tell you anything!" he yelped. "Don't even think about trying to pin that shit on me!"

"It's all right, Leonard. You haven't died yet, have you?" She tapped her overgrown fingernails against the salt tub again. "Maybe it's because there isn't such a thing as a geas after all. You'd be surprised what we've learned about the magical world. Tell me, have you ever actually met anyone under a geas?"

A second or two of hesitation. "No."

"And judging by the way you pronounced it, you've never heard the word spoken aloud. So, what, an e-mail? Someone sends you a message saying you've been placed under a geas, and you believe it?" There wasn't any scorn in her tone. Given the kind of things they were dealing with, Abby knew there were plenty of odd stories she'd believe if someone she trusted told her. "And that e-mail would have to be from someone you knew well enough to believe could place a geas. Your boss?"

"... yes." Leonard shook his head like he was trying to clear water out of his ears. "Look, I can't say anything about that. I can't. You don't know what she can do."

"But I learn fast. Brick walls, for example. Dead sorcerers. Not something you want to play around with."

He laughed a little at that, the sound bitter. "Why do you think I didn't give a shit about what happened to Mulsey or her friends? Fucking sorcerers. Think they're so fucking amazing with that shit, don't care about the rest of us."

"That's usually how it goes," Abby said quietly. "When you've got something everyone else doesn't, it makes them seem less important."

"Yeah." Scott coughed, spitting out a few drops of blood. "Like anyone cares about their problems, right? 'Boo-hoo, I can do magic and make tons of cash. I'm sooo sad about it.' She can't kill 'em fast enough."

"So your boss is a sorcerer who wants to kill sorcerers? Dividing-and-conquering through her. Very sneaky."

"Fuck, no!" Scott seemed personally offended by the idea. "I wouldn't work with a fucking sorcerer. She's something better than that. Way better." His face flushed, seemingly remembering something, and he clamped his jaw shut. When nothing appeared to strike him down, though, he relaxed again.

"It doesn't look like she's going to kill you any time soon," Abby said softly. "I can't say the same for my friends upstairs, Leonard. Please. Who is she, and what's she planning?"

"I'm not ..." He chewed on his lower lip. "I don't know much. I'm just the backup guy."

"The backup guy who happened to move in next to one of the few sorcerers in town?"

"She had me scoping her." The words tumbled out in a rush, as if escaping before he could grab them back. "Not every sorcerer is a good candidate for... whatever the hell she has going on. I don't know, it's part of the plan. But she had a list of sorcerers for her commissions."

"Commissions. What kind of commissions?"

"I don't know!" Scott shouted. "She didn't tell me, and I didn't ask. I don't want to fuck with that magic shit, it messes with your head! I just scoped the sorcerers and helped clean up when they were done."

"So you were a backup guy and an accessory to murder." Abby's voice had an edge to it. "Did you really do all those things you said you did? Drive Sarah around and take her to the mall? Or was that just a lie, like the trap in the basement?"

He hedged for a moment, rocking back and forth in the chair. "I, yeah, I did. I mean, I had to get to know her. She was the only one of the first wave of sorcerer contacts who was really private. But I'm not an accessory to anything! I didn't kill anyone!"

"No, you just helped. Helped arrange a death involving a crippled woman having her eyes and brain burned out." The edge was sharpening. Abby had to stop and breathe. "You can see how that would upset some people, Leonard."

"But she was a *sorcerer!* And it's not like that, 'cause—" Once again, Scott struggled and seemed to lose his train of thought. "I didn't. I mean, I wasn't. Look, I was a scout, okay? I did the thing. I set up meetings with the sorcerers and got the commissions going, that's all. I passed messages and instructions to 'em. And I tried to clean up when it was over. I never touched any of 'em!"

"So you didn't know anything about the commissions, but you met with the sorcerers about them." It was getting harder and harder to keep her composure. Every word out of Scott's mouth grated on her, reminding her of what she was doing and why she was there. The constant push-pull of thoughts (*but he's bad, but this is wrong, but he tried to kill us, but this is illegal*) made it harder and harder to keep herself focused. She had to get the information and get out now, or she'd scream. "Tell me what happened, Leonard."

"I can't—look—" He gabbled more, panic seemingly knotting his tongue.

"Look. I meet up with them, hand over the instructions she sent or the instructions they need. I don't know what's in the letters and I don't ask because my boss trusts me not to look. She knows you can't give that kind of work to fairies. I'm supposed to be meeting one *today* and if you don't let me go, my boss will know you got me!"

"Tell me about the meeting."

He stammered out a few details which she noted down on the back of an old envelope. Her hand felt slow and oddly clumsy as she wrote, hampered not just by the overlong nails but by the chill in the basement and the sick feeling in the pit of her stomach. Scott didn't look too good either: he was paler than ever, and bruises were quickly rising on his lips where he'd gnawed at them. The bandages were soaked with sweat.

"Why the commissions, Leonard?" She couldn't keep her voice neutral any longer. It was flat and hard, and didn't sound like her at all.

"I don't know!" He squirmed in the chair. The bruises on his face were deepening. "She wanted something from them!"

"And then killed them so they couldn't talk?"

"Yes. No. I don't know!"

His hands were trembling, nails scrabbling at the arms of the chair. For a moment Abby wondered if he was feeling caffeine aftereffects. She couldn't have caused that much panic with a few dead animals, not without ever hurting someone. Could she?

No. She couldn't. As the bruises on his lips darkened, a fresh chill swept over her.

"Her name, Leonard. What's her name?"

"I—"

His words were lost in a hoarse squeak. Purple and greenish lines spread across his face, deep and strangely geometrical. As Abby jumped to her feet, the lines spread further and the colors darkened. Blood appeared in the center of the lines as the skin thinned and split.

"Grace and honor to the old ways!" he choked out. Then his mouth clamped shut and his head lolled back, his eyes rolling up in their sockets.

"Mal! John!" she shouted. "Someone's trying to kill Scott!"

The ceiling shook with a violent crash accompanied by an outburst of swearing from John. Scott spasmed in his chair, reddish foam dripping from his lips. When she tried to grab his arm, he bucked so violently that she lost her grip and her nails left tracks on his skin.

She fell back against the workbench and scrabbled along it, searching for anything that might help. Wires, knives, autopsy tools, chemicals. The ceiling shook again as someone scrambled to get to the basement door. Hydrogen peroxide, a bag of jelly beans, tons and tons of salt.

Salt! As the door slammed open and footsteps pounded on the stairs, she scooped double handfuls of salt out of the nearest tub and flung it over Scott. The chair wobbled back on two legs, and she grabbed for it as quickly as she could. Salt sprayed across his lap.

The dividing door crashed open and John came charging in, wide-eyed, Desert Eagle in one hand and a cell phone in the other. Mal was right behind him, also armed but substituting a baseball bat for the phone. A cloud of genie swirled around them like a malevolent fog.

"The fuck?" John demanded. He jerked to a stop at the sight of the man in the chair. "Is he dead?"

"Nearly!" Abby shouted. "He said there's a curse on him and then *this* happened!"

The spasms were dying down a little, but not nearly enough. Mal hurried to the prisoner and tilted his head back, peering into his face. "Ruptured blood vessels, nose and mouth. No clotting. Kit!"

Abby quickly flung open the cabinet under the workbench and hauled out a massive metal-clad suitcase, unlatching it with a flick of her thumb. Inside, packed like sardines, were dozens of carefully-padded vials, pill bottles, and various unprescribed drug compounds. Most of it wasn't street-legal, but Mal knew people.

"Got it!" she said. "What do you need?"

"Blue vial with the green-and-white label, ten ccs." Mal briskly jammed two fingers into the roof of Scott's mouth and held down his lower jaw with the other hand. Scott made a gargling noise and tried to bite down, but Mal held on. Abby uncapped a fresh syringe from the sterile packet and drew the liquid from the vial.

"Into his throat," Mal grunted, tightening his grip. Scott's teeth had ripped jagged lines in his hands, but he held on like grim death. "The big vein. Hurry!"

Scott's thrashing was weakening, but it was still taking all of Mal's strength to hold his head still. John lurched out of his momentary surprise and moved to grab Scott's shoulders, doing his best to help keep the therian steady. Abby pressed two fingers against the bulging vein and slipped the needle into it.

The three of them hung onto Scott until the spasms began to die down. When Mal let his head loose, Scott sagged backwards, unconscious. The spreading lines of geometric bruises had made a diagonal grid across his mouth. The X shapes seemed to stitch his mouth shut.

Mal grimaced as he examined his hand. "Perhaps we should consider issuing padded gloves as required equipment."

"That might help." Abby poured hydrogen peroxide onto a folded piece of gauze and pressed it against Mal's hand. Her own hands were shaking so badly that the tall man nodded to her and took the gauze.

Silence fell in the basement as the three agents looked at each other. All of them were sweaty, bruised and flecked with their prisoner's blood. Two were visibly injured. Scott was streaked with bloody froth and the X marks stood out almost black.

John mopped a bit of blood off his scarred cheek. "All right, that's over with. Adam! Get your arse in here!"

When Adam appeared, John surveyed the group. His mouth was a thin line. "Abby, we'll talk. Adam, clean 'im up and make sure he doesn't swallow his tongue. Then draw some blood and tissue samples from Mal—he's been bit by a therian, an' who knows what that'll do. Mal, you're quarantined until we know what we're dealing with. Period. Any questions?"

Nobody had anything to say. Abby shot a glance at Mal, who seemed unruffled as he cleaned his hand. She tried to picture him sprouting fur and fangs, but the image didn't square. Even flecked with gore, the man exuded a kind of glacial calm that seemed unassailable. Mal as a were-anything just didn't seem to register.

But there was the limit of their knowledge to consider. Nobody bitten by the werewolves in the '80s had ever been confirmed as turning into a werewolf, but that was open to question because most of the victims had just been killed outright. Iris Liu, the werecobra, had never bitten anyone that they knew of. And not only was this a werecoyote, it was one which had narrowly survived a sudden attack by someone or something unknown. Mal might not be a prime candidate for fur, but it was still something they had to be careful about.

From his expression, he was wholly unfazed by the prospect, and Abby envied his even temperament. Every muscle in her body seemed to be aching, and the ever-present smell of the salt flats had turned from a background annoyance to an active assault on her senses. She didn't want anything but a good long nap, a couple of pain pills and a gallon of either ice cream or alcohol. Either way, she wanted the kind that was pink and bad for you.

Still, they all had jobs to do. She hastily sponged the remaining blood off herself and followed John up the stairs. Jimmy, sprawled in his corner, hadn't even woken up. Harvey collected himself into a thick band of fog and dribbled back into the jar. "That was anticlimactic," he muttered almost too softly to hear.

Chapter Ten

Upstairs, the main office looked like even more of a mess than usual. Someone had knocked over a desk, Mal's to be exact, and one edge had taken out the side of a bookcase. Twenty or thirty assorted files, books, and a jam jar full of pennies had spilled across the floor.

They moved into the kitchenette and John, to her surprise, made her a cup of coffee. Three sugars: a touch rich for her blood, but gift horses and so on. He waited while she sipped.

"All right," he said finally. "What happened down there?"

She set down the coffee and, quickly and bluntly, laid out the facts. He shook his head.

"Bloody hell."

"That's about the sum of it, yeah."

John settled into a chair and thought, tapping his fingers against the scarred tabletop. "So these sorcerers were all scouted for some kind of commission by a woman. No name, though. Funny that you could get all that other information, but not her name."

"I know. It's suspicious that the geas would only kick in at that point." She chewed on her lower lip. The burn of coffee lingered, but it was mostly overwhelmed by the cloying taste of the sugar. "If it was a geas. But there are legends on the books about the power of the name in magic. Considering that we were overrun by bogeymen just last month, I'm willing to believe it."

"It's possible," John conceded. "But we don't know that, and this case is already enough of a mess. We need facts. Did he say anything else?"

Abby's mouth twisted a little at the memory. "He said something when he was choking. 'Grace and honor to the old ways,' I think."

"That mean anything to you?"

"'Old ways' is pretty nonspecific. Since he's a coyote therian, maybe he means Native American traditions? But he said it when he was in the middle of choking, like it was the most important thing he could say. Maybe it was a spell."

"Well, that's one more thing to add to the heap." John sat back in his chair with a sigh. "What about this rendezvous with the new sorcerer? Tell me about that."

She pulled out the envelope and ran an eye over her scribbled notes. "He's supposed to meet her at 6 PM this evening outside the Cultural Center, across from Millennium Park. He said he's delivering instructions, but swore he didn't know what those instructions were. Her initials are T.B."

"Do we have anyone matching that in the files? Please tell me we do."

Abby shrugged. "You don't need me to tell you we don't have enough on sorcerers, John. Ninety percent of it is theory, and the other ten percent is based on four cases of spellcasters and a whole lot of dubious interviews that the Rev never gave us the source for. I can recheck the records just to make sure if you like, but we haven't even had a problematic human for almost three years."

"Oh, right. George Salk." John scratched his temple. "What'd you call him? A puppeteer?"

"Poppeteer. With the little dolls that had peoples' nails in them." She wrinkled her nose at the memory. Salk hadn't been able to influence the living, but his poppet dolls had snared the ghosts of the people whose body parts he had in them. Unfortunately, one of the ghosts he caught had been a bloody-minded poltergeist, and the SSR had had to destroy the poppets after one of them choked Salk to death.

"I remember him. Got a cold after sitting out watching his building overnight." John shook his head. "Hate human magic. It's easier to handle when they've got fangs and all."

"So are we going to watch the Cultural Center? See if someone else turns up to meet this T.B. person?"

John shook his head. "Whoever Scott's boss is, we have to assume she knows we've got 'im. Can't afford to just watch. You up for another bit of undercover?"

"Oh, always. Though I might be sort of useless." She hefted her cast with her free hand. "Unless you want to help me tape a butter knife to this."

"Won't be necessary. I'll need your eyes more'n anything else."

"You'll be there?" She didn't frown, but she wanted to. Twelve hours ago he'd been dragging Jimmy into the middle of a fight with a werecoyote, and now he wanted to go meet a sorcerer with her? She quickly looked him over, checking for the twitches or too-bright eyes that meant he was riding a temper high.

He seemed to know what she was thinking, because he leaned back, mouth twisting. "There's nobody else," he said. "Mal has to be benched until we sort out that bite, and Adam needs to look after him. And I don't want him in the field anyway, 'cause he's a little too squirrelly for ..." He caught her expression and smiled, the look tinged with a hint of bitterness. "Yah, yah, I know. It's been a rough couple of days, right?"

"Yeah." She checked her watch: 2:27 PM. "Look, if we're going to be meeting a sorcerer at six, I need to do some prep work. I know I left the Salk records at my house, and I can see if there's anything else there as well. Maybe the *Tarwell's* volume on witches. Okay?"

"Sure, go ahead." John sipped his own coffee. "Be back here by quarter to five. With any luck Scott'll be awake by then and we can get some information about the meeting."

She nodded and stood. The atmosphere was thick and distinctly awkward, which was fine by her. She wasn't sure she wanted to do too much talking or thinking about anything that had just happened.

As she turned to go, though, John stood too. "Abby?"

She paused. "Mmm?"

"You did good." She half-turned, surprised, and John shrugged sheepishly. "I mean, picking at Scott like that. Smells and all. I would've gone with sewing needles under the fingernails or somethin'." That got a start from her, and he held out a hand. "Wait, wait, not literally! I mean... look... Hell. You were smart. You know."

"Okay," she said softly.

• • •

Jimmy was still asleep. She considered waking him up to go home, but she wasn't sure that was a good idea: it would mean leaving him alone at the house while she went downtown. At least this time Mal and Adam would be with him at the office, and John would be safely out of the way. Maybe it would be good for her son to see some more stable agents doing their jobs.

But that still left a couple of questions unanswered. Bending over the cot, she gently pulled the green glass jar out of Jimmy's hands and backed away before he could notice her.

"Hey," she said softly, knocking on the jar. "Awake and speak to me, djinn so wise, Of myriad dangers and possible surprise."

A tendril of mist came creeping out, trailed by one bobbing yellow eye. "Not bad," he said. "Your meter was off in the second line, but it's pretty good for ex tempore. What's up?"

"Harvey, I need you to tell me the truth." She bit her lip. "Did Jimmy get hurt?"

The eye blinked. "What? When? Is this a bogeyman thing?"

"I mean yesterday. Was Jimmy okay? Was he scared? Did anyone try to hurt him?"

"Honestly? I don't know." Abby's shoulders slumped, and the second eye rushed out of the jar to join the first one. "He wasn't banged up, if that's what you mean. Nobody even touched the kid. But was he fucked up in the head? Scared to death? Dunno. Not my department," He paused, and a ring of mist rose higher to loop around Abby. "Unless you want me to take a peek at his thoughts?"

"What? No! Don't be ridiculous. I'm not going to read his mind!"

"Look." The two yellow eyes rose higher, sliding along the belt of mist to hover level with Abby's face. "I've already read it, okay? I've read everyone's mind. I have to, because that's what I am. I've got this information, and the best way to get that information is for me to drop it into your head. You won't be hurting him. He doesn't even have to know. And we can get this over with quickly, rather than talking about details for twenty minutes and possibly waking the kid up while you get all sad again. Okay?"

Abby swallowed. She was remembering that the wispy creature in front of her—normally just an odd little quirk of light, a pet, a program, a resource—was older, and less human, than the rest of them. He might have thought through her concerns, but he didn't share them, or he wouldn't be offering in the first place.

"All right," she said. "Just quickly show me what happened. And no commentary."

"Silent as the grave," he promised.

Abby wasn't a fan of his choice of words, but she didn't have a chance to object. The world gave a lurch as something cool and damp swished into her ears and glowing yellow swallowed her vision. She stumbled and reached out blindly, but her limbs weren't cooperating and she couldn't control her hands. Bolts of pain shot through her head and down her back.

Then, as quickly as it had appeared, the pain and blindness vanished. The world around her had changed. She was standing in Scott's apartment, locked in place, and she could see Mal and John on either side of her. When she looked down, she glimpsed a pair of folded arms in denim holding an open messenger bag. Inside the bag was a familiar glass jar. Jimmy. Jimmy was holding Harvey.

John was advancing on Lenny Scott, who wasn't backing down. His fists were clenching and his teeth were bared. A thought arrived in Abby's head, in a voice not her own: *he's gonna go flying. He's dead meat. Sawyer's nuts.*

But Lenny didn't cower. He hunched as if he was a runner on base preparing to steal home and met John stare for stare, eyes narrowing, teeth bared.

For a moment, she thought John had hit him too fast to see. Blood welled up in Lenny's mouth, dripping over his drawn lips and onto the linoleum. But John hadn't moved forward or thrown a punch. In fact, he took a step back.

Lenny's teeth were falling out.

They stared. The teeth wiggled loose, trailing droplets of red as they clacked onto the floor and bounced away. Fresh teeth, glinting sharklike triangles, were already pushing through the gumline.

John snarled and lunged, but he was jerked back by Mal. The thespian's face was papery-white and drawn, his grip on John's arm like a claw.

Lenny's hands dropped to the floor. Fur sprouted on his bare forearms and spread from his jaw down his neck and chest. His nose and jaw bulged out as if something was trying to burst out through his face, color leaching out of the skin even as more fur rippled up to coat his face. His nails touched the linoleum with an audible clack.

In seconds, the agents were facing two hundred pounds of animal. Its jaws were open in a canine smile. It seemed to be saying: *your move, human.*

"Holy shit," Jimmy whispered. "He's a werewolf!"

"Coyote, I believe." Mal's grip on John's arm was still tight, but the agent had stopped struggling. His face, too, was pale and drawn, but his stare hadn't wavered from Lenny-the-coyote's and his hand rested on the butt of his gun.

The coyote's mouth opened wider. Blood still coated its gums, but the teeth there were fresh, stark white and murderously sharp. It paced forward, claws clicking on the linoleum, mustard-yellow eyes fixed on John's.

John pulled his gun as the coyote leaped. A single shot cracked through the apartment, muffled by the body of the animal. Jimmy couldn't hold back a yell, Mal drew a second too late. The coyote crashed to the floor on top of John, blood staining both of them.

One paw swiped heavily at John's face, raking lines across his cheek and chin, and John let out a yelp as it tore his skin. He squeezed the trigger again, and a second shot ripped right through the coyote and made it jerk wildly. Jimmy's mouth tasted like acid as he pressed his back against the door.

With a grunt, John heaved the writhing coyote off him. More claw marks were revealed on his chest and collarbones, and the slanting, livid wounds on his face made a gruesome tic-tac-toe board with the scars left by the bogeymen.

The coyote staggered to its feet and began to shift. Its teeth dropped out, littering the floor along with the human ones, and hair sucked back into its body. This time, though, the transformation stopped halfway through and a bald, hairless creature crouched on the floor, holding clawed hands to its newly-repaired stomach.

"Well," Mal said. "Abigail will be sorry she missed this."

The cool words seemed to shake John out of his momentary reverie. He shuddered and unclenched his muscles, blinking for the first time in a minute or two. "Yah," he said. "She can read the obituary."

"Try it," the creature rasped, baring its fresh set of human teeth. "You'll be dead before you can reload, you son of a bitch."

"Who needs to reload? Got a twelve-round mag. And since only one of us has four legs, I'd be careful whose mum you're callin' a bitch." John raised the Desert Eagle, heedless of the blood spotting its muzzle. The stink of gunsmoke in the room made Jimmy's throat tight.

"Fuck you," Lenny said hoarsely.

It was way too familiar: the figure of John looming over the snarling attacker, blood on the floor... His mom in pain... He shook his head and blinked hard.

"That's not helping your case," John said. "You set us up. *You set us up.* But something's even more interesting, eh? If you knew our work, you might guess we could manage one little bonepicker." Lenny's eyes widened, though he tried to hide it. "Which means that as far as you knew, you were running a couple of inquisitive normals into the nest of a war zombie. That's unfriendly."

"John," Mal said. Not so much the Good Cop as the Not as Bad Cop, which was still creeping Jimmy out. "This man is a confirmed shapeshifter. He's useful, mainly if he happens to be alive to give us answers and submit to testing."

"I'm not submitting to shit!" The new set of teeth began to loosen and drop, but John gestured with the Desert Eagle and the shift stopped. Maybe even a werecoyote couldn't heal a .357 round to the head.

"You knew that bonepicker was down there. It's the only reason you would've sent us to that place. And that bonepicker told us he was put there by fairies, which I'm not too happy about 'cos this whole case is too damn complicated already. Talk."

"Fuck off and die!"

"Okay. Mal, cover him for a mo, would you?"

Mal loomed up, tall and stone-faced, as John stepped back and pulled an eight-inch cylinder from his coat pocket. "Really should've done this earlier," he said almost conversationally as he screwed the cylinder onto the end of the Eagle's muzzle. "'S a pain to get these, too. Had to have the barrel threaded specially. Luckily I know a guy who lives in a basement with a lotta tools. Thanks, Mal, you're a friend. Now." He readied the Desert Eagle again, now sporting its brand-new suppressor. "They usually call these silencers, but it's not silent... Quiet enough to not go through these walls, though. A suppressed Desert Eagle sounds a lot like snapping a big stick in half. Now you're going to be helpful an' share your thoughts with us, or I'll shoot you in the crotch. Okay?"

"Holy fuck, man," Jimmy said. "You can't *torture* someone."

"It's not torture, it's punctuation. Adds emphasis." Lenny's eyes were fixed firmly on the suppressor, whose aim had definitely moved south.

Jimmy backed away. A sick feeling was welling up in his stomach, and his eyes were burning. He thought he was going to throw up, but he wasn't sure why. The world felt unsteady under his feet.

His mom worked with these lunatics? What the fuck? What kind of people did this kind of thing? The world was full of things that bled on the ground and dropped teeth all over the place and *kidnapped kids,* and this guy was waving a *gun* and it was all bringing it back.

He clutched the bag with the jar in it. It was a flashback from hell. Everything was crashing in together and making his hands shake, making him wonder what he was even doing there. Why would his mom do this? Why did these things *exist*?

Lenny was babbling and swearing, almost trying to back through the wall. His claws were out again, digging into the cheap plaster as John stared him down impassively. Jimmy hugged the bag tighter and tried to get his legs to move, but they seemed stuck to the ground.

"*Hey! Kid!*" a voice hissed. Jimmy started and almost dropped the jar. Light was leaking from it. Hands trembling, he opened the jar and found himself staring at a cloud of gray mist with glowing golden eyes floating in it.

"Oh damn," Jimmy said.

"My thoughts exactly," whispered the jar. "Listen, Sawyer's gone nuts. We have to stop him or he's gonna do something we'll all regret. Tell me to stop him!"

"I—he—what are you?"

"Now is so not the time for this!" the jar hissed. "Say it, or this place is getting redecorated in Frontal Lobe Gray!"

Jimmy swallowed. He desperately wanted to drop the jar, run away, pretend none of this ever happened, go to his dad's where life was sane and nobody could walk through doors or grow claws on a whim. But... He swallowed again, trying to ease the horrible burning sensation in his raw throat, and nodded. "Go," he said.

Several things seemed to happen at once. A voice yelled *"Hold it right there, buddy!"* as the room filled with fog. A loud snapping noise echoed through the chaos, followed by an animal yowl. Someone said "God's wounds!" in a tone more appropriate for "Fucking hell!" Jimmy dropped the jar, and it bounced off the toe of his combat boot and rolled away into the mist.

As fast as it had appeared, it vanished. Jimmy flattened himself against the wall.

Lenny Scott was on the ground and unconscious. His claws were still out, but there was no more blood than there had been before. Mal had one hand against the wall and the other on his own gun. No injuries on him either, though his face was drawn and pale.

That left John. Injured? No. Not that that reassured anyone.

The agent was standing bolt-upright in the middle of the room, his arms stiffly at his sides. The Desert Eagle was still in one hand, but his finger was off the trigger and the barrel was aimed dangerously close to his own foot. Gray mist wreathed his head and shoulders, and his dilated pupils glowed sickly yellow. His muscles and joints were locked tight, but he was still trembling as if he was trying to break out of his own skin.

"Down, boy," said the gray mist creature from John's own mouth. The voice was unmistakably the same as the one from the jar. "We've already been through this, okay? You're freaking everyone the fuck out. I get you're upset about Marquise, but if you get yourself torn up or arrested because you couldn't hold back on the Charles Bronson impression, what'm I supposed to do? Huh?"

Jimmy couldn't help it. Moving as slowly as possible, he pulled his smartphone out of his pocket and held it up to film.

An incoherent growl ripped through the mist's last words, and John's features trembled for a moment as he fought to regain control. Within five seconds, he lost the fight. "Relax," the unJohn voice said chidingly. "Relax. Okay? I'm not letting you go unless you can behave, and we both know that if I have to restrain you like this for more than a couple minutes, someone's gonna wind up brain-damaged. Think logically about this for a minute. Do you really think you're so mad just because Abby is in the hospital? Be serious. That kid over there kicked her in the face a month ago, and you haven't even laid a finger on him. This isn't you, buddy. Snap out of it."

A shudder seemed to run through John and he wavered, the mist rippling around him. Then, with what seemed to be a full-body sigh, he gave up and slumped backwards. The mist poured out of him and the yellow glow streamed from his eyes. John landed awkwardly on the tile and scooted backwards, pressing his shoulders against the wall. His eyes were closed.

The mist collected in the air, and the glowing orbs refocused. "I'd smile for the camera," it said, rotating to face Jimmy and his phone, "but I'm kinda short on facial muscles. Sorry about that."

"Harvey," Mal said. His slow, deep voice made Jimmy start, almost dropping the phone in the process. "Thank you. What was wrong?"

The indistinct shape of Harvey swirled in midair like a small tornado. "Some kind of ripple," he said. "I think. There's something freaky-deeky going on here. Everything feels kinda off, like the world got dropped and glued back together with some pieces missing."

Mal's gaze flicked to the unmoving John for a moment. "Reality is being altered?"

"Maybe. Not rains of frogs, but something's definitely screwy." The cloud lost shape and spread out as one eye wandered off in another direction. "There was more crazy in that head than I'm used to. Were you able to get anything out of Fuzzy?"

"Scott? Not yet. Can you?"

"Are you kidding? I'm a *human* parasite. Therians run like humans, but their brains are already dual-processing with the whole human-animal schtick. I was able to knock him out, but that's about it." Harvey coalesced again. "I hate to say this, but I can't do shit with this. You're gonna need to actually get info from this guy."

"Understood." Mal nodded to the talking cloud. "Jimmy?"

"Uh—" Jimmy fumbled with the phone again. "Yeah?"

"Turn that off, please. We have work to do." Mal moved across the room and crouched down next to John, whose eyes were still closed.

Jimmy couldn't hear what they said. Mal's words were too low to catch much of, and John's replies were short, snapped whispers that consisted mostly of profanity. Eventually, though, Mal offered a hand up and John managed to clamber back to his feet.

"Okay," John said heavily, mopping his sweaty face on his sleeve. "Now what?"

"Now we retreat," Mal replied. "Quickly. You're certainly not yourself, and we can't continue the investigation here."

"Not without him." Before anyone could say anything else, John grabbed Scott by the arm and jerked him to his feet. The werecoyote growled, baring fresh, bloody teeth. "Mal, grab him some pants. Please."

The world reeled again, and Abby's eyes opened.

She was lying on the basement floor. Her head ached, cold jolts of pain were still shooting down her spine, and the ceiling was dim through the thick mist of Harvey. The genie was hovering a few inches over her head.

"Hi," he said. "You were out for about thirty seconds. Feeling okay?"

"Jesus Christ."

"I'll take that as a no."

Abby rolled over and pressed her face against the cold concrete. Her head ached, but that was nothing compared to the thoughts and images rattling around in her skull. Jimmy pressed against the wall, Jimmy afraid, Jimmy watching and holding a genie bottle while her coworkers viciously subdued a therianthrope who'd tried to have them killed. Jesus Christ. *Jesus Christ.*

"Never again," she said hoarsely. "Never. Again. Don't even ask me. Got it, Harvey?"

"Oh, come on, it wasn't that bad." The misty form retreated a foot or two, eyes bobbing cheerily. "Didn't you get what you wanted?"

With an effort, Abby pulled herself into a kneeling position. Her hands were shaking. She didn't say anything to Harvey, just shook her head and braced herself.

"Uh huh." If he had eyebrows, he'd be raising them. "Okay, well, if you have any questions you know where I'll be. In my jar. Waiting. Because that's where I always am."

"Just as long as you behave yourself," she said as she climbed to her feet.

• • •

The drive home went faster than she had expected. A low fog was clinging to the ground, but the air was much warmer than it should have been and a lot of the more treacherous ice patches had melted. Pedestrians had their jackets unzipped and scarves unknotted, embracing the unusual weather but not trusting it enough to leave the heavy coats at home. Smart of them: Chicago always enjoyed knocking people for a loop during winter.

Her house was just as she'd left it, complete with her bedclothes still strewn all over her room and an untouched pile of dishes in the sink. She shot them a glance and did some quick mental math; after years of late nights and quick meals, she knew exactly how long a dish could be left in the sink before it started growing mold, and these looked like they still had a couple of days to go.

It had long ago become impossible to keep her work and home life separate. Books, papers, newspaper articles, diagrams with question marks all over them, and the occasional dried or pickled specimen from the office collection had all been on her kitchen table at one point or another. Last month's cleaning spree had given her an opportunity to organize some of it, and the important things had been moved up to the attic. She reached up to the corridor ceiling and unfolded the ladder.

The attic was small and cramped. Even Abby, who was just five foot five, had a difficult time standing anywhere but in the center of the room. The sloped ceiling, lined with splintery support boards and spotted with dusty webs and patches of exposed pink insulating foam, would snag anything that touched it. She had settled for packing everything to the sides and leaving a narrow alleyway in the middle of the attic where she could actually stand up and look through everything.

Here were the records from the Salk case. She peeled open the first carton, sneezing at the sudden puff of dry dust, and removed a glass jar half-filled with pure salt, silver shavings and iron. Inside, coated in holy potpourri, was a crude doll made of denim wrapped around a handful of twigs. A face had been drawn onto it in lipstick, but it was mostly faded after three years in the jar.

It was the only poppet they hadn't destroyed, and that was just because it was a dud. Salk hadn't really figured out his process when he made it, or so the theory went. That didn't mean they were going to be careless with it, though.

Underneath the jar were several manila folders in no particular order. Given that each of the ghosts had caused various kinds of trouble while under Salk's control, the agents had opened a file for each. It took some digging to unearth the folder on Salk himself, which was the thinnest of the bunch.

George McLerran Salk. Born in Dublin around 1950, emigrated to America with his parents when he was two years old. A slight learning disability, possibly undiagnosed ADHD, held him back in school. Average or bright in most things but crippled by academic failure, Salk dropped out of high school. His two marriages both ended in acrimonious divorce. He spent most of his life in service positions, usually janitorial work at various schools, until stumbling on a latent talent for poppet magic while taking a learning annex wood-shop class.

With ghosts to serve him, it had been a quick trip to the top. Once he started killing people whose ghosts he wanted, it had been an even quicker one to the bottom. The SSR had started out investigating his crimes and wound up investigating his murder.

Unfortunately, the case of Salk was a bust when it came to usable data. Human magic was hard to analyze because the sample group was small, and each case on record had involved different skills and different groups. Sorcerers only came onto the agency's radar when someone died, which didn't leave much opportunity for interviews and research.

Fairies, on the other hand, were a little more predictable. They were living proof that observation didn't always change the group observed: they did what they liked, when they liked, to who they liked, and rarely batted an eye at the agency's attempts to slow them down. Many of them did possess unusual gifts, but it seemed to run along breed lines: selkies with their sealskins, kelpies breathing underwater, banshees with their eerie voices that could make your ears bleed. One theory on the books held that they, like bogeymen, were influenced by human belief. No proof had ever been found.

But while stories of fairies emerging from trees or casting magical thralls over people were common in folklore, the SSR had never seen anything like that happen in real life. Fairies with sorcerer-like powers were pure legend as far as they knew, and none of the stories or actual sorcerers had involved anything like the strange tattoo magic from the hospital. There were just too many factors in this case that didn't square with any of the available data.

But that was how it always went. All the agents could ever do was focus on the here and now, picking out the little problems they actually understood.

So someone, possibly a fairy, commissioning sorcerers. Fairies violently murdering sorcerers—to keep them quiet?—after the commissions were done, and for some unknown purpose. Fairies using sorcerer magic, and committing the aforementioned violent murders in very uncharacteristic ways. Skinning? Tearing in half? Why?

She glanced down at the Salk file. He had died violently too, and they'd thought he was murdered by a coconspirator or disgruntled accomplice. It turned out to be his own fault, really. John had called it "aggravated suicide." Had Neill, Mulsey and Petrovich been in the same situation? What had they made for the fairies that required them to die? Something she was missing here, something tugging at her thoughts …

Her arm gave a twinge again, and she sighed. The hospital had given her a prescription for Percocet, and while she didn't relish the idea of going on a mission half-stoned, it was probably better than being in too much pain to pay attention to the job. Anyway, John had *his* pills, and they didn't seem to make him any less efficient. She could get the prescription filled on the way back to the office.

By the time she had the boxes of files loaded into her car, it was four PM and the sky had begun to darken. The mist was still thickening, and several icicles dropped from the eaves when she closed the front door. Across the street, her neighbors' silent houses looked like watercolor paintings, half-hidden as they were in the fog. The background hum of car horns, traffic and the el trains now had a new component, the patter of running water. The storm drains were beginning to flood as the snow continued to melt.

Well, that was Chicago for you. Abby didn't doubt that it would all freeze again in a few days, and then there'd be black ice all over the roads. With any luck the case would be finished by then and Abby could cocoon herself until spring like a sane person.

Chapter Eleven

The Chicago Cultural Center was a massive Neoclassical facade on a plain box of a building, like someone had tried to dress it up enough to disguise the bureaucratic function of the place. Huge slabs seemed to have been carved out of its sides, creating sleek arches and broad colonnaded gallery windows in the pale tan stone: ancient Greece by way of the 1890s. Inside there were government offices and art galleries, all crowned by a Tiffany green-and-gold glass dome. The dome wasn't visible from street level, but even without it the elegant curves of the exterior stood out against the sheer metal and battered brick structures that crowded the Loop.

Three broad lanes of Washington Avenue divided the Center from the white terraces and silvered glass of Millennium Park. In the distance, spotlights gleamed off the mirrored surface of the Cloud Gate sculpture. A broad reflecting pool, flanked by thirty-foot rectangular towers with projected images of male and female faces, was supposed to be a seasonal skating pond in the colder weather. Several blocks down, the Art Institute of Chicago loomed over the park.

Abby shivered and tucked herself more deeply into her coat. John was playing the role of criminal contact for the evening, lingering by the Center's brass bull statue in relative safety from the wind, but she was stationed by the reflecting pool as a lookout and the cold wind skimming off the lake seemed to aim right at her. The sky was dark, but the orange and white streetlights left everything at pedestrian level clear. The lights leaking through its own broad windows had left the Art Institute outlined against the dark sky, giving Abby the feeling that it was watching her.

At least the tourists were having fun. Black November had thrown cold water on the nation's spirits, but there was always a ready crop of out-of-towners eager to fool around on or near the Magnificent Mile, and the Center's brass bull was one more opportunity for them to take photographs doing silly things in public. Abby didn't envy the jeans-wearing college kid who climbed onto the bull's back (and, from his expression, flash-froze a very personal area) but at least he and his friends seemed to get some good pictures out of it. Maybe discomfort didn't matter as long as you looked good on Facebook.

Her phone vibrated. With the other one fried by the energy surge in the hospital, she was down to using her burner phone for everyday use, and the caller ID displayed only the incoming number. Fortunately it was one she recognized.

"See anything yet?" The voice was low and hoarse, with a bit of a drawl overlaid on top of the hard Midwestern r's and flat a's. It sounded a lot like

Leonard Scott's voice, though not exactly: John wasn't that good of a mimic, and even if he could sound like the sorcerer's contact he'd never be able to look like him.

"If I had, I would've called you," she said. "How about you?"

"If I had, I wouldn't be calling you." He huffed loudly, making the phone crackle. "Just tourists, hobos, office workers and a couple of guys who look like they're this close to soliciting prostitutes." A pause. "From the looks of things... male prostitutes."

"Everyone needs a hobby," Abby said. "Focus."

That got an honest-to-God hearty laugh from John. "Lighten up!" he said. "Why so glum?" The cheerfulness sounded nearly sincere, maybe even fully sincere to someone who didn't know him, but from John it was hard to swallow. She didn't want to joke with him, not after what had happened yesterday.

The image of her son curled up on the cot, cradling the glass jar of a thousand-year-old angry genie, made her hand tighten on the phone.

"I think we're rushing into this too quickly, that's all." she said. "This isn't exactly something we've been planning for a long time. And contractors can be difficult."

The trick to discussing monsters, magic and extralegal operations against spree-killing fairies in public? Keep it vague. The world expected comfortably-dressed white people in a trendy district to be talking loudly on cell phones about petty interpersonal drama. They were far enough apart that nobody would connect them as two halves of one conversation, and even a really determined eavesdropper wouldn't stick around long enough to figure out that "contractor" was code for "fairy."

(Another recent addition to their vocabulary of code words: "bogeymen" was now "asbestos." As in, "of course the parents are upset, nobody wants asbestos in the city." Home insulation was second only to homeopathic medicine on the list of things no one wanted to hear about.)

"I know, I know," John said. The wind slapped at Abby, momentarily snatching away his words. "—an't back out of it now, right? And if it can help, we have to give it a try. This is important to everyone. Anyway, who's it gonna hurt?"

"Us."

"Well, sure, if you want to be negative."

Abby smiled despite herself and double-checked the envelope in her hand. "I know, that's usually your job."

"Listen, is this about the kid?" The accent slipped a bit. "Because I told you, he's fine. Nothing happened."

"No, it's not about him. Focus, remember?"

John said nothing more, but he stayed on the line; she could hear him breathing. The two of them silently scanned the streets around them. T.B. was a woman, but near Michigan Avenue, that didn't really narrow things down.

Two women had joined the men by the bull and were taking photographs, laughing and mugging for the camera. A Baba-Yaga-like old lady in rags was curled up on a steam grate, staring dully at nothing. A small group of middle-aged women with bulky coats and bright red hats were standing on one of the park terraces, having an animated discussion that seemed to involve a lot of impassioned hand gestures. A college-age girl with a backpack on was walking a large collection of dogs. A woman carrying an artist's portfolio stopped to pat the bull on the nose, but continued on to a nearby Starbucks. Another woman, heavily bundled-up even for a Chicago December, slunk along close to the buildings in a vain effort to keep out of the wind.

"Hang on a bit," John murmured. "Think I've got something."

Abby held up her phone and switched to camera mode. John appeared in the shot, standing by the bull with his own phone still pressed to his ear, and his gaze was tracking someone.

A tall woman with striking red hair had emerged from the Starbucks and was walking down the street towards the Washington Avenue junction. She was wearing a long dark wool coat and high-heeled leather boots which ordinarily should have been a hazard on the slick sidewalk, but she moved with perfect grace. Her eyes were fixed, laserlike, on John. One hand dipped into a pocket and dropped a folded bill into the sleeping old lady's lap without her ever looking around.

"Yeah, that looks about right," Abby murmured. She lowered the phone and moved to the crosswalk. The line was still open, but she wasn't about to distract John with their target moving in. Her job now was to sneak in closer and provide backup if things got hairy.

The woman flicked a hand almost imperceptibly at the bull, and the tourists all seemed to get the same idea at the same time. The teenager currently straddling it hopped off, complaining about something Abby couldn't hear, and his friends gathered around him and moved off in a group. The light was taking entirely too much time to turn green.

There was a strange static crackle over the phone. Then the woman's voice came through, light and clear. "Are you Leonard Scott?"

"No." They had no way of knowing if this contact had met Scott before, after all; she might be asking as a test. Fewer lies kept things simpler. "I'm here to take over his shift. His last job got a little out of hand."

"That does happen sometimes with amateurs. Do you have the things I need?"

The light had finally changed. Abby dashed across the street as quickly as she could, hampered by her awkward balance and the slight dizziness of the painkillers. John made some kind of answer she couldn't quite overhear, but the woman raised an eyebrow and crossed her arms.

"Boring," she said. Her tone was distinctly familiar, in a "broke into the hospital room to kill me" sort of way. Abby skidded to a stop on the curb and sucked in some air, trying to quell the sudden rush of adrenaline as John lowered his phone.

The pair were about forty feet away. John had parked himself on the far side of the bull, putting T.B.'s back to Washington Avenue, but that didn't mean Abby was free to sneak up with a gun. The plan was to talk the sorcerer into taking things somewhere quieter where they could question her, but if the sorcerer was actually the fairy woman from the hospital, Abby wasn't sure she wanted that happening. Not when she'd shown a striking lack of reluctance to use magic in small spaces.

On the other hand, she couldn't just pull a gun in the middle of the Loop. Police presence was already heavy; the Black November protest in Daley Plaza had turned into a small shantytown days before, and that tended to make the authorities a bit nervous. Abby didn't blame them, but it severely limited her options in public.

John was suggesting they move the discussion off the main street, couching it as a security concern—"Cops might think we're dealing drugs or something," with a bit of a laugh that said he didn't take the idea of the authorities too seriously. She could hear him now without the phone, so she ended the call and paused to snap a quick photo of the two of them.

There was no woman in the picture.

She almost dropped the phone. There was John, caught in mid-gesture and with a rather silly expression on his face, typical for what was essentially a single frame from the middle of a video. There was the brass bull. There, however, was no fairy sorcerer.

Holding her breath, Abby pretended to glance up at the looming facade of the Cultural Center and quickly snapped another picture. There John was again, but the fairy was nowhere to be found. Even her shadow, lying visibly dark across the sidewalk in real life, was nowhere to be found in the photo.

Her hands shook a little as she dipped her left hand into her pocket. Flashlight, no good. Paper, too light. Folded envelope with her notes on it, dead giveaway, and with her fingerprints on it to boot. With no other options, she pulled the elastic hair tie off the end of her braid and, still pretending to study the building facade, moved closer.

When she was within range, she shot the hair tie at the back of the fairy's foot. It flicked right through and snapped loudly against the tip of John's shoe.

He looked up. Their eyes met. His gaze darted to the hair tie, then to the fairy, and his stare hardened as he took a step back. One hand went to his side, where the Desert Eagle would be hiding.

The shape of the fairy began to break apart. One second she was there, live and three-dimensional, and in the next she was drifting into pieces like an image projected on a cloud layer. Her mouth froze as it opened, and the fragmenting picture was just as absurd as the pictures Abby had taken.

"An illusion," John said. "Well, fuck me." His jaw tensed, drawing deep lines in his face as he tucked away his own phone. "I'm feelin' a mite ticked off here, Abby."

"I noticed. Count to ten."

A minor commotion made them both turn. The crowd in front of the Starbucks had been disrupted as a woman knocked someone's coffee over. She clutched her portfolio under one arm. Abby recognized her, too. She was the art student who'd patted the bull on the nose.

"John—" she began.

"I see her." His eyes narrowed. "Be right back."

She nodded and moved closer to the bull, scanning the perimeter for any other possible attacks, as John took off at a jog-trot after the art student. Putting a hand on the bull's back, she prayed a little. She wasn't in any shape for a chase, but that didn't mean John was the ideal choice either. A man chasing a woman in public looked bad. It *was* bad, albeit not in the way the cops would think, and if John wasn't careful he'd get himself arrested and the sorcerer (if it was her) would slip through their fingers.

Once again the zoom mode on her phone's camera came in handy. She raised it and followed the action for as long as she could. The artist wasn't flat-out running, but weaving a complicated path through crowds, under awnings, and right past a group of police. John, in his khakis and parka, might have been a tourist in a hurry. She kept her gaze fixed on the darting pair and made an addendum to her prayer: *God, if you're listening, please let this end without someone getting arrested.*

The art student cut left and vanished into a department store. John slowed to a walk before following her in, and the two of them were lost to Abby's view.

With nothing to do but maintain a perimeter, she texted updates to Mal and Adam. Mal quickly responded with a laundry list of questions about the strange illusion of the fairy sorcerer, and Abby sent him the photographs she had taken.

Thinking back on the encounter just confirmed what she'd thought before: the projected image was the woman she'd seen in the hospital. Was it possible that the fairy had actually been there, and just teleported out? Maybe the camera couldn't pick her up? They'd debunked that old fantasy about vampires being invisible to mirrors, but it wouldn't be the first time traits of one legend had been assumed by a different one.

She was so caught up in her own thoughts that she barely noticed the clopping sound.

"Ma'am?"

Abby jumped, almost dropping her phone. Her first thought was *Wow, that's a big horse.* And it was: a massive blood bay with black socks on its forelegs and splashes of white on its hind legs, easily seventeen hands high. The mounted policeman seemed a little too small for it, though he was still plenty imposing on the back of the huge animal. The badge and gun didn't hurt, either.

"Yes?" Abby said, trying to settle her racing heart. The horse made a whuffling noise and sniffed at her hair.

"You look worried, ma'am. Is there a problem?"

That was a surprise. Abby couldn't remember a single time when a policeman stopped her just because she didn't look well. That was the kind of thing that happened back home in Daimler, Montana, population 3300 on a good day.

"Uh." She glanced down, feigning embarrassment. "Sorry, officer, I'm all right. I'm just waiting for a friend of mine to get back, and he's always late."

The policeman nodded. "All right. Sorry to disturb you. Sunny!" This was directed at his horse, which had abandoned her hair in favor of licking Abby's gloved hand. The policeman looked embarrassed. "Sorry, ma'am. He should know better."

She smiled at the horse. The Daimler area had a short growing season and heavy winter, but there were still plenty of local farmers. She'd done a season in 4H and spent most of it mucking out horse stalls. Cows kicked and she didn't like the way pigs looked at her, but horses she'd always gotten along with. Apparently Sunny was no exception.

Her phone vibrated, stopping the nice little moment in its tracks. John was calling. "I think that's my friend," she said, smiling again and patting Sunny on his velvety nose. "Thanks, officer."

The policeman nodded and directed his horse back into traffic. She turned her back to him and answered the phone.

"Hello?"

"Hey." John sounded out of breath, and his fake accent was slipping a little around the edges, slicing off the H. "I've got her. She's really unhappy, though, and I might have her cornered in a back alley off Macy's. It's awkward as anything and I feel like a sex offender. Get here now, please?"

...

Cell phones can only do so much. When you have to meet and publicly discuss magic, monsters and murdered sorcerers, your options for staying under the radar are limited. Fortunately, America has Starbucks.

Not the Starbucks by the Cultural Center, of course, but it took them only two blocks to find another one. The SSR had long ago discovered that you could discuss anything, including violent death, in a Starbucks. No matter how many fairies or bogeymen you name-dropped, people would just assume you were writing a screenplay.

According to her wallet, T.B.'s real name was Terra Burns. She was shorter than both of them at five foot two, with short gingery hair, warm fawn-brown skin and long lashes. Her portfolio had contained several thin canvases with intricately-painted abstract symbols on them, and her jeans and shirt were both spotted with matching paint. She regarded Abby and John with open suspicion, which surprised neither of them. John had, after all, chased her into the women's bathroom at Macy's.

The three of them gathered at a small table in the otherwise-uninhabited back section. John got the drinks: bottled sodas, easy to get and hard to tamper with. He offered Terra her choice, but she didn't take any of them.

"Not happening," she said. She had the merest touch of drawl to her tone, perhaps a downstate Illinois accent.

"All right, but it's safer for everyone than an open-topped coffee cup." John nudged one of the bottles towards her. "Sure you don't want one?"

Her lips twitched. "You know, all I have to do is scream and you two are going to be dead meat. Kidnapping's kind of a crime."

"So's murder." John nudged the bottle again. "Which one d'you think the police'll be more worried about?" A muscle leaped in Terra's cheek. "What with the whole dying sorcerers, murderous fairies business."

"I don't know what you're talking about," Terra said. "I haven't killed anyone or done anything wrong."

"Sure you haven't." John uncapped his own bottle and took a swig. "So you've got a rendezvous with Lenny Scott—" Another twitch at the name, though she tried to control it "—a werecoyote who's linked to fairies that've been killing sorcerers. And you show up to that rendezvous with an illusion of a fairy that Scott probably already knows, supposedly as you. Which means either you, Scott and maybe that fairy had something on the side that his bosses don't know about, or you knew Scott wasn't going to make the meeting and wanted to smoke out anyone who tried to sub in."

He laid the words out very calmly and bluntly, like he was a doctor explaining the pros and cons of a new cancer treatment, and then took a drink of Coke while Terra stared at him.

"I don't see what your problem is," she said finally. "It's not illegal to work on commission, even if the people doing the buying aren't human."

"No, it's not." Abby jumped into the conversation while John's mouth was full. "But the people you've been dealing with have been killing the sorcerers they commission from. Do you know Sarah Mulsey?"

Terra faltered. "That was an accident. She didn't know what she was doing."

Abby shook her head. "I'm sorry, but I don't believe you. We picked up Lenny Scott this morning, and you didn't even flinch when someone else turned up in his place. Since you're sitting here with us and not still climbing through department store bathroom windows, I think you're on the level as far as the murders go—" John nudged her under the table, which she ignored "—but there's still plenty of unanswered questions. We need to know everything about the commissions and the fairies."

"And how do you know I won't lie?" Terra demanded.

"We don't," Abby said frankly. Terra's dark eyes met hers, her gaze clearly skeptical. The sorcerer had deep brown eyes, large for a normal human, and her pupils showed an oily sheen. "But let me ask you something. Are you human?"

That got her another nudge from John, but Terra leaned back. "Are you serious?"

"Usually," John said. "I get to be the crazy eccentric one. How about it?"

Her eyes darted back and forth between the two of them, her mouth twisting. "What am I supposed to say?" she said. "I thought mixed blood wasn't a crime any more. Should I have some kind of license? Registered mulatto?"

Abby ducked her head a little, acknowledging the sting in the other woman's words. "This isn't about skin color," she said quietly. "I've never seen a human with fairy eyes. Not a live one, let alone a sorcerer."

There was a moment of silence. Then Terra sat back, shoulders slumping. "We're not common," she said. "It helps if there's magic in the blood to smooth things over. That mist image I used was my mother."

"Your *mother?*" That was John, incredulous.

"My mother. Yeah, I'm not proud of it, so don't say anything." Terra finally took the last bottle and uncapped it. "She abandoned me when I was little. Want to see any other pieces of my dirty laundry? I've got sob stories about my dead dad and time in foster care, if you're into that kind of thing."

"Considering what your mother tried to do last night, you might've been better off away from her." Abby rested her cast on the table. Terra's eyes flicked over her right hand, now unprotected by a glove and showing vivid green-and-purple bruises.

"Not gonna argue with that." Terra took a swig from her bottle. "So the big question is who are you people, anyway? And don't say you're magicians, because it's obvious you don't know anything about the craft. Not fairy, either, because you only chased me through a window instead of trying to kill me. What's the story?"

Abby opened her mouth, but John got there first. "You could call us an independent faction," he said. "Sort of a third option."

"Uh huh." The sorcerer's words carried all the enthusiasm of someone ambushed by a persistent timeshare salesman. "And I'm supposed to, what, be impressed by this? You guys have got some kind of back-alley political thing going? I'm not gonna see you on the news, am I?"

"If you ever do, it's probably just John happening to someone." Abby toyed with the plastic cap of her soda bottle. It informed her, in unnecessarily cheerful lettering, that she was not a winner. "Look, Ms. Burns. It's a pattern. This mysterious woman, working with fairies, commissions sorcerers who then turn up in unhappy circumstances. Sarah Mulsey, Richard Neill, Owen Petrovich."

Terra's grip on her drink tightened just a little. "What do you know about Owen Petrovich's death?"

"I think the question is what do *you* know," John said. He'd apparently lost interest in his own drink and was idly folding a paper napkin into some random shape. "Because the cops don't seem to have found him yet if the police band is anything to go by, but you seem pretty clued-in about him being dead. Sorcerer grapevine?"

"As if I'm going to tell you," Terra retorted. "I still don't even know who you guys are or what you're doing here. You gave me an answer that's not an answer at all and you want me to just roll over and tell you everything I know? Like that's gonna happen!"

John opened his mouth again, but this time it was Abby who did the under-the-table nudging and left John rubbing his bruised shin. While he was occupied, Abby turned to Terra. "We're not political," she said. "We're more like animal control." Terra's eyes narrowed at that. "Ghouls," Abby added quickly. "Doppelgangers. Sometimes fairies, if they're killing people."

The sorcerer relaxed a bit at that, though her gaze was still sharp. "Well, that explains a lot," she said. "'Moved away' my ass—thirty-plus fairies don't randomly decide to go off, not even to New York. I was beginning to think the Big Apple was the fae version of that upstate farm Mom sends your old dog to. So how do you know I'm not gonna go running to my fairy contacts and rat you guys out? I could get a decent reward for turning you in."

"You could," Abby agreed. "But I'm betting you don't like the fae any more than we do. You want to know more about Owen Petrovich? We can tell you. But we need a fair trade of information here, or nobody will get anything done and the Fair Folk get to keep killing sorcerers."

"So basically ..." Terra tapped her fingers on the tabletop. "You scratch my back, I scratch yours."

John grinned. "That's the way it always goes," he said, putting down the napkin. It teetered delicately on the table, resting on a crisp fold while two triangular fans of paper spread out like wings and gave it a bit of balance. The shaped corner that made its face and neck seemed to be aimed at Terra, cocking its eyeless head in an inquisitive manner. "Far as we know you haven't tried to hurt anyone we like, so a flat information-for-information trade should set us all up a treat. People should be friendly, yah?"

From Terra's expression, the timeshare salesman had only gotten more persistent. Finally, though, she nodded. "You already know my name, and you that the fairies commissioned me," she said. "That's enough from me for now. What've you got for me?"

"Nu-uh. That came out in the conversation, not as part of a trade. Not our fault you didn't work out the terms beforehand." John's tone was almost playful. It momentarily tempted Abby to give him a good hard smack: being a condescending jerk wasn't going to get them anything. Terra, however, just picked up his little napkin crane and tore it in half.

"Petrovich," she said. "I want to know about how he died. Who killed him?"

"We don't know yet," John said. He didn't seem all that ruffled about the loss of his crane. "Fairies were probably in on it, though. He was skinned alive and left on a rug in the middle of his living room. What about your commission?"

She crumpled the remainder of the crane in her left hand. "Leonard Scott contacted me four months ago. He wanted a magical item, one he said only an illusion magician could make. A magic ring." Her gaze was defiant, as if expecting them to make fun. "One that could alter the wearer's appearance."

"Making them invisible?" John guessed.

She shook her head. "I asked the same thing, but Scott said they already had that covered. He wanted a ring that could make you look like someone else. Called it a polymorph ring. It's not the normal way you use illusion magic, but I've got student loans to pay like everyone else. So I said I'd try. The money was too good."

"Why would a fairy want that?" Abby mused. "I've never heard of one of them wanting to change their appearance. I suppose it's one way to hide their distinctive features, though."

"Too bad it can't do anything about their personalities," John said as he started on a second crane. "How's that project going for you?"

"I scratched," she said. "Your turn. Have you caught the person who killed him yet?"

"No. We're looking."

"What'll you do when you do catch them?"

"That depends."

"On what?"

"How many pieces we have left."

It was almost silly to hear, but it seemed to be an answer Terra liked. She relaxed a bit and nodded, taking another sip of Coke. Maybe it was what she needed to hear. "'Revenge is mine,' saith the Lord", but knowing that revenge was possible tended to be calming.

"Now the important question," she said. "Do you know anything about what's going on here? Who's running the show?"

Terra's lip curled. "If I knew, trust me, we wouldn't be sitting here talking about it. Something's been stirring the fairies up real bad, though. The phrase I keep hearing is 'old ways.' Bring back the old ways, be respectful of the old ways. A few redcaps started a fight with some Sox fans on the Red Line, too, and redcaps have been pro-Sox since forever, so no one saw that coming. But it's not like there's a government you can complain to when fae start getting out of hand, right?" Abruptly, she let out a short laugh—not unlike one of John's. "You guys are the closest thing to cops I've talked to about it. How sad is that?"

Chapter Twelve

They grilled Terra Burns for another forty minutes, but their information about Petrovich's case was quickly exhausted and she wasn't willing to trade for anything else. When John had tried to give her the number to one of their many spare cell phones, she'd refused it. "I don't want to talk to you again," she'd said flatly, gathering up her portfolio and bag. "If we meet on the street, I don't know you. I want this done."

Abby and John waited until they were back in the car to talk about it. John drove while Abby wrote, putting down as many pieces of information as she could remember.

"John?" she said finally. The car had just swung off Lake Shore Drive, and the traffic was thicker and slower. John absentmindedly flipped a lane hog the middle finger as he turned to her.

"Yah?"

"How much of that do you think was lies?"

John frowned as the offending lane hog screeched off, flashing its taillights at them. "Good question. Thirty percent? Forty?"

"The trick will be figuring out which is which." Abby flipped back through the last few pages in her notebook, rereading her own hurried scribbles and making a note here and there. "I think I know a place to start, though."

"Not surprising. What's on your mind?"

"The SSR has been active for more than twenty years. We've dealt with fairy cases, sure. But in the last five years, we've only handled ..." She took a moment to silently tally them up. "Ten fairies in the city. Eleven if you count Crazy Ivan."

"I thought we were calling him Creepy Ivan."

"Well, they both work."

"Very true. That thing with the clockwork?"

"Yeah." Abby looked down at the page again. Creepy (or Crazy) Ivan Czerwien a fairy of unknown bloodline, fixated on clocks and intricate machines. He made good money selling his creations to steampunk enthusiasts, but he'd gotten on the agency's radar when he tried to steal a donated human heart from the hospital where it was about to be transplanted. Something about the potential of an organic pump mechanism. Since he hadn't actually hurt anyone and the undamaged heart went into the patient with nobody the wiser, they'd let Creepy Ivan go with a warning. They still tried to keep an eye on him, though, in case he wanted any other human bits for his projects.

Something niggled at her about that, but she brushed it aside quickly. "The point is, we don't deal with fairies much. It's mostly just the animalistic monsters or anything from the undeath category. But Terra said thirty-plus fairies have gone missing, and she made it sound recent."

"Maybe they did move," John suggested as the car pulled to a halt again. The traffic was thinning a little as they moved out of the office districts and into the residential areas. "Let some other place deal with 'em is what I say. Too busy freezing my arse off to care if they like it in Florida better."

"I don't know." Abby chewed on her lower lip. The niggling was getting more insistent. Something about a fairy, all right, but what? "She's fairykin, and seems pretty plugged into what's going on with them. If she noticed fairies going missing, and it wasn't us doing it, who could it be?"

"Could be just fae killing fae." The thought seemed to do wonders for John's mood. "Or it could be someone else like us. The Rev always said there had to be more'n just us doing this sort of thing, after all. If there weren't, the country would be in a mess."

"That's only if we assume a consistent level of supernatural population all over," Abby reminded him, biting her lower lip a bit as she thought. "Chicago might just be really, really unlucky. But even if it is another group like us out there, how would we get in touch with them? What could we do?"

"I don't know." The words came out quietly. "And that's a fact, Abby. Sorcerers and fairies and people going through walls and all that shite. I'm stuck for answers, and I'd much rather not be."

Abby turned in her seat, examining John with fresh eyes. The circles under his eyes were darker than ever, and the fine lines in the corners were turning into definite crows' feet. He was thirty-five, but looked ten years older. And, not to put too fine a point on it, he was starting to smell. She probably was too, but it was easier to notice on someone else.

"You know," she said, "there's something my grandpa used to quote at me a lot. 'Mornings are wiser than evenings.'"

"Uh?" said John. They turned onto Western Avenue, and the traffic thickened again. It was the tail end of rush hour, but Western was still one of the bigger streets in the north-central district of the city, and a lot of people were going home or out to dinner.

"It's something that crops up in the Russian fairy tales a lot."

"Ugh. Change the subject, Abby, or you'll wind up summoning that old ghoul again."

"I don't think so." Abby had been doing a lot of reading on Baba Yaga ever since coming face-to-face with the ancient spirit-witch not so long before, and she was pretty damned sure that she couldn't be summoned. *You* went to *her*. "My point is, you look horrible. Worse than usual, I mean. And I know I haven't slept well in weeks. I think we all need to clock out for the night."

At that, John glanced over at her. His expression was faintly disappointed. "What, really?"

"Yes, really." Well, this was a change. Last time they'd had a big case, it had been him telling her to sleep. Maybe they should draw up some kind of schedule. "And before you say anything else, yes, I know that someone else might die while we sleep." Her good hand clenched on the armrest at the thought, but she kept her voice as level as she could. "Believe me, I've been thinking about it a lot. But at this point, I don't know what else we *can* do. If we run ourselves into the ground, we won't be awake or sane enough to put together any clues when we do find them. And what if we meet another fairy? I'm on painkillers and you look like the walking dead."

John was silent, thinking. The ghost of a smile twisted his thin lips as he shot a quick glance her way, brown eyes brightening in their deep bruised sockets. "You know me too damn well," he said. "Nice and pat, that little speech."

Abby snorted. "After this long, I'd better know you. Or I should probably start looking for another line of work."

"Yah, well, when you do, don't forget to pass your resume 'round the office. That should be some funny stuff. How're you going to explain what you've been doing for the past six years?"

"Shouldn't be too hard. Office manager, research specialist, folklore archival expert, personal assistant... nanny..."

"You think you're clever, but you're not."

"Believe me, John, only a very clever person could've put up with all of this for so long." She stretched and leaned back in her seat. "So are you going to get some rest?"

"Maybe."

"That's a start. But if I come in tomorrow and find you asleep in the file room, I'm going to yell at you. Maybe I'll use your full name, too, because if you're going to act like a kid I might as well act like your mom." She frowned. "Except I'm not sure about your middle name. Do you have one?"

"Yes."

"What is it?"

"Moshe."

"Jonathan Moshe Sawyer." She tested the words carefully, making him grin again. "Yeah, I could yell that. Jonathan Moshe Sawyer, get your butt down here right now!"

He flinched at that. "All right, you *do* sound like my mum now. I'll try and get some shuteye if you do the same, all right? Can't say we'll be in good shape if I'm all bright-eyed and you're snappin' at everyone."

"Deal. Adam and Mal too, okay? You'll need to help me talk them into it. Mal might listen, but Adam needs convincing. And maybe he should get his prescriptions checked."

John shook his head. "Shouldn't we all."

• • •

It was only eight o'clock, but in December it might as well have been midnight. The sky overhead was a washed-out purplish-black with not a single visible star, and the orange streetlights seemed to only make the patches of shadow deeper. The unseasonably warm weather was still too chilly for comfort, and the agents hurried into the office to warm up as fast as possible.

Mal was sitting on the basement cot with Dummy's blue blanket wrapped around his shoulders. His sleeves were rolled up and several fresh Band-Aids spotted in the undersides of his arms. Judging by the number of them and the locations of the clusters, Adam had gone a little blood-sample-happy. His bitten hand had begun to swell, and when Abby peered over the edge of the stairs, she could see him taping a fresh pad of gauze into place. He, too, had dark circles under his eyes. It seemed to be a popular fashion statement.

To her surprise, Adam had company at the workbench. Jimmy was standing next to him, watching the blond man with a mix of skepticism and curiosity as Adam prepared a slide with a single white selkie hair. Harvey's jar was propped up on the bench next to him, but the lid was off, and Harvey himself was drifting casually over Jimmy's shoulder in a heavy damp mist. It was an oddly comforting scene, if not wholly expected. At least nobody was yelling or visibly bleeding.

"Where's Scott?" she asked the group at large.

"Still sleeping," Mal informed her as he neatly snipped off the end of the tape with his free hand. "Adam brought out the spare cot and we have him trussed up in the library upstairs. After his hemorrhage, it seemed unwise to leave him in the salt flats. The air in there isn't precisely healthy for a man with his senses."

"Did you really torture him, Mom?" Jimmy was still watching Adam. His posture was casually confident, but the words came out soft and uncertain.

Abby looked down. She probably should have expected that question once she saw her son awake. Half a dozen answers rose to the front of her mind, but they were all lies.

If she was going to make anything of this, and get them both home to sleep in one piece, she had to be honest. She had what she'd wanted for years: Jimmy here in the office, participating, or at least not hindering the work. He was following Adam's movements easily enough. Maybe he recognized some of what he was doing from high school chemistry.

"No," she said. "I made him uncomfortable. Something hurt him, but it wasn't me."

Jimmy's shoulders slumped. "I want to go home."

"Me, too." He looked up at that, a little surprised, and Abby gave him a smile. "We're not going to get anything done here, are we? And sleeping on that cot's bad for your back. C'mon, grab your stuff—we're going to clock out."

"Fuck yes!" Jimmy exclaimed, pushing away from the workbench. Adam, who was trying to concentrate on his slides, gave the teenager a dirty look that had no effect whatsoever on him. "Let's go already!"

"In a minute." Abby eyed her other coworkers. This might take some delicacy.

Mal, as John had predicted, was easy enough to talk into getting some sleep. His main problem was his swollen hand, which had an unhealthy shiny look: until they had an answer about the nature of the bite, he wouldn't risk exposing civilians to any kind of wereanimal contagion. Abby helped him move a cot up to the main office and, with his guidance, administered a couple of injections to reduce swelling and combat infection. She offered him a couple of her antibiotic pills, but he declined. If agents were going to keep getting bitten, though, they should probably stock up anyway.

It was after nine o'clock by the time everyone was settled. Jimmy gathered up the things he'd brought to the office and Abby drove them home. She snuck the occasional glance at her son as they went, but Jimmy didn't seem to be in the mood for responding; he was leaning on the window, staring blankly out at the street as he huddled into his jacket. The mist had thinned, but there was still more than enough of it to dim the edges of the world and diffuse the lights.

"Looks like Silent Hill," Jimmy muttered.

Abby glanced over again. "What?"

"Nothing."

They pulled up to the house in silence. Abby had been in such a hurry that she'd left the lights on earlier, and though it was a waste of electricity, it was nice to see the warm glow beaming through the fog at them. Inside, the small house was actually warm enough for once, and mother and son both collapsed onto opposite ends of the couch.

"Mom?"

"Yes?"

"Have you *ever* tortured someone?"

Abby leaned back, resting her head against the back of the couch. Absolutely everything seemed to ache. "No, honey," she said softly. "I haven't."

"But you've killed people. Right?"

She turned her head and, this time, found him looking back at her. He was still gangly, looking younger than he usually did, but his bony shoulders and oversized feet promised that he wasn't done growing yet. If he ever got into weight training, he'd be a real force to reckon with. The upturned nose and deep-set eyes were just like hers. Blond roots were showing heavily through the fading green dye, making his hair look like bleached moss. Her son, honestly asking her if she'd ended someone's life.

"Yes," she said after a moment. "I have."

Abby expected another outburst, but nothing happened. Jimmy just tilted his head. His gaze was distant as he said "But they were monsters, right?"

This one was harder to answer, especially since she didn't know the truth herself. Well, honesty was supposed to be the best policy, right? "I don't know if that's the right word," she said. "Ghouls are like feral dogs, really. They even drool. And there was that ghost, the one who wanted euthanasia. Yes, you can euthanize a ghost, you just need some cathode ray tubes… Anyway, he wasn't a monster. But the fairies? The vampires? I don't know, Jimmy. And that's the truth. But they wanted to kill me, and a lot of other people besides."

"Vampires?" Jimmy said. There was a crack in his voice. "Vampires are real?"

"Yes, but not like you think," Abby said quickly. Her son's face was twisting, his thoughts apparently running wild with that idea. "We don't know much about them. They might not even be vampires, really. That's just what we call them."

Jimmy shook his head, his overgrown bangs flopping. "This is fucked-up, Mom."

She thought about telling him to watch his language, but right then she was too tired. "It is. It's been like this for years. And—" She hesitated. "I'm sorry, Jimmy. I never wanted this to happen. If I could go back in time and change all this, undo it all, I would. Do you hear me? I *would*."

"Mom, I …" He swallowed. "I… look, I …" He flinched and scrubbed at his eyes with the back of his sleeve. "I'm going to bed, okay?"

"Okay. Sleep well."

"Thanks. You too."

Then he was gone.

Abby sat, blank, for a few minutes. With the insistent throbbing redoubling in her arm and the long, long day, just sitting still felt like one of the greatest things in the world. Every muscle in her body seemed to relax and settle, letting her sink back onto the couch in something close to actual comfort.

She was so tired and so comfortable that it took her several minutes to process what had just happened. Once she had, though, she couldn't quite keep a wide smile from tugging at her lips. Somehow she'd managed to have a whole conversation about a dangerous topic with her son and not seen it devolve into a screaming match. It was sad that that was her yardstick of a good family experience, but heck, it was a change. Maybe they could make this work. Maybe it wasn't too late to build a relationship with her own son.

The thought, as warm and comforting as a blanket, made it hard for her to get off the couch. Her legs didn't seem to be responding to her stern orders to move. Eventually, she just scooted to the side and lay down, curling into the cushions and breathing out a soft sigh. Nothing much had changed, but all the same she felt so much lighter. It wasn't long before she drifted off.

Chapter Thirteen

The woman watched quietly over the top of her desk as her men conferred. At least this time she hadn't been in bed when the news started arriving. It was easier to keep everyone under control when she was seated, fully clothed and in her right mind. They were less *concerned*.

And most of them had a right to be concerned. As her strength increased and the bond between them all grew, she had begun to catch snippets of their thoughts. Emotions, mostly, but every so often there would be a rush of thought that was almost speech. They hated seeing her at anything less than her best, because it reminded them that she was the center of it all and the center had to hold. She'd already proven to them time and again that she was a good leader in the model of the old ways. But when you introduced magic into work, well, the usual rules stopped applying and anything might happen. Any sign of weakness in a leader was bad news for them all.

But some of them were smart enough to know that what she had wasn't weakness at all. Those were the ones she liked best. Though she really shouldn't, she knew. It was arrogant and close-minded of her to bring personal issues into such an important operation.

"Gentlemen," she said, and the gazes turned her way. "Have you found Burns yet?"

Cox shook his head. "No, ma'am." Bowers nudged him. "Conscript mother."

"You don't have to call me that, Mr. Cox. Nothing is finalized yet." She sat back in her desk chair and tapped her fingernails against the worn leather of the armrests. She wouldn't have had leather at all, but the chair had been left behind by the former occupant of the office, and there was no point in wasting it. "Where's Silkwillow? I asked you to bring her up for her report."

"She wouldn't come, ma'am. She's locked herself in her room. One of my employees tried to talk her out." Cox looked at the floor. "She turned him into a tree."

"Really?" The woman sat forward, surprised. "Do we have confirmation of that, Mr. Cox? Eyewitnesses?"

"Three people saw it happen. And since there's a willow rooted to the carpet on the 27th floor of the building, yes, I'd say we have confirmation." Cox's words were sharp, but he still wasn't raising his head. Unsurprising, given some of the rumors she'd been hearing around the office.

"Get rid of it." The woman paused for a moment, thinking. "The employee was killed tragically and accidentally in... an elevator malfunction, maybe. Something gruesome that ought to discourage his family from wanting to see the remains. Pension and generous compensation to his spouse, if he has one. If anyone even whispers the word lawsuit, call me, understood?" Nods all around. "Good. And someone go tell Silkwillow that it's *me* who wants to talk to her, and if she values her life she'll get up here as soon as she can. She'll behave."

More nods, these with accompanying expressions of badly-concealed relief. This was a risky venture, and everyone involved knew there might be trouble when they signed on, but employees going terminally green hadn't been one of the possibilities on the table. She was pleased to say that her people had no reason to fear her. The contractors were in a different boat, especially if any of them pulled another stunt like this.

Silkwillow was good, though. Too good to get rid of. She herself was helpless right now, but with Silkwillow's help, she might be able to crack open a small mystery. Her fingers tightened on the chair, her heart stuttering at the thought.

She kept her expression neutral, of course. The thing to remember was to maintain control. No pain, no gain.

"Which reminds me," she said. "Are there any updates on Scott?"

This time it was Phillips who answered. "No, conscript mother," he said. "But the description given by the witness matches the group he reported sending to the bonepicker."

Of course it did. She could feel the rush of nervousness from Phillips, and a flicker of thought: *this wasn't supposed to happen*. Silkwillow and Kotik had been sent out for the specific purpose of cleaning up that loose end. Now a mess was officially being upgraded to a problem, because someone had dared to kidnap one of her people. Her grip on the armrest tightened a bit more.

But there was no point in getting angry in front of the others. She wasn't going to be some kind of dictator or despot, controlling her people with a show of rage. She knew how *those* stories usually ended. So she restrained herself and, calmly and quietly, began to lay out her plans.

• • •

Abby Marquise didn't dream much these days, which was fine with her. When she was younger, she'd sometimes been afraid to go to sleep because of the nightmares that would inevitably find her. Always the same nightmares—images of empty beds, silent houses, being alone in the world except for judging, staring eyes. After the attack, her court-ordered therapist had said the dreams were her subconscious's reaction to her "transitive family situation." Thinking over it later, she realized he'd probably meant something like "tenuous," but at the time she'd just agreed with him. It was easier than explaining yet again that no, her tenuous family situation *then* had nothing to do with her tenuous family situation *now,* and she definitely hadn't imagined whatever put those marks on her back. If her therapist could know what she'd seen since then, the man's head would probably explode.

Still, she'd gotten used to facing her fears head-on and, where necessary, shooting them. Exhaustion would make her sleep so deeply that she rarely dreamed, and when she did, she almost never remembered it.

This time she did dream, and for once, it was the kind of odd thing she wouldn't hate remembering. She was doing her laundry in the basement of the office for some reason, and her son and ex-husband were playing Monopoly on the workbench. Though she didn't look too close, she knew that if she did, she would see that the pieces they used were tiny copies of her coworkers. In other contexts it might have been ominous, but the sense of serenity hanging over her made it hard to be afraid. Jimmy deposited a tiny Adam on Free Parking and won $750, which her ex disputed. Apparently they were playing by John's house rules.

She didn't remember awaking so much as sliding gently out of sleep. Her back and arm were stiff and tight, but she was lying still and warm and the pain seemed to be a long way away. The dream lingered on the edge of her awareness, still half-real in the space between sleeping and waking. Monopoly? What? Oh, well, it didn't matter. She was floating in the haze, lazily flicking through thoughts like a collector in a junk shop: pick them up, turn them over, blow a bit of dust off the edges and put them down again.

As she examined one thought, though, something caught her interest. Reluctantly, Abby looked more closely at it. The soft edges of the world started to wear away even as the dust cleared.

Fairies. Fairies that they knew of. People like Creepy Ivan...

Creepy Ivan, who'd vanished two months ago.

Her eyes shot open. A link. It was tiny and tentative, but it was someplace to start and God almighty did they need that.

Creepy Ivan had been on their radar thanks to that heart business, but he'd been good for a while and there'd been no indications that he was about to leave town suddenly. But Terra Burns said there were fairies vanishing, and likely fairies the SSR hadn't touched. Very, very tentative. But a place to start.

With a grunt, she rolled off the couch and immediately regretted it. Sometime overnight her muscles had turned into jelly. She sprawled sideways onto the floor and rested her forehead against the carpet.

After some help from the coffee table, Abby managed to stand and reach for her phone. Seven AM: with any luck, he'd gotten some sleep too.

John responded more quickly than she anticipated. By the time she'd shaken herself awake, changed her clothes and made coffee and toast, he was on the doorstep with an armload of books and files. Abby wasn't sure if he'd slept or not, but his clothes were different and he didn't smell any more, so she took that as a good sign and let him go to town on the food while she paged hurriedly through the things he'd brought.

After thirty minutes of futile discussion and file-hunting, they gave up and made a chart. It took up half of the living room wall and was rather impressive, in a they're-coming-to-get-me sort of way. There were photographs, names, timelines, diagrams, and notes about the various pieces of evidence or ephemera they'd collected. There were were even pieces of string (all right, dental floss) tied around pushpins to link various pieces and, hopefully, make some sense of the mess. It didn't help much, but eventually they thought they had something.

"All right," John said finally, stepping back from the chart and crossing his arms. "Let me see if I've got this right now. Petrovich dies first, near as we can figure. He was the least fresh, anyhow. Then Mulsey, then Neill. Each die after making some kind of commission thingummy for someone, possibly fairies. Patches of melty brick were found at two of the three crime scenes, and general suspiciousness abounded—Mulsey suddenly getting all those dolls, like. And you said the melty brick comes when fairies get into places they don't belong."

He tapped the picture of a young Gina Torres, who was standing in for Terra Burns. (He insisted there was a definite resemblance which in no way stemmed from his secret love of a few canceled TV shows. Looking at the picture, Abby had to agree.) "Burns, she knows Petrovich somehow. She's also one of the commissionees. But she also knows something's fishy, because she sends that illusion to make her meeting. She also says fairies are vanishing, and most of 'em we probably aren't responsible for."

"Right." Abby pinned up a picture of Creepy Ivan. "Here we have one who's gone mysteriously missing just like Terra mentioned." She stretched a strand of floss between Terra's pin and Ivan's.

"And here's four more that haven't been heard from." John fanned out the pictures. Two were sketches, one was a still from an ATM camera, and one was a Facebook profile photo of a grinning man with a beer bong. "Jane Gray, Webheart, Jupiter Spotts and Blue Man Banshee. All known offenders and hangers-on, mostly theft and fighting, but none of 'em have made a peep for months. Unless a report got lost 'cos our records are shite." He frowned. "Should do something about that."

"We should," Abby said. "But if we're making changes, I vote for better insurance first." She pinned up the four pictures but didn't tie them to anything. "File those under tentative. Now, Neill was in contact with both Petrovich and Mulsey—" More floss "—and there was some communication going on there. Petrovich asked Neill if he was sure about getting involved in some project, probably the commissions, and he cited Mulsey's opinion on it." She stood back, examining the web they'd created. "Petrovich was the oldest of the sorcerers. He was a leader among them, I think."

"A leader with a mysterious bricked-up second story in his house." John tapped his front teeth with a spare pin. "You got any plans for today, Abby?"

"None that I can't cancel."

"Mom?"

Abby turned quickly, fighting the urge to throw a blanket over the wall of conspiracy. Her son was standing in the doorway with a piece of toast in one hand. He was wearing thick socks which had muffled his footfalls some, but considering how much the floorboards in the corridor creaked and groaned, he must have moved like a cat for neither of the agents to hear him.

"Holy shit," he said, looking at the wall. "So *was* 9/11 an inside job?"

John took a sip of coffee. "Damn Freemasons."

"Did you sleep well, honey?" Abby said quickly. "Want more breakfast? We're out of waffles, but I can pick some up while I'm out."

Jimmy seemed to guess that she was trying to change the subject, because he didn't take the bait. "So you're going out to investigate this... whatever, right?" he said, jerking his head towards the wall. "And Dad asked me to call him if I ever thought you were going off the deep end. I'm pretty sure this counts. Normally people stay home and rest when they've got broken bones and stuff."

His tone was light, but Abby wasn't taking the bait either. "Your dad means well, but I don't think he'd really understand what's going on here," she said. "Anyway, we're shorthanded right now. Lenny Scott bit Mal, and he's sidelined with Adam."

Jimmy stepped back. "That wolf guy bit him? He's a werewolf now?"

"Coyote, honey. And we don't know that for sure. But until we know, he's got a bigger problem than me." Abby rubbed her right hand with her left, working out some of the aches. "And if we want to get any of this figured out, we have to go looking for answers."

The teenager glanced back and forth between Abby, the wall, and John, who was looking back over the rim of his coffee cup with what he probably thought was a mild, inoffensive sort of neutral expression. He couldn't quite pull it off.

"Right," Jimmy said finally. "And even if I call Dad, you're going anyway?"

"I wish you wouldn't," she said. "But yes. I have to."

Another long moment, so cold and stiff they might have all been frozen alive by the winter chill. Then Jimmy said "Whatever" and vanished into the hallway, chomping loudly on his toast.

"Y'know, sometimes I wish I could go back to being eighteen again," John said softly, setting down his coffee cup. "Then I remember that I was a complete tit at that age."

"Me too. Except part of that was pregnancy hormones." John raised an eyebrow at her, and she gave him an exasperated look. "Are we going to go do this or not?"

"Lead the way. Although maybe we should stop off at the office first."

"Why?"

"Two words: sledgehammer."

"That's one word."

"Fine. Sledgehammer *and* pickaxe."

• • •

Owen Petrovich's house looked just like it had a few days before. The only difference was that the pile of mail on the front mat was a little higher and the sharp, coppery smell in the air had taken on a ripe note of decay. Abby and John moved past the open living room door quickly, not wanting to stop and look at what condition the body of the homeowner might be in now.

Abby stood back as John grinned and hefted the sledgehammer, which he had christened Natasha. (The pickaxe was Boris.) She took a look at him and shuffled back farther.

The wall went down in a thunderous crash, shaking the landing and sending clouds of white and reddish dust billowing out over the two agents. John got a lungful and started coughing again, but as he cleared away the edges of the brick with Boris, he couldn't quite keep himself from grinning.

When the dust cleared, Abby stepped carefully over the litter of brick rubble and snapped on her flashlight. John followed behind, the sledgehammer propped on his shoulder.

The two of them found themselves in a narrow corridor. One wall was angled sharply with the line of the roof, and a pair of frosted skylights admitted weak gray light and gave a blurred view of the house next door. Pale blue wallpaper had spot-faded in squares where the windows let some sun in, creating a dappled wash of blues and old grays.

Three doors lined the left-hand-side of the hallway. Abby fit neatly under the slanted roof, but John had to crouch, and she motioned him behind her before putting a hand on the first doorknob. Moving slowly, checking for charms as she went, she opened the door. The hinges squeaked in protest.

Inside was a small bathroom. There was no shower, only an oversized bathtub with a hatch in its side and a hand bar. It looked like the kind of thing you'd see in a hospital or a nursing home. A bath chair was propped inside, etched deeply with more of the symbols they'd seen in Petrovich's files. Abby thought she recognized a partial symbol for good health, and another for clean energy flow. The person who used this bathroom was an invalid, and Petrovich wanted them to be better. The medicine cabinet was stuffed with expired prescription medications, most with labels twenty years old.

Then next room was a combination library and what seemed to be a playroom. A bench sat under another frosted window, dotted with well-worn cushions, and several old toys were still scattered around. Abby spotted a Barbie dream house, a Cabbage Patch doll, and a few other things that screamed 1980s. She'd had a couple of them when she was young.

The walls were lined with inset bookcases. Unlike Petrovich, who seemed to have focused on magical texts and history books, these shelves held everything from Aesop to Zelazny and in between. Dog-eared paperbacks were piled up around the shelves, so old that their edges had turned almost goldenrod from sheer age and cheap printing. Science fiction, fantasy and romance were well-represented—Abby found a battered copy of *The Flame and the Flower*, which fell apart in her hands as she picked it up—but the occupant had clearly not been limited in their choices. There were books on astronomy and astrology, mythology, weather science, internal medicine, American law, battle techniques of the ancient Romans, and everything else. They seemed to have been jumbled on the shelves in no discernible order.

The third room was the bedroom. It was the smallest room, and so thickly coated with dust that Abby sneezed. It took a few seconds for her watering eyes to clear enough to take in the details, most of which were pink.

The centerpiece was a high hospital bed with a grip bar dangling from the ceiling, perfect for a wheelchair patient. The comforter was pink. The pillows were pink. The headboard, rather awkwardly tacked to the wall behind the raised bed, was pink with a rainbow painted on it.

"I'll have a go," John said, "and guess this was a girl's room."

Abby pulled open the small (pink) dresser. There were a few items of clothing still in there, gray with dust. "A room for a girl, all right," she said, "but I'm guessing not one the girl wanted." Most of the clothes were black. "Or maybe not the one she wanted once she got older. Whoever lived here must be our age now, easily."

"If she's still alive." John's good mood visibly faded as he glanced around the small space. "Why would Petrovich have a girl's bedroom upstairs? He wasn't married, was he? He better not have been playing Lolita, because I get pretty uninterested in finding out who killed someone like that."

"Let's not jump to conclusions," Abby said. If she was honest, though, the bedroom was making her uncomfortable. The sheer pinkness of it, with rainbows and cheap lace-edged curtains, made her think of a dollhouse.

Her coworker frowned. "Well, there has to be a reason this lot is here," he said. "If you've got another explanation, please, share it. 'Cos I'm getting creeped out."

"Well, there might be something in here ..." Abby moved back to the pink dresser and ran a finger across the top. The dust was thick across most of the wood, but a clean square towards the back showed where something might have stood not long ago. She hooked the fingers of her good hand around the edges of the dresser and rocked back, tilting it away from the wall. Something was lying there. "Gotcha! John, would you—?"

John quickly grabbed the dusty object and wiped it off with his sleeve. Underneath the dust, the object was pink.

It was a picture frame. The wood was so cheap that years of being handled had deformed it, and someone had been able to carve a few unreadable letters into one side. Behind the glass was a yellowing Polaroid of a rumpled dark-haired man with a small smile. Tucked into his side was a pale, pretty little redheaded girl in leg braces, beaming toothily at the camera. She had a two-and-a-half-foot, well-used wooden club balanced across her knees.

"That looks like a shillelagh," Abby said, squinting at the picture. "What kind of man lets a kid play with a club?"

"Maybe her Christmas came early." John peered over her shoulder. "Does that look like Petrovich to you?"

"It might be." She fished out her phone again and used the zoom function to closely scan the surface. "If it wound up back there, though, it was either knocked over or someone hid it. Between the freshness of the bricks and the level of dust on this thing, I'd say it was put back there around the same time this story was walled off."

"Which raises an interesting question." John stepped back and knelt down, running his fingers over the carpet. "Dust thick on the floor in the library and loo, but not here. Why's the carpet so clean?"

Abby's eyebrows shot up. She hadn't even noticed the state of the carpet, not with all the pink distracting her. "Maybe there's something underneath it?"

The thin man scooted across the carpet in a sort of crablike crawl, investigating the edges of the room. "Nope. All tacked down. But—hang on a mo—" He worked his fingers under the pink ruffle on the box spring and pulled it away. "Hah! My turn to shine. Look at this, Abby."

She knelt down next to him. The box spring was old and cheap, just a fabric-covered frame of wood meant to keep the mattress off the ground. There didn't seem to be any actual springs involved. Someone had cut a long slit in the cloth, half-concealed by the lace ruffle, and a scrap of paper was just visible.

John pulled on his winter gloves before reaching back in. The first thing out was a battered spiral notebook, each line crammed with scribbled chicken-scratch and occasional sketchy diagrams in ballpoint pen. Abby recognized Petrovich's handwriting and began to flip through the notebook as John continued fishing through the hiding spot.

This was going to take time, she could tell. Petrovich had been writing for himself, and the notes were littered with abbreviations and random little comments that probably wouldn't make any sense unless she could get inside his head. Many of the diagrams were just intersecting circles with letters sprinkled here and there, and a few equations on the side. In places the paper had wrinkled or the ink had run, usually with associated staining from a coffee cup or—she sniffed the page—ketchup.

Some of it, though, she could just make out. Her eyebrows shot up as she read.

Theoretically the sacrifice effect could spread +1k? +10k? Limits unknown. Is blood key? Or is it just because we think it is? Chaos bruise (CB) effect = age of sorcerer x skill type P / trauma of death? When the world is bruised, it becomes thinner because a bruise is just damage.

"Hey, Abby, look at this!" The words jolted her out of her concentration and made Abby jump. John was holding out a heavy cloth-bound book flecked with dust and pink threads from the torn fabric. "There's a title, but it's all faded, and I don't read German."

Abby flipped open the book and was greeted with a very familiar frontispiece. "*Der Hexenhammer*," she read aloud. "That means 'the hammer of witches.' This is just the *Malleus Maleficarum*, that old witch-hunting guide." She paged through it. "Section two's been pretty heavily annotated, though, and the spine is broken where that part starts. Looks like he was interested in the part of the book that had to do with witches' methods. All this information about how to forge pacts with the Devil, make mens' genitals vanish, that kind of thing." John's expression was a picture, and Abby couldn't help rolling her eyes at it. "Look at these margin notes. I think he was *testing* this stuff."

"Testing how to—" For a moment, John's words failed him. "Hell, maybe he committed suicide."

She opened her mouth to reply, but her words trailed off. Something was pricking at her brain again. It was close, and she had to go slowly or she would scare it off. "I think," she said, "he was the scientific type. Look at this." She opened the notebook and showed off the page she had been reading. "He talks a lot about sacrifice and blood. He seems to have been studying it, all very carefully. He says there's some kind of effect, he calls it a chaos bruise, that happens in the vicinity of a blood sacrifice. Something about the source of power and its effect on the world." She shook her head. "It has to be connected."

"How, exactly?" John said. He sounded exasperated and, to Abby's surprise, a little helpless. "Neill was ripped in half, and someone tried to keep him from being identified. Someone stupid. Mulsey got her brain burned out and Petrovich was skinned, but nobody tried to hide *them*."

"No, but something ..." Abby walked to the window and back, chewing on her lip and trying to think. It was there, just out of reach, she could feel it. "Petrovich studied blood sacrifice. He was working on a commission for the fairies. We don't know what it was, though. The only commissions we have confirmed is Terra's. Neill had a commission page, but ..."

The penny dropped, and Abby's heart clenched. "Oh my God. John— Neill. Neill was ripped in half. His commission page, it mentioned magic boots. *Neill was making seven-league boots.*"

"Who in the what now?" John frowned at her. "Not making much sense."

"It's a fairy tale thing, John. Just trust me. Take one step, and you're seven leagues from where you used to be. Which means that for a minute, your legs are seven leagues apart."

"I don't think—" John stopped. His eyes widened. "Well, fuck me."

She didn't even bother to correct his language this time. "Think about it," she said quickly, pacing. "He's commissioned to make these boots. He tests them out. Takes one step. And suddenly his right half is seven leagues from his right." She swallowed. "Seven leagues is about twenty-four miles. His other half probably ended up in Wilmette."

John ran a hand through his disheveled hair. "You mean it was an accident? What about Petrovich and Mulsey?"

"I don't know. But I'm having a hard time believing it's a coincidence." Abby stared at the windowsill, thinking hard. The glass panes were frosted and let in light, but nobody could see out. Or in. "It sure spilled a lot of blood, though. And Petrovich's notebooks talk about this chaos bruise thing, this theory that messing with sacrifice magic creates some kind of effect on the world. Things get odd. What would you call photos and papers turning negative? Or an apartment filling up with dolls for no good reason? Or maybe—?" She wiggled her fingers at him, displaying the ragged stumps of her once-overlong fingernails.

"I don't know, Abby. That's pretty fucking tenuous." John's face twisted a little as he thought. "Blood sacrifice? Really?"

"Petrovich was skinned alive. That looks pretty sacrificial to me."

For a moment, there was silence in the small bedroom. Abby was feeling lightheaded again. Time for another pill, maybe.

John shook his head. "There's more books and things in the bed," he said. "Let's grab 'em and get out of here. This place is making my skin crawl."

It took them another forty-five minutes to clean out the cache in the box spring. Several more books in Latin, German, and Greek ("Grimoires," Abby said), a sheaf of additional Polaroids featuring Petrovich and the red-haired girl at various ages, two more notebooks filled with scribbled notes, a box of loose rings, necklaces and talismans and, tucked right in the back where John had to scramble and strain to reach it, a much-abused reprint of *The Black Pullet.*

When she hefted it, though, Abby knew something was wrong: *The Black Pullet* was a fairly short text, but this book was the size of a Bible.

"Clever," she murmured as she opened it. The first few pages were French text and magical diagrams, but the rest were from a biography of Franklin Roosevelt. Their content didn't matter, though, because the last three-quarters of the book had been hollowed out. More Polaroids, tightly bundled together, crammed the space.

The pictures showed Petrovich again, this time ten years older and much closer to the person they'd seen in the photos from his website. And once again, there was a red-haired girl with him, smiling into the camera. This time, though, the girl had dark fawn skin and the hair was curling and gingery. Instead of holding a club, she grinned up at them with a paintbrush in hand.

"Terra Burns," Abby said softly. "So they were friends."

"Or lovers. Or co-victims. Or conspirators." John grimaced at the photos. "Let's bring 'em back to Adam. Maybe he can pull fingerprints or something."

"Hopefully." Abby gathered up the last of the items and piled them all into her duffel bag. "Do you think she might actually be Scott's boss? She's certainly good enough with illusions."

John shot her a sharp look. "That's a nasty thought. Anything's possible, I suppose." When Abby tried to lift the duffel bag, he quickly slid a hand under the strap. "Come on, none of that. Give it here." He slung the duffel over his right shoulder, resting the bulk of it against his back, and moved towards the door.

There was a *pop* like a flare going off and John recoiled, stumbling back and hitting his knees on the edge of the awful pink bed. The room filled with the thick smell of ozone and Abby felt the fine hairs on her arm stand on end as the light sputtered overhead. Smoke leaked through the ceiling as old, underused wires fried.

The air in the doorway shimmered as an image faded into existence. It was a humanoid shape, outlined in golden-orange light and blazing so brightly that Abby squeezed her eyes shut before she could see any details. A dazzled John tried to take another step backwards and fell over the bed, cracking the back of his head on the wall. The smell of smoke filled the room.

"You were warned," hissed a ragged voice. "Stay out of my room!"

And then it was gone.

Abby sat up dazedly, rubbing her eyes. The glare had burned white spots into her vision. Fumbling around half-blind, she grabbed one of the fallen pieces of clothing and awkwardly threw it towards the doorway. It sailed through and landed in a dusty heap against the far wall.

"What the fuck was that?" John said. He struggled to sit up, the sprung mattress creaking under his weight. "Booby trap?"

Abby crawled towards the door and poked a finger through the gap. Nothing. "I think," she said, "that was a Scotch-taped Keep Out sign for the junior sorcerer."

"Oh, brilliant." With a grunt and another clunking chorus from the springs, John finally managed to get to his feet. "Let's get out of here before the walls start bleeding."

• • •

Adam couldn't pull fingerprints off the photograph. Or rather, he could, but wouldn't. There was a twitch under one eye.

"Do you know how much I have to do right now?" he demanded. "I had a shit-ton on my bench even before this case started, thanks to you assholes leaving all those weapons in the museum last month. Then there's the original samples from Petrovich's house, samples and photos both from the Mulsey scene, Mal's cell slides and blood, and all that goddamn brick dust and mortar that you somehow think is going to magically give up answers when you make me look at the same stuff a third time! And that's not all! This isn't *CSI*, guys, I need time to actually pull this kind of shit off! Not to mention government resources we don't have! And the next person to ask me for a DNA sample is going to have my boot so far up their ass that they're gonna be brushing shoe polish off their goddamn teeth! Okay?"

John had tried to argue, but Adam threw a paperweight at him. It was a pretty hefty paperweight, too. At that point the agents decided that discretion was the better part of not getting beaned with A Present From Hawaii and backed away.

There wasn't much better news from the rest of the office. Lenny Scott was still sleeping, and while the bruises on his mouth had faded slightly he stayed unconscious no matter what they tried. Mal checked his pulse and pupils every half-hour with the same results: he wasn't in a coma, he just wouldn't wake up. John asked what the difference was, but when Mal began talking about REM cycles he lost interest. Mal himself seemed not to be sprouting extra hair or sets of teeth, but the bite marks on his hand had turned purple.

"I suspect a significant immune response," was all he said when Abby asked how he was feeling. Since he was the one with the medical training, Abby left him to it.

Unfortunately, that meant she had nothing to distract her. Bits and pieces of thought were whirling around in her head. Her new theory was so strange to her that she wasn't sure she should even think too much about it, in case it crumbled under close examination.

But if the chaos bruise theory was correct, it meant that the three sorcerers' deaths might be sacrifices. And whichever way she looked at it, human sacrifice was really not something Abby wanted to contemplate dealing with.

Well, no point in putting it off. She booted up the computer and started Googling. Mulsey hadn't been a very public person, and variations on her name turned up almost no hits. Everything she found seemed to come from family tree websites or law firms. Even Neill's extensive links pages had no reference to her or to "the crystal lady."

When she searched Neill's full name, though, a handful of new links appeared. News sites. Abby's heart sank as she clicked on the first one.

FOWL PLAY AT LOCAL GROCERY

Wilmette, IL – Local residents are demanding an investigation after a series of gruesome discoveries recently resulted in the shutdown of the Plaza del Lago Jewel-Osco grocery, police say.

The store was temporarily closed following the discovery of the mutilated body of local artist Richard Neill, 39. Less than twelve hours after its reopening, the Jewel was forced to close its doors again after disturbing reports of unprocessed poultry carcasses being sold in the frozen foods section.

"It was horrible," said area woman Tallulah Dixon, 34, who purchased two bagged frozen chickens. "The bags were sort of lumpy, but that wasn't too strange, so I took them home and opened them up. They were whole chickens! Feathers and beaks and feet and everything. I threw up in the sink."

Ms. Dixon has not yet announced whether she will file charges, but three other local residents who also purchased unprocessed whole chickens are filing claims against the store and the poultry manufacturer.

Local ASPCA members have also notified the Tribune that they will press animal cruelty charges based on the apparent mistreatment of the chickens.

"I don't know what sick mind thought this up, but it's completely unacceptable," said Daryl Ramirez, president of the Wilmette chapter. "These animals were likely alive when they went into those bags. They suffocated, and then their corpses were shipped to the store like nothing happened! Everybody is at risk from this kind of shoddy, unethical behavior."

Representatives of Jewel-Osco and Larson Farms Inc. have yet to make a statement.

"Hell," Abby said.

Chapter Fourteen

A new version of the Paranoia Web quickly sprouted on the office's north wall. Fresh photographs, mostly from the Polaroid stash, gave this one a slightly more professional look. The supposed sacrifice victims had computer-printed labels, and red thread was used to mark fairies who had mysteriously disappeared. Style, John said, was everything.

"Sacrifice," he mused, standing back from the wall and examining it like an art critic assessing the work of a talented but overenthusiastic amateur. "That's a nice and nasty sort of thought. Funny paper and dolls could be coincidence, but chickens rewinding is new to me."

"Rewinding?" Abby said. She was perching on the edge of her desk, which was pushed against the south wall. She'd obliquely hoped that somehow getting a fuller look at the whole picture would give her a bolt of insight. So far it didn't seem to be working.

"'Brought back to life' makes me feel like I should be cackling on the rooftop in a thunderstorm." John tapped a printout from the article, showing a slit plastic bag with feathers and a frozen head poking out. "Although even saying 'rewinding' is a bit off. Are we sure this is even possible? Mal, you have a secret former life as a poultry processor or what, eh?"

Mal was replacing the gauze dressing on his hand. "I apologize, but no."

"I think we can safely say this wasn't just factory oversight." Abby shook her head. She had spent thirty instructive but creepy minutes on YouTube watching videos about chicken processing, and while she'd learned a few useful things she was also beginning to understand Adam's vegetarianism. "There are a lot of steps between the chicken being killed and going into the package. Different machines, different places, all kinds of oversight. Stuff like thumbs in chili usually happens when food is being prepared on-site, and that's usually not a very automated or regimented process. And look at the pictures of the plastic bag. It's all stretched out. That chicken grew after it was packaged." She swallowed. "And then it probably suffocated or froze in the grocery case."

"Which means that if you're right, this chaos bruise business is powerful enough to bring something back from the dead." John raked a hand through his hair. It stuck up around his ears, making him look as if he'd been struck by lightning "It's aliiive! Or was, anyway."

"Actual, legitimate reanimation." Abby bit her lip.

Zombies were real enough. Her broken arm was proof of that. But ninety-nine percent of the time, there was very little to them: just randomized muscular twitches persisting long after death. Even the rare active ones, like the bonepicker in the basement or the crow in the salt tub, were more like automatons or puppets than people. They didn't really think, they didn't heal, and they certainly weren't alive in the way a biologist would think of it. They didn't eat, excrete, or reproduce.

Ghosts weren't much better—vague impressions of personalities on an endless loop. Nobody she knew would want to spend eternity as a meat puppet or a repeating hologram. But real life after death, not in Heaven but here on Earth, was something someone would kill for.

"The amount of power it would take to do something like that is... unimaginable." Abby worried her lip between her teeth, thinking hard. "Magically or otherwise, I mean. I don't think it's possible for those chickens to get to the store without being actually cleaned, but if they weren't, that means we might have to believe that they came back to life in the freezer. And if the chaos bruise is powerful enough to do that, I think I speak for all of us when I say we're in deep trouble."

"Something about killing a sorcerer." John was pacing, chewing on a stub of pencil. "That goes with the sacrifice theory. Killing a job lot of sorcerers somehow gets you some kind of power. I'd like to know why, but I think we'd need some of that government funding Adam wants. Petrovich was an expert on this kind of thing, and I'd say he's our number one suspect, except that he's a touch dead right now."

"Which means the sacrifice theorician was himself sacrificed." Mal tied a neat knot in his fresh bandage. "In the colloquial sense, sweetly ironic. That would argue for a certain amount of personal issues bound up with it."

"Irony. Revenge. Good strong motives." John's gaze moved to Terra Burns's photograph. "Maybe someone getting their own back on Creepy Uncle Sorcerer with a thing for underaged redheads?"

"God, I hope not."

"Any other bright ideas?"

"Unfortunately, no. I think we have to beat the bushes." She, too, looked at the picture of Terra. The girl couldn't be more than ten years old, and she was laughing as she daubed paint onto Petrovich's shirt. "Let's put the word on the street."

• • •

When she was young, Abby imagined policemen and secret agents as dashing, literally and figuratively. People who protected the law and did the right thing would do so by running down corridors in Russian nuclear silos and punching out crazed dictators. When detectives put the word on the street, it usually involved shaking down a squealer or making a tense deal with a double agent.

In her professional life, it mostly seemed to consist of posting on message boards. She couldn't be too disappointed, since it had been a message board posting that first led to her finding the SSR, but the part of her that had idolized Sean Connery still demanded a little more excitement from the business of investigation. Although perhaps she should be grateful, given the amount of excitement they'd had lately.

You could find anything on the Internet if you looked hard enough. The SSR sometimes ventured into the Deep Web if they needed something even Adam's or Mal's contacts couldn't get, but for the most part they stuck to research and a handful of forums and message boards. An anonymous post with a description of Terra Burns and a few words about her magic use were enough for many places: the Internet was full of conspiracy theorists of all kinds, and plenty of them believed in magic well enough to keep an eye out for anyone matching the description of a rogue sorcerer.

"The trick'll be finding her in their moms' basements," John said. Abby gave him a dirty look.

After that, she paced. The painkillers had left the world agreeably soft and fuzzy, but her worrying was enough to cut through the mild narcotic haze and she almost wore a hole in the carpet before John told she was making him nervous. With nothing else to do, she went down into the basement to check on their newest tenant.

Mary had escorted the bonepicker to its new home before going back to her aunt's store, and her touch was evident. The spare safe, a creaky old relic left over from the office's clinic days, had been dusted off and moved next to Harvey's shelf. Its door was closed but not locked, and when Abby opened it an inch she could just glimpse an empty screw-top wine bottle half-full of what looked like withered gray spaghetti and a scattering of cinnamon potpourri. When a sliver of light touched it, the contents stirred slightly. Abby quickly closed the safe and locked it for good measure.

Adam, looking somewhat calmer than he had before, was at his workbench. It was colder than ever in the basement, and he was wearing full desert camouflage with a bathrobe and a fur-lined ushanka. He was examining a mottled set of bonepicker phalanges with a magnifying glass and occasionally jotted down notes in a hand worse than Petrovich's.

"If you're here to guilt me into trying for those fingerprints, you're wasting your time," he said without looking up from his work. "If you don't believe in my backlog, you can take a look for yourself." He waved a hand at the workbench, where piles of paper and file folders tottered between boxes of bonepicker pieces.

"Relax, I'm not," Abby said. She moved to the workbench and squinted at the pile. "I'm sorry, Adam. We really need more people who know their way around a microscope. It's the old recruiting problem."

"Uh-huh." The sound could have been skeptical, but Adam seemed to just be acknowledging what she'd said. It was never easy finding agents who a) acknowledged the existence of the supernatural, b) were passionate enough or unhappy enough about it to do what the SSR did, and c) would work for not much money. For the most part the agency got around that problem by recruiting people who'd acquired that passion after a face-first encounter with the worst parts of the magical world (such as Abby, Adam and John), but that was a pretty scattershot and, frankly, unethical way to look for personnel. Mary had been actively recruited, but Mary had already known about magic when she joined and was enthusiastic by dint of youth and inexperience.

Although it seemed like they might have a new member. Abby picked up one of the ropy femurs, examining it with a certain amount of curiosity. Mary had better hope that the bonepicker decided to behave. His wine bottle had been surrounded with rock salt to foil any tracking spells on him, and there wasn't much he could do without any bones and inside a lead-lined safe, but it still wasn't comfortable to have him in the office. She hoped that this wasn't going to backfire on them.

"Hey, pass me the cervical vertebrae," Adam said.

"The what?"

"The neck bones."

After a few moments' rooting through the box, Abby found the bonepicker's lower jaw and spinal column. The pointed teeth were still stained rust-red, and crusty flecks were lodged in the crevasses between them.

Adam frowned at her as she passed him the vertebrae. "You don't look good, Abby."

"People keep saying that. I'm still working, aren't I?"

"I hear you. If you don't keep going, you don't have anything." He turned one of the vertebrae over, scraping a flake of bone off one spiny protrusion. "Though you're probably not going to find anything to do down here. I have a lot of crap to go through, but most of it's not your kind of thing."

Hint taken. "All right," she said, stepping away from the bench. "Anything you have that *is* my kind of thing? I feel like I'm about ready to jump out of my skin."

"Sure, if that's what you're after." Adam put down the vertebra and pawed quickly through a pile of folders. "I've got that thing you wanted me to look into a few days ago. The glass pane in the foster services office?"

"The glass—" Abby paused. "Foster services office?"

"Yeah, the janitor guy who went skydiving. I wasn't sure what kind of frame might be in those windows, so I dug a little deeper and it turns out your mysterious breaking glass was in the downtown office of the Illinois Department of Child & Family Services. The guy must've been a pancake when he hit the pavement, that shit's like fifty stories up. They would've had pretty good glass in there, too, especially in a government building."

Foster services. Her brain fizzed at the words. A mysterious death in the department of foster services, with glass that shouldn't have broken.

"So what you're saying," she replied slowly, trying to keep her thoughts from running away with her tongue, "is that there's no way this could have happened? In a normal world, I mean?"

"Define normal. But yeah, it's pretty unlikely." Adam opened the folder and pulled out a printout, showing an arrangement of tightly-packed molecules. "Remember the gorilla glass in the hospital last month? This looks like it was pretty much the same stuff, and the crime scene photos show that it was completely shattered. I redid the calculations for an ogre like you asked, but even one of those throwing him probably would've popped the frame out first. The last thing to bust glass like this was a bogeyman, and they don't really play by the usual rules."

"It couldn't have just been a manufacturing fault in the pane?"

"No suits were filed. If crap glass in a government agency killed a guy, the lawyers would be all over it."

"True." Abby leaned against the bench and thought hard. Breaking industrial-strength, nigh-unshatterable glass sounded like a good candidate for a chaos bruise, even just a minor one. And nobody had been able to confirm who the dead man was or if he actually worked there. If he was a sorcerer, what would he have been doing in the department of foster services in the middle of the night?

Foster services. Terra had said she'd been in foster care, and that her father was dead. So how had she ended up with Petrovich? What about that other red-haired girl, the one in the leg braces?

"That bedroom was made for her," Abby said aloud. Adam opened his mouth, but Abby ignored him. "She came first, not Terra. And not just the bedroom, either. The whole place. But he decided to wall it up. What happened?"

"Uh," Adam said. "That's a little vaguer than the stuff you usually ask me."

"Sorry, thinking out loud." She turned away and slapped her good hand against the wall, trying to work out some of the sparking, fizzing energy that seemed to be dancing through her muscles. There was something there, she just had to find a way to grab it. "Where's Mal?"

"In the library, but I—"

"Thanks!" She pushed off from the wall and headed for the stairs, her head still swimming.

The small office library was still a mess, but someone had clearly been doing some cleaning up since the last time she'd been and that someone was obvious. Lenny Scott was on a cot in the corner, still asleep. Mal sat in the middle of the floor, looking vaguely befuddled and dusty as he examined a pair of fabric-jacket albums the size of coffee table books.

"Hello, Abigail," he said without glancing up. "Did you know we have four different collected editions of *Days of Future Past?*"

"Do we? I didn't know." Abby maneuvered around a stack of encyclopedia volumes. "Mary did say we needed to thin out the philosophy section."

Mal opened one of the albums, showing off a bright sixteen-color picture of a clawed man having the flesh seared off his bones by a giant robot. "Not precisely philosophy, I must admit, but still an excellent example of Chris Claremont's work at Marvel. What confuses me is the four editions."

"And from the look of that cover, library editions." Abby contemplated that. "Maybe this place grows new books when we're not looking. But that's not important. Mal, do you have any adrenaline?"

That got him to look up. "Everybody does, provided their glands are functioning. But I suppose that's not what you meant to ask."

"Not quite," she said. "Listen, we have to wake him up." She nodded at Scott. "We're this close to being out of options and if we don't figure out a way to get some names from him, we won't have anything. Does your magic medical kit have a syringe of adrenaline, or triple-distilled caffeine or something?"

"Something like that," he said, putting down the book. "I considered the use of it, but there are always potential side effects. Too much can cause heart palpitations, and we don't have dosage tables for shapeshifters."

"Well, maybe it's time we started putting some together." She tugged on the hem of her shirt, thinking. "We need to wake him up, Mal. Even if we can't get any more concrete information, it's not natural for someone to be asleep that long. He might be sick."

"If he is, it would be to our advantage," Mal said as he stacked up several more books. "A sick man will say almost anything in exchange for medicine."

"Mal!"

"It should be worth considering," he said. It might have been her imagination, but there seemed to be a coolness in his tone.

"Are you crazy? That would be ..."

"Torture? We've already interrogated him, Abigail." Mal added another book to the pile. "I admire your ingenuity in harming him without touching him, but to pretend what we've done here is not some form of extracting words by violence? That would be, I think, impolitic. We are of *l'ancien regime*, engaging craft for the purpose of death. Compared to that, a threat of withholding medicine is hardly something to balk at."

"Mal." She swallowed, mouth dry. "It's not like that. We need to stop a killer."

"I know." His expression tightened. "Believe me, Abigail, I know. And you know I'll help you do it. But we shouldn't forget."

Abby swallowed again, trying to force down the lump that seemed to be caught in her throat, and moved forward a step. Mal turned his back to her as he slowly and methodically began to restack books. "Mal," she said. "Scott?"

"Take him back down to the basement," he said, piling up the extraneous library editions. "I'll meet you in ten minutes. Make sure he is securely restrained and be prepared to cover his mouth."

• • •

With only one good arm and an agency history of being bitten by nonhuman creatures, Abby wasn't prepared to cover his mouth. Not with her hands, anyway. A few minutes' pawing through the random store of junk under Adam's workbench yielded a battered catcher's mask, which she slipped onto the unconscious Scott's head and secured with some packing straps and luggage clips. The result was somewhere between *Field of Dreams* and Hannibal Lecter.

Once Scott was back in the chair and secured, Mal rolled up the therianthrope's sleeve and uncapped another syringe. "This will need time to clear out of his system," he warned as he shot the drug into Scott's arm.

The effect was immediate: the veins on Scott's arm began to bulge, his fingers twitched, and a line appeared in the middle of his forehead as his face contorted. A low grunt, though maybe more like a groan, came from him as he blinked owlishly up at them.

"Owlishly" was definitely the word, too. His pupils were the size of golf balls.

"Mal," she said, "what exactly did you give him?"

"I decline to answer on the grounds that it may incriminate me," he said, dropping the syringe into a glass of mineral spirits. "I can assure you that its separate ingredients were, for the most part, harmless."

"So harmless that you're disinfecting the needle before you throw it out?"

"Something along those lines, yes." He swirled the glass of clear fluid, the needle clinking against the side like a macabre swizzle stick. "But he's awake now."

Scott was definitely awake, but he didn't seem too aware. He blinked dazedly and sagged forward against his bindings. A thin droplet of drool lingered on his lip.

"Leonard," Abby said gently, leaning forward and putting a hand on his shoulder. "Leonard, I need you to look at me. Do you remember where you are?"

He shook his head, tried to focus on Abby and failed. His eyes seemed to be independently interested in opposite sides of the room. "Dunno." When she moved, he tried to track her motion and failed. "I think I'm stoned."

"Just a little bit," Abby said. "The good news is, it's free." Mal muffled a cough that sounded suspiciously like a laugh. "I need you to pay attention to me, Leonard. I need to ask you some questions. Can you do that for me?"

Scott blinked hard and managed to lock both his eyes on her for a moment. "Oh, it's you," he slurred. Abby waited for the inevitable demand to unprintable-word off or unprintable-word herself, but whatever Mal had given him seemed to have blunted his edge. Instead, he licked his lips and blinked again, sleepily. "Nobody calls me Leonard."

"Well, that's too bad," she said. "It means 'brave lion.' Which sort of fits, I suppose. I don't know any names that mean 'coyote.' Well, except for the word 'coyote' obviously, but I don't think many people are actually named after an animal. Except in books, anyway."

That seemed difficult for Scott's hazy brain to follow, because his eyes unfocused again. Abby tapped gently on the catcher's mask to bring him back to her. "Leonard, we need information."

"Last time I talked to you, I started horking up blood," he said. "So no."

"I'm not going to push you too far, I promise." Abby produced a sheaf of yellowed Polaroids. "I just want you to look at some pictures, okay? And you don't have to say a thing. Just nod or shake your head."

Scott shrugged one shoulder. "Okay. Anyway, if it happens again, I'll just rip your fucking head off."

"Better men than you have tried," Abby said. She held up the first picture: Petrovich with the red-haired girl and the shillelagh. "Do you know either of these people?"

After a moment's concentration, Scott shook his head, making himself dizzy. "Nope."

"How about these?" She held up another picture, one of the newest ones in the little collection. It showed just the girl, now almost a teenager and wearing some of the black clothing Abby had found. Against her bright hair the black looked dull and unnatural, which may have been the effect she was going for. She was sitting in a wheelchair and scowling at the camera over the edge of a book.

Another blink from Scott. "Uh, yeah."

Abby's heart leaped, but she kept her voice calm. "Do you work for her?"

"No." The therianthrope scoffed a little at that. "She doesn't tell me what to do. I just help her out sometimes."

"Can you tell me her name?" Abby said softly.

He opened his mouth, but no words came out. An expression crossed his face: dawning fear, draining the blood from his face. He quickly closed hiss mouth again and shook his head.

"So this *is* your boss," Abby said. "Or someone who works for her."

Scott shook his head again.

"So she isn't?"

Another headshake.

"You're contradicting yourself now."

More headshaking, vehement. He might as well have sewn his lips shut. Even through the haze of Mal's concoction, the look in his eyes was clear: you're not getting anything else out of me.

Come on, Abby thought. *Come on, we were doing so well.* "What about this girl?" she said, showing him the picture of young Terra. "She was living with one of your victims for a while, and she said she met you. Do you know anything about her?"

He hesitated for a split second, but shook his head yet again. No. He was done talking.

"Please," she said, trying not to let fear color her words. "I know you can't say it, but can you write it? Sign language? Charades, for God's sake. We're trying to save lives!"

Another moment's pause. And then, emphatic, one more final headshake. The muzziness was beginning to fade from Scott's face, and there was a steely quality to his stare now. No. No, he wasn't going to say anything at all.

There was always the crow, she knew. Or maybe something else: how would he react with a selkie's half-desiccated corpse in his lap? But even as the thought formed, she glanced across the room at Mal, who was stoically sorting through his medical kit and not saying a single word.

She wondered what he'd meant by *l'ancien regime.*

She could justify torture, she knew. People were dying. She never wanted to see a corpse like Petrovich's or Neill's ever again. But somehow, withholding medicine—*that* would cross a line?. The thought made her want to throw up. So much for being a good Christian.

Abby took a deep breath. Then she stood and walked away. The eyes of the two men followed her, but whatever they were thinking, she didn't want to know it.

Chapter Fifteen

She was making a timeline, sort of, when John came clumping into the main office with water streaming from his hair and clothes. "It's a fucking monsoon out there," he said, shaking himself and spraying water droplets onto the carpet. "Five minutes I was out, an' I'm soaked to the skin. There's hardly any snow left."

"Really?" Abby glanced up, surprised out of her dark thoughts. John looked like a wet dog, his hair matted and damp, and his sour expression almost startled a laugh out of her. She quickly turned the laugh into a cough.

"Really." John wiped his face off and flung the collected droplets away, spattering an old poster and creating a sudden blank spot on the office whiteboard calendar. "Never seen anything like it. 'S almost bearable out there now."

Abby got to her feet and checked the window. Water was pouring down, smearing the glass and distorting the gray daylight. She pulled the window open and leaned over the sill, reaching a hand out into the downpour. Her hand recoiled as soon as the water touched it.

"It's warm!" she said, swinging back from the sill. "I've never seen that before. Not in December!"

"Like I said, monsoon." John went back to wringing out his shirttail. "The weather's been cockeyed anyway lately, but not like this. What d'you think? Global warming?"

"No, I don't think so." Abby dried her hand on a stray dishtowel. "Not unless something really, really big has changed in the last week."

"Chaos bruise, then?"

"God, I hope not. If we're right about this sacrifice business, the effects left by each death are localized. To change weather patterns would require more power than ..." She trailed off.

"Than bringing something back to life?" John finished. "'Cause if we've actually done our homework right this time, we've already had that." He flopped into his chair and began to unlace his boots. The smell of damp, unwashed sock filled the office. "What a week. Happy Christmas, have a nightmare."

"Sure brings back memories," Abby muttered to herself, shaking her head.

"So." John peeled off his socks and tossed them over to the heating grate, where they gently steamed. "What do we do now?"

Abby sighed. "That's a really good question, John." She showed him her half-finished timeline and, as best she could, explained what she'd just learned from Scott. Or rather, not learned. Her words, a lot like her timeline, were a tangled mess.

"Foster care office..." John tapped the desk, thinking. "And Terra was in foster care, all right. But she's not the wheelchair redhead in the photo. Or is she? She's big on illusion magic, ain't she? Could they be the same person?"

"I'm not entirely certain, but Scott did mention her to me the first time. The geas didn't activate until he started giving out information about his boss. Maybe this guy in the foster office was a sorcerer, and he was sent in to try and pull her files?"

"Doesn't wash." He took the timeline from her and spread it out. "Let's try looking at this from another direction. What's involved here? All this happens, right, but what do you get?"

"Sorcerers making magical items and then being killed, possibly with fairy magic if the bricks are anything to go by. Sacrifice theory, maybe. But on the other hand, a lot of fairies have gone missing, and you'd think they'd need all hands on deck for this kind of thing. "

"Not just fairies, problematic fairies. The type of people who were on our books." John's eyes brightened. "Abby, it's not just magic. It's *power.*"

"You're repeating yourself."

"No, I'm not." John's finger stabbed into the timeline, tearing the paper. "You know as well as I do that fairies don't cooperate too well, Abby. And there's other kinds of power than magic. Think about it! It's not *fairies* that're doing this, it's a *group* of fairies. They've got magical artifacts, they've built up a great stock of juice from all this sacrifice business, and now they've purged their ranks! Creepy Ivan and his lot were the kind of fae we'd catch. They're not good soldiers."

"But fairies aren't soldiers at all. They're always random—"

"That we know of. If there's one thing this case ought to teach us, it's that we don't know as much as we think we do." John rocked back on his heels. "This sacrifice stuff is about magic, sure, but magic is just one form of having power over someone else. Killing undesirables, eliminating a local leader like Petrovich among the sorcerers, buying commissions and then wiping out the folks who made 'em. That sounds like politics to me."

"Cui bono," Abby murmured. "My grandpa used to say that. Who profits?"

John shook his head. "Right now, it's whoever's makin' the power play."

"It could be our mysterious redhead." Abby pulled out another of the Polaroids and settled it on the timeline. "I like this theory, John... OK, that's a lie. I hate it. But it could work. Too bad Scott isn't talking."

"And you can't torture him."

The question was remarkably blunt, and it took Abby a few seconds to dredge up a coherent response. "I can," she said. "But I won't. And I won't let you or the others do it, either."

"Not even to save lives?" John's tone was oddly light. Maybe he, too, was remembering another argument they'd had last month, when the bogeymen had been on the march. To end that argument it had taken a minor explosion in the office and a helping hand from a power they really couldn't afford being indebted to. Abby would have almost preferred taking another loan from Baba Yaga if it would get her out of this.

"I don't know," she said finally. "Maybe there'll be another time to cross that line. He-who-fights-monsters, right? But not today. Not now." She swallowed. "There has to be another way to get the information we need."

John nodded, and in some unspoken way, the tension in the air began to thin. "All right," he said softly. "If we can. But look, there ain't much a shapeshifter is gonna be afraid of. That scent trick worked once, but he's wise to us now. And I don't know if there's any other avenues we can follow."

"Maybe." Abby tapped her fingers on the paper timeline, thinking. "He was living in that apartment to monitor Sarah Mulsey. And he knows this redheaded woman, whoever she is. So how does the redhead know about Sarah Mulsey?"

"Now that is a good question." John's expression relaxed. "Hell, what do we even know about Scott himself? What's a werecoyote doing working with a bunch of fairies, anyway? He didn't seem too fond of 'em."

"Right. Right!" Thoughts were sparking again in Abby's brain, and it was with a strong sense of relief that the idea came to her. "Listen, we need to know more about Scott. How long was he in that apartment? Maybe there was an alternate contact number or something!" She jigged in place, suddenly more energetic than she'd felt in days. It was like doing something, anything, would somehow keep her thoughts moving as well and perhaps find her an answer. "Okay, look. I'll go back to Mulsey's and Scott's places, see what I can find. Maybe talk to the superintendent. You start looking for more information on him online." John opened his mouth to object, and Abby quickly cut him off. "Yes, yes, yes, I know that I shouldn't go by myself. But my typing is slow as heck with only one good hand, and you should be here in case Mal starts sprouting fangs. I'll call in as soon as I find something."

• • •

She gathered up her kit, hopped in the car, and within half an hour was in front of the weathered apartment building. The rain was still pouring down, a little cooler now that it was late afternoon but still too warm for the season. A Units for Rent sign had been placed on the building's tiny lawn and was sagging damply in the rain. She went inside.

Boxes were piled up in the hall, and there was a low murmur of voices. A couple of tenants, dressed in colorful waterproof raincoats and steaming as their body heat warmed the damp air, were in the middle of moving out.

Abby didn't have to look for the superintendent: he was in the middle of a fight with one of them.

Abby waited patiently while the two men yelled at each other. Evidently someone's security deposit was at stake.

As she waited, the shouting faltered. The two men stared at each other, then glanced over at her. They probably hadn't been expecting an outsider to walk up to them and watch them fight; it was an unwritten rule of city streets and subways that if two people were getting into it, passersby would act like they couldn't see or hear a thing. Abby had spent more than enough time pretending to read ads on the subway while a group of fellow passengers screamed at each other.

"Yeah?" the building superintendent said finally.

"Hi." Abby flashed a police badge. "I'm Detective Brittany Douglas, CPD. I'm here to check on a couple of final details in the Mulsey case. Can you open the apartment door for me, please? Also, I'd like to talk to her next-door-neighbor, Mr. Scott. Is he here?"

The superintendent shook his head. "Sorry, lady. Uh, ma'am. Lenny got in some kind of fight the other day and no one's seen him since."

"A fight? Was it reported?"

"Uh, no. Not really. That happened sometimes. He was a big guy, you know, liked throwing his weight around."

"In that case, I'll need to take a look at Mr. Scott's apartment as well," she said, frowning. "He's a person of interest in this investigation. Could you open it for me, or would you prefer to wait for a warrant?"

The man exchanged glances with his soon-to-be-ex-tenant. Abby could guess a little of what was going on in his head: all these people already unhappy about someone being murdered on the premises, tenants moving out, bad publicity. And while people might pretend they were deaf and blind when an argument started, you could always bet on them listening intently. A public fight was free entertainment in Chicago. If it looked like he had something to hide, everyone would notice.

And worse, it might get him paid additional attention by the cops. Probably prompt some trouble about pesky building codes, too. Abby wasn't prepared to say that he was any less law-abiding than any other landlord she'd known, but pretty much every building had some kind of code violation simply because of the number of regulations and the endless forward march of time and entropy. She could almost pinpoint the moment the superintendent decided that it was more trouble than he wanted to deal with.

He unlocked the two apartments and stood back, hovering in the hallway. She stepped into Scott's and firmly closed the door behind her.

Aside from a few pieces of furniture being knocked over, it looked just like it had before. Abby took a few photos of the main room and moved through to the bedroom, which the agents hadn't had much time to check. It too was fairly sparse and seemed to be decorated in the ever-popular senior-year dormitory style, with Martin Scorsese movie posters and a lot of unwashed laundry draped over folding chairs. His bed was a mattress on the floor, with no box spring or frame to provide a handy hiding place for incriminating documents. Food wrappers had gathered in the corners of the room, and a few of them were starting to smell.

Abby pulled on a pair of gloves and began to search. She went through the dresser, turned over the mattress, peeled back the posters, and stood on a chair to check inside the glass dome of the ceiling light. Nothing.

In the main room, she pawed through the bookcase and checked under the rug. She pulled the cushions off the chairs, opened the cabinets and looked through the collected records. Nothing.

The only thing left were the extensive DVD and record collections. She tipped them off the shelves, but there was nothing behind them. One case rattled when it fell to the floor.

It didn't sound like a loose disc. Curious, Abby turned the box over. *Teen Wolf.*

Oh, come on. Could it really be that easy?

She opened the case. The disc was definitely *Teen Wolf*, and so was the interior booklet, but something was poking out of the glossy paper. She dialed John.

"'lo?"

"I found a computer chip," she said, carefully dropping it into her gloved palm. "No, wait, something else. It looks like a small external drive of some kind. Hold on a second, let me plug it in."

"Got your burner phone with you?"

"Always." Abby dug into her pocket and produced a cheapie preloaded with innocuous numbers. With her ordinary burner doing full-time phone duty after her normal one burned out in the hospital room, this third phone was smaller and older than the others. It took some finagling to make it recognize the drive. "One text file of numbers and some photos," she reported finally. "Definitely fishy. His listing for 'Dad' is 911." She rattled off the numbers, and John took them down.

"Anything else?" he said. She could hear the faint clacking of keys in the background as he typed up the numbers and began the laborious process of searching them online.

"Not much. There's a few photographs, but ..." She paused. "Hello."

"Don't keep me in suspense here. What?"

"I found the redhead."

It was a grainy picture, clearly taken with a low-res camera. Probably originating on a cheap phone like the one she carried. The image showed a red-haired woman sitting behind a desk, caught in the act of writing something while three tall men gathered around and peered over her shoulder. Two of them had their backs to the camera, but the third sent a chill down Abby's spine. He had the eyes of a fairy.

"There's a photo of her with at least one fae. Nobody's looking at the camera, and the quality's terrible. I'm not sure why it would even be on here, frankly." She scrolled through to the next picture. "Here's another one. You can barely see her here, but it looks like the guy next to her has a sealskin on. Probably a selkie."

"Probably?" John's tone was dry.

"Well, he's either a selkie or a Viking." That got a snort from John. "Come to think of it, he has got blond braids, but the jeans sort of ruin the picture. Probably a selkie. And here's a picture of a couple of fairies with those tattoos I told you about. Christ, it's a regular rogues' gallery." She flipped through and couldn't hold back a short laugh. Scott had evidently been experimenting in the medium of the bathroom mirror self-portrait, and had produced a rather fuzzy—in more ways than one—shot of himself in mid-transformation. One claw had half-obscured the lens. "I'm not sure what he was doing here, but there's a couple of pictures of the redhead and a lot more of different fairies. They mostly seem to be taken in an office suite somewhere."

"Any location clues?" She could hear John still typing furiously. "View out the window or something?"

"No, just a beige office. There's some prints on the walls and a lot of blocky furniture. The windows are all shuttered." She kept flipping through the pictures. "Aside from a questionable selfie or two, all of these are just pictures of people meeting. Probably candid photos, too, since nobody's ever looking at the camera."

"Now that's interesting." The sounds of typing stopped, and Abby could hear a scrape of the chair as he pushed it back. "Know what it sounds like to me? Blackmail."

"Linking these people to each other? That's a definite possibility. Here, take a look." She pressed a few keys, beginning to forward some of the photos to John. The ones of the redhead went first. "It explains why he tried to hide the drive. What about those numbers?"

"So far? Junk. Half of 'em are publicly-registered service numbers, probably just in there to pad out the list. One was an organic grocery in County Cork, Ireland. Some of the others are dead. Dunno what we can do with 'em, though. It's not like we have the resources, and—"

"'We're not the cops,'" both of them chorused together, getting another laugh from John. Abby had pitched her voice down, not wanting the superintendent to hear her say that, but she still glanced towards the door. Still closed. Good.

"Too bad we aren't," she said as she dug through the pile of fallen DVDs. There were a few tell-tale rattles, but whenever she opened the plastic cases, it would be nothing but a loose disc or, one time, a menu from a local Thai place. "We might know where to look next. But why would Scott be gathering blackmail material? He seems pretty loyal to his boss."

"Loyal to his own hide, you mean. That geas business was the only thing keeping him from talking, wasn't it? Maybe she put it on him after she caught him sneaking around. Putting him on notice, as it were."

She sighed. "Could be. But there's no way to know, is there?"

"Unless we want to take another run at 'im. Break out the bamboo slivers?"

"John." She stood up, her knees creaking. "I told you, I don't want to talk about it."

"All right, but just so long as you know it's still out there." John didn't seem too upset by her words. Abby had the vague feeling that he had been prodding her purely out of curiosity, as if he was poking a bruise to see if it still hurt. "Oh, good, the pictures finally arrived... Fucking mandatory data plan, this thing's slower'n Piers Morgan... Hmmm. She grew up nice."

"John."

"Just saying."

"Say it while working, please."

• • •

She finished her sweep of Scott's apartment almost forty minutes later. Nothing else had turned up: there were colonies of dust bunnies under every available piece of furniture and several pieces of Sox memorabilia, but neither of those were strictly criminal. With a sigh, she locked the door behind her and moved on to Sarah Mulsey's.

When she opened that door, though, she stopped. The dolls were gone.

No, not entirely gone. A few still lingered on the edges of the room, their fabric heavily decayed and their seams burst. For a moment she wondered if there was some kind of leak in the water pipes, but the carpet was clean. Only the dolls were rotting.

Moving gingerly, she closed the door behind her and locked it. The air was thick with the smell of mold, and she would have preferred to keep the door open, but she wasn't sure the superintendent should know about this just yet. The mold was greenish and fuzzy white rather than black, so she was probably safe for a few minutes. But if a shelf full of dolls was bad, a shelf covered in mold spores and piled high with rot-flecked porcelain heads was definitely worse.

"Jesus Christ," Abby said before she could stop herself. The air smelled stale and damp, like a greenhouse that had been closed up too long. Her hand shook as she raised her phone to take pictures.

A few seconds later the phone rang, and John was back on the line. "The fuck did you just send me?" he demanded bluntly. "Looks like a war crime."

"Mulsey's apartment. The dolls all rotted." Abby clambered up on the sofa and began to prod the ceiling, looking for damp patches or tell-tale leaks. There were none. She checked the bathroom, but the water must have been turned off after the tenant died. "I can't see any reason why. Mold's growing, but it's very dry. It crumbles when I touch it." She peered at one doll, frowning. "And a lot of dead mold, too. It's like it was all growing gangbusters for a few days, then the energy ran out and it's started dying off."

"Fucking hell." John let out a breath that rattled against the phone. "Abby, get out of there, okay? I don't like this."

"Well, I don't either." She muffled a sneeze. "But I'm not done yet. We didn't check this place out nearly enough last time."

Mulsey's apartment was laid out in a mirror-image of Scott's. Two next-door units with their bathrooms next to each other so they could share plumbing, a good economy measure. They probably could have overheard everything that went on in each others' homes. No wonder one of them wound up killing the other. With the dolls mostly gone, she could see more of the apartment's furnishings. The sharp lines of the modern furniture and geometric art prints contrasted with the misshapen pieces of crystal displayed on virtually every flat surface.

Abby laid a hand on one of the crystals. It was warm, oddly so, and vibrated just a little under her fingers. For a second she thought she heard a faint hum, like a malfunctioning radio about to squeal. The Crystal Lady indeed; she quickly pulled her hand away before she could accidentally trigger some kind of magical backlash.

"Lots of crystals," she reported to the phone. "I think she was using them as some kind of power battery."

There was a hiss of frustration from John. "Abby, I feel like I'm in a fucking horror movie here. Will you just *get out of there?*"

"I told you, I'm not done yet." She moved into the bedroom. There were more crystals here, dozens of them in all shapes and sizes. The hum wasn't quite audible, but she could feel it in her teeth. No bookcases or decorations here, just a high hospital bed with a hoist suspended from the ceiling. The covers were the same burnt-orange and umber in geometric patterns, but it looked strange against the stark plastic of the bed.

Abby pulled back the covers. Half a dozen crystals, pulsing with light and warmth, were scattered on each side of the mattress. A large flat geode, also warm but much less so than the others, had been stuck under the pillow.

"Definitely power batteries," she said. "She was sleeping with them, too.

The one under the pillow seems drained." She glanced around at the room. There were tracks on the carpet where something heavy—or several somethings—had been wheeled away. A lone IV stand occupied a corner. "I think she was sick recently. Very sick. It would explain why such a powerful practitioner would take a risk on such a weird, shady job."

"Abby, you need to find something useful in there or get out now. Stuff doesn't just rot for no good reason."

"What about it being magically transported someplace else? That could definitely mess it up." Abby snapped some photos of the room. "We don't know anything about this stuff. We need to—"

"God fucking damn it, Marquise!" John exploded. "When I tell you to do something, you do it! Get out of there *now!*"

Abby froze. Her stomach clenched automatically as her grip tightened on the phone, her heart pounding, but she closed her eyes and counted to five.

"John," she said quietly. "If you talk to me like that again, I'm going to hang up on you."

She could hear him breathing raggedly. "Abby," he said, his voice hoarse. "Just get out of there. Okay? I've got a feeling. I can't explain it. It's in the back of my throat, like." He coughed. "Please. Get out of there."

Abby looked around her. The apartment was dead silent. There was nothing there, just furniture and books and crystals and mold. On the one hand, she was tempted to tell him to shove it where the sun didn't shine. (There, that technically wasn't swearing.) But on the other hand, John had been doing this a lot longer than she had, and she remembered what Mary had said about the fog in his brain. She wondered if all the magic in the air was affecting him somehow.

"All right," she said finally. "But you don't get to yell at me, John. We have to be in this together, remember?"

Another huff of breath against the phone, half sigh and half laugh. "I know. I know. I'm sorry."

After hesitating for a moment, Abby took a few of Mulsey's humming crystals and stuffed them into her pockets. Then she left.

On the way out, she showed the picture of the redhead to the superintendent. He just shook his head. "Looks familiar," he said, "but I don't think I know her. Was she on TV?"

That didn't help much. She thanked the superintendent for his help and left before he could ask any inconvenient questions.

Back at the office, she found Adam and John jointly poring over the photographs and numbers she'd sent. Instead of talking to them, she went to her desk and did more Googling of her own, hoping to turn up some information on Sarah Mulsey's mysterious crystal magic. "Crystal lady" was too general a term for the web; she got a lot of links about antiques, yachts and Olivia

Newton-John. Other sites carried information about the supposed magical powers of crystals, but nothing that would make them hum or glow. On the other hand, she was willing to make a guess at whatever item had burned out the woman's eyes and brain. What would you buy from the Crystal Lady but a crystal ball?

She told John, who didn't look happy. "Wish we could know for sure," he said. "But it's all speculation at this point, ain't it? Can't bring her back from the dead."

"I should hope not." Abby grimaced, thinking about chickens freezing to death in shrink-wrapped plastic shrouds. "What about the pictures, then? Do you have any ideas?"

"Tried doing a back-end search on some of 'em, but no luck." John turned his computer monitor to show her the blurry photographs from the phone. "Quality's too low and there's too many bloody redheads out there. If we had a suspect to check 'em against, maybe, but right now we're dead in the water."

There was a "hmm" from Adam. "I might be able to help with that," he said. "Come look at this."

It was like getting a shot of coffee directly into the bloodstream. Both Abby and John jumped up and hurried over to Mal's desk, where Adam was seated with a list of telephone numbers and a pile of scribbled notes.

"Photos might be a bust, but some of the numbers are legit," he said, handing Abby the list of numbers. John must have handed them off to him for database trawling when the photographs demanded his attention. "There's only eight that I could find which are still active. Those are the ones labeled Mom, Dad, Home, Emergency, Tapout, Jake, Cherf and Pizza. Pizza was pretty obvious, and Cherf and Jake seem to be unlisted private numbers. They might be in a database we don't have access to, but unless the Director has connections, we'll need to sideline those. The others, though?"

He opened up a new window, showing a colorful web page with pictures of smiling mothers and children in the header. "Dad is 911. Home is the newsdesk at the *Chicago Tribune*. Emergency is the listed contact number for a crimewatch blog. Tapout is a legal aid service."

"Quite a list," Abby said. "It sounds to me like he really was getting ready to flip on his boss."

"But the odd man out is Mom." Adam pointed to the printed number. "Or it would be, if Mom wasn't a direct line to the office of Kelly Buchanan, a senior coordinator at Family Services." He nodded to the open Internet page. "And Kelly Buchanan is interesting, because when I looked up her official bio, it touted her thirty-five years of service to the community. Mostly in the Wrigleyville area, where she worked to remove children from unfit homes."

Wrigleyville. Petrovich's neighborhood.

"Foster care again," John said slowly. He stared at the pictures of happy families, seemingly waiting for them to tell him something helpful. "First there's some bloke dies in the foster services office, maybe killed by sacrifice magic. Then there's this business of the vanishing redhead, who was living in an area where she might've been scooped up by foster care. She was sure in a home that didn't really fit the standards of child welfare, did it?"

"And Terra Burns was in foster care," Abby reminded her. "So our mystery redhead lives with Petrovich for a while, then vanishes out of the photographs. A few years later she's replaced by Terra, the daughter of the fairy woman with the tattoos. So why would Petrovich take her in?'

"Maybe he felt responsible." Adam pulled up one of the fresh photos of young Terra and put it side-by-side with the young redhead. "Look at the shape of the chin. Both kids share the fairy eyes, but Petrovich's chin matches the mystery girl's. And the ears, too. Sort of. I'll bet they were related by blood."

John snapped his fingers. "And Lydia the Tattooed Fairy doesn't seem the family sort. Say Petrovich has a daughter by her an' takes the kid in. He was raising her in that second story, got it all set up for her needs. Explains the wheelchair, too. Cross-species breeding almost never goes smooth."

"But the redhead disappears," Abby put in. "Only to turn up years later in Scott's photographs, bossing around a bunch of fairies. Even her own mother."

"Meanwhile, Terra's wary of fairies and wants to know who killed Petrovich." John stared at the two photographs. "Terra had to have lived somewhere before she moved in with Petrovich. Bet it was done on the sly, too, since if he's had one kid taken away by social services he ain't gonna get handed another. He takes her in, say, knowing how Lydia ain't into this taking-care-of-kids business and her dad's gone, and when he dies 'cause of this fairy business she wants revenge." He turned to Abby and Adam. "What d'you think?"

"It's a theory," Adam said, understated as usual. "But where does Scott fit into all this? And why does he have Kelly Buchanan's number on speed-dial?"

"Well, Buchanan was a social worker." Abby tapped her fingers against the back of the chair, thinking of all the social workers she'd known. There'd always been one or two kids in the neighborhood whose parents were drinking, fighting or missing, so the Daimler under-twelves got to know the usual suspects pretty quickly. They'd come to see her, too, when Mom had been dying and Dad was getting a reputation for his bad temper. Later on she'd been visited again, this time as the neglectful parent. Talk about a role reversal. From a parent's point of view, they'd been suspicious and intrusive, but to a kid they could sometimes help you when no one else would. How had the mystery girl seen her?

"If Buchanan was the redhead's case worker," she said slowly, "then there'd have to be a reason for Scott to be in contact with her. Juvenile issues wouldn't apply, not now. So how did they meet?"

She thought about Scott, unconscious in the basement. He was loyal to his boss for personal reasons, but even so he'd begun collecting photographs of her circle and compiling a list of emergency numbers. Divided loyalties. A case worker. "Was Scott a foster kid?" she said finally.

"Now that's a very good question," John said. He turned to Adam. "Run a search on Scott and Buchanan, would you? I'm gonna get some coffee."

"OK, but it'll take a while. Those names are generic as hell, and there's only five billion people on the planet right now." Adam opened a new window and began to type as John wandered into the kitchen. He'd probably be a few minutes: they were out of instant.

Abby went back to her desk and began rifling through her case notes. She had barely reached the second layer of paper when Adam said "Well, hello."

It was a newspaper article about twenty years old. A round-faced middle-aged woman was standing with a young family, all of them gathered around a wooden table in what looked like a public park. Two kids between nine and twelve were working busily on a puzzle. The boy had cropped brown hair and a vague expression; his companion, a redheaded girl in a wheelchair, had most of her side of the puzzle completed already.

Abby's heartbeat sped up as she looked at the picture. The angle was bad on the redhead, but she definitely looked familiar. As Adam zoomed in on the photo, Abby grabbed a couple of the recovered Polaroids and held them up to compare. Not perfect, but...

"It could be her," she said softly. "Adam, how'd you find this?"

"I just searched their names with some social work keywords, and there it was." He shrugged. "It's an article about some community mixer for local blended families. Puff piece."

He zoomed in further, and the photograph's caption. displayed in large letters. "'Caseworker Kelly Buchanan helps new siblings Leonard Scott and Sascha Dolan with a Blended is Better puzzle,'" Adam read aloud. "'Sales of the puzzles will go to aid local families who are in the process of fostering and adoption.' Sascha Dolan. Name rings a bell."

Abby glanced down at him. "It does?"

"Yeah. I don't remember from where, though. Sort of familiar. Maybe she's on TV?"

Now that Abby thought about it, though, the name *did* seem familiar. If this really was the redhead they were looking for, then her being any kind of public figure would work in their favor.

"Maybe," she said. "The building superintendent said the same thing. Start looking, okay? JOHN! We might have her!"

There was a whoop from the kitchen, followed immediately by the sound of breaking china. "S'okay!" John called out quickly. "All clear. Nothing important. So who is she? What's her name?"

"Twenty years ago, it was Sascha Dolan," Abby told him. "Adam's following up on that now. Drink some water, too. Caffeine dehydrates."

She went back to cleaning up her desk and tried not to look over at Adam's computer too often. He was buried in Google searches and wouldn't welcome any interruptions, no matter how well-intended they were. Hopefully the obvious casualty hadn't been his Ranger mug.

John emerged from the kitchenette, coffee in hand, just as Adam closed a couple of windows and leaned back with a sigh. "I found her," he announced. "But you're not gonna like it."

"Who gives a good goddamn?" John demanded. "This isn't Deal or No Deal! Who is she already?"

Adam had opened another website. This one was sleek and professional with soft, tasteful graphics of stylized stars and stripes. There was a photograph in the sidebar.

"Here we go." Adam tilted the monitor towards them. "Meet Sascha Dolan Carter, Cook County District Attorney."

Chapter Sixteen

"Fuck," John said. The word itself seemed to encapsulate everything that needed to be said: the world was in a state of Fuck, and that was all that needed expressing. His shoulders sagged as he sat down.

Abby looked at the picture again, hoping it was a mistake. Redheads weren't exactly rare in a city like Chicago, which had a rich history of immigrants making it that far west before running out of money. And "Sascha" wasn't such an impossible name either. It was entirely possible that they were looking for another redheaded woman in the same age bracket who happened to be part of the foster system and named Sascha.

The picture was neat, clean, and professional. Sascha Carter had been photographed from the chest up, wearing a sea-green tailored jacket with a white blouse and a chic silvery-gray silk scarf. Her curly red hair was pulled back in a bun with a pair of lacquered chopsticks in it. There were fine lines in the corners of her bright green eyes, but not enough to make her look haggard. She was smiling faintly, and had her head tilted slightly as if she was waiting to hear what news Abby had to share.

The biography was impressive. Born Sascha Dolan, now age 40. She'd been in office for two years and had represented Cook County in several lawsuits, most of which Abby only vaguely recognized from *Tribune* headlines about the insert-name-here scandal. She'd studied law at Yale, done postgraduate work at Oxford and the University of Edinburgh, and lived for a short time in Galway with her husband Jack Carter. After her husband's untimely death, she moved her practice back to the United States and quickly made a name for herself as a well-rounded and fair-minded lawyer who never took a case she didn't believe in. She was passionate, intelligent, and possibly not corrupt, which got some attention in Chicago.

It was silent on the issue of her childhood. Politicians usually milked any available youthful trauma to humanize themselves for the voting public, but Sascha Carter either didn't have any trauma to milk or didn't feel like sharing. Abby could respect that.

But if she was the mystery redhead? Abby's heart sank as she stared at the list of legal accomplishments. A powerful lawyer. A city official. A voice in the government, however minor. Someone with the respect and love of the population, to judge by her approval ratings. Abby tried to map the idea of Lenny's boss, who laid geasa on her people and might be sacrificing sorcerers for power, onto this woman.

"Oh, hell," she said.

"What she said." John slumped over his desk, head in his hands. "Politics, maybe. I can live with that. But a politician? A fucking politician? Ever get the feeling we're cursed?"

"At this point, about once a month." That was Adam. "But seriously, who's surprised? We're looking for someone who ruthlessly exploits other people and doesn't mind lying, cheating, stealing and murdering to get what they want. Sounds like a politico to me. And a lawyer, which is a bonus." He shook his head and adjusted the collar of his bathrobe. "I'm surprised we didn't think of it before."

"But *this* politician?" Abby argued, pointing to the screen. "I've never seen anyone so squeaky-clean. I mean, I think I voted for her!"

"You think you voted for her?" Adam said. "You don't remember who you vote for?"

"You vote?" That was John, the words muffled by his hands.

Abby flushed a little. "Sometimes. If we're trying to make the world a better place, shouldn't we start by getting ourselves a decent government?"

That got a shrug from Adam. "Don't ask me. I haven't voted since the '90s. John?"

"Illegal alien." John raised his head. "So, congratulations. If this turns out to be our girl you can have one three-millionth of the guilt for getting her into power. Doesn't mean we actually have a prayer of finding out, though." He shook his head. "Lawyers are bad. Politicians are worse. Politicians will take you apart, and they'll do it nice and legal. Fillet you, take your stuff and make it legal precedent. We can't *fight* politicians!"

"But we have to do something." That was Mal, slow and calm as ever. He had moved to the bookshelf and was thumbing through a small hardback volume, his eyes flicking over the page. "Decaying dolls, the dead coming to life, bizarre weather. If sorcerers continue to die, I believe we will be unable to contain the situation."

"Go piss up a rope!" John snapped. "What d'you expect us to do, then? This ain't bogeymen and fairies and all that. This'd be going up against people who can destroy you and don't need to be quiet about it, neither. And some of us ain't on too solid ground already!"

"Obviously." Mal's eyes never wavered from his book.

That got John out of his chair. "D'you have something to say to me?" he demanded. "'Cos I'm not hearing anything helpful out of you!"

Mal turned a page. "Neither do I hear any such thing from you," he said. "Abigail, your thoughts?"

The blonde woman paused. A coffee mug had been knocked over when John started slamming around, and she was in the middle of rescuing some papers from the spreading pool of French roast. "I don't think this is our culprit," she said. "But if she is, we have to do something. Anything. There's been too many deaths already. But if it's her ..." She dropped a clump of wet paper into the wastebasket. "Whoever arranged all this? They deserve to die too."

"Indeed." Mal turned another page. He seemed to have found what he was looking for and carefully inserted a happy frog bookmark before setting the book down. "If this is indeed the cause of these deaths, and if power is what she seeks, then her ambition has murdered these people. By that sin fell the angels... Or perhaps, *Let death be felt and the proof remain.*"

John glanced back and forth between them, his face twisted. "Is there something going on here I'm not allowed to hear?" he demanded.

"English poetry," Mal replied with a shrug.

"Apparently," Abby said. She shot a glance at Mal, who just shrugged again. "Look, John. We have to do something. We had this argument a month ago, remember? When the bogeymen kidnapped Mrs. Shepherd. We have to try doing something, because we're the only ones that *can* do something. And even the bogeymen weren't skinning people."

There was a heavy moment of silence before John flopped into his chair again, face a mask. "All right," he muttered. "Point taken. How, then, d'you geniuses propose we investigate—" He waved a hand at the screen, where the list of commendations awarded and lawsuits won was still visible "—that?"

"Sack up or shut up." Adam seemed to have officially run out of damns to give. He poured the last of the cream into his own coffee and added three sugars as he spoke. "We're not even sure she's the one doing the murdering, right? So go check it out. Me, I have work to do."

He opened the basement door and, with a certain amount of finality, slammed it behind him. Footsteps echoed as he clumped down the stairs. The three remaining agents looked at each other.

"Ouch," John said finally. "Point taken."

Mal turned his head away, trying hard not to smile. The tension had been broken, at least for now.

"Sometimes I think we don't deserve him." Abby settled into her own chair. "So let's talk strategy. We have a target we need to approach, but it's high-profile. She's been in the public eye a lot. What do we do?"

"Strike at the heart," Mal suggested. "Where does she live? Perhaps we can enter her house."

John grunted. "Don't think so. Politicians and suchlike have a bad habit of havin' guards, security systems, all that. Harvey maybe could get us through, but it'd be near impossible without her realizing something's gone wrong."

"At her office?" Abby suggested. John shook his head.

"Same problem. I don't want any of us caught in a couple of rooms full of angry bodyguards and cops. Better if we're in the open air, where we can leg it."

Abby and Mal exchanged glances. The prospect of getting in any kind of confrontation with the authorities wasn't pleasing at the best of times, and with the group at half strength, John seemed determined to keep them all as safe as possible. The problem was that serial killers, especially serial killers playing at human sacrifice, typically took some catching. The light, cautious touch might not be what they need.

On the other hand, John had been at this longer than either of them. And who knew if he really was an illegal alien, but if he was it explained his familiarity with the mechanisms of law enforcement. If he said an indoors meeting was too risky, then they should probably believe him.

"The schedule page on her site says she's speaking at the Black November rally tonight," Abby offered. "She's been making appearances there every couple of days. I remember seeing her on the news, saying there was stuff the government wasn't telling us."

John barked out a laugh. "Oh, yah. Yah, I see that."

That got a raised eyebrow from Abby. "Am I missing a joke?"

"More'n one. The woman who might've killed people is part of the group trying to dig up that bogeyman mess. And she's out there with the Save Our Children posters, too." John shook his head. "If it is her, the world's got a terrible sense of humor."

"I wouldn't read too much into it. Politicians are supposed to be pro-children; it's kind of a requirement." Abby shifted, trying to get comfortable. Her arm still ached, but at least the swelling was going down. "So what do you think? Try and talk to her at the rally?"

"Bodyguards again. Too risky. Although if it's out in the open …" John glanced over at the guinea pig's cage, where a green glass jar was sitting. "We send someone in there with Harvey to look in her mind. It'll be suspicious, sure, but with a lot of people in the crowd and a jar-carrier in there to give him a place to hide? Could be possible. Any volunteers?"

Mal and Abby both tried to speak at once. John jumped at the sudden chorus and held up his hands. "Wait, wait, I didn't actually think you'd *answer* that. Right. Mal, are you feelin' hairy?"

"Absolutely not," Mal said.

"Good. You're our genie carrier. Abby, what was it?"

"I was just going to say that I probably shouldn't be the one doing it," Abby said. "Since if Carter really is Scott's boss, she must've been the one who sent the sorcerer and Kotik to kill me at the hospital. She'll know who I am."

A short silence fell.

"Damn," John said. "Forgot about that." He ran his thumbnail over the edge of the tattooed B on his forefinger, looking grim.

"However," Mal said slowly, "this leaves us with an intriguing possibility. Abigail is an obvious target. A known stalking horse could be valuable. If we give her the genie, that leaves the rest of us at liberty to monitor the situation."

Both of them looked at John, anticipating an objection. As they watched, though, he uncapped a small bottle and swallowed a couple of pills. Then he nodded. "All right."

"You're not going to argue?" Abby said.

"Oh, I am. But it's still the best idea that's come up so far, and if that's not sad, I don't know what is." He closed the bottle and tucked it back into his pocket. "Abby goes in with Harvey. They could be watching her, which'll make it hard to deploy, but if it does get noticed it'll keep them from pinpointing anyone besides her. Keeps the damage limited." He tapped his fingers on the edge of his desk, thinking. "That means the rest of us watch her an' everything else. I'll set up a lookout post up high, and Mal and Adam do ground work."

"Feasible." Mal, of course.

"All right," Abby said. "But are you sure we want to use Harvey for this? Taking him out in public is always a risk, and we've been working him pretty hard lately."

"We have to," John said. "He's all we've got."

"Sad indeed," Mal murmured.

John stabbed two fingers at him. "Don't start with that shite, Barrymore. You have something to say about the way I do things?"

"All right, all right," Abby said again, quickly forestalling a real argument this time. "No fighting! That's our plan."

It was pointless to keep up the conversation after that. There was too much to do before the operation began, and the agents scattered.

John pulled up satellite photographs of Daley Plaza and the surrounding area. Recent pictures showed only the first days of the protests, but it was easy to place the stage and the protestors' encampment based on news footage. Mal and Abby went to the basement to check on Scott and prepare some equipment.

Adam was there, fiddling with something on the workbench. He grunted as Abby filled him in on the plan and began opening cabinets and drawers. He didn't seem inclined to talk, and Abby and Mal left him to it.

Scott was still unconscious. His color was better, but he barely twitched when Mal touched him. "I dislike the idea of leaving him unattended," he said frankly. "This is hardly a normal condition, and if he recovers while we're all gone, he'll have freedom of the office."

"We need a babysitter." Abby sighed and massaged her forehead. A knot of pain was beginning to form over her right eye. "And I don't think we can leave any of us four behind, either. Either we lock him up or we call in reserves, and we don't have any."

"Perhaps Dummy," Mal said, peeling back one of Scott's eyelids to examine the pupil. "He is also quite capable with emergency medical treatment, which may be helpful. I suspect that if Mr. Scott remains asleep much longer, we'll have to administer an IV or hand him over to a hospital."

Abby's stomach dropped at that. "But if we turn him over, he might wake up and tell someone about ..." She cut herself short, but the thought had already escaped half-formed.

"Mm." Mal let the eyelid droop back into place. "Better for us if he never awakens, perhaps."

She turned away from him and wrapped her good hand into the fabric of her sweater so he wouldn't see the fingers clenching. "Mal, we've been over this."

"We have. But have not yet found a solution."

"Babysitter," she said firmly. "I'll call Mary again and see if her family will loan us Dummy for the evening. We can figure the rest out after tonight. Okay?"

She didn't wait for him to respond, brushing past him through the dividing door and reentering Adam's half of the basement. The microscope was still sitting on the workbench, and a box of labeled slides sat next to it. One of them contained only a tell-tale wisp of selkie fur. Just yesterday, Adam had been showing her son how to prep that slide.

And now today, she was involved in yet another dangerous mess. Jimmy wasn't going to be happy about this.

She threw a glance at the clock. Only a couple of hours to go. This really wasn't the best way to go about an operation, but lately it seemed like they'd been flying by the seat of their pants a lot of the time. If she wanted to call her son, she'd better do it now.

The phone rang several times before picking up. "Yeah?" Jimmy said.

"Hey, honey."

"Oh, great, what's happening now? Did someone die?"

He was getting too used to this stuff, she thought. "No, everything's fine. But I'm going to be home late, okay? Something's come up. Will you be all right for dinner?"

"Yeah, fine. What came up? Is this about the wolf dude in the basement?"

"Coyote. And not really." Abby hesitated. But if she was going to have a good relationship with her son, honesty was key. Or so multiple therapists had told her. "We may have found the person who's responsible for all these attacks. We're going to be doing some reconnaissance, that's all."

"Mom?"

"Yes?"

"Can I talk to Sawyer?"

She almost dropped the phone. "What?"

"Can I talk to Sawyer?" he repeated with exaggerated patience. "I just want to ask him a couple questions."

"Why?"

"What, don't you trust me?" His tone took on an air of hurt. It was obviously feigned, but did its job anyway: his mother felt guilty enough to take the question seriously. "Look, if you're going to be late, I want to make sure he's not trying to fuck with you or something."

"Jimmy. Language."

He sighed. "Whatever. Look, Mom, can I talk to him? Or do you *not* trust me?"

For a moment, Abby badly wanted to swear herself. Then she sighed, said "One minute" and went looking for her coworker. Whatever Jimmy was after, it wasn't worth getting into a trust argument over, and John would be able to tell her what he'd said anyway.

She found John in the library, digging some ammunition reserves out of their hiding place in a hollowed-out encyclopedia set. "Jimmy wants to talk to you," she said. Then she tossed him the phone and walked away, knowing that if she stayed she'd try to eavesdrop.

With her phone occupied, she went to borrow Mal's to call for Dummy, but Mal had disappeared. The only thing he'd left behind was the little brown book with the frog bookmark. Sighing, Abby leaned against her desk. Dummy's hand was still sitting there, twiddling its lone thumb. She tapped it on the palm to get its owner's attention before using the office phone to call Mary's aunt's house.

It took a little persuading to get the rest of Dummy to come down to the office. The big mute had been attached to Mary for all of the girl's life, and since there was no chance of Mary coming along to help babysit a werecoyote, he was reluctant to go anywhere. Eventually the psychic herself, relaying Dummy's part of the conversation to Abby, chipped in her two cents and asked him to do it. "I'll be okay," she promised, her voice only wavering a bit. "Abby said she didn't want us to be part of this, right? If she's asking now, it *has* to be bad."

Harsh but true. Dummy promised he would be on his way, and Abby hung up with the distinct impression that she'd stepped in something nasty.

Mal still wasn't back. Frowning, she picked up his little book and began to leaf through it. He'd been acting strange lately, even for Mal...

The book itself seemed to be a collection of English poetry, with the frog bookmark holding the line between Robert Browning and Thomas Burke. Burke's offering was a poem headed "Of Inaccessible Beauty," but Abby's eye was drawn to the Browning. It was titled "The Laboratory—L'Ancien Regime."

Now that I, tying thy glass mask tightly,
May gaze thro' these faint smokes curling whitely,

As thou pliest thy trade in this devil's-smithy—
Which is the poison to poison her, prithee?

"Cheerful stuff, Mal," Abby murmured. When the tall man had first mentioned "l'ancien regime," she'd imagined something about history or the ancient world. This, though, made her skin crawl.

The poem began with a woman talking about how her former lover and his new lady were enjoying her misery, and her anticipating a counterattack against the people that wronged her. But the further she went, the more unhinged she seemed to become. More names were added to the list of people to kill, seemingly for the crime of being attractive or annoying her. *Let death be felt, and the proof remain,* Mal had said. She'd thought he was talking about the execution of a criminal, not *murder.* Which was what it was, no matter how righteous this woman thought she was. Even for Mal, this was dark.

Anger coiled in her gut as she dropped the book. What was he thinking when he quoted this crap at her? That things weren't as morally cut-and-dried as she'd like them to be? That, oh my God, she might be walking a fine line? She knew that. She'd known it since her first kill went into the salt.

Bastard. She wanted to punch him.

With an effort, she pulled herself together and took a deep breath. Now was very much not the time to pick fights or let herself get worked up over imagined insults.

Mal came back a few minutes later, carrying several books. Apparently he'd been hunting through the library for more on fairy magic. Nothing in the books provided any advice on what they were facing, but paging through them killed some time and settled Abby's temper.

All too soon, Dummy had arrived and it was time to get ready. John returned her phone and made a noncommittal grunting noise when she asked him what Jimmy had wanted to talk to him about. "Guy stuff," he added eventually.

"Guy stuff?" she asked.

"Lad stuff, really." He shrugged one shoulder. "He doesn't like me an' he wanted to be sure I knew it. He still in therapy?"

"Both of us are, on and off. Do you think he's a danger to anyone?"

That got half a laugh from John. "Not much chance. I remember being that age—hated everyone and wanted 'em all dead. But him, he's spooked now. He'll hold his peace for a bit."

"Good." It surprised Abby to hear herself say the word. But if Jimmy was scared, well, Abby was scared too. It was part of human nature to be scared by scary things. She would make it up to him later.

"Thanks," she added as she headed for the equipment cabinet. "I mean it."

John said something, but his words were lost in the clanging of metal as she pried open the bent cabinet door, and before she could ask him to repeat them he had turned and disappeared into the other half of the basement.

...

Equipment was more important than ever. Not only were the agents setting out on a potentially dangerous operation, but they were launching that operation in a public place. If they weren't careful they could be arrested, and if that happened, their whole agency would be in jeopardy.

Abby went back to the Christmas sweater. The bulky knit concealed a money belt that carried emergency cash, her phone, and a small Taser. Fleece-lined tights under jeans provided some cushioning in case she fell, and her pockets and purse were filled with useful items that most people wouldn't find suspicious: a metal pen (good for what Adam called "a shank-mergency"), a disposable camera, a necklace of beads strung on deceptively thin-looking steel wire, and a spray bottle of perfume that contained water, alcohol, rose oil and capsaicin.

The perfume had been another of Adam's innovations. The best pepper sprays were restricted in Illinois, but some of the world's hottest peppers could still be bought online for a couple of dollars each. Adam had ordered ghost-pepper and scorpion-pepper seeds, cultivated several windowbox crops that caused serious angina in the neighborhood squirrel population, and distilled a capsaicin solution custom-tailored to hospitalize an attacker.

He could have bought pure capsaicin crystals for the mix, but his way was cheaper and left less of a paper trail. Or so he said. Abby privately thought he'd just wanted an excuse to play with chemicals.

The rest of the team was kitted out for inconspicuousness. John had added a woolen stocking cap and scarf to his parka, and if you didn't notice the lines around his eyes he might have been a college student. The illusion was somewhat spoiled by knowing what lay underneath the coat: John would join a golf tournament before he gave up his Desert Eagle.

Mal had more trouble. The clothes were perfect—chinos and a rumpled long-sleeved T-shirt with scuffed snow boots and a heavy wool coat, all pulling together to make him look like a slightly lost geography teacher. The look was completed by a Lincoln Park High School backpack. Unfortunately, nothing could take the starch out of his personality.

To avoid being noticed, they went in two separate cars. Abby took her Camry, once again with freshly-swapped license plates, and brought Harvey with her in a diaper bag. John, Adam and Mal followed a few minutes behind in John's Saturn. They would rendezvous later, at the plaza, but for now it was just Abby and the silent genie. She half expected one or both of the men to call her, but her phone remained silent, and she drove quietly into the night.

Chapter Seventeen

Daley Plaza glowed. A dozen floodlights ringed the square and the dais, their high beams bouncing off the glass of the buildings and fracturing the central sculpture's shadow into thin, overlapping shards. The crowds gathered around the sculpture were touched with color where the light hit them, and with people jammed-shoulder-to-shoulder their shadows blended until the colors stood out against heavy darkness.

On the very edge of the plaza were yellow-painted riot barriers, and at the barriers were cops. A solid ring of them surrounded the area, facing outward and watching the passersby warily. A few were on horseback, and Abby caught herself looking hopefully for the friendly policeman with the blood bay horse. No sign of him.

"Are they searching people?" John said softly. Abby followed his gaze. There was only one entry point to the rally, and it was lined with cops. Several pairs of officers were methodically checking everyone who entered, opening bags and patting down coats. "Is this legal?" he whispered to Abby. "I thought you lot were land of the free, home of the brave and all that."

"Well, sometimes they go through bags at Navy Pier or the museum campus. But since this is technically a political event, who knows?" Abby shrugged. "I guess they're afraid someone might bring in a gun. But there's a lot more of them than I ever imagined."

As they watched, a policeman opened a young woman's backpack and rifled through it. The bag was crammed with art supplies of all kinds, and it took the policeman only a moment or two to find a craft knife tucked into the bottom. He shook his head and gestured to another officer, who gently but firmly took the surprised young woman by the arm and escorted her around the side of the plaza and out of view. The woman looked familiar, but by the time Abby turned her head she was gone.

None of the agents bothered to say it: this was bad news for them. Only Abby was supposed to enter the plaza, but she had to do it while carrying Harvey. And while a genie wasn't technically a weapon, none of them could imagine those worried-looking cops taking a look at a jar full of mysterious glowing mist and not wanting to ask some questions. If they formally arrested her they'd discover Abby's priors, and then it'd be straight to the police station while they asked a lot of questions about what it was she did for a living and what exactly was in that jar.

"Maybe Harvey can scrub them," Abby suggested. There was a snort from her bag.

"What, twenty-plus super-alert cops in the open air, with hundreds of witnesses to them being attacked by a strange amnesia-causing gas cloud? Brilliant, Holmes. Totally not suspicious at all."

"Harvey, if you have any useful suggestions, I'd love to hear them. If you're just going to be rude, maybe we should install that air purifier Adam keeps asking for." The bag just made a "hmph" noise and subsided into silence.

"You know ..." John had his arms crossed and was staring up at the sky, seemingly addressing himself to the constellation of Cygnus. "I thought this might happen."

"How helpful of you to inform us so promptly," Mal said. "I take it you also intend to favor us with a solution?"

Even for Mal, that was dry, and John was taken aback. "Well, yah," he said, shooting Mal a brief glare. "But I didn't bring it up because you lot aren't going to like it very much. Back this way."

He led them back to the parking lot and, with a flourish, unlocked the Saturn's trunk. There was a person in it. A very familiar, disgruntled-looking person, the green tips of his hair poking out from under his camouflage knit cap.

Words failed Abby for a second or two. John, apparently sensing that it wasn't going to last long, quickly jumped into the gap.

"Look, he asked to come, and he's old enough to get involved. And I thought, well, we might need an extra body, just in case it all went to hell like it usually does."

Her breath came back in a rush, and with it came the anger. "Jonathan Moshe Sawyer," she said, and the words were exactly as serious as they hadn't been before. "Did you drag my son into an operation again? By *putting him in the trunk?*"

"Hey!" Jimmy interjected, sitting up and glowering. "I didn't get dragged anywhere, all right? You need to stop treating me like a kid!"

"Jimmy, it's too dangerous—"

"More dangerous than handing me over to a freaking monster? Or him?" John yelped in protest, and Jimmy rolled his eyes. "Accept it, dude. You're an international manhunt waiting to happen. Look, Mom, if you're going to go get yourself killed—whatever. But what's gonna happen to me and Dad and Diana if you guys don't win? We're screwed. Those guys are going to freaking *kill* us. I don't know about you, but I like being alive! And do you think Diana is gonna know what to do when monsters come after her? Or her kids?"

It would've been nice to lose her temper. Shout, scream, tell everyone exactly what was on her mind and what they could do with their arguments. But she couldn't, because her son (and her coworker, who was going to be getting salt in his coffee for a very long time) had a point or two. She stamped firmly on her petty impulses and thought about the weight of the jar in her bag.

"All right, John," she said. "What are you thinking?"

· · ·

The cop at the barrier was one of the tallest people Abby had ever seen. Rain cascaded off his hat brim and plastic poncho but clung to his skin, which was as dark as oil with the bright lights behind him. Jimmy was beside her, tense as a guitar string and almost vibrating with nervousness, but Abby put a hand on his shoulder and gave him a squeeze as they approached the officer. "He's just doing his job," she whispered. "Like we are. Don't be rude and everything will be fine."

"Bag, please," said the cop. With him between them and the worst of the light, Abby could see his features clearly for the first time. He looked faintly embarrassed.

"Sure, no problem." Abby unslung her purse and held it out. She swayed, and Jimmy steadied her.

The officer looked up from her bag. "Ma'am, are you intoxicated?"

"No, it's just my vertigo." She gave him a self-deprecating smile. "You know, you get to be a certain age and things don't work as well as they used to."

"All right." He ran his gaze over her but didn't seem to spot any obvious red flags. Another win for the Christmas sweater. "Are you sure you want to be going in there?" he added after a moment as he opened her purse. "It's going to be a pretty tight squeeze. People are worked up."

"I'm sure," Abby said honestly. "This is such an important cause. Right, honey?"

Jimmy jumped as he was addressed. "Uh, yeah," he said when she prodded him. "Sure."

That got a chuckle from the cop. "My kid's just the same. All right, go ahead." He handed the purse back and waved the two of them forward. "Be careful."

"Thanks, officer," Abby murmured. As they moved past him, feet slipping just a little on the wet pavement, the blaze of lights grew brighter.

She looked into the crowd and immediately regretted it. This close, the contrasts were even deeper: the campaigners, protestors, political activists, news reporters, homeless people and dozens of others were so closely packed that their touches of color against the shadow made her think of life arising from the primordial ooze. The lights were bright enough to dazzle her, but she couldn't help following their beams as they traced across the mass and picked out points. If she concentrated, she thought she could see the individual photons, cutting through something that wasn't so much a thing as an absence of a thing. That's all darkness was, not a power or a force but just a place where something wasn't. And now the scene was worse, because the floating heads and shoulders and arms carrying placards weren't connected to anything, just pieces of disjointed humanity that could only remind her that there was a horrible logic to the world. Everything she saw, everything she felt and touched, was nothing. There was no life, just a collection of atoms in a certain pattern. No life. No soul. No God.

She blinked and paused. "Harvey," she said softly, "cut it out."

You're no fun, said a voice in her head, but the dark thoughts eased back. She blinked hard and watched the world recover some of its shades of gray.

"Mom?" Jimmy whispered beside her. "Mom, your eyes are kind of yellow."

"How obvious is it?"

"They're *yellow.* They look like badass contacts, but still."

"Sorry about that, hon. Harvey was messing with me." She pulled down the brim of her cap as the world wavered again. Having a genie riding along inside her head was turning out to be a strange experience. "You may have to steer me," she added softly. "I'm starting to have trouble seeing straight."

"You know, most people my age just have to worry about their parents giving them curfew," Jimmy said as he gingerly took her arm again. "Not this …whatever."

Abby huffed out a laugh. "That's because those parents aren't as cool as me," she said. That got a sarcastic laugh from Jimmy. "What? I'm not cool?"

"Cool parents don't exist." He pulled her to the side as a group of twentysomethings went hurrying past, following a man who was holding up his iPhone like a beacon. They were into the edges of the crowd now.

"But I kill monsters," she pointed out. "Isn't that cool?"

"Maybe if you got more money for it. Dad found out we were shopping at Salvation Army and said he was worried you couldn't handle stuff."

Abby waited for another surge of worry and frustration, but felt only a small hollowness in her stomach. Maybe the parts of her brain that normally generated those emotions were currently occupied by Harvey and too busy to be worried. She hoped so. Being afraid was tiring.

She was getting light-headed. John had carried Harvey in his head once before, and he'd lasted almost twenty minutes before showing any signs of distress. How did he handle it so easily?

He doesn't, really, Harvey's voice informed her. *But on Sawyer, it's just harder to notice.* And while he was communicating in a voice that really didn't make any actual sound, Abby somehow got the impression that he was rolling his eyes.

And to think she'd been worried about bad behavior from the *young* agents.

"Mom?"

"What?" she said as she looked up. Jimmy's face swam into view, his expression strangely contorted.

"Mom, you look sick. Do you want me to, uh, take over?"

She shook her head. "No. No, not yet. I know how to do this, okay? I just need to get closer."

Jimmy looked like he wasn't buying it, but he didn't say anything else. Instead he took her arm again and led her forward.

The crowd was so thick that they had to shoulder their way through. There had to be thousands of people in the plaza, all packed tightly together as they pushed to reach closer to the stage. A man Abby didn't recognize was giving a speech. She pushed through the rising haze to pick out some of the words: something about pulling together and making a better city in the new year. She could support that.

Of course you do, Harvey drawled. Every word sent a fresh knife of pain through her head. *Mom.*

If I was your mother, you'd be in big trouble, she thought back.

It was almost impossible to move now. A large contingent of twentysomethings in black hoodies and Guy Fawkes masks were having a loud discussion near the stage, elbowing anyone who got too close and vetting each others' placards. Several Black November protesters, their home-printed organization T-shirts partially obscured by reflective vests, had taken up regular positions around the dais and were listening intently to the speech. One appeared to be livetweeting it. Curious rubberneckers mixed with hardcore political activists, tourists, food vendors, concerned parents, skeptics, and other variations on the theme of human curiosity.

Abby checked her watch. The speaker on the dais was beginning to wind down (the words "so we can continue to move forward" had been used) and, with any luck, Carter would be prompt. Then they could have Harvey do his thing, get some information, and go home.

Unless Sascha Carter really was their target. Then what would they do?

You know, I can hear you, Harvey told her. She loudly thought a word that hadn't passed her lips in fifteen years and was rewarded with momentary silence from her mental passenger.

What would they do? She remembered John's dumbstruck expression, and she sympathized. What could someone like her or John or Mal do if a powerful public figure was slaughtering sorcerers for their own gain? Their chain of reasoning only worked if you accepted the existence of magic, and all of their evidence had been acquired illegally. The idea of making their case before a judge was almost funny, in a demented sort of way, but she couldn't help her thoughts bending that way. How else do you take down a politician?

Well, there was the other option. But though the shades of Lee Harvey Oswald and Gavrilo Princip would probably approve, Abby still balked at political assassination. More risks to negotiate, more planning, more possibility that they'd be caught. And it was easier to wear the label of agent than assassin. Must've been the Catholicism talking.

A stir in the crowd broke through her thoughts. The speaker had flung out one arm and was stirring up the listeners, a broad right-to-the-back-row smile on his face. "But we're going to get through this!" he shouted exuberantly. "We're going to make this work! Chicago is a city of warm hearts and strong arms, and anyone who underestimates the power of this city and its people is in for a big surprise! *We are strong! We will not give up!*"

His next words were drowned out by the crowd. People shouted, applauded, stamped and clapped, making Abby sway as the wall of sound pressed in on her. Jimmy's grip on her arm tightened. "Mom, c'mon!" he shouted in her ear, barely making himself heard over the tumult.

"There's someone else here who knows!" the man was saying. "She's been with us since this started! She's overcome so much already, and she's not going to stop until every child in this city is safe to sleep in their own beds! Ladies and gentlemen, mothers and fathers of the Windy City—District Attorney Sascha Carter!"

The cheering rose to a fever pitch as the lights tilted, focusing on the ramp next to the dais. A small figure in a black wheelchair was rolling herself up the incline. As the light touched her, there was a flash of bright red that lit up in Abby's enhanced vision like a supernova. She flinched and ducked her head, blinking tears away.

The shouting had reached the point where it wasn't sound any more, more like a tidal wave rolling over them all. Carter reached the center stage and turned neatly to face the crowd, giving them a broad, grateful smile, and if anything the cheers got louder.

A whisper of thought from Harvey. *They're in love with her.*

Looking at her through watering eyes, Abby could see it. Sascha Dolan Carter, with the lights shining on her, was beautiful. She was barely five feet tall and perched in her wheelchair like some kind of rare butterfly: elegant and unmistakably delicate. Her creamy white skin covered slim, almost sticklike limbs, and her bright forest-green eyes seemed too large for her face. She wore a neatly-tailored, professional suit in ash-gray, but the businesslike effect of it was offset by the masses of curly, cherrywood-red hair flowing loose over her shoulders.

She held up her hands for silence, but the din took almost two minutes to subside. Cameras set up at the edge of the stage snapped on, projecting her image onto a massive screen behind her. As they watched, her smile faded.

"Thank you," she said softly, her voice echoing around the plaza. "Thank you so much for being here and showing your support. But please, don't cheer. We're all here to focus on something so important to everyone. Everyone in this city, in America, in the world."

The hullabaloo started up again, but this time, they quieted down when she gestured for silence. She tucked a curly strand of hair behind her ear and smiled out at the crowd.

"Nobody expected Black November. We've been faced with something that none of us planned for, because we never wanted believe that somebody could be that twisted. Thousands of our children were in danger, all because of something that no normal, loving parent would ever imagine.

"We've been told that there were no fatalities. But who's telling us? Government agencies. News bureaus. People with an agenda." There was a hitch in her voice. "I don't want to believe that we're being lied to. I hope we're not. But whether we're hearing the truth or not, *our* truth is that we have to protect our families. We need to do everything we can to keep ourselves and our loved ones safe. Because if they can come into our homes and take our children out of their beds, what's going to stop them doing it again?"

This time, when the crowd applauded, she didn't silence them. She looked down and mopped her eyes quickly, smearing her mascara.

Abby's heart wrenched even as her head gave another warning throb. Despite her immaculate makeup, Carter looked like hell: this close to the big screen, they could clearly seen the signs of dark circles under her eyes and deepening lines in the folds of her cheeks. She seemed weighed down by her responsibilities.

"It's almost a new year," Carter continued, leaning forward in her chair. "We need to make it a good one. I promise you—and you can write this down, put it on YouTube, whatever you like to hold me to it, because *I promise you*— that I will fight to make sure it will never happen again. Not here. Not to anyone. Ever."

The last word was almost a whisper into the microphone, but the plaza exploded again. The sudden press of sound was too much on Abby's aching head; she staggered and Jimmy clutched her arm and babbled something. Abby couldn't hear what he was saying, though. The world through her eyes was turning red.

Harvey's words, when they came, seemed to arrive through a thick layer of cloth. *Uh, hey, I don't want to start a fight or anything, but it's starting to look really bad in here and I'm having trouble focusing. Marquise, you're cracking up.*

"Don't you think I know that?" she hissed. "Jimmy. It's time."

His grip was bruise-tight on her arm as he paled at the words. "Mom, don't!" he said, but it was too late. Abby breathed out a great cloud of steam, and spread out on the wisps of breath came the genie.

He swirled into the air, mixing expertly with the fog and the steam from the grates, his yellow eyes reduced to mere sparks that were barely visible in the bright glow from the high-beams. Even Abby and Jimmy could barely follow his progress as he snaked through the air, riding the brisk wind and wrapping himself around the struts of the dais. One more gust and he was at his target.

The crowd's cheering was slashed through by a squeal of electronics. Sparks flickered as one, two, three, four of the huge floodlights exploded, showering the crowd with broken plastic and bits of burning wire. Cables detached, smoke filled the air as fuses blew, and the massive screen drooped as one of its supporting guy ropes was snapped by a falling microphone. Carter ducked and covered her head. The live feed cut.

Screams erupted and the crowd surged. Abby and Jimmy were pulled away from each other, Jimmy yelling and waving for his mother, Abby still half-blind. Someone slammed hard into her right side and she yelped as pain flared through her arm and shoulder.

"Please! Stop!" Carter was yelling, but she could barely be heard above the crowd. Abby reeled as someone crashed hard into her back, almost throwing her to the ground. "Please, don't panic! It's going to be okay!" Carter shouted. Abby hoped that the other woman was right.

Someone screamed, someone else let out an exclamation in a language Abby couldn't place, and the stage lit up like a sunset as the biggest speaker erupted into flames. Silhouetted against the leaping orange glow was Sascha Carter, standing in front of her wheelchair and supporting herself with the microphone stand. She was clinging to it, but she was still standing, and tears were streaming down her cheeks. Her lips were moving, but it was impossible to tell what she was saying. With the flames behind her, she might have been an ancient goddess. Her eyes were blazing green mirrors.

Abby wavered, but someone slid an arm around her shoulders. One glance over her shoulder showed her green hair and a camouflage jacket: Jimmy, with tear tracks on his cheeks. She squeezed his hand as tightly as she could.

Carter was still clinging to the microphone stand. As calm spread across the crowd again, she raised her voice. "Don't you see?" she shouted. "We can't be quiet any more! There's more here than we're being told! I won't rest until every child in this city is safe, and I don't care what I have to do to see that done! And if they think this—" She jerked her head towards the tangle of destroyed equipment "—is going to stop us, then they've got another think coming! *Are you with me?*"

They were.

Chapter Eighteen

Mal met them outside the barrier. Paramedics were everywhere, hastily tending to the dozen or so people seriously injured in the aborted riot. The cop who'd checked Abby's bag tried to wave her towards an ambulance, but she shook her head. "Just got hit by someone's elbow," she said. "Need to go home and lie down." Mal gently intercepted her and lent her an arm, which she gratefully leaned on. Her grip had left bruises on Jimmy's arm.

She moved in a daze, and it wasn't until cold concrete touched the backs of her legs that she realized she was seated on a curb. Mal knelt down next to her and peered into her eyes, watching her pupils in the light.

"How are you feeling?" he said. "Was it Harvey?"

"Yes, I—oh God!! We forgot Harvey!" She tried to get to her feet, but stumbled again and sat down hard on the curb.

"No, you didn't," Jimmy said as he crouched down next to her. "I'm right here." There was a familiar glow in his eyes. "And fucking hell, Marquise, did you see that? That's some spooky crap right there."

"What?" Abby managed get herself upright this time, leaning heavily on Mal. "Harvey, what are you doing? Get out of his head right now!"

"In public? With police all riled up after that shit went down?" Jimmy crossed his arms. "It's okay, Mom," he added in his own voice. "It feels weird, but it doesn't hurt. He's freaking out, though. It's like there's a bunch of bees bouncing around in my head."

Abby scrutinized Jimmy's face, looking for any signs of bulging veins or strange bruising, and found nothing. Yet.

"All right," she said finally. "But the second, the *second* you feel sick, I want you to give him back, okay?"

"Okay," Jimmy said. He shook himself and rubbed his eyes. "Mom, I think he really wants to talk to you. He's yelling and—" He swayed again. "Shut up! All right, all right, you asshole, one second! Mom, you should sit down again."

Well, that wasn't a good sign. With Mal's help, she lowered herself back onto the curb and folded her legs under her. "You too," she said. "You're going to start feeling sick in a minute. Trust me." She waited until Jimmy had plopped down next to her. "All right, Harvey. What the heck happened back there? Did you cause all that?"

"Are you shitting me?" Harvey hissed as the golden glow came back. "I wouldn't do that! You're lucky I even survived that fucking thing!" He leaned forward, slamming his fist into the curb. "Ow! Crap! I forgot how much it hurts to be physical. Incidentally, your son's brain is a nice comfy place to live. You should let me rent him more often."

"Harvey," Abby said. "Please. What happened to you?"

"I was traumatized, that's what!" He frowned exaggeratedly, clearly unused to facial expressions. "I didn't even know that was possible. Pain? I don't like it. It lingers. I definitely prefer boredom." Abby glared, and Harvey shook Jimmy's head. "Fine, fine, fine. Look. I zeroed in on her mind and boom." He made a little explosion gesture with his fingers, expanding them outwards and throwing in some jazz hands for good measure. "Hey, that's kinda fun."

Abby's eyes widened. "She attacked you?"

"No, not really. I don't think so, anyway. I tried to get into her head, but, well, boom." He made the gesture again. "There might be some kind of barrier there, but the real problem is cross-platform compatibility. I don't think her brain is wired like a human's, anyway. Though I can't guarantee anything because I got maybe point zero zero zero one seconds' worth of a look at its vague outline before kablooey! And when I got blown back, everything did. There was a wave of power from her, just ..." He shook Jimmy's head. "I've been around the block a few times. I mean, back when I had my first amphora the infant mortality rate was *hilarious*. But I've never, ever seen a mind that's shaped like that. Like a perfect energy conduit. I poked it, and the automatic backlash was insane. An immune response, almost."

"Great." Abby rubbed her aching face. "So she's not human? She had fairy eyes—I think, anyway. Could she be our killer?"

"In a wheelchair?" Harvey snorted at that. "That'd be a new one, sure. But I told you, Marquise, I only got a momentary look and even what I could see wasn't much. Sort of like how you can see the shape of a glass once you pour whiskey into it, but you can't tell how the whiskey tastes from the shape of it?"

Abby made a mental note of that. Harvey was their most powerful member, no question, and any kind of limitation that might apply to him needed to be remembered. The thought of a mind that automatically expelled the genie wasn't comforting.

"So definitely not human," she said, trying to focus on the upside. At least they'd discovered something new. "But, uh, to expand the metaphor, could you tell what kind of glass it was from the shape the whiskey made?"

Harvey shrugged awkwardly, moving Jimmy's shoulders separately like he was clicking pieces into place. "I don't know. The problem is that a lot of glasses are shaped the same. But she's probably not drinking Old Scotch Therianthrope 1887."

"Oh, good." One possible race down, only a few hundred or so to go. "What about sorcerer? Could she be a magic-user of any kind?"

"Couldn't tell you, Marquise. I was too busy having my atoms shredded." The eyes blinked and their glow faded. "Mom? Mom, my head hurts."

Abby's lips thinned. "All right, Harvey, you heard Jimmy. Out of there right now."

"To where, genius? Sawyer has my jar." Harvey glanced over Jimmy's shoulder. "Hey, where is Sawyer, anyway? He should be right here getting in my face for not grabbing Carter's social security number and blood type while I was in there."

Mal unslung his ridiculous backpack and, after a moment's rummaging, produced a zip-top plastic lunch bag. "Here," he said. "John is watching us from a distance. He must have been very unhappy when the fireworks began, so I dare say we'll see him shortly. In the meantime, if you would oblige?"

"Hell, no," Harvey sputtered. "What were you carrying in there? I don't want to wind up smelling like tuna."

The lunch bag was overturned. A pair of razor blades and a battery charger fell out.

"Kinky."

"*Harvey,*" Abby said again.

"Fine, fine."

Jimmy breathed out, and the glow went out of his eyes. Curls of gray smoke flowed from his nose and mouth, collecting in the air between them before drifting into the open lunch bag. The last thing to go were the two bobbing lights, one of which somehow managed to eyeball both Abb

"*Harvey,*" Abby said again.

y and Mal before following its brother into the bag. Jimmy slumped, rubbing his face.

"That was weird," he managed to say. "Mom, I hate your job."

"Me too, honey." She put her good arm around him and he didn't flinch too much, which counted as a win in her book. "Come on, let's get going. We can go home, but we're gonna sleep at the office, okay?"

"'Kay." Jimmy's head was resting on his knees. Abby tousled his sweat-dampened green hair before reaching for her phone and dialing John's number.

It went straight to voicemail. Abby ended the call, waited thirty seconds and redialed. Voicemail again. She glanced up at Mal, who was watching her curiously. "This is probably a stupid question, Mal, but do you think John forgot his phone today?"

"I doubt it." Mal turned to survey the building behind them. "He should be in the bookstore on the second floor there. That was the lookout point." A corner of his mouth twisted. "I don't see him."

A chill skated down Abby's spine. "He probably lost his phone or something," she said. Even she didn't believe it. John might be a little strange sometimes, but their phones were their lifelines. She would sooner bet on him losing his pants.

"Although," she added, clambering to her feet, "knowing our luck this past month, we probably shouldn't bank on it. I'll go check on him. Jimmy, stay here with Mal."

Mal frowned. "Abigail, you're not in fit condition. You should stay here while I investigate."

"I'm feeling better," she said. "Look, this is about Jimmy. I wouldn't be very good at watching his back if I stayed here with him while you went looking, okay? And he doesn't need to be involved in anything more, so I can't go check it out with him in tow. But I can do the looking. I'll bring Harvey with me in the bag, and he can brain-melt anyone who tries to hurt me." Jimmy and Mal both started to object, but she just grabbed the lunchbag of genie. *"No arguments.* Let's just get this over with so we can all go sleep. Okay?"

There was another protest from Jimmy, but Mal laid a hand on his shoulder. "I believe," Abby heard him say as she turned away, "that discretion is the better part of valor here."

Darn right, as far as Abby was concerned. Everything hurt, but she could walk without stumbling again and she was itching to do something. Sascha Carter might be one more dead end, and if she wasn't then their next course of action might not bear thinking about. Some women jog or box to get out their aggression and work through their issues; Abby was going to hunt down John and find out what he'd done now.

The nice thing about the Loop was that it had almost everything you might need. Restaurants, banks, department stores, art supply stores, video rentals, purse shops, framers, decorators, and a world-famous diamond district. If you wanted to spy on Daley Plaza without being noticed, though, the best way to do it was to get off the ground. That meant staking out the huge multi-level bookstore a block away, where a would-be secret agent could monitor activity from the second-floor cafe. At this time of year, a warm place to sit and watch couldn't be overvalued.

She relaxed as she moved into the bookstore. It was nice to be in the warm, but it was just as nice to be in a place with a lot of cover and crowded sightlines. It would be easy to lose a tail in a bookstore.

Up on the second floor was the cafe, with one bored barista and a glass display case of chocolate cake and biscotti. A handful of post-Christmas-sale shoppers were sitting around drinking coffee and reading their new books. Floor-to-ceiling glass windows showed a beautiful view of Daley Plaza, but nobody was looking at it. None of them were John.

Well, if he wasn't in the cafe, he had to be somewhere along the only wall that offered a view of the plaza. She glanced around, noting the sections that bordered the broad windows: Children's Literature, Self-Help and Biography. He wouldn't be hanging out in Children's Literature, because an unaccompanied man with an occasional worrisome odor wasn't going to be very popular there and would probably get the police called.

(They knew from experience, too. Creepy Ivan worked in a toy store for several months, and Mal had almost been arrested while checking in on him.)

Self-Help, on the other hand, was a perfect place for him to hide but would have caused an endless stream of sarcastic commentary and complaining over the phone. Abby headed for Biography.

No sign of him. She pulled out her own phone, dialing his number.

There! In the distance, somewhere along the opposite wall. The opening guitar lick of "I Ran (So Far Away)" was definitely coming from somewhere on that floor. Still holding the phone to her ear, she followed the sound. Out of Biography, through a stationery section, past trendy brick-walled restrooms until she finally ended up in Economics.

What the heck would John be doing in Economics?

The answer, it seemed, was nothing in particular. The ringing phone was lying on a shelf at eye-level, nestled neatly between two copies of *The General Theory of Employment, Interest and Money.* John Maynard Keynes' bemused smile was reflected on the plastic surface of the smartphone, apparently enjoying Abby's frustration.

"Oh, Christ," she said. She grabbed the phone off the shelf and pulled up its call history. The last outgoing call had been just around 6 PM, and it had gone to her: John confirming their rendezvous time before turning back to, as she now knew, grab Jimmy. Nothing since then. A handful of incoming calls, though, all of them from her number.

No. Wait. There was one call from a number she didn't recognize. It had come in a few minutes before seven, just about the time she and Jimmy had been heading into the crowd. John should have been in position and watching by the window, but someone called him and he... What? Headed back into Economics to take the call? Unlikely. He wasn't the type of person to just abandon an important job.

She selected the anomalous number and hit redial. It rang eight times before picking up.

"That was quicker than I expected," said a woman's voice. A chill ran down Abby's spine.

She cleared her throat, carefully rearranged her grip on the phone, and said "District Attorney Carter, I presume?"

"And not Dr. Livingston. You must be Mrs. Marquise."

Abby didn't answer. Her throat seemed to have seized up. The voice on the other end of the line was cool and collected, but it was also unmistakably the voice she'd heard in Daley Plaza not even an hour ago. Not this, please. Not the one person in the case that they couldn't touch.

"I take it you thought you were invisible," Carter continued. "Mrs. Marquise, I'm sorry to have to tell you this, but you aren't as quiet as you think you are. And you're certainly not the only ones in this city to know about things that go bump in the night... although it seems my approach is a little more nuanced than yours."

Abby finally found her voice. "And what is your approach, exactly?" she said, putting a sharp edge into her words. "Because if Richard Neill's death was your idea of subtle, I'll need to send you a dictionary."

"Neill died when his project went wrong," Carter said. "And if you're thinking of talking about motive or opportunity, don't bother. There's no court in the world that would listen to anything you have to say."

"Never mind the courts. We've got your group linked to the deaths of at least three amateur sorcerers, and I bet if we kept looking, we'll find more." Abby leaned against the bookshelf and prayed that she was saying the right thing. They didn't have a link, not really, but Sascha Carter couldn't know that. "If you know anything about us, you'll know that the sentence is death upon finding. Period."

"Yes, I know," the other woman said. "And it's disgusting. Don't you ever get tired of playing cowboy cop, Mrs. Marquise? You and your friends have been killing people for years, and yet you still haven't achieved anything. At what point do you get sick of blindly hating everything different from you?"

Abby bridled. "I'll stop hating it, as you put it, when it stops trying to kill me," she replied tightly. "Every single target is definitively linked to its crimes before we take any action. We're not crazy people shooting up the streets. We're taking care of a problem nobody pays any attention to."

"Don't be naïve, Mrs. Marquise, you're not Clint Eastwood. You don't understand how the world works. Aside from leaving behind a few dead fairies, what are you going to accomplish with your life? If you understood the finer points, like —"

But Abby had had enough. "*Finer points?*" she exploded. "Finer *points?* One week ago I shot a selkie who murdered two women for fun, and they were just the ones we knew of. Show me the finer point of that! Or how about the nuances of Richard Neill, Owen Petrovich, and Sarah Mulsey! Finer points? Their finer points were all over the *floor!*"

"All right, it was only an expression," Carter said. "And, yes, the finer points, so don't scream at me like a crazed housewife. But there's always a bigger picture."

"Which is it, a nuance or a bigger picture?" Abby said sourly. "Some crazed housewives can tell the difference."

"Never mind. Listen, I'll agree that occasional deaths are a problem. We do have to be practical. But this is all part of a plan, don't you see? With these sorcerers' help, I'm opening a path for something bigger and better. I know that's difficult for you to understand, but, well, eggs and omelet as the saying goes. Can you see that?"

Abby wanted very badly to rise to the bait. John would've, and possibly gotten some information out of her to boot. All Abby had was the plain truth, and it wasn't a precision tool.

"I don't know," she said. "But I do know that if you're sane, the idea of something bigger and better should scare you. There are a lot of things out there that're bigger than us, and believe me, no human wants to let any of them in."

"But I'm not human," Carter said coolly.

"That's not much of an excuse."

"It's not an excuse at all. I wield the elemental forces, Mrs. Marquise. I'm something nobody counted on."

"You're a sorcerer, or maybe a half-blood fairy." Abby's hands trembled as she spoke. Her heart was hammering, and for a moment she badly wanted the comforting softness of the pain pills. "Sorcerers aren't exempt from the law."

That got another sigh from Carter. "I'm sorry, Mrs. Marquise, but it's not my job to explain things to you. I may not be human, but that doesn't mean I'm not concerned about the fate of humanity. It's all part of the long game."

"It's never been a game," she said. "Where's John?"

Carter sighed once more. Abby was beginning to hate that sound. "Listen, I... I had hopes, all right? People are stupid, but I can save them from so much. I put up with your interfering, but maybe you can help me. I can create peace, real peace, if I just have a little more time. Don't you want to be a part of that? I mean, you're a mother, you must have some kind of protective instinct." A pause. "So what do you think?"

"I think you can go to hell."

"Of course you do." The pretense of cordiality dropped from Carter's voice, leaving a sharp coldness. "In that case, I think we'll have to agree to disagree."

"Kind of you. Where. Is. John?"

"That's none of your business, frankly. You kidnapped my brother and interfered with my plans, and that's not going to make me want to explain anything to you, is it?"

Abby lowered her voice. It was quiet enough in the stacks, but she still couldn't risk attracting the attention of someone who might feel the sudden, burning need for a copy of Adam Smith. "Do you want a trade? Leonard for John?"

There was silence from the other end of the line, followed by a soft exhale. "I wish," Carter said finally, "that you'd made me that offer forty-eight hours ago. Then we might have played ball. But time is running out, and this will be difficult enough to manage with substandard material. No, there's not going to be any trades. Tell Leo I'm thinking of him."

The phone went dead. Abby stared at it for a moment before dropping it back onto the stained workbench. Her whole body felt strange: shaken, off-kilter, like she'd been slapped in the face and the pain hadn't yet fully registered. She put a hand on the bench to steady herself as she dialed Mal.

"John's gone," she said. "Sascha Carter took him. I don't know how, and I don't know what she's planning, but I don't think we're going to get him back."

Chapter Nineteen

They were supposed to go back to the office, but somehow it didn't happen. Maybe none of them could face Dummy and his questions, or Lenny Scott and his sleeping silence. Abby went home, and the rest of them followed her.

It was the first time that any of them other than John had ever been in her house. Mal, glancing cautiously around her living room and trying not to touch anything, looked as if he'd been crudely pasted onto the wrong backdrop. He wasn't saying much.

He accepted her offer of coffee, but Adam declined. Being in an unfamiliar environment put him on his guard and he probably didn't need anything to be any more alert. She caught him looking through her family photo albums, but instead of telling him off, she just shrugged. No doubt they'd all have to clear out soon enough, and there was no point in starting a fight.

Jimmy retreated to his room. She knocked on the door, but stubborn silence greeted her. If she concentrated she could hear the rustle of clothes that told her he was still in there, but he didn't seem to be in the mood to talk. Not surprising. She left medical wipes and Band-Aids outside his door and called out to him whenever she passed—"Do you want coffee, honey?" "How about toast?"—but given the choice between breaking down the door and leaving him be, she let him have his space. She remembered all too well what it was like to be seventeen and scared.

The only cheerful one seemed to be Harvey. He'd done his job exactly as ordered and now he had a new environment to explore, one which he could later tease Abby about. Heaven for a curious genie.

"Hey, Marquise!" he called as she was rinsing out a coffee mug in the kitchen sink. "Nice vase. Can I have it?"

She frowned and turned around, not bothering to wipe her soapy hands. "I don't have any vases, Harvey. They just collect dust."

"Sure you do. There's this cool blue one with all the fishes on it."

"Harvey, that's my great-aunt's urn."

"So?"

"So someone's already in it. Weren't the ashes a tip-off?"

"I thought you were just bad at hiding your cocaine stash."

"You think you're clever, but you're not." The words came out before she could quite stop them. John said that a lot. Maybe because it was usually true. They weren't the smartest people when it came down to it.

What the hell were they supposed to do?

Something unfamiliar welled up in her throat. Not tears, she hoped. She'd sworn off tears a long time ago, though they still came at odd times when she didn't want them to. This was something else, something strange and forceful. She swallowed and put a hand to her throat, dripping dishwater and soapy bubbles down the front of her shirt.

They hadn't said much after her call. They'd all just followed her, like it was a given. Even Harvey. Being leader of the SSR meant that the genie went with the job, like the world's worst company perk, and even though John was the only one who could ever issue a direct order to him he had followed Abby home.

Of the humans, John been with the organization the longest. Ten years, easily, since he'd been recruited back when the Rev and his second-in-command, Oliver Kendrick, were running things. He'd been there when Mal joined, he'd been there when Adam came looking for work, and he'd been part of the group that voted on Abby's admittance.

He'd voted against her, she remembered. He later admitted that at the time, he'd thought she couldn't pull her weight. She'd disproved him.

John wasn't the smartest of them, and he wasn't the strongest, but more than any of them he lived the job. Nobody had elected him leader in the days after the Rev died and Kendrick left; they'd simply assumed he would be, and he'd gone along with it for reasons of his own.

He wasn't a very good leader in many ways. He was impulsive, abrasive, and frankly kind of annoying. But because he had nothing outside the work, you could always rely on him to back you up. John might not have actually liked any of them, but as far as Abby could tell, he tried to do right by them.

She turned off the sink and rested her wet hands against her forehead, enjoying the chill of the water against her skin. It had been a long, long couple of days, and she was starting to think she had an air-cooled brain. There had to be something they could do, no matter what.

They'd all followed her home like lost puppies. With John gone, they should have turned to Mal, but he seemed as stunned as the rest of them. Now the sum total of the active SSR was in her house, and a nice encouraging group they were: a gunsmith who lived in a basement, a medically-trained thespian of uncertain provenance, a genie stuck with them because he had nowhere else to go, and per Carter, a crazed housewife.

"Crazed housewife." The woman was a government official who could access all the records she needed. She probably knew about Abby's old drunk driving conviction, the attack in the alley, the divorce. She'd likely sent the fairies to kill Abby in the hospital. And in her expert opinion, Abby's life and accomplishments could be summed up as "crazed housewife."

Unable to hold back a growl, Abby whipped off her wet dishwashing gloves and flung them across the room. They hit the back door with a damp splat and slid to the linoleum, leaving a trail of soapy bubbles behind.

Sascha Carter had kidnapped John and was going to do God only knew what with him, and all they could do was sit around waiting to find out when his body turned up? Maybe that's what housewives did, unlike glamorous, intelligent, well-loved district attorneys who seemed so sure of themselves because never mind being a serial killer, you were sure you were doing the right thing, whatever that was—son of a bitch!

She was a housewife, all right. She was a housewife and a mother and a chubby blonde on the wrong side of thirty who hated swearing, went to church as often as she could, and wanted to have a better relationship with her son. She had also slapped a bogeyman in the face, gone toe-to-toe with a war zombie, repelled an evil spirit with only the power of faith, survived an attack by a hungry ghoul, chased down a murderous selkie and successfully navigated a nasty divorce despite a husband who was convinced she was insane and a lawyer who was probably a school of piranhas in a human suit.

Abby hadn't survived in the agency without learning a few tricks. She tried to think of herself as a good person, and Carter had made fun of that, but Carter didn't seem to realize that good didn't mean weak. Or stupid. Or nice.

"All right," she said to herself. "You can do this."

She had to.

"Hey!" she shouted! "Mal! Adam! Harvey! Get in here now!"

There was a general shuffling of feet and clinking of glasses and mugs. Adam was the first to emerge. He'd been in the spare bedroom, probably going through Abby's books, and from the way he jogged in place he was still full of nervous energy. Abby pointed at the kitchen table.

"Sit," she said. "And stop twitching, please." He sat.

Mal was next, carrying the lunch bag with Harvey streaming out of it. Abby held out her hand, and he put the bag into it.

"All right," she said. "Here's the situation. We're down to four active members, or three if we count the ones with bodies. John's been kidnapped by someone with more power and political influence than we'll ever have. Frankly, I'm surprised she hasn't used the hospital records to track us down here and have us arrested, but maybe she thinks we're not enough of a threat. She's wrong."

Mal sat down next to Adam. "I take it you have a plan?" he said.

"No. Not yet. But you guys are going to help me come up with one, and when we have it, we're going to cram it down Sascha Carter's throat."

Adam and Mal exchanged glances. "Uh, all right," Adam began cautiously. "So what do we do now?"

"First we assess what we have." She opened the lunch bag and looked Harvey in the eye. "Harvey, John is our leader. You're always the one who's linked to him. Do you know where he is?"

"Nope. I could probably triangulate if you took me around the entire city or something, but it's not an exact science. I mean, do you guys know which part of your brain is running your thought processes?"

"What if you possessed us? Can you find him that way?"

"And again with the nope. When I possess people, I can only work with what they already have. Enhance their natural gifts. Senses, that kind of thing."

Adam coughed. "What if he possessed Mary?"

Silence fell. It was a beautiful idea, in an awful sort of way. Mary was already powerful; her natural gifts, as Harvey had put it, were the ability to peer into peoples' thoughts. She'd already told Abby that John's mind was distinctive to her. If they got permission to put Harvey into her head, her abilities would be turned up to eleven. How much of the city could she scan? Would she even be powerful enough to get into Lenny Scott's head?

And that was the awful part. Having Harvey in her head for only ten minutes had been a nightmare for Abby. What it would do to a young psychic didn't bear imagining. Yet it wasn't just sad, semi-anonymous victims on the line this time—it was John. It was personal. That must make it different.

L'ancien regime. She could feel Mal's eyes on her.

"No," she said. "We've already involved her too much."

"In that case, we don't have any other options," Adam said bluntly. "We're not exactly swimming in personnel or equipment here, you know. Harvey is the only magic-user left on the premises, and he's not even technically a magic-user, just a parasite."

"Fuck you very much too," the genie grumbled. "Marquise, I say you and me ditch these losers and go solo. I can hijack the kid for a couple of hours. It'll be great!"

"I don't think so." She shook her head. "All right, Mary's off the table. Involving her with the bonepicker was bad enough ..."

And she trailed off. A thought had just begun to surface in her mind, gleaming in an enchanting sort of way, and she was almost afraid to approach the thought in case it decided to pop like a soap bubble. A thought, an idea, a psychic, a connection.

"Harvey," she said slowly. "Harvey, I think I know someone who might have information we could use. Can you possess the bonepicker?"

"I don't think you get the whole 'human' thing," he began, but stopped. "Wait a minute. It *is* human."

"Sort of. It's a little, uh, mutated."

"But if it's still got a human-shaped mind, then you bet your ass I can!" Harvey surged out of the lunch bag in a gleeful cloud. "Why the hell didn't any of you bozos think of this before? I can be the Incredible Hulk here!"

"NO," Adam, Mal, and Abby said together.

"Better make it just the brain," Abby added quickly. "We're trying to rescue John, Harv, not get him killed in a one-genie rampage."

"Spoilsport."

"That's me," she said. "All right, it's worth a shot. Let's get back to the office." She mopped her hands on a dishcloth. It had a picture of Santa Claus on it. "You guys get to the car. I'll be a minute."

The men, and asexual gaseous spirit, left. She shrugged into her coat, double-checked her cast and bandaging, and then knocked on Jimmy's door.

Silence. Of course.

"Jimmy," she said softly. "I'm going back to the office, okay? We might have a lead for finding John."

Silence again.

"I love you, honey. I don't want you to be in here by yourself. Do you want to come with us?"

Silence still. She could just make out his breathing, but nothing else.

"Please," she added. "Look, we're about to do something... well, pretty stupid. I don't want you to be here where someone could come after you."

"So don't do it," Jimmy said. His voice was hoarse, and he sounded like he'd been crying.

"I can't." Abby rested her head against the door, praying for help, or understanding, or something. "He might be killed."

"So you're gonna do something that might get me killed instead? Fine. Whatever." Something hit the wall, hard, and crashed to the ground with a clatter of plastic. Anything that heavy and plastic had to be expensive.

"Jimmy, it's not like that. This person is a *killer*. If we don't stop her, John could ..." She took a deep breath. "Please, honey."

"This shit is fucked up, Mom!" her son snarled. He yanked the door open so hard that the knob flew out of his grip and the door clashed hard against the wall. She took a step back, surprised and a little scared despite herself. Jimmy's eyes were red and his mouth was twisted into a grimace of grief. "You talk and talk and all that shit about wanting me to understand what you do 'cause you love me, but then you say you might get me killed! Wow! I'm really feeling the love here!"

She didn't have an answer for that. "It's just—"

"Just what? Just ruining my life? I didn't want to be part of this! This was my stupid luck because I got a fucking lunatic for a mom!"

"I wanted you safe!" she shouted. "I didn't *want* you to be part of this, just to understand! You were the one who decided you wanted to climb in the trunk!"

"'Cause I thought you were gonna *die!*"

They glared at each other. Jimmy dropped his gaze first, but it was a near thing.

"Look," Abby said quietly. "We can fight about this later, okay? Come back to the office. We can put you in the safe room. I'd rather have you angry at me than sitting here alone and ready for something to come after."

He nodded stiffly and stepped out of his room. "I hate you."

"I know."

・・・

Abby could have made the drive to the office in her sleep, which was good, because her thoughts were anywhere but on the road. Jimmy's stony silence from the other seat was a big part of it, but most of her was trying hard to focus on the task at hand.

She wasn't sure she could be the SSR's leader, even in a temporary capacity, but it seemed to be the job she was being handed. Now she was trying to think about what to do next: tactics, possible pitfalls, weapons and equipment. Another part of her was turning over the problem of John and Sascha Carter.

Sacrifice theory and political power. Neither of those explained what she might want John for. If it was just revenge for Scott, why would she refuse to make the trade? Even if Carter was indeed the one who put the geas on Scott—and a pretty vicious geas it was—it didn't make sense to Abby that the woman would prefer a single hostage over getting a valuable informant back.

No, there was still something they were missing, and she didn't like it.

Back at the office, she put them to work. First priority was equipment, and she sent Adam to check on what they had available. They were still severely depleted after the half-cocked raid at the museum the month before, but that couldn't be helped. Mal examined the sleeping Scott and changed his bandages. Dummy quickly explained in ASL that there had been no change.

Harvey she took down to the basement. The safe was in the smaller half, but after some consideration, she moved both the bottled nervous system and the boxed-up skeleton into the salt flats. If something went wrong and David Bonie got out of hand, the bare concrete and metal tubs could take a beating better than the equipment on Adam's side. Harvey's pickle jar had never turned up, but he'd willingly moved from the lunch bag to a spare Erlenmeyer flask with a thick rubber stopper. "Badass," he opined as he curled into it. "I feel like I should be on a table with a crazy guy cooking meth in me. Or maybe sitting next to a severed head. Where's Dummy when you need him?"

"Busy doing his job, like everyone else." Abby put the flask on the autopsy table. "Now relax, all right? You'll need to bring your A-game for this."

He scoffed. "Don't I always?"

"Yes, you do, but an hour ago you were telling me how bad Sascha Carter's brain was for you." She patted the side of the flask. "So take a few minutes and pull yourself together while I set this up."

She knelt and opened the safe. The lumpy gray mass inside the wine bottle vibrated slightly when the dim light of the basement fell on it, but other than that it didn't do anything. She double-checked the screw top on the bottle and gently picked it up.

"All right," she continued, setting the bottle down on the autopsy table. "Can you hear me?"

A tendril of gray poked out of the bottleneck. "If you can hear me," Abby said, "tap the side of the glass." The tendril did so. "Good. Now, I'm not going to hurt you. Mary wanted you kept safe, and I agreed with her. But we're going to try something to help one of our people, and if you can work with us on this, we'll take good care of you. You'll be able to sleep for as long as you like. Do you understand?"

The tendril tapped once more and retreated slightly. Abby aimed a frown at the Erlenmeyer flask. "Harvey?"

"I think he gets it," Harvey said. His mist was dribbling out of the flask again, and the yellow eyes were fixed on the wine bottle. "Dude. Wow. There's some heavy mojo in there. Can I jump him now? Can I, Marquise? Please? Just say the rhyme and I'm there."

"In a second." Abby mentally parsed out the lines she had come up with. "All right. My friend, I entreat you to take up your post, And possess you this dead thing for use as a host, But take care how you act in this unforeseen brain, And sever connection when I call you by name."

"No fair with the rules lawyering," Harvey complained. "Are you seriously trying to build in a safe word to make me disconnect? Do you really think I'm that bad?"

"Just being cautious," Abby said. "As the current leader, I'm going to keep all of us safe if at all possible. We don't know what it's like inside a zombie's head, let alone a war zombie. So do you accept the summons?"

Harvey spread out in what was, for him, a sigh. "All right, all right. I accept. But I'd really like some more interesting rhymes next time."

She smiled. "I'll have Mal write you a sestina."

"A what?"

"A really complicated... Never mind. How about a limerick?"

"How about no," the genie said. He gathered into a cloud above the wine bottle and then, before she could say anything, flowed into it.

Almost immediately, the bottle cracked. Abby ducked as it shattered, glass shards scattering across the autopsy table. The gray mass threw out strands like rubbery octopus legs as it scrambled towards the edge of the table. Inches from the lip, it spasmed and collapsed into a heap. Abby couldn't hold back a yelp as it sent more glass flying.

"Ha—" She bit down on the name, trying to keep herself from accidentally pulling the plug on the experiment. "Jesus Christ. Are you okay?"

The tangled mass didn't say anything. Of course it couldn't, since it didn't have any vocal cords, and she resisted the urge to slap her head as she remembered that. Now Harvey was in a body that she could barely communicate with.

After a moment's pause, the mass began to move with purpose. It slithered to the edge of the table, flopped onto the floor and shuddered. As it began to uncrumple itself Abby drew her Tomcat and flipped the safety off, just in case. It didn't seem about to pounce, but she'd been wrong before.

As she watched, gun ready, the tangles began to smooth themselves out. Soon there was some semblance of order: a central lump around the desiccated bulge of the heart, with four branching limbs and a twisted brain stem on top.

Wow.

She jumped. It wasn't so much a voice in her ear as a thought that inserted itself without permission. She kept the Tomcat trained on the twitching mass of nerve tissue. "Can you hear me?" she repeated.

Wow. Wow. I AM A GOD OF HELLFIRE.

"Talk to me," she said. "Are you in control in there?"

A rush of emotion flowed through her, hot and furious and gleeful all at once. Abby took another step back. "Okay," she said steadily. "You have five seconds to either answer me, or come out of there. Five... four... three ..."

The twitching nervous system lashed out with all four limbs and, gripping the edge of the autopsy table, pulled itself upright to crouch on the metal like a ropy gray spider. *I am*, said the voice. *I am. I am. And I can do this, Marquise. This is amazing. This is amazing.* Another wave of emotion, this one touched with what felt like awe. *Is this what it feels like to have a body? You lucky bitch. I never feel like this when I possess you people.*

"What about the bonepicker?" she pressed. "Is he resisting you?"

She.

"What?"

She. This body was female. You better tell Mary to rename it Bone Derek or something.

Abby wasn't sure why the information gave her pause. Maybe she just hadn't expected an eight-foot-tall construct of twisted bone spikes and bulging nerve tissue to be female. Or maybe it worried her that Harvey had thrown out the information so easily. "How do you know?" she said cautiously.

Are you kidding? The gray spider flipped over, bent backwards and crab-walked across the table. *I can sense everything. Bonepickers are incredible! Not much brain left, but what there is is cockroach-level tough.* That sounded more like Harvey, and Abby let herself relax a small fraction. *There's a couple of memories stored back here, ones it probably can't access or doesn't understand. Hah, even MARY couldn't grab these. She can't go deep enough.*

"What happened to it—her?"

The spider flexed its neuron tendrils as Harvey thought. *Lot of mixed-up images here. I think... bone cancer. Long time ago. Fast-growing cells, all getting out of control, perfect for someone who wants to make a mutant zombie out of the leftovers. Been passed around a lot, moving between collectors. Black market, very quiet. Seems you can piss a lot of people off if they know you're buying one of these. A fairy told her she was an expensive investment.*

"Jesus." Abby rested her hands on the edge of the autopsy table. "But is she resisting you? Are you scaring her?"

I don't think so. She just wants to go back to sleep.

Abby shook her head. She wished Harvey hadn't spoken. Turning the bonepicker from an "it" to a "she" in her mind had suddenly raised ethical questions she wasn't sure she should even be having. "Then let's get this over with," she said. "Start looking. Is there any information there about where Sascha Carter could be? Can you sense John?"

Well, let's find out.

The genie went quiet. Slowly, slowly, the strands of gray began to untwist from each other and coil together in different patterns. It was like watching a charmed snake swaying back and forth, winding itself into shapes that bled into each other and separated smoothly. Tendrils of nerves and withered muscle moving on their own, with none of the herky-jerkiness she had seen in the bonepicker.

Harvey was silent, but she could feel his concentration pressing in on her brain. He seemed to be straining with the effort and as the bonepicker's gray strands moved, the pressure intensified. Abby's vision started to blur.

Then, in an instant, the sensation vanished, The tendrils fell flat onto the table, flopping a little in seeming exhaustion. She thought she heard (felt?) two voices sigh in unison, but it was gone before she could even begin to focus on it.

"Are you okay?" she said. No response, just a tired wriggle of nerves. "Can you hear me?"

Silence. She took a pen out of her jacket pocket and carefully prodded the coil of bonepicker guts, but this time there wasn't even a twitch from it. The gray string had gone entirely limp.

She took a deep breath. "Harvey!"

The effect was immediate. The pile of nerves jerked as if electrocuted and began to tremble as mist flooded out of it. The eyes flickered into existence and immediately turned to Abby. They didn't look happy.

"What'd you do that for?" the genie demanded. "I was getting somewhere!"

"Were you? Because it looked to me like you were shorting out," Abby retorted. "And there's been enough of that already today. Are you all right?"

"I was until you cut me off," Harvey said sourly.

"Then why weren't you talking to me?"

The genie roiled in an angry cloud. "It's not like I can explain, can I? There aren't really words for what we're doing here. So why don't you get off my back and let me work!"

"Harvey," she said flatly. She hated to take this tack, but she didn't see what choice she had otherwise. "This is a new trick we're trying, and nobody knows what's going to happen. When you wouldn't respond to me, I got nervous. I wanted to make sure you were all right. After all, we're trying to find your host here."

It was hard to distinguish expressions on a creature made of mist, but the look Harvey shot Abby was pretty clearly lethal. "I can do this, Marquise, but not if you're gonna keep yanking my leash. Okay?"

• • •

Contrary to her grandfather's favorite fairy tales, Abby knew you can't squeeze blood from a stone. After half an hour of watching Harvey swoosh in and out of the bonepicker's brain, she was relieved by Mal. He was reading the poetry book again, though she couldn't tell which poem he was looking at. At least he didn't say a word about laboratories or regimes.

They traded off shifts throughout the night. The kitchen was out of coffee, which was probably a good thing since they were keyed-up enough without caffeine jitters. Abby went through the cupboards and found a half-empty container of instant lemonade, but after mixing it up she remembered that they hadn't finished it because it tasted like Pixy Stix and battery acid. She poured it out and curled up on the couch in the main office, trying not to think about anything.

Just before dawn, she was startled out of her doze by a hand tapping her shoulder. She blinked blearily and tried to focus. Eventually, the looming blue-and-white shape in front of her resolved itself into Dummy, who was proffering a glass of ice water and a granola bar.

"Lifesaver," she croaked as she accepted both. Dummy nodded and waited while she wolfed down the granola bar. "Any news?" she asked as she ate..

Dummy nodded and began to sign. *H-A-R-V-E-Y says for you to come. He has something.*

"Oh, thank God." She washed down the last mouthful and clambered to her feet. The room swayed, but her arm didn't hurt as much as she expected it to. Some of the swelling in her hand and wrist had eased, too, which was all to the good. She crunched the last ice cube between her teeth as she hurried down to the basement, Dummy trailing behind.

The bonepicker was lying quiet on the table. An outlying tendril or two fluttered occasionally, prodding the metal surface in a way that reminded Abby of someone tapping their fingers impatiently. Maybe she was bored. Could you be bored if you didn't have much of a brain to be bored with?

Harvey hovered over the table in a low fog. The bobbing lights of his eyes had dimmed somewhat, and his form was thin and wispy.

"Before you ask," he said, "no, I didn't find Sawyer." His voice was flat and reedy, as if his voice box had been damaged. Since he had even less of a voice box than the bonepicker did a brain, all Abby could guess was that it was a symptom of exhaustion. "And I want a raise. Actually, I just want a salary, period. And something classier than a pickle jar to live in. Maybe one of those bulb-shaped liquor bottles with the wax on it. And if you ever make me do this shit again, whoever's hosting me is going to spend the rest of their natural lives thinking they're a cud-chewing ruminant with perpetual indigestion. Got it?"

"I'll have to talk to the Director about a salary," Abby said. Since Harvey had no bills, food, rent or physical needs aside from a brain to run off, she had no idea what he would do with money, but now really wasn't the time to raise the issue. "What did you find?"

"Bunch of stuff. Turn your little recorder thingy on, I'm only saying this once." Abby did so. "Right. She can't confirm that Sascha Carter is the one who bought her or had her set up in the basement, 'cause she never met the boss in person. I showed her one of your memories of that tattooed sorcerer chick, though, and we got a hit. Her name's Silkwillow, and whoever she is, she's the mother of the queen."

Mal made a little noise at that and muttered something about tithes and hell. Abby ignored him. "The queen?" she repeated. "Were those the exact words? Because Neill's site claimed he was making magic for a dark queen."

"That's the one. Silkwillow only does what her darling daughter says, too, so at least you can have the satisfaction of knowing that hospital hit was ordered by the highest level of lowlife. What they want Sawyer for, no idea. There's definitely blood magic going on, though. That's what the funky tattoos mean—blood magic, however that's supposed to work."

"Blood magic ties in with the sacrifice theory. And political power?" Abby grimaced, her stomach feeling hollow at the thought. "You can't get much more power than an absolute monarch. If Sascha Carter is setting herself up as a queen, then a queen of what?"

"La belle dame sans merci," Mal said.

Harvey squinted at him. "The pretty dame without thank you?"

"Not precisely." Mal turned to Abby. "The old ways, Scott said. Grace and honor to the old ways. Do you recall what fairies were like in the old stories,

Abigail?"

"I do." She swallowed. "They had queens. Powerful, ruthless queens."

"Ones who were not averse to killing men for their own ends."

The hollow feeling intensified. "I know, I know," Abby said quickly. "But we can't count on old stories for a game plan. When I talked to her, she kept going on about nuances, better things, bringing peace, that kind of stuff. Fairy queens don't talk like that in the ballads."

"That depends," Mal said, "on whether or not she means *eternal* peace."

"All right!" Adam broke in. "Whatever she's doing or why she's doing it, who gives a shit? She's got one of our guys. What are we gonna do about it?"

"We're going to get him back," Abby said firmly. She refused to let herself imagine anything else. "Harvey," she continued, turning back to the genie. "You have the chance to do more than just save John's life. If we can find him we might find Sascha Carter. You can make or break this case. Is there anything you can tell us? Anything at all?"

She'd hit the right note. "Maybe," Harvey said slowly. "There's an image of a house in there. A street of houses, actually. They delivered her somewhere to show her off, but she was bundled up to hide the fact that they were, you know bringing in a giant spiky skeleton. There's some details, though."

"Share. Please."

"Do I have to? I'm tired."

"Harvey, if we solve this, I'll pay you a salary myself."

"Deal." A tendril of mist snaked in front of her eyes and the blurred, distorted image appeared in her mind. She grabbed a pencil and quickly made a sketch.

The drawing showed a large boxy house with enormous two-story windows, standing in the middle of a miniature grove of trees. A few more houses were visible on either side, some with For Sale signs in the windows. One, boarded up, appeared to be abandoned.

"Yeah, that's it," Harvey said, examining the drawing. "Definitely not in the city. Tons of trees, big lots everywhere."

Adam was unrolling a huge map of northern Illinois. "Sounds like the suburbs. Maybe even a separate town."

"She was picked up in Springfield," Harvey volunteered. "The drive took less than five hours by the sun."

Abby's eyebrows went up. "She could see the sun?"

"Felt it through the trunk lid. It was fall, they started after noon, and she has memories of feeling the warmth fade around the time they arrived at the house. Sun was going down when they got there. Ergo, less than five hours, give or take. Try to keep up, Marquise."

"How John puts up with you, I have no idea," Abby muttered. She didn't even feel bad for saying it. "Do we have any more details about the area? Tree types, street numbers, anything?"

"Tree types? Isn't Starczynski always bitching about how we're not actually *CSI*?"

"Not helpful, Harvey."

The genie replied with something sarcastic (what a shock), but Abby momentarily tuned him out. She was looking over the drawing she had made, trying to sort out the details of the information. "Lots of trees, five hours or less from Springfield. Were there a lot of houses for sale, Harvey?"

The cloud roiled as the genie thought. "Yeah. I mean, I don't know what's normal for humans, but she saw a bunch. And some broken-down lots."

"Economically depressed. Probably a small town." For Sale signs. The thought tickled her brain. "Wait a minute! Harvey, what did the For Sale signs say?"

"Uh. For Sale."

She rolled her eyes at that. Probably juvenile, but she was past caring. "Harvey, signs say more than that. If someone is selling a house, they probably have a realtor."

"And realtors," Mal added, "have territories. And numbers."

Abby shot him a quick smile over her shoulder. Her hands were trembling, but as she watched the genie think, a curious feeling of elation was beginning to kindle in her stomach. The world was shifting around her as thoughts and perceptions reordered themselves and one more beautiful, bright little notion made itself known.

The world held its breath. Then Harvey let out a gusty sigh and settled onto the table, turning into a kind of sulky fog. "224-555-0161."

Adam dived for the computer and began to type hurriedly, the keys rattling like machine-gun fire. It took only seconds for him to pull up the realtor's home page. "Bingo. Farrell Brothers of Waukegan, Illinois," he said. "I love the Internet."

Abby quickly located Waukegan on the map. It was well within the plotted circle.

"Sale listings," Mal said quickly. "There should be photographs."

It took Adam only a couple of minutes to locate a photo of a house that looked very much like one from the drawing. The house next to it, the one the bonepicker had been taken to, was just visible on the edge of the image.

"All the features check out," he reported. "And when you look at the satellite maps, it fits the layout of the neighborhood. I think we have our house."

Abby shook her head as she stared at the screen. "Let's double-check. Search Carter's name and the town together. If she was D.A. at the time, there might be an article about the sale."

"No problem," he said, throwing a rare smile over his shoulder. It had a mirthless, gleeful quality to it. "Oh, hey, look at this! What a shocker. Puff piece from eighteen months ago. District Attorney Sascha Carter, 39, loves Waukegan because it reminds her of 'the rolling green hills of her husband's native Ireland'—cute."

Leaning forward, Abby put her hands on the back of the chair. "All right," she said. "Knowing is half the battle." Adam stifled a laugh. "I think I know how this is going to go. Mal, I want you to put out a new message to the boards. We have some information that might buy us help. Adam, I'm going to need you to get ready. If you're hiding anything really good, now's the time to bring it out."

Cats could look at kings, and crazed housewives could go up against queens. Not just could, but should. She remembered the look on Terra Burns's face when she talked about her onetime guardian's death: that was the legacy a would-be queen was leaving behind her.

Abby had joined the SSR not out of hate, but because a ghoul decided she would make a good dinner. Maybe vampires were lovely people at home, but Abby had only met two, and both of them had had lists of victims as long as her arm. You don't hate something like that because of what it's called or what it looks like. You hate that there are things in life that are willing to do that to living, breathing creatures. Cats could look, and housewives could do what needed doing. If they didn't, who would?

It was all in the planning. She wrote out the message for Mal and, pulling herself up by her bootstraps, followed Adam down to the armory.

Chapter Twenty

Jimmy didn't say goodbye. When she went looking for him, he was curled up on a cot in the library, and when she touched his shoulder he curled up and put the pillow over his head. "I love you, honey," she said, "but I have to go now."

She wondered if she should tell him she might die. It was true enough, but the thought of saying it out loud made her cringe. If she did die, she didn't want to leave behind a last memory of blatant emotional manipulation. All she could do was squeeze Jimmy's arm (he flinched away) and tell him again that she loved him. Then she picked her weapons.

There was an art to going armed in Illinois. True, handguns were fairly easy to conceal if you dressed in layers, but whatever they might find at that house Abby was willing to bet that it wouldn't be simple to deal with. That meant going in prepared for anything, and that meant hiding some illegal weaponry.

They all had their own tricks. John, who could pass for a hipster or aging art student in the right light, tended to favor a laptop bag: a bit narrow, but more than enough to hide a small automatic weapon. Mal's gravitas and obvious middle age made things more difficult for him, but a large briefcase or an architect's blueprint tube usually did the job. Adam could carry almost anything and look natural, but his twitchiness made people think of clock towers and sniper rifles, so he tended not to bring guns. Mary and Dummy never carried.

The diaper bag was Abby's favorite carry-all, but considering what they might be facing, she would need more space. Luckily there were other options. A man holding an instrument case made people think of mafia gunmen, but a chubby blonde woman with, casually slung over one shoulder, a yoga mat bag? She could be walking down the street at midnight in a war zone and nobody would think she was up to anything. The fact that the mat bag concealed a H&K MP7 made no difference. The embroidered *Namaste* on the strap was as good as an alibi.

• • •

The outskirts of Waukegan made for a lonely scene. Houses stood in the middle of large, wooded lots, heavily fenced, and the city itself was just a distant glow on the horizon. Life was visible in the form of lighted windows and the occasional passing car, but several houses were deserted and one, the victim of a fire, had been boarded up. A young deer had circumvented the chain-link fence and was doing its part to keep the neighborhood beautiful by eating down the overgrown shrubbery.

By the time Abby parked her car it was after nine o'clock. There was a tinge of smoke in the air with a gunpowder aftertaste: someone in the area had been letting off New Year's fireworks a little early. The smell carried well in the warm damp air, reminding Abby of rained-out Fourth of July barbecues back home in Montana. Twenty-five years ago, perhaps. Practically ancient history.

The town seemed to unravel at the edges. Streets that formed somewhat orderly grids wandered off and vanished, while houses became more scattered and empty lots more prominent. Sascha Carter's property was on the edge of a miniature forest preserve, and with the wild-looking woods and boarded-up houses she felt like she was standing on the edge of the world.

The preserve helped isolate Carter's house from the rest of the neighborhood, but it was also an unexpected bonus for the agents. By parking a few streets away on the curving edge of the woods, Abby could get a clear look at the house without being seen loitering on Carter's street. She pulled out a pair of high-powered binoculars and surveyed the scene.

It certainly stood out. Set back from the road and fringed with bare trees, the house was an almost perfect box nearly twice as big as any other house on the street. Brown shingles dripped from its flat roof, sliding aside to form rough arches that crowned high windows. Instead of chain link, the property was edged with a board fence, the paint old but looking shiny and new after being washed clean by the heavy rain.

A medium-sized garden shed occupied a corner of the property, and as Abby watched, a tall man ducked out and hurried toward the house. The door swung closed behind him, but she glimpsed a sliver of light and what looked like a desk with a computer.

She dialed Mal. "Guard shack in the north corner," she reported softly. "Curtains are drawn at the house, but I can see shadows pacing back and forth pretty regularly. Looks like they have people walking a perimeter inside. Hard to tell from this angle, but I think there's two guys on the roof." She shifted the binoculars, wishing for better light. The intermittent streetlights glowed only faintly, and men in dark clothes on a dark roof in shadow didn't exactly show up. Still, by unfocusing her eyes and tracking motion, she could spot what looked like the movements of two men gesturing as they talked.

"I see them," Mal replied. His words were muffled by the sound of the wind. He would be up high, she knew, watching and waiting while Adam put the first part of the plan into action.

Most of it was Adam's plan. They didn't have many options or personnel, but Adam had been a Ranger once, and he still remembered his training. The trick, he'd said, was to go in as silently and grab the high ground as quickly as they could. But before they could do that, they needed to ensure that the local authorities were distracted.

Sascha Carter might not be willing to call the police if she was in the middle of hatching some strange plan. If she did call, though, they weren't likely to shrug off the Cook Country district attorney. That meant something was needed to draw the cops away, and Adam had plenty of ideas on that score.

Abby checked her watch. Twelve minutes after nine: nearly time. She looked back to the house.

"Two more guys going out to the shed," she reported. "Definitely a guard shack of some kind. They're both kind of humped up under their coats; I think they've got furs on their shoulders. Could be selkies." The shadows on the roof shifted, and a small square of light appeared, hovering four feet in the air. Abby bit back a laugh. "One of the roof guards is playing Angry Birds."

"Careless," Mal observed. A metallic noise, like a kitchen timer being wound up, cut through the rustle of the wind. "Waiting on Adam's signal."

Maybe it was her imagination, but Mal sounded different. Some of the polish had rubbed off his words, leaving a colorlessly neutral voice that reminded her of a newscaster. Abby shook her head and checked the perimeter and the roof again. The guard playing on his phone had just aced a very difficult level.

Her phone vibrated. The text was from Adam: *we r go. sw of gr0.*

Abby turned and oriented herself. Southwest of the house. She frowned, seeing nothing for a moment, then stopped. A glow was rising on the horizon.

After carefully considering the neighborhood, with numerous abandoned houses on large isolated lots, Adam had been given the go-ahead for his part of the plan. In other circumstances, Abby would have put her foot down, but Adam had pulled up three likely sites with two minutes of Googling. "You're sure you can do it?" she'd asked him when they pinpointed the best option.

"You'd be surprised," he'd said.

So she gave him the okay, and he set an abandoned house on fire.

Her confessor would never believe her. It was probably a good thing she didn't have one.

The house was only two streets away and at an angle to Carter's. For a few minutes it lingered as a vague glow on the horizon, recognizable as a fire only if you were looking for one. Abby waited patiently, hoping that they hadn't made the wrong decision, as the glow grew.

The men on the roof noticed first. Thick black smoke was growing more visible as the rain-dampened wood fought the fire, and one of them spotted the plume and pointed it out to the other. There was a hurried consultation between them and one leaned over the edge to shout, but his words were inaudible. The fire convulsed, setting up a sudden burst of green-tinged smoke and flame, and a man poked his head out of the guard shack and shouted to the roof men.

She tapped at her phone: *Green?*

i like green.

You need a hobby.

i have one. blue next.

She didn't wait for the blue. She turned to watch the Carter house instead. Four men had come hurrying out of the guard shack, all with the strange lumps of furs under their clothes, and were staring at the colorful fire. One of the roof men opened a hatch and disappeared down a ladder into the house, while the other gazed across the rooftops with his glowing phone dangling from his hand.

After a quick consultation among them, three of the four guard shack men took off at a sprint down the hill towards the fire while the last one went back into the shack. Abby watched like a hawk, but no other people came out of the house.

She checked the time again. Eighteen minutes after nine. An icon was blinking on her phone, signaling a new text message from a number not in her listings, and her stomach clenched. *I'm in,* it said. *Be there in 30.*

Thirty minutes was too late. That fire wasn't going to burn forever. Still, she texted back with a rendezvous point. Then she called Mal again. "Mal, how are things looking for you?"

"Ready to go."

"OK. We're going to have company soon, so be on the lookout for her." She hesitated. "And... you may fire when ready."

"Yes ma'am," Mal said. "Fiat justitia, ruat caelum." The line went dead.

Abby swallowed the lump in her throat and tucked the phone away. The weight of her yoga bag hung hard against her shoulder; the HK wasn't heavy, but she was keenly aware of it after she'd given Mal the go-ahead.

For a minute or two, nothing happened. Then the last man on the roof stiffened, jerked, and silently crumpled to the ground. If Abby squinted, she could just make out the line of the feathered shaft protruding from his chest.

The compound bow was Adam's. The hand and eye, though, were Mal's. Sometimes Abby thought that if Mal was shipwrecked on a desert island, he'd have a solo Industrial Revolution in six weeks. And Mal never shied away from being the executioner.

The roof hatch opened again and the second man climbed back out, looking around. The moment the hatch was closed, the man lurched and collapsed onto it. At this angle, she couldn't see the arrow.

"Clean," she murmured. The cold breeze snatched the word away.

Now came the hard part. With a distraction provided by the burning house and Mal having picked off the roof guards, a nice chaotic scene was developing down there. But that left one person to do what had to be done next: get Harvey into the house.

Only an idiot would stage an assault with three semi-trained civilians, but when you added a genie into the equation, things looked more even. Abby had hoped to avoid it, but he was crucial for something like this. If they could get him into the house, he could find John and disable any other humans on the premises. It might tip the scales in their favor.

Abby opened the diaper bag just enough to see a gleam of glass. With his pickle jar gone and the flask needed for Adam's lab work, Harvey had been relocated to a sieve-topped powdered cream dispenser. It wasn't perfect, but it gave him an easy exit without unscrewing any lids, so it would do for tonight.

"Ready?" she whispered.

A glowing eye winked on in the depths of the bag. "Ready. You mean it about the salary, right?"

"Wouldn't you know if I was lying?"

"Well, yeah. But it's nice to hear it."

Surprised, she couldn't quite hide a small smile. "Yeah, I mean it."

"Then what're we waiting for? Hurry up before I get bored and ditch you losers." The words trembled, but Abby pretended not to notice. Her own hands were clammy as she closed the bag again.

It was only a short scramble down the grassy bank to the bed of a small stream that flowed out from under the road and into the forest preserve. The rain had swollen the stream, but its bed was lined with gravel that made it a firmer path than the deep, slippery mud on either side.

The woods were surprisingly thick and dark. In seconds the trees had closed behind her, and the vague noise of the street was muffled by the thick undergrowth. The little stream was flowing against her, and despite her boots, damp began to seep into her socks.

Abby checked the compass on her watch and climbed up the left bank towards a stand of maple trees. The leaf litter was thick on the ground, packed into a spongy layer by the weight of now-melted snow, and a pungent smell of decay rose as her feet churned up the rotting vegetation along with the mud. Abby sneezed, swiped a few droplets of sweat out of her eyes and kept going.

Soon the trees began to thin again. Peering through a clump of alders, she saw the grass sloping up towards the backyard of the house. Two guards had been posted by the edge of the woods. One was clearly a selkie, and the other was an enormous bald man with a tattoo of web-like cracks spreading across his scalp. A gang member of some kind, maybe.

Abby stepped back into the woods and put down the yoga bag. It was only a moment's work to prep the H&K and sling it, casual carry, over her jacket.

Adam had recommended the gun specially for her: more power than her little Tomcat, semi-automatic, and capable of being fired one-handed if she really had to. She had never been fond of guns, and now she was carrying something that most people wouldn't even sell to civilians. Necessity made strange bedfellows.

Still, a gunshot would alert the rest of the guards. The big bald one was an unknown quantity and had to go down as quickly and quietly as possible. Leaving the H&K slung, she readied the Taser in her bad hand and palmed the perfume in her good one. Then she stepped out of the alder stand, marked her target, and fired.

Tasers of this kind weren't strictly street-legal either, but they did the job. The clips struck the bald man's back with an instantaneous effect. Jaw clamped, back arched, muscles twitched horribly, and he wavered for a brief unbalanced moment before crashing to the ground unable to do anything but shake and scream through clenched teeth.

Surprised, the selkie did what selkies often did and pounced. He was fast, faster than anticipated, and Abby barely had enough time to raise the perfume bottle. He took a full dose directly in the eyes as he slammed into her. The two of them went rolling down the grassy slope into the woods.

Abby clawed herself free of his grip and scooted away, but the selkie was no longer interested in her. He curled up, clutching his nose and mouth, making gasping noises.

She probably should kill them. That was what John and Mal would do. These were fae, they were working for the other side, they could possibly identify her. Three strikes. Looking down at the contorted, whimpering shape of the selkie, though, Abby reached for the gun and couldn't make her fingers grip it.

Her Taser victim was already unconscious. As the selkie yowled through his fingers, she leaned down and pulled the sealskin off his back. "Sleep," she said, running her fingers through the soft fur, "and when you wake up, you won't remember anything from the last day." Obedient to the commands of whoever held his skin, the selkie passed out.

She dragged the bald man into the woods, ziptied both of them and covered them with leaves. The selkie had a black jacket and ball cap which she took, stuffing her ponytail under the cap and draping the stolen skin over her shoulders. Then she circled right and began to hurry towards the house, looking like she had someplace to be.

A shout from the roof told her someone had discovered the dead guards. She was almost out of time.

There was a long porch wrapping around the back of the house, with a couple of picnic tables and a patio set below on the grass. A steep wooden stair with a motorized chairlift attached led up to the porch. Perfect. Abby made for the stairs.

"Hey! You!"

Her blood froze. Three more bald men with scalp tattoos (new fashion? Group? Species?) were racing across the lawn towards her. Two had collapsible batons, but the one in the lead was carrying a rifle.

She brought her gun up and fired a warning burst. The kickback of the weapon jarred her arm and made her ears ring, but it halted the men just long enough. She backed up the stairs, her bag heavy against her hip. With her bad arm she fumbled open the zipper on the bag. "Get ready to go, Harv," she said quietly as she lined up another shot. This one she couldn't afford to miss.

Then a band of iron locked around her throat. Abby jerked as her air was cut off. A huge hand, with a palm the size of a salad plate, knocked the gun out of her hand. Her bag fell to the ground, tumbled down the steps and landed in a crumpled heap in the bottom. The smell of burned paper overwhelmed her.

The three men were laughing now, but Abby couldn't focus on them. Air was becoming a problem. She jerked her good arm back and connected with something soft and yielding, but her assailant just gave a small grunt and loosened his grip a fraction of an inch.

The man with the rifle rattled up the stairs. "Her Majesty was right," he said over Abby's head. "Good timing, too. Stefan, let up a little, you won't be paid if the specimen is ruined."

The massive fingers loosened just a fraction, and Abby gasped for breath. Stefan's other hand fastened hard onto Abby's wrists and held her pinned as the lead bald man rifled through her pockets. Abby hissed and tried to knee him in the groin, but he pushed her leg aside with ease and relieved her of her weapons.

"What about the others?" a voice said from behind her. It rumbled in her captor's chest, but when it reached the air it sounded thin, almost crackly and breathless. Maybe she'd hit him harder than she thought. Abby ignored the coiling knot of fear in her gut and fought for another lungful of air, determined not to faint. Any opening, anything at all, and she would be ready to lunge for it.

But the bald man didn't seem ready to oblige her. He snapped back an answer in what sounded like Spanish, and from the tone of it, he was telling her captor off for talking in front of a prisoner.

Prisoner. Great. Couldn't she have a month go past without being captured by a mysterious group with a grudge?

Abby tried to call out for Harvey, but she still couldn't gather enough oxygen to force the words out. As she struggled, one of the other men turned Abby's bag upside-down and pawed through the spilled contents. Her heart seized again as he picked up the cream jar.

It was empty. Abby almost let out a sigh of relief but caught it just in time.

At a nod from the leader, Stefan—whoever or whatever he was—pulled, dragging Abby backwards towards the porch door. The leader snapped a few more Spanish words to the other men and followed, carrying Abby's wallet and phone. His maroon eyes searched Abby's face, seemingly looking for something, and he grunted softly when he didn't find it.

The porch door closed behind them, and Abby found herself in a cream-paneled hallway with deep carpet. The back of the door was layered with foam padding, and the walls around it sported thinner layers of the same stuff. The minute it closed, the distant noises of the street and the rising wail of sirens vanished as if a switch had been thrown.

Soundproofing. Wonderful. Abby breathed as deeply as she could and concentrated on keeping her feet under her. Stefan was pivoting, putting her in front of the little procession, and the forward motion was as implacable as a tidal wave. Whenever she stumbled, her feet were pulled from under her and Stefan's grip on her arms and neck suddenly took the full weight of her body.

Stefan pushed her forward from corridor to corridor, passing room after room. In another time Abby might have admired the place: less a house, more a small castle, and the rooms were simply but beautifully decorated with old wood, misty watercolors of hillside scenes, and small paper screens.

People were everywhere. A businesslike bald-headed few were talking into phones or guarding doors, but fairies of every possible type seemed to fill the house. They jostled and laughed and started small scuffles or just smiled at the world. Row after row of smiles, blank and glassy-eyed, followed Abby as she was pushed along. None of them seemed to know her. They were simply looking for the sake of looking. Abby swallowed hard and looked right back, hoping to spot a way out, a weapon, a weakness. Anything she could use.

Jesus. Six years of scrambling to come to this. Why couldn't she have just accepted the serial-killer-with-a-railroad-spike story instead of chasing after the ghoul? She could be home with a functional family.

But the smiles, happy and vacant, put a stop to those thoughts. If not her, someone else would probably be in the same position.

The last door was finer than the rest, an intricate screen of carved mahogany with a pattern of curling flowers and trailing vines as fine as lace. Stefan halted, and the bald man carefully unlocked the door with a brass-plated key.

The world turned upside-down as Abby was pushed through. The grasping hands released her. She stumbled, gasping in her first real lungful of air in what felt like hours, and fell to her knees. The door clicked shut and locked behind her.

She knelt with her bad arm cradled to her chest. Her neck was throbbing where Stefan's fingers had bruised it. If she ever met him she'd know him, face or no face; it would be impossible to forget those hands. She gingerly probed the rising ring of bruises around her neck, feeling for broken skin. Nothing. Good.

When her head had stopped reeling, she finally looked around. She was kneeling on granite tiles. High above her was a skylight, but it had been fitted with tinted glass and showed nothing of the outside world. Around half the upper level ran a high balcony, while a sweeping staircase flowed down from one side. There was another door across the room, locked and much sturdier than the delicate screen. A tall pair of glass doors opened onto the balcony.

The familiar shape tickled Abby's brain, and she let out a small chuckle. *Beauty and the Beast!* It had been Jimmy's favorite movie when he was too little to be self-conscious about "girl stuff." The colors were different, but the chamber was unmistakably palatial.

Only the best for Her Majesty, no doubt. Abby climbed to her feet and turned, surveying the room. No furniture and no sign of anything she could use as a weapon. The screenlike door was apparently unguarded, but it was the obvious weak spot and she doubted she could just walk through it. Instead, she headed for the stairs.

But the moment she put her foot on the first step, the door across the room clicked open. A shaft of light streamed in but was quickly blocked out by two massive figures. Another pair of bald men, enormous and grim-faced, entered with a drooping sack of old laundry between them. She caught a whiff of the same burned-paper smell on the air as they dropped the sack in the middle of the tiled floor and retreated. Their gazes slid right past her, and their eyes were hard. Abby's good hand reflexively tightened.

She carefully made her way over to the bag. When she looked closer, though, she realized it wasn't a bag at all. Someone had wrapped up a large bundle in a blanket, like Cleopatra in her rug. The ends had been tied with heavy twine.

It took a few minutes of careful picking to undo the first knot. Abby rolled up the twine and tucked it into her pocket, then, carefully parted the folds of cloth.

John's pale face looked back. His skin was cold.

Oh God.

She sat down hard. John was lying on his back and looking up at the skylight, but his stare was blank and unmoving. His face and neck were decorated with purple-black bruises, some flowing into lines and some the plain ugly marks of strangulation. They formed a band all around his throat, like a collar. His nose had been broken and dried blood stained his mouth and shirt.

Silence fell inside her head. At first she registered the thing in front of her as plastic: a doll, a mannequin, some kind of strange item stolen from a store and dropped here by equally strange people. Dimly her mind connected it with the furs worn by the selkies, and she wondered about the odd stylized figures used for store displays. Maybe if you were buying fur, it didn't matter what the mannequin looked like.

But a slight twitch of skin brought the world rushing back to her. There was a pulse under the damaged skin of the neck, erratic and small but definitely there. Abby cautiously put two fingers against his throat and felt the pulse again. He was alive.

Hands shaking, she pulled the rest of the blanket away and began to methodically check him for injuries. One broken rib, maybe more. Significant bruising and swelling. When she tilted his head towards her to check his jaw, she saw that the fresh wounds left by Lenny Scott's claws had been reinjured. The scrapes around the edges of the wound looked like nail marks. Someone or something had scratched his face open.

Dried blood had collected under his nails. By its color it was probably human, or at least not fairy, but all that told her was that he'd gotten a few licks in before being subdued. Good for him.

"Come on, John," she said as she mopped the blood off his face. That seemed to be happening a lot lately. This time she didn't have any quick-and-dirty disinfectant, so she made do with a clean handkerchief that the bald men had somehow neglected to take away from her.

Time was passing, but she had no way of knowing how fast. There were no clocks, her phone was gone, and in a windowless room with a darkened skylight there was no changing sky to follow.

She checked all three doors. Locked. She looked John over again. No change. She inventoried her available weapons and wasn't encouraged. One handkerchief, one metal pen, one crucifix with attached metal chain.

And one bottle of perfume. Or so they'd thought, anyway. Abby had shoved it back into her pocket after dealing with the first of the bald men, and none of them had tried to take it away from her. Maybe they hadn't yet found the two missing guards under the leaves; if they had, someone would doubtless have relieved her of what was essentially homebrewed Mace.

She quickly uncapped the pen and twisted it, bringing out a deceptively blunt-looking metal point. Then she opened the perfume bottle, dipped the pen into the clear liquid and swished it a few times to make sure it got into all the nooks and crannies. Then she quickly capped both up again and stowed them away in different pockets, certain she was being watched.

She sat back down by John, checked his pulse again, and waited.

Chapter Twenty-One

A crashing noise startled Abby out of her doze. She found herself still sitting on the floor, hunched over her bad arm. How had she been dozing? What time was it? Blinking sleep out of her eyes, she glanced up at the tinted skylight, hoping for some change that would indicate daylight outside. Nothing.

John was gone. Abby's eyes snapped open and she jumped to her feet, scanning the room. If she'd fallen asleep and they'd taken him away again, she was going to charge right through that *damn* door and break some teeth.

But no, there he was, standing below the sweeping staircase and gazing vaguely up at the stained-glass door on the balcony. Abby took a step towards him.

"John?" she said. "Are you feeling okay?"

He didn't say anything, just kept staring upwards.

"John," she repeated as she took another step. "I know this is a pretty terrible rescue attempt, but we came to get you. Whatever happened, we can get you fixed up. Okay? You know the Director will take care of everything. Can you look at me?"

Silence. If it hadn't been for the gradual rise and fall of his shoulders as he breathed, he might have been a waxwork.

"John," she said, "Look at me. It's Abby."

He swung in place, head bobbing, and she bit back a yelp. He moved like a puppet with its strings tangled: jerky, reluctant and awkward, with no rhythm to anything. The bruises on his cheeks and neck had flowered into stark, familiar tribal symbols, now so deep that they were purple-black against his skin.

"John," Abby said softly. "John. John, it's me. It's Abby. Can you hear me?"

"He can," a voice said. "He just can't do anything about it."

It came from above, up on the balcony. A soft, feminine voice, calm and reasonable. Abby kept her gaze on John, but her fists clenched.

"What did you do to him?" she said. John's throat spasmed as the bruise band tightened, his eyes rolling in their sockets.

"I made him honest," said the voice.

"Looks like honesty doesn't suit him." That, too, was honest. John looked like a dead body, and not the kind of dead that had been granted a fresh (short) life by a chaos bruise in a supermarket. If it hadn't been for the pulse in his throat, she would have been checking for rigor mortis again.

"Save us the one-liners, Mrs. Marquise." The voice turned brisk with just a hint of irritation, like a teacher dealing with an obstreperous student.

"Honesty is an underrated quality these days. It's certainly rare enough. Can't you appreciate how nice it is to actually have someone look like what they are?"

As she watched, John made to raise his hands to his face. Then he stopped, pawing instead at his shirtfront like he was trying to get rid of a spider. Blood under his fingernails. She wondered if he'd been the one to scratch his face open.

"And what is he?" she said.

"A useful asset. Provided you know how to keep him on a leash." From the landing came a creak of wheels, a dull scrape, and then twin thumps. Then two more. Footsteps.

She moved slowly into Abby's view as she descended the stairs, one hand resting on the guide rail the chair lift had used. Her movements were slow but graceful, with the odd lightness of a dancer moving underwater. Her legs were wrapped in black braces with deeply-carved sigils standing out as dark marks against the glossy plastic. Ritual markings, identical to the ones littering John's skin, had been carefully painted onto her face in what seemed to be liquid eyeliner. In one hand she held a two-foot, whip-slender wand made of some golden wood Abby couldn't identify.

"I'm sorry," Carter said, waving to the leg braces and the wand. "It's a little cliché of me, isn't it? Descending the stairs for a confrontation." She rolled her eyes at the words. "But closeness is supposed to be important in things like this. And I couldn't stand to have this lovely old ballroom ripped out when I bought the place, anyway." She gently touched the tip of her wand to the back of John's neck, and he stiffened, freezing. "That's a good little fanatic."

Abby took a half-step forward, and the effect was immediate. John let out a warning growl and tensed, teeth bared. Carter nodded to herself and withdrew the wand.

"Just testing," she said. "If there's one thing I learned in law school, it's to never assume that anything is working like it should." She smiled at Abby, almost companionably, and Abby stared at her.

"What do you think you're doing?" she finally managed to say. "How can you claim to be any kind of public servant and order peoples' deaths? How can you do this to my friend?"

Carter's smile slipped a notch. "I could ask you the same thing," she said. "The problem is that you'd lie to me, because you can't comprehend anything outside of your narrow little worldview. At this point, I don't think there's anything either of us can do to fix that, so we'll have to settle for following our own consciences." She prodded John again, and a fresh marking in the shape of an eye bled into existence on his forehead.

Abby was willing to argue, but not while Carter had her friend. "You know," she said, "if you keep raising those bruises, he won't have any blood actually left in his veins. He's no good to you dead, I bet."

"Actually, he's better that way." Carter studied John thoughtfully for a moment. "The problem is, it's important that his death is at least partially of his own free will. That's the part Owen missed, you know. They have to die willingly, or at least unaware of it, for there to be any kind of power generated by their death. Executing somebody dulls the effect."

She ran a hand through John's hair, seemingly checking something, and then grimaced and wiped the hand on her pants leg. "Ugh, dandruff. You've been working with him for years, and you never once had a talk about his shampoo issues?"

"Call me stupid, but didn't seem important," Abby said. "You can't sacrifice John. He's not a sorcerer, and I'm pretty sure he'll come back and haunt you anyway."

"Now that's where you're wrong." Carter's smile reappeared, this one smaller and more genuine. "He's got the gift, or something like the gift, anyway. The bloom never lies." She tapped the tip of her wand to the eye marking on John's forehead. "My guess is mixed ancestry. Perhaps vampire, but more likely, one of his grandparents or great-grandparents came from my people. He should be grateful, really. Once he's finished, he'll be helping to bring peace by restoring the Fair Folk to power."

Abby's throat was dry. "Speaking of cliché," she said, "finished with what?"

"Well, I need him to die willingly," Carter said with a shrug. "And he won't. So I have to ruin his life. Push him 'til he snaps, then put a collar on the animal and aim it in the right direction." She shrugged again, looking embarrassed. "I know, I know, it's such a crude way of getting this done, isn't it? That's another change I'll need to make once I've assumed my place with the Folk behind me. No more eye of newt, toe of frog."

Abby didn't reply, and Carter frowned. "Eye of newt? It's from *Macbeth.*"

"I know," Abby said. "But no matter how angry you make John, he's not going to ruin his life for you."

"I don't know about that." She pressed a hand to the third eye marking. "You'd be surprised what people will do when regret and self-hate are kicking them in the balls. *Maraigh i,* Mr. Sawyer."

Abby didn't know what language the other woman was speaking, but John did. He came to life with a hiss and charged.

She had known John Sawyer for years. He was sarcastic, bitter, addicted to Cartoon Network and whiskey miniatures, and sort of her friend. He was also stronger and more experienced than her, and she had seen him kill. She ran.

There wasn't nearly enough space in the ballroom to dodge forever, but she wasn't about to make it easy for Carter. Abby rocketed into the door and tugged frantically at the knob; when it didn't give, she slammed her weight into it. The thin screen-cut wood snapped in several places and Abby broke through, ignoring Carter's shout.

The guard, a fairy woman with scale-like markings on her skin, let out a squawk as Abby came crashing through the door and into her. They tumbled to the floor, rolling in the shards of wood, but Abby jammed her knee into the guard's stomach and scrambled to her feet while the other woman was gasping.

The fairies had gone, and she didn't stop to question why. She ran to the closest door and tried to open it. Locked tight. The corridor stretched out, freedom beckoning in a way that might have been more than just her imagination, anything to get away from the staring, bloodied maniac pushing his broader frame through the broken remains of the door—

Another yelp from the fairy woman as John collided with her. Abby wanted to look, but she was afraid of what she would see. She barreled down the hall, trying one door after another, hoping she could find something. Someone was shouting in the distance while someone else intoned a droning consonant-less chant. The sound was hovering right on the edge of her hearing and digging into her eardrums like the feedback from a microphone.

She ought to be running, but if she left now, she might never find her teammate again. Even through pain and fear and anger, she couldn't let that happen.

The hall doors here were too sturdy to break, but one had been left unlocked. She crashed through the open door and shoved it closed behind her, wedging a heavy metal-framed chair under the knob. The door vibrated hard, and she heard an incoherent snarl from the far side.

She backed away from the door, almost tripping over a heavy metal toolbox. Surprised, Abby turned around. Her eyes widened.

"I didn't know fairies used voodoo," she murmured.

But it only took a second for her to correct that assumption. She was standing in a stone-floored cinderblock chamber with an altar at one end, a couple of workbenches on either side, and an array of well-used power tools neatly arranged on a mat in the center of the room. Every flat surface had been carefully daubed with ritualistic sigils identical to the ones she had seen on Silkwillow and Lenny Scott.

And John. The door vibrated again, the wood creaking.

She crossed the room in a few quick steps and crouched down, reaching for the nearest power tool. It was an autopsy saw, and there were several nicks on the blade. No sign of an outlet anywhere in the room, though, and her hands slipped on some strange oily substance when she tried to pick it up. She sniffed her fingers. Sandalwood? Yes, sandalwood, and some other blend of mixed oils with tiny flecks of dried herb in it. Some kind of ritual blessing, maybe, for whoever blessed a bone saw.

Probably the same person who brainwashed her friend. The door was cracking through now, slivers of wood grinding and creaking against each other as repeated blows split the grain. There was no snarling from him now, just the thud of fists and feet while Abby's own breaths echoed in her ears.

So she was going to have to fight him. This wasn't supposed to happen, but it was, and until she could undo what had been done to him she would have to stay alive. She dropped the useless bone saw, kicked aside a few other pieces, and went straight for the toolbox. A pen was good, but ...

The door broke in and what used to be John crawled through, completely ignoring the shards of wood jammed into his knuckles. He pushed over the useless chair and charged. His face was a set mask of blood, bruise and tight-drawn skin. Abby crouched by the workbench and waited, her posture as terrified and submissive as she could make it.

John certainly was stronger and more experienced than her. But the thing driving John wasn't the mind she knew, just a ravening id with no sense of tactics and its lizard-brain instincts in the driver's seat. John would have known that Abby didn't sit and wait for people to kill her. But this John just saw a frightened woman and pounced, and that was when Abby swung the heavy steel toolbox into his face.

Instinct is a powerful thing, but it's also not very cunning. Instinct, not conscious thought, will make us recoil when someone jumps out at us. And instinct hates it when someone goes for the eyes.

There was a wet *crunch* like stepping on a fat spider. It was a perfect physics lesson: two opposing forces meeting and momentum transferring between them. The toolbox jerked in Abby's hand, almost wrenching free from her grip. John's head snapped back and his legs skidded out from under him. His charge turned into a barely controlled crash as his feet tangled with Abby's, knocking her backwards. He landed hard on his back, fresh blood streaming from his nose and rapidly purpling eyes, as Abby collapsed against the workbench.

"I'm so sorry," she panted, clutching her crucifix in one hand and the toolbox in the other. "I swear, I'm really sorry."

His eyes half-opened again, but he couldn't seem to get his feet under him. Redness suffused one eyeball, and when his gaze moved towards her, it was unfocused. A half-hearted hiss twisted his lips, displaying some skewed teeth.

"I'm sorry," she repeated automatically. "Are you okay?"

A crash at the door startled her enough to glance away from John. Three broad-shouldered selkie men were kicking away the remains of the door debris. Their gazes were hard and blank.

"God damn it," said Sascha Carter, stepping over the damaged threshold. "Of course he isn't okay!"

"Sorry to ruin your plans." Abby wanted to kneel and check on John, but while partially stunned he definitely wasn't unconscious. His breathing was regular, shallow and raspy, and the air whistled through his crushed nose. Swallowing another surge of guilt, she kept the workbench to her back and planted her hands against it, ready as she could be for another charge. Concealed by the thick folds of her sweater, a stolen screwdriver rested against her left wrist.

Carter sighed. "I was afraid something like this might happen. You people have been making a hobby of messing things up, after all. It's just lucky for us all that it's not impossible to fix."

She twirled the golden wand and John stiffly rose from the ground, once more a marionette. His eyes were closed, but Carter murmured something and the bruised lids opened.

Abby breathed out, long and slow, and let the tip of the screwdriver touch her furled palm. "And that's it?" she said as calmly as she could. "You just... use him like a puppet until he kills me, then kill him for your weird fairy-power ritual? That's sort of silly." It came out pettier than she meant, but in her defense, she had fair enough reason for pique.

"Almost." Carter stepped back as John reanimated. "He'll kill himself. You don't think I'm having him chase you for fun, do you? There's only so much I can do with a mind like his. But once he's finished with you I'll help bring him back to himself. I've gotten good at bringing minds back; it's one of my talents, honestly. I like to help people when I can." She tightened her grip on the wand, knuckles white. "Once he sees what he did, he'll be ready to kill himself, and I'll... well, I'll let him. It's more efficient."

The selkies and Carter both jerked a little when Abby barked out a short laugh. "Didn't I see this in a movie?" she said, unable to stop the hysterical sarcasm from creeping into her voice. "But it's not going to work, Sascha. John *is* my friend, and that's how I know this stupid, stupid, *pointless* plan won't work. Because no matter what you make him do, he's never going to hate himself as much as he hates you."

"I disagree," Carter said flatly. "You'd be surprised what I can make him do to you."

"You mean torture? Rape? Again? I got that kind of threat from Leonard Scott for a while, and it didn't do anything for him."

And *there* was the spark she'd been hoping for: the widening of the eyes, the tensing of the mouth, the deepening lines as muscles flexed with the effort of repressing a grimace. A fairy beginning to lose her temper. "I suppose you think you're smart, bringing that up," Carter said through thinned lips.

"No. It's been a long time since I thought I knew what I was doing."

Carter blinked, perhaps surprised by that blunt admission. "But I've learned a lot since I started. Some of it was from your brother. Mostly I learned that you're ruthless bitch who'll give her brother a hemorrhage to keep his mouth shut, and that whatever the hell John does when he wakes up isn't enough for what's coming to you."

"You don't get it, do you," Carter snapped. "This isn't about something as small as one or two people. It's about the *world*. When this is done, the world will be a better place for everyone. Did you think I was kidding when I said I wanted children to be safe in their beds?"

"I don't know." Abby met her stare and refused to waver. "But people are dead because of your plans. I think you've lost the right to decide what's right for anyone."

Now Carter was the one who laughed. "You're such a hypocrite. Or have you forgotten all those fairies you and your hate group have killed?"

"Never. Ever. But I'm going to have a hard time shedding a tear for people like Luka. I think Alicia Gonzalez and Rebecca Cartwright would agree."

"Who?"

Something seemed to burst behind Abby's eyes, and the floor wavered under her. The single syllable shot through her brain like a red-hot bullet and scrambled her thoughts in its wake. "How can you not know that?" was all she managed to say.

"Well, I'm not omniscient," Carter said. "Are you going to be deliberately obtuse?"

"I can't believe..." Abby raked her good hand through her hair, feeling the fabric-cushioned steel of the hidden screwdriver against her forehead. "Tell me something. Please. You want to be queen somehow and you're using fairies and sacrifices as part of it. But will your queenship make any of your fairies kinder? Smarter? Less likely to kill?"

Another long moment, this one stiff as burned skin.

"I think," Carter said finally, "you don't understand what I want to do, Mrs. Marquise. I wouldn't violate them by trying to change the way they think. You can't judge them like humans. But when the fifth man dies and the ritual is complete, I will be the first true fairy queen in centuries. I can be the queen they need. With a queen, they can finally be a force for positive social change."

Abby gaped. "Some of them hunt people, Sascha! For *fun!* How do you make that positive?"

"Well, for a start," the other woman responded, "we can point them at the right people. *Maraigh i,* John."

He was slower and more awkward this time, but not by much. The words jerked him into motion, and he lowered his head and snarled as he leaped for her. There was a spark in the reddened eyes.

Abby tried to punch him in the stomach, but the heavy crack of his forehead against hers sent her reeling backwards. As she fell to the ground John crouched over her, his hands going for her throat.

She blocked him as best she could, cracking her cast against the back of his hands and making his grip slip. His fingers were slick with sweat. The face inches from hers seemed hardly human.

Struggling, she let the blocking cast slip just an inch. As he lunged forward to get a grip on her throat, she braced the screwdriver with her good hand. There was a wet squelch as a fresh trickle of warm blood dampened her clothes.

But it wasn't enough. John was too far gone, the bruise markings black now, his face a mask as he tightened his grip. Abby's world began to go fuzzy as her air was cut off again. She choked and jammed her knee into his groin.

That got more of a response. Attack the face and the eyes close, but attack the groin and all bets are off. John fell to the ground, curling up in the fetal position around around his wounded torso. The screwdriver clattered to the floor, the first two inches of its shaft smeared with blood.

Abby barely managed to get to her knees. Her vision was still swimming, but she could make out the blobs of white that were the sealskins and the bright red of Carter's hair.

"Are you stubborn, or just ignorant?" Carter was shouting. "*Mac soith!* Don't you understand how important this is? Cristobal! Auslan! Take her to the ritual circle. Starik! Help me get that mess on his feet." She twisted the wand between her fingertips, her lips set in a thin line. "I'm going to get this right if it kills me."

That was what John would have called a golden opportunity, but Abby couldn't seem to make her lips move. She hung limply as two bald men grabbed her arms and pulled her into a standing position. She half expected a joke or a smile from the pair, but they seemed oddly silent for fae. Maybe they had something on their minds?

She was vaguely aware that her thoughts were tending in odd directions. That last knock on the head must have scrambled her brains a little.

Abby couldn't stand on her own, but that didn't stop Cristobal and Auslan. They were tall and they were strong: between them, her feet didn't even touch the floor.

Chapter Twenty-Two

Sascha Carter called it a ritual circle, but a realtor would have called it a dining room. The space was twice as long as it was wide, but even at its narrowest point there was more than enough space for three people walking abreast to move freely. The blue carpet was pulled up in the center of the room to reveal slightly scarred wood, but there were still divots in the remaining squares that showed where a table, chairs and sideboard had gone not so long ago. Carter might have been planning this for a while, but here in the visible part of the house, the remodeling had been recent.

The circle itself, though, couldn't have stood out more. It was crudely carved into the wood in a furrow an inch wide and almost as deep again. Metallic shavings glittered in the bottom of the cut. The four cardinal directions were each marked with a hatchet—one with a stone blade, one bronze, one copper and one silver—driven deeply into the floorboards. Inside the circle a pentagon had been neatly laid out, and at each point was a small ceramic dish. One was empty, but each of the others contained something that made Abby's heart sink.

A pair of boots. A crystal ball. A folded cloak. And, lying awkwardly across its undersized dish, a pushbroom etched with symbols.

"Neill," she said to the boots. "Mulsey. Petrovich. And that must be for the fourth man, right? A broomstick." She looked up at the slightly bigger of the two—Auslan, whose crack-shaped tattoos were much smaller than his partner's and who also smelt noticeably of burnt hair. "So he was a sorcerer after all. Did he make the commission and then go looking for answers? Or did a test flight just go wrong, like everything else does around here?"

"No comment," said Auslan, drawing a rumble of amusement from Cristobal.

"Of course not." Abby kept the rest of her thoughts to herself. The apparent cool of the two couldn't be counted on, not when faced with something like this.

A flicker of light caught her eye, and she squinted, curious. For a moment she thought her eyes were playing tricks on her: it was freezing cold, inside and in the middle of the night, which meant there couldn't be a hovering heat shimmer in the middle of the room. But there it was.

As she watched it, the little patch began to expand. It warped and twisted in midair, radiating a cold white light that was somehow familiar. Looking through it, the world on the other side seened warped. It was a flaw in the world, giving the impression that someone had warped a pane of glass.

She swallowed, trying to work past the lump that was rising in her throat.

That looked familiar, all right, and not in a reassuring way. The last time the air warped like that, the agents had been thrown a relic of incredibly unstable power and had wound up owing a debt to an unsympathetic old woman who was as far from human as one could be while still being shaped like one. And that had been a gift from someone who wanted to *help* them.

"It's not going to work," she said to Auslan, trying to keep her voice level. "Even if she manages to become some kind of mythic queen, it's not going to help your people one little bit. If she's willing to kill to get that kind of power, imagine what she'll be like when she has it."

"No comment," said Auslan.

"She's already killing off her own people, isn't she?" Abby demanded. "Ivan Czerwien the organ thief, remember him? Or Jupiter Spotts, the corrigan? They were both troublemakers, and they weren't the only ones who mysteriously vanished."

"None of our business if she kills the fairies," said Cristobal. He gave her arm a twist, making Abby hiss in pain. "Now be quiet."

"No commenting," said Auslan. That got another chuckle from Cristobal, who nudged his partner behind Abby's back.

So the men weren't fae after all. Abby blinked lingering tears out of her eyes and studied the two of them. They were tall and built slim, but their thick ropy muscles betrayed a lot of time spent doing heavy labor. Their eyes were yellow, and in addition to the crack-shaped symbols, Cristobal had a tattoo of a mouse over one ear. Both smelled burnt. The unnatural stoniness and heat of their skin definitely argued for nonhuman status, but beyond that, she couldn't guess.

As much as any of them could be called experts, she was the agency's mythology and folklore expert, but she couldn't even begin to identify what Auslan and Cristobal were. And that meant she had no idea what they might be able to do if she got on their bad sides.

But at least now she knew that there were other factions involved. Why would a sorceress, a would-be queen of the fairies, hire muscle that wasn't fae? Did their group have special skills she hadn't seen yet, or was Carter just playing it smart by diversifying and bringing in smarter outside talent? Or maybe they were tied to her by something else, the way family bonds had pulled Lenny Scott into the conspiracy. There had to be *something* she could use here.

A long, high chime cut through her thoughts. The rift in the air was widening again, its edges bulging and warping as it emitted a clear tone like a wet finger circling the rim of a wine glass. Light shifted within the glimmering patch, and Abby wondered if something would come flying out. But the noise faded away and the motion of the distortion subsided as the moment passed.

The door opened again and Sascha Carter strode into the room. Behind her came two selkies who dragged John between them. He was unconscious again, his battered face swollen. His shirt had been cut open and bandages, sealed with a number of charm symbols Abby couldn't identify, were wrapped around his torso where she had stabbed him.

"I hope you appreciate how hard I have to work at this," Carter said she stopped just outside the circle. "I'm trying to save lives, and you'll knife your own friend to stop me. This might've been avoided if you'd just spent some time with a good psychiatrist."

If *she* had—? Abby resisted the urge to say exactly what she thought of that. Whatever was going to happen next, she had to be ready with every scrap of strength and concentration she had left.

Carter knelt on the edge of the circle, putting one hand just above the folded cloak. It was made of plain black cotton and looked like something you might buy in a Halloween store for a witch costume, but when Carter's fingertips brushed the fabric, pink spots appeared on the skin. Seconds later, blood welled up in the marks.

The victims had to go to their deaths willingly, Carter said. Fairies gave the sorcerers instructions to follow, Terra said. So Neill had been making seven-league boots that tore him in half, and Petrovich created an invisibility cloak. Abby swallowed. An invisibility cloak that made his skin vanish.

Carter sketched marks onto her face and arms with the bloody fingertips. As she completed the shape of a third eye, a subtle thrum went through the room. The gleaming patch widened slightly.

More fairies were filing into the room now. Some of them crowded forward, but others pulled them back and hissed harshly at the offenders. Instead of their usual bright colors, the gathered fae were dressed in an oddly subdued fashion: mostly tough, hard-wearing materials in muted shades, incongruous next to the animal skins draped over some shoulders. One or two were sporting camouflage jackets, and almost all of them wore army boots. Each had a patch on their left shoulder of a lotus flower growing through a crown.

They surrounded the ritual circle, their backs against the walls, and they watched Carter hungrily. Many of them were holding hands, clasping each other even as their gazes were fixed on the woman in the center of the room.

Carter slipped her wand out of her sleeve and tapped the edge of the ritual circle with it. John stood up again.

Before, he'd looked dead. Now he looked exhumed. He trembled where he stood, still restrained by the pair of selkies, and the fresh blood was drying into a mask on his nose and mouth. Carter snapped a command and the selkies let him go, but he didn't move, just swayed slightly in place.

Carter shouted and snapped out her wand like a whip, smacking John in the leg. He swayed again and, moving like a robot, shuffled forwards.

His eyes met Abby's as he moved towards her, and she felt her gut clench. No toolbox or screwdriver now. Cristobal and Auslan were going to hold her tight while her brainwashed friend did whatever Carter wanted him to do. She had one weapon left, though. Her mouth.

"You think you're clever, but you're not," she said.

Abby's eyes met John's, and his steps faltered. "I remember," she continued, trying to keep his gaze on her. The pupils contracted. "I remember how much you hate having your leash yanked. I know you, John. Aren't you angry enough? Can't you break it?" He rocked back on his heels and stopped dead.

"What is your problem?" Carter demanded, smacking him again with the wand. John blinked swollen eyelids and wobbled, looking as if he was caught in a stiff breeze. The gathered fairies watched him with fixed gazes, one or two licking their lips or whispering to each other. Their reactions didn't seem to touch him.

Carter frowned and pulled a sheaf of folded notebook paper out of her purse. It was standard cheap stuff, but somewhere along the line someone had dyed it black. So Petrovich was the one she got her information from after all, Abby noted. She'd probably grown up surrounded by it, for the first few years anyway. She couldn't help wondering if Petrovich had known he was incubating the agent of his own destruction. Maybe he'd guessed, right at the end, because he'd walled up her part of the house and tried to hide all evidence of the girls he'd fostered. Hiding Sascha, and hiding Terra from Sascha.

The paper crackled as Carter pawed through them. "This isn't supposed to happen," she murmured, too low for almost anyone to hear. A few of the fairies exchanged glances, and Abby felt Auslan and Cristobal stir beside her. "He can't disobey the commands. He can't. Unless—" She turned over one of the papers, read a few lines, and glanced at Abby. "He doesn't have any medical conditions, does he? Seizures, epilepsy, autism?"

Abby stared. "You really expect me to answer that?"

"You're right, I suppose. Auslan?"

The world went white. Pain flooded down her broken arm as Auslan twisted it. His clawlike fingers dug into the swollen skin of her hand, raising fresh drops of blood. Good God, how did she even have any left after the last few days?

"Let me put it this way," Carter said. "You can help me, or my people can help you. And I'm sorry I have to put it that way, honestly. I feel like Scarface doing that. But there's more than just you at stake here, you know." She leaned down and grabbed Abby's chin. Green eyes bored into her, making Abby flinch. The pupil was just like Terra's, a greasy sheen over the black, but on Sascha Carter it looked like a painted detail. She might have been an exquisitely-crafted mannequin. "Medical conditions. Does he have any?"

Abby shuddered as Auslan's claws dug a little deeper. She wanted to lie, but the pulsing agony in her arm and shoulder seemed to blot out every reasonable argument for doing so. Instinct, her friend against John, was screaming at her to just give in and make the pain stop. She tried to say something pithy and defiant, but the words never managed to make it past her lips. "I—ahh—I—no! Nothing!"

"You're not lying to me, are you? I can get sodium pentothal, but that takes time. Auslan is more reliable." Carter shot a glance over her shoulder as the humming tone rose again slightly. The ripple was widening still further. "Talk, and I'll try to make it quick."

"No!" Abby burst out. "None of us do! We're all sick in the head, and so are you, but I don't know what goes into his pills and none of us ask! That's what friends do!" Her head sagged as tears began to gather. Traitors.

Carter knelt and put a hand on her shoulder. "I'm sorry," she said softly, and for a second or two Abby almost believed her. "You know, I think we could have been friends if things had worked out a little better."

Abby had no reply to that. She was trying not to let the tears fall. They wound a slow track down her nose and cheeks, skating around the puffy spots and flecks of dried blood, before collecting at her chin and silently dripping onto the floor. Her nose was beginning to run.

"All right, then." Carter stood up again, her braces creaking, and put her hands on her hips. "It looks like we'll have to do this the Scarface way after all." She moved over to John and gently touched the tip of her wand to the center of his forehead, where the third eye marking still stood out in livid blue-green. "Verdigris green," Carter noted with satisfaction in a voice almost too low for anyone to catch it. "For life and death both. Ancestors, let this be a sign."

Light flared at the tip of the wand. No, it didn't. Abby blinked through her tears, trying to focus. Something strange was happening.

It wasn't light at the tip of the wand, it was a blot. A light-colored blot, but a blot all the same, like someone had dripped paint on the world. Abby moved her head, but the shape of the blot stayed the same.

Absence, Harvey had said. Darkness is absence of light. Whatever it was gathering there, as Carter muttered words in languages Abby didn't recognize, was an absence of *real*. They hadn't dripped paint, they'd scraped it away, and the canvas underneath the painting was showing. The scent of ozone filled the air as the patch of unreality blended, spread, and was sucked into the third eye marking.

John swayed again, and for a moment, the world was dead silent. Then he squared his shoulders, stood upright, and opened his eyes.

"Hell," Abby said softly.

He swayed a little as he moved towards her. Carter was watching him intently, keeping her gaze fixed on his back as she spun intricate gestures with her hands. When she moved, he moved, when she stopped, he stopped. A true marionette now.

This was a stupid way to die. Killed by a friend as part of a blood sacrifice for a ritual to raise a Chicago politician to the level of a fairy queen? It was original, sure, but it wasn't the way she would have chosen to go. All because of a damn grocery run that took her past the wrong alley at the wrong time, putting her in the path of something she didn't know existed. She'd gone looking for the truth, and through years and years of fighting and running and watching her loved ones fall away from her, the truth had stripped her of everything she had. And now one of her only friends was going to kill her, just to have a burden of guilt laid on him that would make him end his own life for someone who thought she deserved all the power she could bleed out of the world.

God, where was Giovanna when she needed her? The old woman had been something else, a strange blend of dignity and rage who hadn't been intimidated by bogeymen or anything else. Abby had slapped El Cucuy, but Giovanna had terrified him and turned his own magic against him.

Abby looked up. John had frozen again, his strings tangled, but he would be on her soon enough. She looked her death in the face and couldn't be afraid anymore.

Maybe all the fear had dripped out with the blood she was leaving everywhere these days. Maybe there was something freeing about the finality of it all. Or maybe—and in her secret heart of hearts, where the dark impulses and jump-Abby-jump lizard-brain thoughts of her own lived, squashed into cages made out of family and religion and laws and *thou shalt not*—she was just too angry. Angry at a truth that killed, angry at John for being captured, and most of all, angry at Sascha Carter for thinking she was better than anyone else and putting them all in this position.

She had no weapons left, really. But she knew as well as any other agent that magic had its rules and needs, and this ugly magic was no different. Giovanna would have known that.

Not much time, Carter said. She could've had a better sacrifice, but there wasn't much time. Abby straightened up and stared across the circle, basking in the warmth of her tight little ball of lizard-brain rage.

"Hey! You!" she shouted. Her gaze picked out the biggest, toughest-looking selkie in the front row. He was six foot ten if he was an inch, with a lanky frame that betrayed basketball-player genes but was now muscled like a crazed bodybuilder. The sealskin draped over his shoulders was pure white and magnificently long, the fur around the shoulders curling into a striking mane. The effect was slightly spoiled by the Bananaphone T-shirt, but people that size generally had the confidence to wear whatever they damn well wanted. "You, in the T-shirt! Why aren't you the one doing the killing around here? Not man enough for your queen?"

The effect was instantaneous. Tendons bulged in the selkie's neck as his jaw clenched. A couple of the other fae snorted and poked each other.

"Shut up," Carter said shortly. She gestured, twisting her fingers and accidentally flicking droplets of blood over the floor, but John had lurched to a halt again. Carter's face was pale as she repeated the gesture. "Move, damn it!"

"It's not going to work, Carter," Abby called out. A couple of heads turned, and more glassy fae eyes were being aimed in her direction. "John has more experience being crazy than anyone here. Find another sacrifice, or—" Her words were cut off by another vicious arm-twist, and Abby sagged, hissing out the pain through clenched teeth.

"You didn't leave me a choice, did you?" Carter snarled. She slid her bloodied fingertips down the slender wand and snapped it like a whip again. The hole in the world was still widening, light bending through its sickly gleam.

Sweat trickled into Abby's eyes, but she raised her head and blinked it away. "You mean you didn't have a backup plan? Some queen!"

"Bitch!" The wand slashed out and slapped Abby across the face. Energy crackled and sizzled through the thin wood and delivered a sharp shock even as Abby's head snapped back with the force of the blow. The side of her face stung, and her left eye began to swell shut. The runes carefully etched into the wood had probably imprinted themselves on the skin.

"Some queen!" Abby repeated, not even pretending to be talking to Carter anymore. "Is this how you solve your problems? Hit things until they go away? That's fun, sure, but your fairies already know all about fun. A queen has to *think!*" She was almost babbling the words out, trying to say as much as possible before the next inevitable attack. "What kind of queen can't control her own prisoners?"

She ducked her head again just in time, and the lash of the wand struck her scalp instead. Impossibly, she felt a surge of furious triumph, and she seized that feeling between her teeth and held it in a mirthless grin. "And then it's all over but the arrests!" she called out to the world. "Luka's gone! Ivan's gone! Kotik's skin is being cut up in a workshop! How much fun can you have when you're dead?"

The last words were drowned out by a roar of voices from the assembled crowd. Half a dozen of them were pushing and shoving each other, trying to get to the front row to do God only knew what, and others were keeping them back as they all shouted at each other. The big selkie had whipped his sealskin half-on, claws unfurling and murder in his golden eyes. He looked ready to charge across the circle and punt Abby's head like a soccer ball.

Sascha Carter stood there motionless in the light of her growing power. She had gone, if possible, even paler. The bruises on John's face were rising into welts, but Sascha's seemed to be sinking into her skin, leaving her gaunt and skeletal. Her eyes were fixed on Abby's, and they burned with hate.

"*Silence,*" she said, and the soft word cut through the room like the first crack in a frozen pond. Struggling fairies stopped and dropped their hands, looking at the floor or the ceiling or anywhere but at the other people they had just been trying to pummel. *Who, me?* They seemed to all be saying.

"I was wrong about you," Sascha told Abby quietly. Once again, the low voice somehow echoed throughout the room, and the fairies swayed and whispered among themselves. "I thought we might have been friends, because I thought you were sensible at the bottom. That you'd understand what it means to be fighting for a cause, for something bigger than yourself. But you won't, will you? You're just a petty little fanatic who can't see how things really are, who willfully *blinds* herself to it, because you can't stand the idea that you might be wrong!

"This is what ignorance does!" she called out, and to Abby's surprise there were tears shining in her eyes. Lovely tears, beautiful and perfect as drops of crystal sliding down a porcelain cheek. "It makes you ugly and small-minded and shallow! And you say my fairies are evil, when things exist like you?" She raised the tip of the wand. "I have a better plan. John?"

John's head turned, slowly, but his gaze was distant and blank. Sascha touched a finger to the eye marking on his forehead and he focused, if only briefly.

"John," Sascha said softly. "This is your fault. You know that, don't you? I saw it all in your head, you poor deluded idiot. You let her stay with the group. You taught her. You created her. And if you hadn't, she would still have somewhere to go. Now I have to clean up your mess for you."

Abby struggled to her feet. Auslan and Cristobal weren't giving her any leverage, but after being knocked back and forth so many times, their grips on her had shifted a little bit. If she faked a stagger—just enough to get her fingers into her pocket—

"On your head be it," Sascha whispered. Then she rounded on Abby and reached for her throat.

Abby's hand snapped up. A tiny glass bottle gleamed in her fingers. There was a fine hiss, and a smell of rosewater.

Sascha's expression didn't change for a moment. She halted, sniffed the air, and wrinkled her nose. Blinked once. Twice. Again and again. More tears formed. She choked and clapped both hands to her face, nails digging into the skin. Her wand dropped from her hands and landed on the very edge of the ritual circle. John collapsed.

Abby moved. Cristobal had her bad arm and she stamped on his foot as hard as she could, heavy sensible boots carrying the full weight of a woman with a grudge. Cristobal howled and his grip loosened just enough for Abby to whirl in place. As Auslan let out a shout, she gave him a faceful of rose-scented Capsaicin #5.

She was free and Sascha was there in front of her, screeching and blubbering incoherently through a full dose of hot-pepper agony, and the lizard brain screamed *bite her, scratch her, gut her* but the spirit of Giovanna-La Donna Nera was in the back of her head whispering *no, girl, you know what you have to do.*

Abby snatched up the wand and gave the other woman a hard shove. Carter stumbled back into the ritual circle.

"No—" she began, but it was too late. One of her windmilling arms touched a shimmering tendril of warping air and stopped. She struggled, but she was held.

"Sacrifice," Abby said hoarsely. "A sorcerer who causes their own death willingly. And an artifact from their hands." She held up the wand. "Will this do?"

"Brothers!" Carter shouted, her voice hoarse. "Sisters! Help me!"

The fairies in the back ranks surged, but the ones in the front were less eager and the packed mass of bodies held them back. Their glittering eyes fixed on Carter as she struggled to free herself from the gleaming distortion.

Abby stood at the edge of the circle, wand in hand, and met Carter's gaze. Hate and fury and fear sparked between them.

"Alicia Gonzalez," she said, "And Rebecca Cartwright. Alicia was a physical therapist. Rebecca was a babysitter saving up for cosmetology school. Luka killed them both, and he laughed when he ran away."

She snapped the wand in half and flung it into the pulsing distortion. It gave a heave and crackle as sparks danced around its edges. The glare was almost blinding.

"Help me!" Carter screamed. "Help me! Stop them!"

The fairies still hadn't moved. Finally, a voice spoke up from the back of the crowd. "Do we still get a queen?"

"They're going to kill me!" Carter yelled, tugging futilely on her trapped arm. "For the love of the old ways, *help!*"

"But do we still get a queen?" another voice said. "You promised you were going to be queen, and then we could do anything we wanted. You said we were going to have the whole world."

Abby crouched down by John and put her good arm under him. Carter was saying something, promising them anything, anything at all, but the glow was getting brighter and the rumble of the crowd was drowning her out.

"Quitting time," Abby said in John's ear. He responded with a groan, but one bruised eye cracked open and there was a spark of life in it. "Come on, John, we've got to get out of here!"

"Marquise," he croaked. "Hate my job."

"Me too." She rearranged her grip on him and pulled him into the crowd, glaring fiercely at the fairies in her way and perfume at the ready. Few seemed inclined to stop her now. The glow was so bright that nobody could look directly at it, and a couple of humans were much less interesting than the shouts of the would-be queen. Abby clutched her partner and begged herself not to look back.

They had reached the ridiculous ballroom again when the world seemed to *flex* around them. Abby and John crashed to the floor as the ground underneath them rippled, stone tiles flowing like water and walls bending and bulging to the shriek of protesting wood and plaster. Light ripped through the world, hot and bright and irresistible, flowing through them and scorching them inside and out. Abby could feel her skin crisp as she clutched her hood over her face.

For a moment she lay unmoving, stunned by the wash of power that had flowed over them. The rush of fear and anger were fading rapidly, and Abby couldn't seem to find anything to replace them. God almighty, she hurt.

A guttural croak from John brought her back to her senses. He was struggling to sit up, his eyes screwed shut against his own pain and exhaustion as he groped blindly for something to hold onto. The sight pushed her into action. Staggering, she braced herself against the wall and heaved him to his feet again. They picked a door at random and headed for it.

Not that way, a voice said. Abby blinked and tightened her grip on John even as she fumbled for the perfume bottle. *Marquise! Can you hear me?*

"What—Harvey?" Abby managed to say. "What's going on? Where are you?"

I hitched a ride. She could hear the grin in the genie's voice. *Head for the front door. Or, you know, don't. And die. Whatever floats your boat.*

Abby could think of a few things to say to that, but none of them would help. She could hear voices and a rising ruckus of pounding feet as the last of the fearsome glow leeched out of the world. Politics, it seemed, was getting back to its old cutthroat self. She dragged John in what she hoped was the direction of the front door.

A shape loomed up out of the dimness and Abby couldn't restrain a shriek. It was a man, ghostly pale, lurching as he hurried towards them. His black parka was damp with blood and the snapped-off shaft of an arrow protruded from his chest.

"Hi," the man rasped, and a familiar yellow glint appeared in his eyes. "Sorry it took me so long to find a good one. Not exactly a lot of compatible humans around this joint. Are you okay?"

"Do we look okay?" Abby said hoarsely. The last dregs of energy were draining away. The long hallway ended in a branching staircase and the locked front door, but she couldn't take another step towards it. John's weight slid bonelessly from her shoulder and fell against the edge of the steps. Abby wavered and then, with a small sigh of relief that no one should have felt in the presence of a zombie, wound her good arm around the banister and leaned against it.

"Where are the others?" she said breathlessly.

"Coming this way." Harvey's borrowed face was twisted into a scowl. "Couldn't do shit 'til I found a body, but I heard a lot. They knew the fire was a distraction. The big guys had orders to capture you for some kind of creepy …" He trailed off. "Holy shit, what happened to Sawyer?"

"Carter did. Then I did. Then Carter did again." Abby clutched the bottle of perfume. The following feet were coming closer, and she could hear angry voices. "Harvey. please. Help us."

The zombie-djinn cracked his new knuckles. "Got a rhyme for me?"

Now? Abby's brain was fried. Roses are red? Violets are blue? She couldn't think of a rhyme.

"I... I would not, could not, win this fight," she slurred. "How about you? I think you might."

"Fucking *Green Eggs and Ham?*"

Abby didn't say anything. The power of speech seemed to have temporarily deserted her. Harvey flexed his stolen shoulders, blinked his dead eyes, and gave her a smile that promised hell. "Eh, it'll do."

The door behind them burst open and selkies came pounding into the room, teeth bared in snarls, hands already melting into paws. The one in the lead checked himself almost imperceptibly when he saw the glowing-eyed zombie, but the others were too eager or crazed to do even that much. The force of the rush slammed their leader headfirst into Harvey's new body.

He didn't even flinch. One arm swung back, and with a smoothness like a lead-weighted pendulum he slapped the charging selkie off his feet. There was a crack, and the selkie left the floor sideways. He crashed into the wall and lay still, his head at an unhealthy angle, his eyes half-closed. The sealskin slipped off his shoulders.

By the time the selkie landed, Harvey was already laying into the next two. Pale hands wrapped around their throats, one for each, and the genie just lifted them off their feet in one liquid-smooth motion. He cracked their heads together, dropped the smaller one, and hurled the larger into his still-standing friends. More cracks and snaps, this time accompanied by yelps of pain.

But he was too slow. Three more were on him before he could reach for them, and he let out a howl as their claws dug into his borrowed skin. He seized the grasping hands in a relentless grip and crushed their fingers. Even as the selkies screamed, they bit and kicked and clawed at him.

Note to self: zombie body armor, Abby thought.

Cristobal came skidding into the hallway. His eyes went wide at the sight of the screeching struggle, but instead of jumping into the fray, he put his back against the wall. With cat-burglar caution he flattened himself to the wood and slid past the embattled zombie, eyes fixed on Abby and John.

Abby reached for the perfume bottle, but she had dropped it somewhere in the ritual chamber. Hands shaking, she pulled out the metal pen. Not that it would do any good. She was barely upright.

"Harvey!" she managed to choke out. "Incoming!"

Harvey clacked his jaws furiously, but it was hard to say anything with three angry fae on your back. She needed to do something, anything, but nothing was working. She was beyond the point of exhaustion. Cristobal smiled a little, scales rippling across his face as he moved closer—

Then the door blew in.

Someone shouted something, but the words were lost in the thunder of the explosion. The door, the lintel, and chunks of the wall on either side just erupted into splintered wood and masonry, sparks flaring in the shrapnel. Cristobal was slammed back into the wall by the blast, and Abby's arm was nearly pulled out of its socket as she was thrown against the stair.

Another sound cut through the background roar: a crackle-pop followed by a second, slightly less thunderous explosion. The shouting voice was clearer now, but it was just an exultant cheer mixed with a few swear words for good measure. Against all odds, Abby felt a smile stretch her stiff, aching face. Adam *loved* his detcord.

And there he was, dressed in battered desert camouflage that smelled like smoke, pelting over the threshold with Mal and Terra Burns at his heels. His prized FN-P90 was raised, and the odd-shaped gun looked comical until it put two bullets through a selkie's leg almost faster than Abby could blink. A double-tap for each and the fairies were on the ground, no longer interested in fighting Harvey.

Cristobal held up his hands, his scales beginning to fade back into his skin. "No sense in being hostile," he said, taking a step back.

The muzzle of the P90 didn't waver. "None at all," Adam said. "On the ground, hands behind your head. Now."

Moving slowly, Cristobal complied. Adam shifted aside and the grim-faced Terra stepped forward. She dipped a handful of powder from a baggie, sketched a sigil on her forehead with her thumb, and flung the powder over him.

The effect was immediate: his eyes widened and he twitched violently, shivering on the carpet. Cold sweat poured down his face. Adam turned away and Abby started to shout, but Cristobal didn't get up. He trembled and gasped for air.

"I thought," Abby said hoarsely, "that you used illusion magic."

"I do." Terra took another palmful of powder and calmly dusted the wounded selkies, who began shivering and twitching just like Cristobal. Mal collected their sealskins and bundled them into a duffel bag. "Right now, they're all under the illusion that they're having severe panic attacks. It'll wear off in... oh... a couple of hours."

Abby shook her head. "Nasty."

"Hey, I'm not hiding my light under a bushel basket. I do what I can with what I'm given." Terra glanced around, shaking her head. "Man, you people did a number on this place. I hope you've all got good lawyers."

"We manage." That was Mal, who was bundling up the last sealskin. His eyes lit on Abby, and then on the unconscious John. "Abigail, can you walk?"

"I—" She tried to stand again, but her muscles felt like spaghetti. "I don't—I don't think so, Mal. I'm sorry."

"Jimmy will help you. I should see to John." Mal quickly knelt beside the other agent, checking his wounds with a quick and methodical touch.

It took a moment for Abby's brain to catch up. "Jimmy?"

"Nice kid," Terra said as she checked the open door. "See, if you'd sent him to talk to me, I might've listened. He knows some good jokes."

"*Jimmy* is here?"

Adam moved past Terra and checked the hallway in a quick, businesslike fashion. "Called him for extraction. He's parking the car."

"You let him drive?" Abby sputtered, surprise temporarily cutting through the pain. "He's on probation for DUI!"

"Well, our two designated drivers were stuck in a house of horrors and I got my license revoked years ago." Adam glanced over his shoulder, brow furrowed. "What?"

Abby shook her head, dazed. "No, I ..." She shook her head again. "I guess he's officially in this now."

Terra grabbed her by the good arm and heaved, and Abby's world reeled as she found herself pulled to her feet. "Can't wait for the kid," she grunted. "Sascha set things up so she wouldn't be disturbed, but you and your buddy made a pretty damn big mess here. On your feet, Mom, we're hitting the road."

"Okay." Abby staggered. "Mal, John—"

"I'll get him to the hospital." Mal's face was grim as he lifted John in a fireman's carry. "You should go too, Abby."

Her heart squeezed a little at the use of the nickname from Mal. "I'll be fine," she said as Terra towed her towards the door. "Just take care of him, Mal. Please. I think ..." She swallowed. "Carter was inside his head, Mal. She was trying to use him for her ritual. He's going to need a lot of help once he wakes up."

"He'll get it." Mal followed her towards the door. Adam brought up the rear, P90 still at the ready, his gaze raking back and forth as he checked the corners. Abby thought she heard him mutter something about clearing the place out, and Mal must have caught more of it than she did, because he shook his head. "No time, Adam."

Adam growled. "There could be dozens more of them in here, Mal. If we can clear the nest out now—"

"No. Carter is dead, which means they'll have their own problems soon enough."

Abby could imagine it. Politics indeed: the unifying figure that had bound them all together was gone, and now there would be a power vacuum at the top. Even through the fog of her dizziness and pain, she knew that life in the fairy world was about to get very complicated.

And then her brain officially checked out and she sagged against Terra, who gave her a shake. "Come on, you," the sorcerer said sharply. "You can't die yet! You haven't even paid me for saving your butt!"

"We'll negotiate a rate," Abby mumbled through her hanging hair. "How are you at lab work?"

"Is she serious?" Terra asked Mal. Abby never heard the answer because as her feet touched the sidewalk, blissful unconsciousness descended.

EPILOGUE

Abby didn't remember much of New Year's Day. A few fragments lingered in her memory, distant and blurred. Mal telling her not to worry as he injected something into her arm, Jimmy looking gray-faced and nervous, the sound of Mary shrilly demanding an explanation. When she woke up around sundown, her aches seemed worse than ever but her head was a little clearer. Mal was by her bedside.

He'd taken John to a hospital under a fake ID and seen him admitted. The prognosis wasn't encouraging: two cracked ribs, a broken nose, a concussion, abdominal puncture wound, three broken teeth, and shock. Mal had claimed he'd found the other man in an alley, presumably the victim of assault. John would survive, though there would be some definite scarring. Since they were injuries sustained in the line of duty, the Director would cover most of the bills. Abby would doubtless be getting a pointed e-mail about her methods.

They had been expected, Mal said. Carter's people had grabbed John because he was the only one who was alone at the rally, and once he'd proven to be a potential sacrifice for the queenship, they'd planned on dividing the attacking SSR and using one as leverage for John's death. Abby had barely disappeared into the woods before Mal had been called away by Adam, who was under attack from a group of fae that hadn't been quite as distracted as they let on. Harvey had gone to back up Mal and Adam, but it still would have gone badly for them if Terra Burns hadn't made good on the promise of her text message and come to help. Abby's message, thrown out into the Chicagoland cyberspace, had found its mark:

Time to settle up for Petrovich. Are you in?

She was. And, as Mal pointed out dryly, the Director wouldn't be too happy with them taking on someone new. Terra was too skilled to not be offered a place with them, but the extra salary was going to strain the budget.

Abby didn't care. Someone who saved her life got an automatic pass as far as she was concerned.

She asked about Jimmy, but Mal assured her he was fine and sleeping off his own post-mission exhaustion. After a cup of tea and a bowl of soup, Abby sent her coworker home and gratefully crawled back into bed.

January 2nd dawned gray and misty. The city was quiet, slumped in relief or simply hungover. The strange warm rain had gone, leaving nothing behind but streets scoured clean in a way city services had never quite managed. With the world back in order, fresh snow would almost certainly be on its way, but for now it seemed like the new year had brought a new world with it.

Abby cradled her bad arm against her side and leaned against the doorframe. Her breath clouded in the cool morning light and was swept away almost instantly by a gust of wind. The world had that sharp tang to it that always preceded a heavy snowstorm, and she was grateful for it. The evidence of the ugliness would be covered up by the normal, and the city would forget what had happened. Maybe.

Everything still ached but at least she could move again, and after almost twenty-four hours of sleep she had some energy back. The scent of the air and the bitter taste of black coffee were something to glory in for the moment. She was alive.

The newspaper landed on her porch with a thump. She sipped her coffee and contemplated picking it up, but decided not to. After a few frantic days and a near-death experience, the idea of choosing to just not do something had its appeal.

She didn't see the paper again until Jimmy brought it into the kitchen while she was making breakfast. He unfolded it, and even from across the room Abby could see the headline: D.A. CARTER REMAINS MISSING IN BLOODY DEBACLE.

"Debacle," Abby said, pouring the last of the pancake batter into the skillet and licking a burned fingertip. "They only ever use that in headlines when they're not sure what they're talking about."

"That's all you care about?" It wasn't an accusation, just a question. "What's going to happen now, Mom? Are we going to get arrested?"

"I don't think so." She topped off two finished pancakes with syrup and handed the plate to Jimmy, who picked one up with his fingers and stuffed it into his mouth. "Honey, just use the fork. That's what it's there for."

"Okay, okay," Jimmy mumbled. While he was trying to wash down the huge mouthful, Abby finished frying the last pancake and turned off the stove. She prepared her own plate, crossed herself automatically, and sat down to eat.

The warm kitchen was silent for a few minutes while mother and son ate. Finally, though, Jimmy pushed his plate away and set down his coffee mug hard. The bang was as good as a loud "Ahem!" and Abby looked up, knowing what was about to happen.

"Mom?"

"Yes?"

"Why didn't you just show me?" He thumped his mug again for good measure. "And don't give me any of that oh-I-couldn't-you-wouldn't-cooperate stuff. You've got a mind-wipe genie and a guy who can pull out his eyeballs. Why didn't you just get them to drag me down to the office and show me it was real? Instead of having the bogeymen ruin Christmas, I mean."

Abby added creamer to her own mug, stalling for time while she thought. She had promised herself that it would be nothing but the truth from now on, but that didn't mean she knew how to strictly explain the truth.

"Because I was scared," she said finally. "Not just of you, either." Jimmy opened his mouth to protest and Abby stirred her coffee, waiting to hear him out. After a moment of awkward silence, he retreated without saying anything. Abby took a sip before continuing. "There's a lot of reasons why we try to help keep the supernatural separate from the regular world, you know. And the big one, as silly as it sounds, is that the world can't handle it yet. The Rev used to say that if he could buy a thousand years of peace with one year of genocide, he wouldn't do it. He made us all swear to do our best to keep everything on an even keel by stopping the monsters who want to hurt people, and he did it because he thought the world would eventually reach the point where everyone *could* handle it. In the meantime, we try to keep the balance. Because if everyone woke up tomorrow in a world where vampires and werewolves and fae and doppelgangers and ghouls existed—" She twitched one shoulder, and the scars dragged against her skin "—there'd be war. Maybe the kind of war that doesn't have a winner."

Her cup was almost empty. She finished the last of her coffee in one long swallow.

"That's what scared me," she said. "I didn't... I didn't know what would happen if you knew for sure. None of this would have happened if I hadn't been attacked, and I wasn't sure I wanted you knowing about magic and being as angry as you are. And I wasn't sure I could handle it. So I convinced myself I couldn't do anything about ..." She gestured between the two of them. "All this."

"And then you rang up the fucking bogeyman." There was a touch of bitterness in Jimmy's tone, but he didn't seem about to throw anything. "What happened to being scared?"

"Do you remember what was happening, Jimmy?" she said quietly. "You were threatening to report me as a lunatic. You took my car keys away and hit me in the face." Jimmy cringed a little, shoulders hunching, and guilt jabbed at Abby's gut. The truth hurt both of them, it seemed. "I *was* scared. Our whole group almost died that night, and then to come home to another fight with you? I couldn't handle it. I was more frightened of you than of the consequences."

"Mom, I—" Jimmy swallowed. "Look, I wasn't gonna—I mean, I—" Again, he couldn't seem to make the words come. He stared at the tabletop.

"Look, this has been hard on both of us." Abby blinked hard, trying to force back the stinging dampness in her eyes. "I'm going to try to be a better mom, Jimmy. You didn't deserve to have your life uprooted by magic and the divorce and all this, and I know that you're angry. But you've seen what's out there and what we're dealing with. Two near deaths in one month is too much for me. Can we... can we try to get along better? Just a bit?"

He nodded, swallowing again. "Okay."

"Okay, then." Her voice wobbled a little. "You know I love you, honey. Right?"

"Yeah. Yeah, I do." He wiped his eyes. "I just don't get what I'm supposed to do now. With my life, I mean. Everything's gone weird."

Abby smiled, a weight lifting, and stood. "Well, you can help me finish off these pancakes, for a start. And then I thought we could go visit John in the hospital. He really needs some company right now. After that?" She shrugged. "If you want to think long-term, I know you have college applications to finish."

"That's it?" Jimmy looked incredulous. "Just pick up and go on like nothing ever happened? Is that what you do?"

"It's what I need to do," she said. "That's how we keep things together." Her voice softened, and she moved around to the other side of the table, putting a hand on Jimmy's shoulder. "The world's a strange, strange place. It always has been, even before the attack. We can't do anything about that. All we can do is try to make pieces of it less dangerous for the people who don't understand that yet. And in the meantime, try to run our own lives without screwing up too badly." At that, her smile turned a little rueful. "This might be one of those 'do as I say, not as I do' things."

He still didn't seem to fully believe her, but Abby hadn't expected that he would. Part of being a teenager was finding out that your parents didn't know everything, after all. "Come on," she said. "Pancakes?"

For the first time in a long time, Jimmy smiled. "Yeah," he said. "If I don't have to do the dishes."

Her son believing in monsters and magic? Check. Tentative first steps towards repairing their relationship? Check. Chicago saved from would-be fairy queen? Check. Teenage boy voluntarily doing housework? Well, no sense in striving for the impossible.

She smiled back at him and went back to the counter, where the remaining pancakes were still steaming a little on their plate. "Deal."

END

www.ingramcontent.com/pod-product-compliance
Lightning Source LLC
LaVergne TN
LVHW011932070526
838202LV00054B/4602